Beauty from Embers

Pamela Hart

POTATO CHIP PUBLISHING

ISBN: 9798988881964 (paperback)

ISBN: 9798988881971 (hardcover)

ISBN: 9798988881957 (ebook)

For more information, or to book an event, contact: pamela@pamelahartwrites.com

Cover Art by 100 Covers

Map by Cartography Bird

Created with Atticus

For Joe, who makes it possible for me to chase my dreams.

Also by Pamela Hart

Beauty from Ashes
City of A Thousand Tears

THE GREAT NATIONS OF ELORAH

UNCHARTED NORTHERN WILDS

THE ICY ISLES

DARDAK

YARKEL MOUNTAINS

ISHTAWA FOREST

TASNA

ROMIK

NAKRA

ORNAL RIVER

AVATHYS

MELICA

SLIPFOOT FOREST

ULEKREW

NEKRAL PLATEAU

PLISK

SKRATTAFELL

ALTA RIVER

GALAVEGA

KIFU

OBSIDIAN CLIFFS

KAHANA PASS

LIIPA

VOSN RIVER

REDTONA

BIRANO

MENPAC RIVER

NEYHORN MOUNTAINS

KATSAWA CANYON

GEHENNA

SEULAH

TACHA VILLAGE

COBASSO

MINTKA

BERGOTH

ALTINROS LAKE

FALLYNWOOD

CURSED BARRENS

ILYON MOUNTAINS

JALRAH FOREST

EIREN

CAPITAL CITY

SAVLAN RIVER

TEKROR

CHUNYA RIVER

DORMIAN RIVER

ARLINVALE WOOD

ALSEHIR

KALFA RIVER

PALESTRUM

NORDUNE

MAHREA PLAINS

ZAJMIK CLIFFS

THE WESTERN WASTES

THE FIERY ISLES

ENTOVA

MALEMAR PEAK

SOLIS

TARRAGOR

Every time you make a choice you are turning the central part of you, the part of you that chooses, into something a little different from what it was before. And taking your life as a whole, with all your innumerable choices, all your lifelong you are slowly turning this central thing either into a heavenly creature or into a hellish creature...

-C.S. Lewis

Chapter 1

THREE TONS OF BLUE steel, whirring gears, and killing intent hunted Acadia.

A long metal corridor stretched in front of her, divided into corrugated segments like an enormous centipede. Acadia could see a junction in the hall about three meters down. Maybe if she took enough twists and turns, she could shake the malevolent sentry bot stalking her.

Acadia veered around the corner at full speed. She'd pinned back her short black hair, but a wisp came free and tickled her nose. Acadia blew it aside. Her thick-soled boots skidded on the polished floor, and she slipped. Catching herself with her left hand, she pushed off the gleaming wall, her palm leaving a dirty smear. Sweat dripped in her eyes, blurring the xenon lights overhead. She swiped at her brow with the back of her hand. Her gray biomesh jumpsuit automatically wicked away the perspiration that dripped onto it. Acadia's pulse battered a staccato rhythm against her neck, and she stopped to listen.

Relentless metal treads clicked along the floor. The sentry bot was close.

Acadia pressed herself against the wall and concentrated on her spirit. It sat in the center of her chest, a tight little ball of energy. Her lips parted, but her mind spoke directly to her spirit, nudging it awake. <Conceal,> she whispered and imagined fiery blue droplets raining over her. The fine hairs on her arms stood up as a tingle of spiritual energy washed over her. If she cast it right, the spiritual concealment should remove any trace of her presence—sight, scent, sound, even her heat signature.

When the bot wheeled around the corner, Acadia held her breath. It was at least twenty hands tall, each body joint encased in armor-plated steel. It would take armor-piercing rounds to penetrate that shell. Acadia shrank back. How was she supposed to defeat this thing?

Why bother? her mind whispered snidely. *It's not like the Eirenians will accept you, even if you succeed.*

Her spirit quivered. The concealment flickered like a broken grid-screen. Chills danced along Acadia's spine, and her stomach twisted in knots. She shook her head, tuning out her pessimistic thoughts. Right now, she needed to focus.

The sentry bot halted. An optic sensor in the center of its bulbous head irised open and closed. The machine thrummed—a deep metallic sound—and a red beam projected outward, scanning the hallway.

Acadia shivered as the beam slid over her. Would her fluctuating concealment hold up against a direct scan?

The sentry whirred. Its treads hummed to life, and the machine rolled toward her. Metal arms snapped to its sides, electricity feeding into the lasers mounted on both forearms. The bot was preparing to attack.

Acadia's nails scraped the top of her knuckles. Then she remembered Arnion's hands covering hers. "Please don't, chimad," he had whispered.

Get a grip! This is for Arnion.

Her spirit flamed around her, fizzing over her skin like tiny bubbles. The concealment solidified, its invisible barrier hardening like battle armor.

The sentry bot let out a metallic purr. Its posture shifted back to patrol mode, and it adjusted its trajectory, continuing down the corridor.

An oily stench of ergon exhaust seared her nostrils as it passed. Acadia grimaced. The fumes left a bitter taste in her mouth.

Her eyes scoured the bot for weaknesses. Its torso and head were heavily armored. A blast from the photon pistol holstered at her side wouldn't even make a dent. Her eyes traveled up the sentry bot's back to its neck joint. A slim red wire fed from the central processing unit in the torso to the optic sensor. If she severed that wire, it could cause the bot to short circuit. Of course, getting that close to a sentry bot was near suicide. They had lasers that could shear through steel-vaulted doors and metal arms that could snap a grown man in half.

She would only have one chance.

Acadia reached for the multipurpose dagger sheathed at her hip and pressed the release catch. Easing it into her hand, she checked the blade, her thumb pressing lightly against the serrated edge. Her dark blue eyes glittered back at her from the mirror-like surface. Acadia swallowed. She stepped away from the wall, careful to maintain her spirit concealment.

The bot continued to patrol down the hall, unaware of her movement.

A knot of tension loosened at the base of her neck. The concealment was working. Her training was paying off.

Since moving to Eiren, she'd learned there were different categories of spirit use. Innate abilities were those that anyone with basic spirit training could do easily. Adepts had specialized training for their craft, such as artisans, analysts, and engineers. Mental and emotional abilities were the field of Ambassadors, and there were some spirit techniques so powerful, they were only passed down to members of the royal family. Acadia had chosen to study the most difficult level of spirit use available to her—Warrior. Her training days were crammed with lessons on combat, protection, and tactics. A seasoned spirit warrior could take out a sentry bot in seconds.

She trailed her adversary, calculating the height of its neck joint. It was at least five hands taller than her. She'd need some kind of boost to sever the wire. Acadia considered the narrow hallway and remembered her training. One of the abilities in her arsenal was enhancement, where she could temporarily enhance physical characteristics for a sliver of time.

If I enhanced my speed and agility . . . this just might work.

Acadia let the bot trundle forward, creating a gap between them. One breath. Two breaths. Three. She opened her stance, leaned forward, and charged.

<Faster> she urged her spirit.

Blue flames rushed down her legs, strengthening her muscles and giving her supernatural speed. Euphoria zipped down Acadia's nerves. She was doing it! But she could only maintain it for a couple of seconds.

The bot stopped short. Its optic sensor clicked.

She was almost upon it.

Now!

Acadia vaulted off the wall and leaped onto the bot. Her right arm wrapped around its head joint as her left hand raised the dagger. The bot screeched and pivoted, its torso spinning around. Long metal hands reached up to tear her away.

Acadia slipped the serrated edge of her blade under the red wire and sawed furiously. Sparks popped as it frayed.

Snap!

The wire split in two. The bot shuddered. Its metallic arms clattered to the floor, and the smell of burning plastic filled the air.

Acadia slid off its back and nudged the head component with her foot. It lolled to the side, the optic sensor a dark pit.

"Yes!" Acadia pumped her fist in the air. She skipped around the bot, her feet practically floating across the floor. That was the last obstacle.

Her prize should be up ahead. She strutted around the corner, arms swinging—

—only to come face to face with another sentry bot. The machine emitted a deep thrum. Optic sensors whirred furiously.

Acadia skidded to a stop, the rubber grip of her boots squealing.

Dral.

The bot's arms shot forward. Acadia dodged to the side. Cold metal fingers snapped shut so close, they stirred the wisps of black hair that had escaped her hairpins.

The machine pulsed again—an angry buzzing sound.

Acadia backpedaled as the sentry bot loomed toward her. It raised its arms, electricity humming through the twin laser barrels. A red targeting dot zeroed in on her chest.

<Shield!> Acadia screamed to her spirit.

An iridescent bubble of spiritual energy washed over her, and the bot opened fire. The blast rocked her backward. Her flimsy shield bounced off the opposite wall of the narrow corridor and knocked Acadia off-balance. She stumbled to her knees.

Where had the second bot come from? There was only supposed to be one.

Pathetic. The voice in the back of her mind rose, like a serpent scenting weakness. *No matter how hard you try, it will never be enough. You'll never make up for the things you've done. Once Arnion finds out—*

Cracks splintered along the edge of her shield, and the sentry bot leveled its laser at her once more. The second blast shattered her shield and slammed her into the opposite wall. The sentry bot rumbled toward her, its hands outstretched.

Acadia winced.

"End of examination," a voice called out.

The sentry bot froze. The red sensory light dimmed, and its arms relaxed along its sides as it powered down.

More lights flickered around the room. A gust of compressed air hissed, and the metallic labyrinth around Acadia began folding back into the ground of the training room.

Acadia pounded her fist on the ground. "Why didn't you let me finish?"

The proctor entered the training floor, her curly brown hair pulled back in a loose ponytail. The blue civil-servant robes of her office swished across the scuffed floor. She pressed her glasses up her nose and gave an understanding smile. "You were close. However, to pass onto the warrior class of spirit mastery, the exam must be completed without injury."

"What injury?" Acadia threw out her hands.

The proctor pointed a finger to the side of her mouth. Acadia mirrored her gesture and felt something warm and wet. Blood. She must have bitten her lip after that second hit. Acadia groaned. Now it would be another month before she could attempt the exam again.

Her disappointment must have shown on her face because the proctor gave her a sympathetic look. "I know it must feel disheartening, but the examinations are designed for your protection. Without the right level of mastery, moving on to more advanced spiritual techniques would be dangerous."

Acadia smoothed the frustration from her face and summoned a docile smile. "Of course," she said demurely. "I just need to practice harder." She stood and dusted off her biomesh pants.

The proctor patted her shoulder. "No need to beat yourself up. You are progressing well. It's only been nine months since you entered Eiren, after all. Most people take much longer to accomplish what you have."

"Thank you." Acadia ducked her head to hide the ire building beneath her forehead. She wasn't most people. She was Acadia Dannon, reformed former Gehennian and the crown prince's— what, exactly, she wasn't sure. Arnion loved her, and she loved him, but ever since they'd escaped from Gehenna and returned to his homeland, things had gotten complicated. Finding out he was the crown prince of Eiren didn't help.

So, she'd thrown herself into spirit training, assuming it would come naturally to her. Acadia had always excelled at everything she'd put her mind to, and Arnion made it look as easy as breathing. How hard could it be?

Ridiculously hard, Acadia soon learned. She had the bumps, bruises, and scrapes to prove it. At least she had something to look forward to after the exam. Arnion had promised to meet her. He had been inundated with diplomatic problems lately but was determined to carve out some time for her today. Her lips tugged into a smile at the thought of seeing her prince.

The metal doors of the training room slid open, and she stepped into the hallway, towel draped around her neck, eyes scanning the corridor. A dark-haired young man lounged against the wall, curly bangs falling in front of his eyes.

Acadia's heart leaped, then it plummeted to the soles of her feet.

Not Arnion.

It was Rhys, Arnion's close friend and confidant. Since Acadia had arrived in Eiren, Rhys had taken her under his wing. His empathetic and kind-hearted nature won her over quickly, but he wasn't her prince. She blinked back tears of frustration. Logically, she knew there was a reason Arnion wasn't there, but her throat pinched in disappointment.

The doors swished shut behind her, and Rhys's gaze flicked up. His dark-brown eyes brightened. "Acadia! How did it go?" He walked toward her, beaming. If cheerfulness was a candleflame, Rhys was a miniature sun radiating warmth.

Acadia shoved her bitterness into a tight little knot in the back of her mind. She rolled her shoulders. "I didn't pass," she said lightly, "but I was close. Next time, for sure."

"I'm sorry. I know how hard you've been practicing." Rhys furrowed his brow. "Arnion wanted to be here, but the conflict between Kifu and Avathys is volatile right now. Sometime during the night, Avathys moved ships to blockade Kifu's primary trading port. Emissary Narhast was pounding on the advisory-board doors at daybreak, demanding military action."

"Narhast." Acadia rubbed her forehead. "He's the emissary from Kifu, right?" She pictured the stocky man with the perpetual grimace, like he'd been raised on sour milk. Narhast had been stumping along the halls recently, stabbing his wooden cane against the marble flooring as he walked. "Ex-military?"

Rhys nodded. "A retired general known for his military strategy. He got that leg injury in a battle long ago. Took him out of the fighting, but certainly didn't take the fight out of him."

Acadia hummed, thinking. Historically, there had always been tension between Avathys and Kifu, but it never amounted to much. Petty diplomatic squabbles and the odd border skirmish. Kifu's lack of resources was the perfect foil to Avathys's agricultural and industrial power. As a child, she often heard Da grumbling about the greedy Avathysians and their blasted technology. "Always making machines to take away an honest man's work," he'd complain. She'd heard in Avathys that "Kifan" was synonymous with stubborn and unrefined, though she'd never visited the country, so she didn't know for sure.

Without Lucien's pernicious influence seeping out of Gehenna to fuel the conflict, Eiren had stepped into the gap and initiated diplomatic talks between Avathys and Kifu. If the two nations could forge a lasting peace agreement, it would certainly help stabilize the region. Still, Acadia didn't envy Arnion having to deal with the political theatrics.

She remembered Emissary Narhast's scowling face. "So, he's the one causing trouble for Arnion today?"

Rhys cupped a hand against his neck. "Among others, yes."

"And you just happened to walk by the training room this morning?" Acadia waved her hand back toward the doorway.

"Arnion sent me to check on you."

Acadia stiffened. "Did he?" she asked in a quiet voice.

Rhys blushed and looked away. He knew she didn't like being nannied. He cleared his throat and held out his hands like a peace offering. "He's worried about you, that's all."

Acadia turned away. Anger flooded her veins, and her cheeks burned. "Great. That's just great." She clenched the soft white towel around her neck.

"Anything you want to talk about?" Rhys angled toward her and waggled his eyebrows.

Acadia knew him well enough to recognize his playful demeanor was an attempt to get her to lower her guard. She dabbed at the sweat on her forehead with her towel. "Not really," she muttered and turned away. "I'm heading to the showers." She tugged on her biomesh sleeve. It might wick away moisture, but she reeked of sweat. "I need to change. I've got a home visit to do."

Rhys wilted beside her, temporarily dampened by her refusal. Acadia knew it wouldn't last long. She mentally counted to three before he perked up again.

He fired another conversation salvo. "You were the one who first suggested home visits, weren't you? To give the former Gehennians more support in Eiren?"

She paused and spoke over her shoulder. "It's easy to fall through the cracks. I didn't want anyone to feel that way. Not anymore."

"I think it's great you have such compassionate instincts. You really put yourself in their shoes," Rhys gushed.

Annoyance nipped at her and she started walking again, faster this time. "I'm not like them," she said defensively. "I don't have any second thoughts about immigrating to Eiren."

Rhys jogged beside her and held out his hands again. "Acadia, relax. That's not what I meant at all." She grunted and he raised an eyebrow. "You worry too much."

Acadia scoffed and crossed her arms, turning to face him. Her friend skidded to a stop beside her. "Worrying kept me alive," she snapped.

Rhys's mouth opened and closed softly. Acadia cursed herself. When would she learn to stop bringing up Gehenna? While Arnion's miraculous resurrection was celebrated, the suffering he endured to free them was still an excruciating memory for the Eirenians. Nine months after escaping Lucien's prison camp, it was still a silent specter that haunted her every step.

Everyone else was moving on. Everyone else was thriving. What was wrong with her?

Rhys winced and pressed a hand against his forehead.

"What is it?" Acadia took a step toward him, concern for her friend overpowering her defensiveness.

"You sent a syna."

"I did?" Acadia stepped back in alarm. Synas were considered an innate spirit level technique, the ability to shape emotions into pictures that you projected into another person's mind. Acadia was used to hiding her emotions, but accessing her spirit seemed to pull them to the forefront. She frequently sent synas to others around her without meaning to. It was like giving the world an open window into her mind. "Dral!" She stamped her foot.

"Don't worry; you'll get the hang of it."

Acadia crossed her arms. "That's what they said months ago. And here I am, still broadcasting my emotions to everyone around me."

"It takes time to master your spirit. Everyone learns at their own pace." Rhys's tone was patient, like a teacher explaining something obvious to a small child.

Acadia ground her teeth. "Everyone's getting the hang of it except me," she muttered, half-hoping Rhys wouldn't hear.

Endearment flashed across Rhys's face. He looked like he wanted to ruffle her hair, but Acadia glared at him. Instead, he cleared his throat. "I wouldn't say that. I work with the former Gehennians. Their spirit mastery is at all different levels."

Acadia looked down and scuffed the toe of her shoe along a line of white tiling in the floor. "What did it look like? My syna." She dug her nails into her arm at the slight tremor in her voice.

"Like a castle on a cliff, crumbling apart and falling into the raging sea."

"Nothing too dramatic, then." She tried to go for careless but couldn't quite pull it off. Rhys knew her too well for that.

"You know you can talk to me about anything, right? It will stay between us."

Acadia knew Rhys was persistent. If she didn't assuage some of his concern, he would follow her around doggedly for days. Her own little cloud of polite concern, emotional support, and herbal tea.

She toyed with the towel around her neck and turned to face him fully, hands on hips. Rhys was so tall, she had to look up to meet his gaze. "You won't relent, will you?"

Rhys flashed her a cheerful grin. "Nope. As close friend and advisor to the prince, I can promise you, I take my duties of friendship seriously."

Acadia groaned. "Diplomatic strategist and encourager; your tenacity scares me."

Rhys tapped her shoulder. "Might as well get it over with."

Acadia picked at her nails. She kept them brutally short so they wouldn't interfere with her training. For a moment, her mind flashed back to Beulah, when she used to get her lacquered red nails sharpened and filed daily. Acadia clenched her hand. Another memory she wanted to forget.

Rhys cleared his throat and stared at her expectantly.

Acadia groaned and rolled her eyes. She picked the lightest of her burdens and shaved it down to a politely repressed version of her true feelings, suitable for sharing without landing her in a psych ward. "Arnion's so busy. I thought once we escaped Gehenna, I'd get to spend more time with him. I thought Eiren was going to be our happily ever after. But it turns out he's the prince of Eiren with all these expectations and pressures. His time is . . . it's not his own. I feel like every moment he gives me is taking time away from someone else. Someone who needs him more. Who deserves him more." She looked down at her hands, frustrated. Even with her restrained version, more of the truth had slipped out than she had wanted.

"Come here, you worrywart!" Rhys pulled her into a hug.

"I'm all sweaty!" Acadia complained.

Rhys chuckled into her hair. "I've worked with ambassadors coming in and out of missions that you wouldn't believe."

"What's that got to do with anything?" she grumbled.

"Believe me, a little sweat is the least of my worries." Rhys gave her a final squeeze and let go. A mischievous grin winked across his face. "Trust me, Arnion loves spending time with you. Anytime you have a date planned, I hear about it for days. Before and afterwards." He put on a long-suffering expression.

Acadia chuckled. A flush of warmth rushed along the back of her neck as she thought about the implication behind her friend's words. She scratched her nose. "Does he really?"

Rhys nodded dramatically. "*Days.* I'm telling you." He paused his theatrics and gave her an assessing look. "He hasn't always been like that, you know."

The sudden shift toward seriousness caught Acadia off guard. "Like what?"

The laughter was gone from Rhys's eyes, his expression contemplative. "As friendly as Arnion is, he doesn't let most people in. You're the first person I've seen him get truly close to in years."

"That's . . . hard to believe." Puzzlement drenched her words. How could that be? Arnion was the most gregarious person she'd ever met. It seemed like he was everyone's best friend. But if there was a hidden side to the prince, his oldest childhood friend would be the one to know.

She opened her mouth to ask for more details, but Rhys waved her off. "That's a story for another time," he said hurriedly. "Wouldn't want you to be late."

"Yeah. Right," Acadia said uncertainly.

Arnion was surrounded by people all the time. What was Rhys talking about? She knew that cryptic remark was going to keep her up all night. At least Rhys had taken her mind off the spirit exam. "Thanks for checking on me, Rhys. I appreciate it." Acadia made the Eirenian gesture for gratitude, and he beamed at her. Maybe those cultural immersion classes weren't a total loss. She looked back and waved before entering the women's changing room.

Acadia stepped out of the shower and toweled off her short black hair. She rubbed the silky tips between her fingers. Having hair long enough to run her hands through was still a pleasant surprise. And now that her tresses brushed her shoulders, she could even twist it into little updos if she wanted. It was still as straight as an iron rod, but seemed fuller, glossier. When she'd lived in Beulah, she used to pamper herself with the latest hair oils. The products had an obnoxiously sweet fragrance and left a sticky gunk on her hair that lingered for days. But now, even with no treatments, her hair was remarkably healthy.

Maybe that was natural after having your head shaved?

She hugged herself tightly, trying to squeeze out the memories of her first day in Gehenna, when they had sheared off her hair and beaten her unconscious.

Focus! You're in Eiren now. Stop thinking about Gehenna.

Her jaw muscles clenched. Acadia forced herself to breathe. She rolled her shoulders back and let out a slow breath. Memories of Gehenna were poisonous. All her efforts to convince everyone she was okay would be wasted if she walked out of here looking haunted.

Acadia took a series of slow, deep breaths. She was about to step out of the stall when a whisper of her name made her pull back. From the sound of it, two women had entered the changing room. Acadia heard the door slide shut behind them. She held her breath and listened.

"... *Lady* Acadia. I can't stand the sight of her." The words were bitter with scorn. "She's got her greedy little hooks into our poor prince." The voice sounded young. Acadia guessed the woman was probably close to her own age.

"Filthy Gehennians. They never learn," a second voice said. This one sounded older, almost matronly, but with a tone of haughty disapproval. "The whole reason they were imprisoned in the first place was for grasping things beyond their station. It's no surprise one of them would be after our kingdom."

"Father says he's wasting his time with that tramp when he should be preparing for war . . ."

Rage flared through Acadia's veins. It was one thing for them to disparage her—she deserved that and worse—but she wouldn't allow anyone to slander Arnion. Not after everything he'd done. Everything he'd sacrificed.

Acadia slammed her fist onto the unlock button, and the stall door jerked open. She jutted out her chin and strode into the communal area of the changing room.

The two women gasped and whirled around, eyes wide. Surprise, then terror and mortification painted themselves across their faces in rapid succession.

After the incident in Gehenna, where Arnion had given his life to free the prison inhabitants from Lucien's deadly blood oath, about half the prisoners immigrated with her to Eiren. The Eirenians had been welcoming—for the most part—but some were less hospitable.

Acadia squashed the fury that boiled within her stomach at the women's callous words and carefully maintained a placid expression. When the two women flinched at her approach, Acadia repressed a bitter smirk. At least she'd been right about their ages. There was a young woman with tumbling brown curls and an older woman with a frizzy gray bun, wrinkles of disapproval lining her mouth. Carved by years of frowning, Acadia guessed. The young woman's face had gone pale as a sheet, while the older woman was starting to look like an overripe plum.

Acadia nodded at them with her head high. "Good morning," she said graciously. "What a pleasant surprise. I'm always interested to hear a new perspective on foreign policy. I'll be sure to share your thoughts with the crown prince." She glided past them, and the two women shrank back in a bewildered huddle.

The young girl stammered and looked like she was about to burst into tears. The older woman gripped her companion's arm and tugged her to her feet. "Come along, Marisol. I think it's best if we continue your training another day."

Acadia turned from the sink and gave them a regal wave. This time she let a hint of viciousness into her smile, deliberately turning it sharp at the edges. "Have a good day, *ladies*."

The two gossips hurried out without another word.

Acadia turned and rested her shaking arms on the edge of the sink. Her throat tightened. She leaned over the sink as a wave of nausea wracked her stomach. Acadia dry heaved once. Twice.

When the spasming in her stomach stopped, she rinsed her mouth out with cold water. Then she cupped some in her hands and splashed her face. Her shoulders trembled. Acadia pressed her forehead against the cold mirror above the sink and closed her eyes.

After a moment, she leaned back and studied her expression. Dark circles rimmed her sapphire eyes, and her freckles stood out starkly against her blanched face. Acadia pressed a hand against her cheek and pressed down, frowning. She'd never liked her freckles; in the past, she'd always covered them up with pashir-shell powder. Arnion, however, couldn't get enough of them. Leave it to her prince. He always seemed to adore the aspects of her physical appearance she disliked. Still, the sickly pallor to her skin right now made her freckles eerily similar to a pox.

Acadia grimaced at her reflection as she replayed the women's words in her mind. Her name wasn't worth defending. But Arnion's was.

That's why she was working so hard. To protect Arnion, so that he'd never have to sacrifice himself again. She could ignore the spiteful barbs of gossip. She could wear a phony smile at Eiren's diplomatic events. She could punish her body and push herself to the brink of exhaustion to master her spiritual training. The next time Lucien crept out of hiding, she'd be ready.

Acadia was determined to be useful to Arnion this time.

But she couldn't protect him from his own people. If being with her caused the Eirenians to despise him and question his leadership, what could she do?

Her heart fluttered weakly, like a bird with a broken wing. The world tilted, and she clutched the sink, suddenly dizzy.

The Eirenians think I'm after the throne.

Acadia took a sharp breath. She pressed her hands against the pressure building like a knot in her chest. A sound, halfway between a sob and a laugh, wedged in her throat.

How ironic that, after a lifetime of lusting after money and power, all Acadia dreamed of now was a life far away from the drama and politics of the Eirenian court. She didn't want a throne. She didn't even want a prince. All she wanted was Arnion.

But Eiren was Arnion's world.

And it was getting harder and harder to pretend she belonged.

Chapter 2

ACADIA EYED HER TRILORID with disdain. The three-wheeled vehicle seemed to stare back at her in benign amusement. Its white ferolyte casing glistened in the sun, reminding Acadia more of a soft cheese than a means of transportation. Since spirit use was woven into every aspect of Eirenian society, spirit proficiency determined which vehicles a person could access. She'd been stuck with the trilorid for months, and because she'd failed her spirit examination, her access to high-speed vehicles was still restricted. The trilorid was the most advanced vehicle she was authorized to drive. It even came equipped with a speed limiter.

"Stupid thing," she muttered and kicked the synthetic tire. "Looks like we're stuck together for another month."

If she had chosen to train at the Adept level of spirit techniques, she'd probably be able to drive something much more interesting by now. Adepts had specialized training in all kinds of Eirenian devices and gadgets. But with Lucien still roaming free, Acadia wanted to focus on spiritual combat. There was a reason he was known as the Heartless King. Her skin crawled as she pictured Lucien lurking outside the walls, plotting his next move. She needed to be ready. Otherwise, Arnion would have to shoulder everything himself and . . . Her mouth went dry, and her eyes stung. She swallowed thickly. Losing him again was not an option.

Acadia brushed her hand over the left steering handle, the porous material soft against her skin. She closed her eyes and sighed. If putting up with this trilorid for a while longer meant she could help Arnion, she'd do it. No more complaining. She slipped into the seat, gripped the steering handles, and focused on her spirit. It was like a small flame, burning brightly in her chest. Acadia imagined cupping the flame in her hands. She drew the ember close and whispered, <Remember our first kiss with Arnion?>

Her spirit flared upward, feeding on the strength of her positive emotion. A roaring blue flame grew in her chest. Acadia smiled. Remembering that kiss never failed to fan the flames of her spirit. Blue sparks trickled down her arms and seeped into the trilorid handles. The vehicle whirred to life with a soft hum.

Acadia activated the onboard computer and flipped open her data pad. She flicked through the calendar and pulled up today's meeting: Petra Ulsk living at Crown Heights, 31 Lusha Avenue. She tapped the address into her trilorid. The navigation system beeped, preparing the optimal route based on current traffic patterns. Acadia clicked off the e-brake and switched on manual drive mode. Even if she couldn't go fast, manual was better than letting the trilorid's self-driving AI cart her around. She leaned forward and tried to pretend she was on a jetbike with the wind whipping by her face.

Golden buildings curved upward from the street in a series of elegant arcs and twists. The ornate spires and whimsical balconies typical of Eirenian architecture still took Acadia's breath away. Even the most utilitarian structures in Eiren were stunning works of art.

She turned the trilorid onto Central Parkway. Giant chiksa trees lined the center of the road. Their leafy branches stretched above her, providing a pleasant, mottled shade. Acadia appreciated how fresh the air smelled even in the most populated areas of Capital City. Spirit-powered vehicles didn't rely on ergon gas, so there were no noxious exhaust fumes. The city was also remarkably quiet. Sometimes it seemed like the entire populace was holding its breath.

When Acadia compared it to her backwater birthplace in Kifu, or even her time at the heart of Beulah's lurid nightlife, everything fell short. The things she had valued then felt so small and inconsequential now.

Eiren is another world entirely.

The trilorid's navigation system guided her to a white marbled parking area. In the center was a bubbling fountain, with three tiers of water overflowing from one iridescent clamshell to the next. The shells hovered in midair, another marvel of melding spirit abilities with engineering.

Acadia gaped at it for a moment before the glittering high rise beyond caught her eye. The gold-and-blue glass structure shimmered in the afternoon light. Each living quarters appeared to have its own little alcove and terrace. Many of the spaces were bursting with plants and flowers. Acadia grinned. Eirenians loved their plants.

She double-checked the address on her data pad then powered down the trilorid. When she'd first started, driving spirit vehicles even a short distance left her exhausted. Gradually, her training helped her develop more stamina, and now she hardly noticed the strain after driving the trilorid. At least that was something.

Acadia pulled up the standard home-visit questionnaire on her data pad and walked to the door. She ran her finger down the list of names on the apartment intercom until she found Petra Ulsk. After a quick check that she had the right name, she pressed the buzzer.

"Hello," a woman's soft voice whispered through the speaker.

Acadia stepped back and waved at the small camera above the intercom. "Hello. I'm Acadia Dannon, sent by the Gehennian cultural integration committee. Are you still available for our scheduled home visit?"

"Of course. Please come up. Room 807."

"Thank you."

The door slid open, and Acadia stepped inside. She took the maglift to the eighth floor and walked down the hall to Room 807. When she knocked on the door, it slid open.

"Please come in," Petra called out. "I'm in the kitchen."

"Thank you," Acadia answered. She stepped inside and blinked. Stacks of books filled Petra's apartment, overflowing from the desk and side table onto dubiously balanced stacks on the floor. The dusty scent reminded her of a library. Curls of parchment splayed across every flat surface in the sitting room. A line of ink pots glimmered on the mantel: blue, red, purple, and green. Hanging above the windows were bundles of dried plants. Acadia recognized a few herbs, but there were others she'd never seen before. The scent of rosemary and lavender tickled her nose.

Following the clatter of kitchen noises, Acadia came to a metallic bead curtain that parted at her approach, inviting her into the kitchen. A tall woman in scarlet robes was standing in front of the heating filament. Gray streaks shone in her dark auburn hair like starlight.

"I'm making a pot of tea. Please have a seat." Petra spoke without turning around.

Acadia spied a teakwood table that seemed to grow organically out of the wall. Plump blue cushions beckoned, and she sat down. "Thank you for your hospitality."

"It's no trouble." Petra placed a blue ceramic teapot and two mugs on a tray and turned to face her. "I'm happy to—" The tray dropped from her hands. The teapot shattered, and tea spread across the floor.

Acadia jolted to her feet. "Are you all right?" Her eyes locked on the older woman's expression.

Petra's face was ashen. Her lower lip trembled, and her hands flexed as if still trying to grasp the serving tray. "L-Lady Sapphyre."

Acadia froze. Dread shriveled her heart to a dried husk. Impossible. She'd taken such care to avoid anything that could connect to her past. No elaborate makeup or extravagant clothes. No pashir-shell powder to cover up the freckles splashed across her nose and cheekbones. She didn't even use nail pigments anymore, opting to keeping her fingertips natural and short. Even her eyes looked different. While they were still sapphire blue, there was a lightness to them that had never been there before.

She was so radically altered from her past in Beulah—both inside and out—that no one had ever come close to recognizing her.

Was it a fluke?

Forcing her lips to move, Acadia croaked out, "Who?" Her voice was hoarse, as if rust coated the muscles in her throat.

Petra swallowed. The vein in her temple bulged. "Lady Sapphyre, I didn't know you'd escaped from Gehenna."

A shrill laugh burst from Acadia's chest. She waved her hand, dismissively. "You are mistaken. Sapphyre is dead."

Petra shook her head and brought a trembling hand to her lips. "I could never forget your face, Lady Sapphyre."

Acadia's legs folded underneath her as if someone had severed her spinal cord. Her lungs burned, and she tried to remember how to breathe.

Petra knelt on the ground beside her and mopped up the spilt tea with a dishrag. Then she flipped the rag into her palm and began collecting the broken pieces of pottery.

Acadia watched, feeling like she was staring from a great distance. Her life was more shattered than Petra's teapot. Once Arnion found out who she used to be—

"You're bleeding." Petra's voice interrupted her thoughts.

Acadia blinked and glanced at her hands. They were pressed against the wooden floor and blood pooled under her right hand. She examined it, surprised. A shard of blue ceramic was stuck in her palm. She hadn't even felt it. "It's nothing, just a scratch," she muttered.

Petra tutted and fetched a clean washcloth, tossing the soiled one in the sink. She ran it under the faucet and knelt beside Acadia. "Would you like me to take it out?"

Acadia glanced at her. Petra's face shone with motherly concern.

"All right." Acadia said woodenly.

Petra reached forward and nimbly plucked out the shard, quickly pressing the cloth onto the wound.

Acadia used her other hand to apply pressure to the injury. "Thank you," she said. Her head bowed, crushed by the weight of self-loathing. "Whatever I did to you in the past, please know I'm very sorry." She pressed her thumb against the cut until it burned. "My word must mean very little to you, though." Misery twisted her voice, making it rough.

Petra sighed and leaned back, seating herself next to Acadia on the floor. "We've all changed since our time in Gehenna. I should not judge you. But when I turned and saw your face, memories I hadn't thought of in years came rushing back."

Acadia shifted, darting a glance at Petra's face. "Did I . . . was I the reason you were sent to Gehenna?"

Petra's jaw tightened. "Not me. It was my nephew you sent. He and his young bride were visiting Beulah on their honeymoon."

Nausea swirled in her gut. Acadia clenched a hand over her mouth. She remembered that innocent young couple and how, for the sake of a bet, she'd thrust herself between them, a poisonous viper among doves.

"I'm so sorry," Acadia whispered.

How many lives had she sentenced to Gehenna because of her selfishness and cruelty?

Guilt gnawed at her like a horde of bloodthirsty fleas. She wanted to dunk herself in her bathtub and scrub until the feeling went away. Though it was doubtful even all the water in Eiren could wash her clean.

Her thoughts spiraled downward, lost in despair, until Petra patted her on the shoulder.

"We all have regrets," the older woman said softly. "But Prince Arnion's sacrifice gave us a second chance. I should not judge you by your past. Perhaps it is as you said. Lady Sapphyre died in Gehenna."

Acadia met Petra's compassionate gaze. It would have been easier if the other woman had looked at her with contempt. Hatred made her numb, but forgiveness burned. She didn't deserve it. "Every day I try to atone for what I did, but it never seems enough." She bit her lip before more of her heart leaked out.

Petra clucked her tongue. "It's not a matter of balancing out evil with good. How can you weigh the pain another person carries? Or measure the impact of a good deed as it ripples beyond its intended reach? That knowledge is beyond us."

"So, you're saying it's impossible." Acadia looked away. She flexed the fingers of her right hand. Her pulse throbbed around the cut in her palm, and she pressed the dishrag down harder.

Petra clasped her hand over Acadia's. "It's impossible for almost anyone. And yet, your debt was paid. The prince's sacrifice covers you."

"Then why don't I *feel* forgiven?" Acadia raised her voice, panic seeping into the words. "My past haunts me every day. Why can't I let it go?"

"Feelings can be tricky." Petra's voice attempted to soothe Acadia's frayed nerves. "It's all right to regret the past, to learn from it. But you can't let it consume your present."

"But how?" Acadia asked in a small voice.

Petra patted her hand and stood. "Talking about it helps. If you bottle it up and try to carry it on your own, you're sure to stumble." She held out a hand and helped Acadia up. "Let me make another pot of tea, and we can sit at the table and talk."

"And *I'm* supposed to be the one helping *you* adjust," Acadia muttered, too low for Petra to hear.

The older woman relit the heating filament and bustled around the kitchen, and soon the delicious aroma of jasmine and honeysuckle filled the room.

Acadia sniffed appreciatively. "That smells wonderful."

Petra smiled over her shoulder. "It's from Ulekrew. My homeland." She set a yellow teapot with two matching cups on the table, along with a plate of plump rosemary biscuits. "Please help yourself."

Acadia thanked her and reached for one.

Petra poured them both tea and sat back. She stirred a lump of sugar into her cup. "How did the prince react when you told him you were a Jewel? Surely his forgiveness should bring you some comfort."

Acadia paused with the savory biscuit halfway to her mouth. Her heartbeat thundered in her ears.

Petra's eyes widened. "You haven't told him."

Guilt soured in Acadia's stomach. "I *want* to." She swallowed, her tongue thick and clumsy in her mouth. She shredded her biscuit into pieces, the flaky bread crumbling beneath her fingers. "Every time I try to find the words . . ." Shame cinched around her neck like an iron chain. She bowed her head.

Pathetic.

Acadia heard Petra shift in her chair and then felt warm hands cover hers. She looked up, surprised to see compassion etched in the older woman's countenance.

"It won't be easy." Petra's voice was empathetic. "But the prince deserves to hear it from you directly. You don't want him to find out through someone else when you've had the opportunity to be honest with him first. And if I recognized you, there are bound to be others. It's only a matter of time."

Acadia winced and pulled her hands free. "You're right, of course," she said stiffly and settled her hands in her lap.

A pained expression flashed across Petra's face. It looked unnervingly like pity, but the older woman let the topic drop. Acadia was grateful to her for that, at least.

The rest of the meeting progressed without incident. Acadia worked through the digital questionnaire on her data pad and recorded Petra's answers.

How was she settling into life in Eiren?

Just fine.

How did she spend her time?

Petra worked at an herbalist shop. It was proving a fruitful exchange for her and the other botanists. She shared her knowledge of plants from the Ulekrew Plateau and was studying Eirenian flora under their tutelage.

Were any factors causing her discomfort?

Sometimes she still had night terrors of Gehenna and woke up in a cold sweat.

Acadia assured her this was quite normal among the other survivors and that talking about it with a trained counselor might help.

At the end of the survey, Acadia's data pad tallied up the information and declared Petra was successfully integrating into Eirenian society. She was in the ninety-sixth percentile for former Gehennians. It spat out a metallic contact disk where Petra could reach out to a counselor if she wished to discuss her night terrors and advised that no further action was necessary beyond another follow-up visit in six to nine months.

Acadia thanked her for her time. When she lifted the dishrag to check on her cut, it had stopped bleeding, though there was an angry red gash in her right palm. She handed the cloth to Petra. "I'm sorry for getting it dirty."

Petra waved away her concerns with a gentle smile and walked her to the door, then lingered in the doorway. Her lips pressed into a thin line, as if she was on the verge of saying something but forcing herself to stop.

Acadia beat her to it. "You're right, Petra. I need to talk with Arnion. I'm not upset with you for speaking the truth. I'm angry with myself." She kept her tone measured and even, but her inner dialogue seethed.

It wasn't Petra's fault she had managed to carve out a happy life in Eiren, while Acadia was barely holding onto the strings of her sanity. Acadia was a walking time bomb, and she had no one to blame but herself.

If only she'd told Arnion she was one of Lucien's Jewels while she was still in Gehenna. Then he could have rejected her before she'd become so attached. Before she'd learned how amazing he was and how much she adored the time they spent together. If only she'd been honest while she still possessed her heart. Before it had entwined inexplicably with his. To lose him now would be worse than severing a limb. It would be like cleaving her soul from her body. Acadia doubted she'd survive.

Petra seemed to read the conflict in her eyes. She patted Acadia's shoulder. "It may feel impossible, but I'm confident you can do it. The chains of our past no longer bind us. In this new life, you are an example to many."

Acadia fought the urge to grimace at the undeserved praise. Instead, she molded her hands into the Eirenian gesture for gratitude. "Thank you, Petra."

Petra repeated the gesture and bid her farewell.

A chill washed over Acadia as the apartment door slid shut. Like someone was watching her. She glanced down the carpeted hallway; it was silent and empty.

Her nerves were raw from her visit with Petra. That must be it. No need to get paranoid.

Acadia decided she'd stop by the market on her way back to the palace. Bantering with the vendors might lift her unease.

The market in Capital City pulsed with its unique heartbeat. Brightly colored tapestries draped between stalls, creating a vibrant mosaic and welcome shade from the midday sun. Fruit vendors sold piles of lush melons, apples and citrus nestled in wicker baskets. Another stall displayed beautiful ceramic plates, each painted with an intricate geometric pattern. Cloth merchants boasted of having the finest silk and softest wool in Eiren.

Acadia sauntered past them. A pungent scent tickled her nose, and she stopped to admire the heaped bowls of aromatic spices in carnelian, fuchsia, and ochre. Her eyes drifted past a jewelry stand with racks of glittering earrings, necklaces, and rings made of crystal. But she couldn't help stopping at a stall that sold ornate ladies' shoes embroidered with glass beads, seed pearls, and gemstones.

"All handmade," the owner said proudly. She squeezed out from behind the counter and gestured toward the rows of shoes. "My daughter draws up the designs, then my husband, son, and I make 'em." The shopkeeper wore an azure robe cinched with a silver belt like a row of coins around her wide waist. Matching silver earrings twinkled on her ears.

"They are exquisite." Acadia brushed a hand along the soft leather of a pink slipper.

The shopkeeper beamed. "If you tell me your size, I'm sure we can find something you like."

Acadia pulled back. "I really shouldn't."

"Nonsense," the shopkeeper replied. "You need shoes for your feet. Might as well enjoy 'em."

Acadia hesitated. She'd focused on denying any part of her past for so long, it felt wrong to indulge herself. Everything she needed was provided by Arnion or the palace. She couldn't remember the last time she'd bought herself a pair of shoes. Not since before Gehenna.

Perhaps this was why she wasn't adapting to life in Eiren. Buying shoes wasn't a crime. Maybe if she started doing normal things, she'd start to fit in.

Acadia opened her mouth, about to concede.

That's when the shouting started.

Chapter 3

ANGRY VOICES ROSE LIKE a swarm of hornets. The crowd of people around Acadia surged, shoving her backward. What was once a slightly overcrowded market became a tidal wave of bodies. A shriek split the air behind her, and she whirled around.

An old woman was rolling in the dust. She struggled to stand, but her long purple robe was caught in the trample of feet. Frantic, she stumbled to her knees, calling out for help, but her hoarse cries were swallowed by the clamor around her. The marketplace grew more chaotic.

Acadia shouldered her way through to the woman. She gripped her gnarled hands and hoisted her upright. "Are you okay?" she asked.

The woman clutched at her, staring with fear-filled eyes, and nodded. Her breath hitched, like she was holding back a sob.

More people began jostling and shouting. Acadia wrapped a protective arm around the old woman and scrutinized the deluge of humanity around her. They shoved past, mouths tight and eyes wild.

What on Elorah is going on?

Acadia guided her charge back toward the shoe stall, where they could avoid the worst press of the crowds. She helped the old woman grip the wooden counter. "Hold onto this until the worst of the crowd passes by. I'm sure it won't last much longer."

She pressed herself against the wall of shoes. Tiny slippers poked into her back. A clanging sound rose against the sea of troubled voices and the shouting molded into coherent words.

"Not our problem! Not our fight!" Rage boiled from the words that were screamed over and over.

And then she saw them.

A group of at least fifty people wearing black hoods with mesh shields to conceal their faces. Some of them clanged cymbals, adding to the bedlam. They wore riot armor over their clothing, like the glossy carapace of a beetle, with a single blood-red handprint splashed on their chests.

Separatists.

Acadia knew some Eirenians were dissatisfied with taking in refugees from Gehenna. Grumblings had even reached the palace. But she had no idea the discontent had progressed this far. The Separatists were a fringe group of hyper-loyalist radicals. They wanted to isolate Eiren from the rest of the world, and unfortunately their numbers were growing.

One of the black-hooded group gestured to the crowd. "Taking in Gehennians is not our responsibility! Why should we pay for their reeducation, training, and housing? We didn't force them to sign over their lives to Lucien. They got what they deserved. Our prince can't see it. He's been blinded by that scheming harlot." The man paced back and forth, working himself into a frenzy. "Gehenna was always Kifu's problem. It's in *their* territory. And now Kifu is calling on us again to clean up their mess." He shook his head in exaggerated disbelief. "I say no more!" He punctuated his words by slicing his hand through the air like a knife.

The horde of Separatists behind him cheered and raised their fists. "Not our problem! Not our fight!" they shouted.

He waved them quiet. "People of Eiren, we can no longer be silent in the face of the imprudent decisions of the palace. It is time for us to rise. Let the Gehennians know they are not welcome here."

One of his number—a great hulking figure with a battered club strapped to his back—stepped forward. He leaned down to whisper in the speaker's ear.

The leader turned and stalked toward the stall selling ceramic plates. "You!" He jabbed a finger at the young woman behind the stand. "You came from Gehenna, didn't you?"

The trembling lady shrank back, her face white. Her dark curls were pulled back in a long braid that fell over her shoulder. She tugged at a loose curl by her ear. "Yes," she stammered. "But I've been going through the rehabilitation program. I'm trying to make an honest living."

Acadia shuddered. It was Marta, a young woman whom she'd visited a few days ago. It took Marta hours to craft a single plate. She poured her heart into each design. Every color, every line had a meaning behind it.

"Really?" the hooded man sneered. "And who pays for all this? Who gave you the supplies and training to make this garbage?" He swept a hand across the counter of her stall, sending plates crashing to the floor.

The crowd watched in frightened silence.

Numbness crept over Acadia's limbs. She was used to displays of violence far worse than this. But not in Eiren. It was supposed to be different here. Tension threaded along her spine and twined up each vertebra.

Why wasn't anyone *doing* anything?

"I get funding from the royal palace," Marta whispered.

"You see!" The leader turned back to the crowd. "Worthless, leaching parasites. And what do you think she does with the profits? She doesn't pay it back into our city coffers, I assure you."

The cord of tension within Acadia strained, like someone twisting a lute string too tight. She shook with anger.

"I send it to my family." Marta's quiet protest was swallowed by the muttering of the crowd.

"Shut up," the man screamed. He snatched a plate from the hanging display and smashed it at her feet. Marta flinched. Tears streamed down her cheeks.

Caustic laughter burst out from the group of Separatists. "Aw, did we make her cry?" a voice jeered.

The cord within Acadia snapped. "Stop!" she shouted and elbowed her way forward. "What kind of coward throws things at a defenseless young woman?"

The hooded leader turned to scan the crowd. "Who said that?" he demanded. His voice lashed out, like a burning whip.

The people around Acadia shifted. She stepped forward, chin high. "I did," she declared. "I'm not afraid of someone who doesn't even have the courage to show his face."

The man turned to her. Even with a mask shrouding his features, Acadia sensed the malice within his gaze. "Bold words, *Lady* Acadia," he replied.

Only her years of training as a Jewel kept her from flinching at the venom as he spoke. She steeled her spine and glared at him as if he were an insect to be crushed under her heel. Sapphyre's glare.

The man paused, then he threw out a black-gloved hand with a laugh. "Do you see their arrogance? This is a Gehennian's true nature. Wake up, Eiren!" His voice crescendoed into a hate-filled shriek.

Acadia had met many power-hungry people over the course of her life. It was amazing how similar they all were in the end. How tempting it was to scorch him with her words, to cut him down in a battle of wits, and humiliate him in front of his followers. Sapphyre would have done it in a heartbeat. But Sapphyre could also snap her fingers and have unruly guests ejected by her muscular Ulekren guards.

Now she stood alone.

But more than that, she was different. Knowing Arnion, loving Arnion, had changed her. She swallowed back the insult burning on the tip of her tongue and cleared her throat. Maybe his anger could be diffused by a calm, rational response.

Acadia inclined her head. "If you have a political grievance, go through the proper channels. Creating a disturbance here is at best, pointless, and at worst, dangerous. Stop this foolishness before someone gets hurt."

"Oh, you'd like that, wouldn't you, my *lady*?" He stalked toward her. People in the crowd scattered out of his way. "You'd like for us to fall back into the shadows where politicians can sweep our concerns under the rug and away from the public eye, while you fritter away your time in the royal palace, whispering honeyed words into our prince's ears." With each word he took another menacing step forward until he loomed over her. He jabbed a finger at her chest. "Your noxious lies are part of the reason we Separatists exist."

Sweat trickled down Acadia's back, but she refused to break eye contact, even though she had to look up. An elbow jabbed in her back. Bitter voices whispered behind her. The multitude was growing hostile. She was outnumbered and losing their sympathy. Would people always hate her, Acadia, just like they'd hated Sapphyre? Her gaze cut to Marta for a second; gratitude shone in the other woman's eyes. Acadia straightened her shoulders. At least she had protected Marta from this coward's assault. Even if the Separatists hated her, it hadn't been in vain.

"Tell me," the man sneered. "Why were you sent to Gehenna?"

Fury and dread coiled like twin serpents in Acadia's stomach. "That is none of your business." Her voice came out in a low, angry hiss. "My crimes are my own. And they've already been paid. Or is the blood of your crown prince an insufficient price?"

Someone in the crowd gasped, and Acadia paused. Maybe there was still hope she could sway them.

She gestured to the people beside her and spoke in a voice regal and strong. "Allow me to correct your misperception. People were sent to Gehenna for all manner of reasons." Acadia raised her chin. "Some of us were criminals, yes, but others were ensnared by trying to help their loved ones. My friend Agatha entered a blood debt to pay for medicine for her family." She touched a hand to her chest. "All of us made a bad choice to trust in Lucien. We made mistakes. But we were also manipulated and abused beyond what you can imagine by that maniac." She shook her head, forcing back the surge of memories that threatened to overwhelm her and opened her hands to the crowd. "You live in this glittering city, but the rest of Elorah isn't like Eiren. It's a harsh, cold place. You've been shielded from so much. Please give people like Marta a chance to start over. She is innocent."

Murmurs from the crowd told Acadia that at least some of her words had broken through the animosity. Hope fluttered in her chest. Maybe she *could* reach the people of Eiren; help them understand.

"No Gehennian is innocent." The man's vehement reply stung like acid flung against her face. "You spread poison and chaos wherever you go. If the rest of the world is as bad as you say, we should cut it off, like a diseased limb. Starting with forked-tongued serpents like you." He pointed at her, and a group of Separatists behind him moved forward, hands balled into fists.

Acadia's pulse rate spiked. She widened her stance, but with this crowd, self-defense would be nearly impossible. And she was significantly outnumbered. Even so, she couldn't back down and leave Marta. She gritted her teeth. This wasn't going to be pleasant.

White flashed at the edge of her vision. Then an arm snaked around her throat and jerked backward, *hard*.

Chapter 4

THE WORLD SPUN. ACADIA stumbled, clawing at the gloved arm choking her. The assailant shifted his hold lower, pressing his forearm against her collarbone. She took a ragged breath. Her feet scrabbled in the dirt, trying to find purchase. If she could steady herself, she could attempt to throw him. But it was impossible while he kept her off balance, tugging her relentlessly back.

"Don't let her get away!" the Separatist leader shouted, but it sounded like he was underwater. People screamed. There was even more pushing and shoving. Acadia struggled in her attacker's grip, swallowed by the chaos of the crowd. Colors and shapes swam before her vision and the metallic taste of panic coated her tongue.

She wouldn't go down without a fight.

Acadia tore at the hand around her neck. Her fingers gouged into the glove, but it was made of thick sagrin hide. The assailant probably didn't feel a thing.

She dug her heels into the dirt and wrenched her body to the left, trying to break free. Amid the crush of bodies, she made out white robes on the arm restraining her.

An analyst?

So, even the analysts were turning on her now. They were supposed to pursue logic and sound reasoning, not be swayed by emotional outbursts of blathering, unhinged radicals.

Was there anyone in Eiren who wasn't her enemy?

The man took advantage of the confusion and dragged her into a deserted alleyway. No one from the crowd followed. Acadia's thoughts roiled in disbelief, before anger shouldered its way to the forefront. Even among the hundreds of people in the marketplace, she was alone.

No one was coming to help her.

Fury smoldered in her chest. Fine, then. She'd rescue herself.

Acadia grabbed her assailant's arm with both hands and bent her knees. She stepped forward, dropped her left shoulder, and heaved her attacker up over her back, slamming him into the ground.

A cloud of dust rose around them. The analyst wheezed and tried to crawl away. "You're not going anywhere." Acadia seized the collar of his robe and jerked him toward her. "Not before I get a good look at you." With her free hand, she yanked the cowl off his head.

Midnight-purple hair tumbled out in messy waves and laughing hazel eyes met hers.

A woman!

"They told me you were tough." The analyst grinned up at her. "But I never believed it until now."

Acadia tightened her grip on the analyst's collar, her knuckles white. "What were you thinking?" she hissed. "How dare you attack—"

"Whoa, whoa," the analyst interrupted. She waved her hands vigorously. "You've got it all wrong. I was rescuing you."

Acadia's jaw clenched. She shook the analyst's collar. "You really think I'm stupid enough to believe that? Who rescues someone by putting them in a chokehold?"

"In hindsight, it may not have been the best option. But I had to think fast before those Separatists got hold of you. We've been tracking their movements for a while, but we never expected their assembly to become violent." The analyst's expression grew thoughtful as she spoke, though her eyes still sparkled with amusement.

Acadia stiffened, her teeth grinding together until it was painful. She didn't like being laughed at.

"I'm Espina, by the way. Eirenian Intelligence." The analyst reached for the golden belt around her waist.

Acadia tightened her grip around her prisoner's collar, wrenching the analyst forward. "Stop that!"

Espina sighed and held up her palms in a gesture of peace. "Relax, Lady Acadia. I was just getting my identification. For proof."

Sirens blared, and Acadia saw the tell-tale flash of red lights. Enforcers! Eirenian law enforcement were on the way. "A little late," Acadia muttered, but her muscles relaxed slightly. The presence of enforcers should send the Separatists scattering. That's how it was with bullies. They only went after targets weaker than themselves. She maintained her hold on the analyst's collar. "We'll see if your identification checks out."

Espina shrugged. "Who do you think notified the enforcers of the disturbance?"

Acadia opened her mouth to argue when an enforcement vehicle rumbled into the alleyway. The one-person vello bike hovered in midair. Its red-and-white stripes identified it as a law-enforcement vehicle. Thankfully the siren was off, but red lights flashed, bouncing off the walls and nearly blinding her. She held up a hand to her eyes.

"Agent Kartul?" The enforcer hoped off her bike and flipped up her visor. "Are you all right?" Her hand hovered above the stunner strapped to her waist.

"I'm fine." Espina gave a facetious wave around Acadia's restraining elbow. "Just reassuring a concerned citizen."

Acadia released her hold on Espina's collar. Her cheeks burned, and she held out a hand to help the analyst up. "Sorry," she said gruffly.

The enforcer strode toward them, pulling a data pad out of her side pocket. "Thanks for the tip off, Agent."

Espina gestured toward the end of the alleyway, where all the commotion had started. "Was anyone hurt?"

The enforcer shook her head. "No. We're tracking property destruction, and a lot of people are shaken up. But thankfully, no one appears to have been harmed. Your message helped us get here before things escalated further."

"I wish I had predicted this pattern of behavior. I might have spared everyone this . . ." Espina frowned toward the market, enforcer lights flashing and clumps of people huddled together with hunched shoulders and wide eyes.

"No one thought the Separatists would sink to this level of petty violence." The enforcement officer clicked her tongue. "It's a shame." She glanced at Acadia and her blue eyes widened. "Lady Acadia, I apologize. I didn't recognize you. Were you harmed?"

Shame seared the back of Acadia's neck. She wanted to melt into the floor. "I'm fine," she said, looking away.

Espina stepped beside her. "I'm going to escort her back to the palace myself. That will attract less attention. I also have to submit my after-action report to my supervisor."

The enforcer looked at Acadia, then Espina. "If you think that's best. I'll leave Lady Acadia in your hands, then, Agent Kartul."

Acadia took a step forward, reaching toward the officer. "What about Marta? Is she all right?"

"The young artisan?" the enforcer asked. "She's fine. Some of our agents are taking her statement now. Then they'll take her for a med check, just to be sure. Rest assured, our people are taking good care of her." Her gaze shifted from Acadia back to Espina. "If you have everything in hand . . ."

"Thank you, Officer. I'm sure you have a lot of work to do." Espina's tone was polite but dismissive. Like she was accustomed to giving orders.

Just how high ranking was she?

The enforcer ducked her head in acknowledgment and walked back to her vello.

Meanwhile, Espina rummaged in her belt and pulled out a holocard that glowed silver in the sunlight, all the while biting her lip, like she was holding back a laugh. She raised her eyebrows.

"What?" Acadia snapped indignantly.

"Still want to check my identification card?" Espina brushed her hands along her robes. The white fabric was smeared with dirt.

Acadia scoffed and crossed her arms over her chest. "Any normal person would be suspicious."

"But you're not normal, are you?" Espina gave up on the brown streaks staining her outfit and turned to face her. Acadia was surprised to see admiration written across the analyst's face. "You're extraordinary. Something our crown prince realized right away. Particularly for a former Gehennian—"

"I wish people would stop calling us that," Acadia grumbled. "I know it's not supposed to be an insult, but it's a constant reminder of a past most of us want to forget."

Espina's mouth popped open in surprise before she caught herself and clamped it shut. She tilted her head to the side, considering. "I can see how that would be the case. Fascinating." She unclipped her data pad and took short, efficient notes with her stylus. "I'll have to bring that up at the next director's meeting. Maybe we can look for another term to begin disseminating into the populace. It could aid our integration efforts."

Acadia rolled her eyes. "You do that." She stretched her shoulders until she felt a satisfying pop. "Let's go."

"Certainly." Espina pointed to the right. "My vello is parked just around the corner. It will be much faster than your trilorid."

Acadia groaned. "How do you know about the trilorid?"

Espina tapped her chest proudly. "Eirenian Intelligence, remember? If you'd like my advice about how to pass the combat test in time for your next exam, I'd be happy to—"

"I'm good. Thanks." Acadia cut her off. She clenched her fists. "And I'm not riding with you. Once I get my blasted trilorid, I'll follow you to the palace."

"As you wish, Lady Acadia." The enthusiasm in Espina's voice was unmistakable.

Acadia huffed and turned away. A knot loosened between her shoulder blades. Espina was definitely odd—like most analysts—but it was still a relief to find a potential ally, even a quirky one, within Eiren's walls.

A frantic bustle of activity met Acadia as she pulled her trilorid into the palace's parking zone. Advisors, staff, and security personal streamed from the palace, bombarding her with a thousand questions at once. A med tech began waving a sensor probe over her chest.

"I'm fine," Acadia protested. She looked around at the turmoil in bewilderment. "What is going on?"

Espina stepped up beside her. "I sent a status report on the way. Intelligence must have notified the palace. Though their emergency response leaves a lot to be desired." She raised a bemused eyebrow.

"Emergency response?" Acadia's thoughts roiled. *What?*

Espina shrugged. "If a member of the royal family is attacked, the palace staff is put on high alert." The data clip on her wrist beeped, and Espina slid a finger across it. Her eyes scanned the small screen. "I just received instructions. I'm to escort you to the clinic for a full medical check. The prince will meet us there."

Acadia pressed her fingers against her temples. All this commotion was over her? But she wasn't even royalty. How did Arnion put up with this? She took a shuddering breath and pasted on a smile. "There's really no need. I'm perfectly fine." She gestured at her dusty clothes. "Not a scratch on me. Just a little dirt. I don't want to disturb Arnion for something so trivial. I know he had an important diplomatic meeting today."

The med tech scanned Acadia's wrist. A holographic display of her pulse appeared above the scanner. "Your body shows signs of stress and exertion. We need to get you checked out. It's protocol."

Beside her, Espina nodded.

A splinter of annoyance jabbed into Acadia's spine. Where had all these *helpful* people been while the Separatists were spewing their hate? Now, after the difficulty was over, everyone was fussing over her. All she wanted to do was get back to her room, curl up in her bed, and press a pillow over her ears, shutting out all the noise.

It was too much.

Eiren was too much.

Panic scraped long fingernails against the inside of Acadia's skull. Darkness flickered at the edges of her vision. She couldn't breathe. Concerned faces pressed in around her, calling her name, reaching for her.

"Lady Acadia, please look this way." A bright flash blinded her vision. Acadia winced and flung a hand over her eyes.

Was that a press camera?

"Can you tell us anything about the attack?" A hand thrust a thin black recorder into her face.

Acadia blinked and tried to clear her fuzzy vision. Why was the media here? She kept her hand raised to shield herself from the onslaught. "I'm sorry, I don't know what you're referring to."

The reporter jostled forward. His short black hair was mussed and sweat beaded his forehead. It looked like he had just run a marathon. "The Separatist attack in the market." His voice was breathless. "Were you the only victim?" He shoved the recording device at her again.

"I think there's been a mistake." Acadia pushed away the recorder. "There was no attack. The Separatists were protesting, and it got out of hand—"

"How many Separatists were there? Were they armed?"

"I don't think— Ouch!"

The med tech had pricked Acadia's finger. "Sorry. Should have warned you first." He dipped his chin with an apologetic look. "I needed a sample. There are a few more measurements I need to take." He tugged her wrist toward him.

Her mind flashed back to her first day in Gehenna. Rough arms had stripped her and shoved her down the hall to a room full of med techs. Rubber-gloved hands had poked and prodded, stabbed her with needles, and forced a tongue depressor in her mouth until she gagged. Measuring tape was cinched around her waist. A cold metal caliper pricked the skin above her hip.

Acadia shook her head, trying to rid herself of the memory. *I'm not in Gehenna anymore.* Spots danced across her vision, and she swayed. Hands reached for her as she tasted vomit in the back of her throat.

"No!" She jerked her wrist free. Her harsh tone cut through the cacophony of sound. The med tech looked up in confusion, and the mob around her fell silent.

Acadia shook her head and tried again. "No med checks, no emergency, no bothering Arnion. I'm fine." She held up a hand amid the protests. "Really. All I want is to go to my room and lie down. Please."

The med tech reached for her. "Ma'am, you need to—"

"Don't touch me! And *don't* make me repeat myself. Or would you like to get prosecuted for harassment?" Fear warped her words into scathing fury. She pressed a hand over her mouth in horror.

That wasn't her voice.

That was Sapphyre.

For a moment, Acadia forgot how to breathe. She'd sworn never to use that voice again. The promise she'd made to herself ricocheted in her mind like angry shrapnel. Was she really so weak? So easily flustered? Her courage withered, flayed to bits as she mentally berated herself. All these months of careful self-control and poise—destroyed.

The med tech gaped at her. He lowered his hand, eyes wide. "I'm sorry, my lady."

The weight of a hundred Eirenian stares pierced Acadia as the palace staff watched in stunned silence.

"I'm sorry. I didn't mean..." The apology shriveled in Acadia's throat. Everyone was staring at her. Looks of disgust and hurt mingled with disappointment and pity.

Nausea churned in Acadia's stomach, and for a moment she feared she would be sick right in the parking zone. "Please forgive my outburst. I'm not myself right now. I need to lie down . . ." The words crumpled against her tongue. Her fingers fumbled, trying to remember the Eirenian gesture for remorse, but her shaking hands made it impossible. Giving up, she turned and fled into the palace. Her vision blurred with unshed tears.

Acadia didn't stop running until she'd barreled through the automatic door to her rooms and activated the security lock. It chimed and blinked red. The mechanical bolts clicked into place. Acadia pressed her forehead against the cold metal door. No one would be able to disturb her until she deactivated the security system. Her pulse throbbed in her ears as she sank into a miserable heap on the floor and buried her face in her hands.

Chapter 5

WHEN THE TINKLING DOORBELL sounded through her suite of rooms, Acadia buried her face into her pillow. She'd just managed to scrape herself off the floor and fling herself onto her bed. There was only one person it could be, and she didn't want to face him.

<Acadia?> Arnion's spirit spoke gently to her mind. <It's me.>

Hearing his voice released a swarm of nervous butterflies in her stomach. Acadia was still getting used to the way Eirenians could speak directly to one another's spirits. Spir-coms had practical uses, but to her, they always felt more intimate than regular speech. Her pulse drummed a staccato rhythm along her veins as echoes of Arnion's voice reverberated inside her. Stars, she'd missed him. But then she remembered why he was outside her door instead of being consumed by diplomatic meetings, like usual.

<I suppose you heard everything,> she sent back. Bitterness tinged her words orange.

A syna filled her mind. Arnion was sending an image from his spirit. Waves bubbled over a pale sandy beach. Froth spiraled around tiny pink seashells that speckled the turf. Footprints appeared as if a pair of invisible feet were walking along the damp sand. Then Acadia noticed there were two pairs of tracks. Two invisible sets of bare toes strolling across the beach.

<Would you take a walk with me?> Arnion's spirit asked, the tone as light as a spring breeze. Acadia could almost feel the wind on her cheeks.

<Now?> She sat up and checked the time. <Don't you still have work to do?>

A flock of brightly colored birds burst in her mind, soaring over the tranquil beach. They chittered and sang, flying high in the sky until they disappeared in the distance.

Maybe Arnion needed a break too. Is that what his syna meant?

<Please come out, chimad.>

Acadia's breath hitched. She wanted to see him.

Badly.

Even though she'd messed up. Even though her mistake had cost him valuable time trying to bring peace to the world. Guilt welled in her stomach. She should be supporting his efforts, not creating distractions.

But . . .

Dral! She wanted to see him!

Acadia yanked out her hair tie and hastily redid her ponytail. Then she straightened her rumpled tunic, frowning at the wrinkles, and trudged to the door. Her finger hovered over the security lock, and she took a shaky breath.

Time to face her prince.

Acadia pressed her index finger against the button. The door chimed and slid open.

A rush of rich purple fabric enveloped her. Strong arms wrapped around her shoulders and tugged her against a firm chest. "Acadia." Arnion's voice was rough with concern. "Were you harmed?"

"No," she mumbled and pressed her check against his silken robe. Arnion's rapid heartbeat thrummed in her ear.

He tightened his arms around her. "I was so worried. When they told me about the marketplace . . ." Relief filtered into his voice and mixed with sadness. "Why didn't you contact me?"

Acadia squirmed. Her gaze flicked up, taking in his golden eyes tight with worry, before looking away. "It wasn't . . ." Her voice wobbled and she cleared her throat. "I didn't want to bother you. I knew you were busy."

She was still getting used to this. Getting used to his bronzed skin, the short dark curls that framed his forehead, and his perfect posture. In Gehenna, Arnion's limp made him about her height. Now, he was at least a head taller. When they stood close together, she had to tilt her chin to meet his gaze. How Rhys had managed to make Arnion look like he belonged in Gehenna was one of life's greatest mysteries. She still didn't understand the technology used to make Arnion have a temporary limp.

One thing she knew: Arnion was gorgeous. And when he looked at her like that—like she was the only woman in the world—warmth pooled in her stomach and a muddled fuzziness invaded her mind.

"Acadia." Arnion traced his fingertips down her shoulders. "There's nothing more important to me than your wellbeing."

She scoffed, annoyed with herself and her schoolgirl reaction. "Don't be ridiculous. There's an entire planet that needs Eiren. That needs *you*. I'm just one tiny person in a world full of broken people."

"You're my world." He traced her jaw with his fingertips and tucked a strand of hair behind her ear.

Tingles zipped down her arms and heat flared across her cheeks. Arnion bent toward her, and she wrapped her arms around his neck. When his lips brushed against hers, Acadia closed her eyes. Twining her fingers in the soft hair at the nape of his neck, Acadia felt him sigh against her mouth.

"Oh! Pardon me," a feminine voice tittered nervously from behind him.

Acadia released Arnion and peeked over his shoulder. Tifa, her hand-maiden, stood in the hallway behind them. Her indigo hair was done up in an impeccable chignon. A deep blush stained her face.

Tifa ducked her chin, averting her gray eyes. "I was coming to check on you, my lady, and air out your rooms for the day. But if this is a bad time . . ." She fidgeted with her hands.

Acadia pinched her lips together. Resentment fisted into a hard lump at the base of her throat. Was five minutes alone with Arnion too much to ask?

Sometimes it felt like all of Elorah was working against them.

Arnion kissed her forehead then turned to the handmaid. "It's all right, Tifa." He slipped his hand in Acadia's. "We were just leaving for a walk."

Acadia took in his handsome jaw and the patient smile that played across his lips. Even when he was interrupted, Arnion was always kind. It had amazed her how he'd taken the time to learn the names of every member of the palace staff. Right down to the elderly man who swept the halls. He loved his people, and she loved him all the more for it.

Still, it would be nice to have him all to herself occasionally.

Arnion seemed to read her mind because he squeezed her hand. "Shall we?"

Acadia squeezed back. "Yes, let's go. Thank you, Tifa, for your help." She gave the maid a friendly nod, and Tifa bobbed a curtsey as they passed.

They strolled down a corridor lined with white fluted columns. Intricate golden metalwork capped each one. The metal shone in the late-afternoon sun through the large windows that punctuated the hallway.

Acadia slid her free hand along the cool marble banister as they made their way down the grand staircase and out into the grounds.

Even though it was late afternoon, the summer sun blazed high in the sky. It was nice to have the long hours of daylight.

At first, Acadia assumed they were heading toward the palace gardens. She and Arnion often took walks there in the evening, where she marveled over the exotic Eirenian plants, strolled under archways twined with ivy, or meandered around bushes dripping with heady pink blossoms. She always loved to stop and dip her fingers in the reflecting pool, watching the gold and silver fish swam lazily around the water lilies. The sound of water might soothe her frazzled nerves.

Maybe tonight she could finally work up the courage to tell Arnion about her past. The thought settled like lead in her heart.

But Arnion tugged her past the entrance to the gardens, and Acadia eyed him curiously. "I had something else in mind today." He grinned and inclined his head forward, indicating they should continue along the walkway.

Acadia pursed her lips. "But there's nothing down there except the training grounds . . ." Understanding struck her with a jolt, and the heaviness in her chest lightened. She clapped her hands. "You want to spar?"

"I thought it'd be a nice change of pace." He kept his voice light, but playfulness shone in his expression.

Acadia bounced up and down on her toes. "What a great idea!" She threw her arms around him and kissed his cheek. "Thank you."

A good sparring session always made her feel better. And after the day's events, she needed it. Living in Eiren felt like being crushed in a vice. Her failure to meet the kingdom's expectations tightened around her each day. She knew Arnion carried an even heavier burden. People looked to him as a savior, someone who could stop Lucien and bring unity to Elorah. He was probably feeling more stressed than she was. Opportunities to slip away on their own—to relax and have fun—were precious.

Arnion laughed and nuzzled her nose. "We'll see if you're still thanking me afterward. I know you don't like to lose."

"Who says I'll lose?" Acadia planted her hands on her hips. "Don't think I'm going to let you win just because you're charming."

He held a hand over his heart. "Wouldn't dream of it," he assured her.

They crossed the blue striped track that ran around the expansive training ground. Acadia breathed in the smell of freshly cut grass as they entered the field in the center. On the far left, the space was dominated by exercise equipment of all shapes and sizes. Arnion and Acadia bypassed the fitness training stations and headed toward a section of wide-open grass marked with painted white lines. The combat training zone.

Arnion walked up to one of the weapons lockers and pressed a thumb against the lock. The door slid open, and he turned to look at her. "Have you ever tried a stunner or a photon pistol?"

Acadia stepped up beside him, stretching an elbow over her shoulder. "I've been taught the basics. We use them sometimes during our spirit warrior training, but I prefer blades." She selected a flux sword and gave it a practice swing. It was only a training one, so the edge was dulled and the undercurrent of electricity that ran along the blade was deactivated. "Flux swords are more elegant, and a skilled wielder can deflect any energy blasts that come their way. Why do you ask?"

"There's a small arms range just over that ridge." Arnion nodded to a grassy berm on the right. "Maybe next time, we could try it."

Acadia narrowed her eyes. Arnion's shoulders tensed under her scrutiny, and he looked away. "Why?" she asked with suspicion.

Arnion sighed and ran a hand through his hair. "After today, there are some who think you should travel with an armed escort—"

"Absolutely not," Acadia snapped. Panic raised her voice an octave. "There's no way I'm having someone shadow my every step."

"I know, I know." Arnion raised his hands as if to deflect her ire. There were dark circles under his eyes and strained lines around his mouth. "I knew you'd never agree to it." She opened her mouth to argue, and he hurried on. "And I'm not asking you to. I promise." He leaned against the side of the weapons locker. Weariness draped around him like a shroud. Arnion rubbed the dark stubble along his jaw, and Acadia could tell he was working up to something. "But after what happened in the marketplace today . . ."

Anxiety skittered over Acadia's skin. She already felt trapped in Eiren. Having an escort around her constantly would be unbearable. She'd have to be even more careful, maintaining a nonstop mask of perfection. Dread pooled in her stomach at the thought. She had to convince Arnion that she was fine.

"Nothing happened." Acadia imbued her voice with nonchalance. There was a fine line between acting calm and coming off as cold and detached, but she knew how to play the game. She twirled the practice blade in her hand, making it sing through the air. "There were some disgruntled Separatists. The enforcers arrived, and that was the end of it. No one was hurt. I was never in any danger." She resisted the urge to scratch her knuckles, tightening her fingers around the hilt instead.

Guilt flared inside Acadia as she remembered Petra's horrified recognition earlier.

I was one of Lucien's Jewels. She almost blurted it out. The secret she kept from Arnion seared her tongue, begging to be set free. She tightened her jaw, forcing the truth back down her throat like a large bitter pill.

Acadia had heard about what happened to Lucien's Onyx in Dardak. After the collapse of Gehenna, the Heartless King's control across Elorah was shattered. His brokers, reckoners, and even his most precious influencers, his Jewels, were left unprotected. Most went into hiding to escape the repercussions for their vile actions. But not all were so lucky. People wanted Lucien's blood, but they were happy to take it out on his lackeys instead.

Acadia repressed a shudder. It was natural for people to want retribution. Lucien had caused untold suffering across Elorah. She had pieced together the news from bits of broken gossip in the market. The Dardaki had found Lucien's Onyx hiding in their capital city, Narsla. The frightened young woman was trying to book a passage across the strait to the continent. But someone betrayed her. They tortured her and burned her alive in the square. Acadia rubbed her hands together, suddenly cold.

Arnion wrapped an arm around her. "No matter what happens, I promise to protect you. Keeping you safe is my number one priority."

She had to get him to relax, to drop this idea of a security escort. Telling him about her past would have to wait. If Arnion thought she was at greater risk of being targeted, who knew the protective measures he would dream up. She leaned into him. "I *am* safe," she insisted. "What happened today was nothing."

"I disagree." Arnion tightened his grip around her shoulder. She tilted her head to glance at his expression. He looked angry.

Acadia swallowed. "Are you . . . upset with me?"

"Why would I be upset with you?" He looked down at her, puzzled.

Acadia opened her mouth, a thousand failures and mistakes wanting to spill out. *Because I panicked and threatened a med tech today. Because I can't master basic spirit combat. Because the Eirenians think I'm not good enough for you. Because I was one of Lucien's Jewels. Because I'm lying to you every day.*

A small squeak escaped her throat as she fought to keep the words down. She bit her lip. "I . . ."

Arnion shook his head incredulously. "I'm upset with the people who tried to harm you; who threatened the refugees my father and I have personally welcomed into our kingdom. I'm angry that I wasn't there to protect you when you needed me. That I was sitting in a hoverchair listening to diplomats argue while you were in harm's way." He clenched his fists. "For something like this to happen within Eiren's walls . . . It's unthinkable." The raw frustration in his voice shredded her heart.

Acadia dropped her practice sword and hugged him tightly. "It's not your fault," she whispered. "The peace talks between Avathys and Kifu are crucial. You're a prince. You have responsibilities. I understand that."

Arnion took her face in his hands and pressed his forehead against hers. "I'm also a man. Who happens to be in love with you."

Acadia looked away. She pressed her palms against her thighs to hide their trembling.

I love you too.

The words stuck in her throat. How could she tell him she loved him when her past was like an unstable klepton reactor that could detonate at any moment? Once Arnion found out, he'd never look at her the same. She couldn't allow him to bind himself to her without knowing the full truth. Arnion was so good; he would keep his vows—even if it hurt.

Acadia wanted to tell him, but fear stole her voice.

Every time.

"I care for you deeply," she whispered and risked a glance up at his face. Pain flickered in his eyes, so quickly that Acadia wasn't sure if she'd imagined it. Guilt soured her stomach. Frantically, she wracked her brain for a way to change the course of the conversation.

Distraction, distraction. I need a distraction.

Acadia clicked her tongue and swatted Arnion's shoulder playfully. "Enough serious talk. Didn't we come out here to have fun?" She bent down to pick up her training blade and nodded toward the field. "Or is all this an elaborate ploy to stall your imminent defeat?"

Arnion studied her, like he could see through her veil of false cheerfulness. She imagined the wheels turning in his mind. It was clear he wanted to continue their conversation. But would he let it drop, for her sake?

Acadia suddenly felt incredibly tired. Tired of maintaining a façade. Tired of the tensions between Eirenians and Gehennians. Tired of looming war and the unending threat of Lucien. Tired of politics. Just plain tired. What a waste, to have this treasured time with Arnion devoured by other people and their problems.

She channeled her heart's deepest desire—to spend time with her prince—and summoned a smile she hoped would melt his heart. "Please?" She tilted her head. "Let it go for a while. Let's spar."

Arnion's shoulders relaxed. "All right." He gave her a lopsided grin that buzzed through her nerves like liquid sunshine.

The chimad grin.

That's what she secretly called it. It was a grin reserved for her. She'd never seen him use it on anyone else. Usually, it popped up after he'd call her "chimad" or when they shared a special moment.

Acadia still didn't know what chimad meant. Arnion had promised to explain it to her, but with his never-ending meetings and diplomatic engagements, they hadn't made the time. Her lessons in Eirenian history and culture hadn't covered it either. She had the basics, but the deeper cultural nuances of their society were hard to grasp. No one in her classes ever mentioned chimad.

Deep down, Acadia was afraid of what it meant. Afraid it was something irrevocable. Something that Arnion had committed to without knowing her shameful past. It felt like a pledge or a promise of some kind. But would he feel the same way after he found out she'd worked hand in hand with Lucien, entrapping people and sending them to their deaths in Gehenna?

Could someone as good and kind as Arnion ever forgive her for *that*?

You'll never belong here, a bitter voice whispered in the back of her mind. *Once he finds out—* She snapped a lid over those thoughts and walked toward the sparring circle in the grass.

They bowed to each other and took up their stances.

Acadia lunged forward, swinging her sword across her body. Metal rang against metal as her dulled blade clashed against Arnion's. The sound echoed through the training yard. They sprang apart and circled each other. Reading the shift in his stance, Acadia knew he was going to attack her left side. She firmed up her guard to block him.

Arnion pivoted, twisting to strike. Acadia parried, deflecting his sword to the right. Taking a step back, she adjusted her grip and raised her blade to a defensive position along her right shoulder.

"You're doing it again." Arnion shook his head.

"What?"

"Swapping your hands."

Acadia checked the order of her hands. Right over left.

Dral.

He was right. She'd started the match with left over right and must have switched positions without noticing. Being ambidextrous was all well and good, but it didn't fit traditional Eirenian sword-fighting techniques. Acadia groaned. She lowered her sword and switched her hands back.

"I can't help it." She shrugged. "My body does it instinctively."

"Being unpredictable makes you a formidable opponent." Arnion stepped back and raised his guard.

"Is it too much for you, Your Highness?" she teased.

"Never." Arnion leveled her with a smoldering look, and Acadia's heart skipped a beat. "You know I love a challenge." He leaped at her and their swords clashed again.

Acadia firmed her grip and went for his exposed right side.

He met her blade. "I knew you were going to do tha—"

She swept her left foot under his and knocked him off balance. Arnion rolled to the side in a crouch. "Well done, Acadia."

"That's what you get for being over-confident, Your *Highness*." Acadia swept into a graceful curtsey. She lowered her sword and flexed her left hand wistfully. "I wish I could fight with two swords at once."

"Our blades are too heavy." Arnion stepped up beside her, considering the sword. "But I've heard that in Alsehir they sometimes use single-handed swords while riding sagrins. I could get you a pair, if you'd like." He looked at her with such tenderness, Acadia's heart wrenched.

She didn't deserve him.

Acadia's throat burned, and she swallowed. "Alsehir. That's the country to the east of you, right?"

"Yes. Lots of wide-open land, perfect for raising sagrin herds." His eyes took on a distant quality, as if he was remembering the view.

"Have you been there?" Acadia asked.

"A few times."

Acadia hummed thoughtfully. "I'd like to see it someday."

"Then we'll go." He held out his hand, and Acadia took it. As they returned their weapons to the locker, Arnion faced her. "Is there anything else you want to tell me?"

You can't keep it from him forever, the hateful voice whispered in her head.

Acadia took a sharp breath. Her prince waited, studying her.

She knew he wasn't going to be satisfied with another deflection, so she tried to find one of her more benign worries to share. "The others from Gehenna seem to be doing so well. Settling in, finding their place." She twined her fingers together, avoiding his gaze. "Everyone seems to be adapting, except me."

"Give it time."

"I know." She suppressed the urge to roll her eyes. Rhys had told her the same platitudes. But with Arnion, she risked a little more openness. She wrapped her arms around herself, feeling small. "I'm not used to it. Normally I'm not the one who falls behind."

"Come here."

She folded herself into his waiting embrace and pressed her ear against his chest. Arnion's heartbeat always calmed her. Ever since that day in his tomb, when he'd torn a hole through the veil of death and come back to her, hearing his steady heartbeat had always lifted her mood.

Arnion's arms tightened around her. "I love you. You're doing great," he whispered. His breath tickled her ear, and he pressed a kiss to her forehead.

When they broke apart, Acadia's eyes caught sight of a pale-blue flower that had sprouted beside the weapons locker. "Aladrius." She breathed out in surprise and bent down to pluck the small plant. "I didn't know it grew in Eiren." She crushed a leaf between her fingers and inhaled the pungent herbal scent. "It complements a rabbit stew perfectly."

She held the leaf out to Arnion, and he sniffed it. "It does smell good." His eyes shifted from the plant to her face. "I've never seen this herb before."

"It grows near Tacha . . . my childhood home." Acadia stumbled over the last word but forced herself to continue. "It's one of my favorite seasonings." Arnion studied her intently and she frowned. "What?"

"I never knew you liked cooking."

Acadia rubbed the aladrius leaf between her fingers, enjoying the familiar smell. It took her back to when she was a child, learning how to cook with her mother. She had never told Arnion about the time she'd tried to enter the palace kitchens. How the staff had offered to fetch her anything she needed and stoutly refused her offers to help. "I haven't cooked my own meals in a long time. But when I was a girl, Ma taught me. We used to cook together every day. She'd sing little songs to help her remember the ingredients." Acadia coiled the aladrius around her fingertip. "It's funny how a scent can hold so many memories." A tear trickled down her cheek, and she brushed it away.

"You miss them, don't you?"

Acadia sniffled. "Of course. Not a day goes by that I don't regret . . ." The lump in her throat choked off the rest of her words.

After a beat of silence, Arnion asked gently, "Maybe, if you reached out?"

"I've written to friends in Tacha. Shortly after I left, Da died of his injury. Ma and my brothers disappeared. No one seems to know where . . ." Acadia sighed. "I hope they're all right, but I don't have any clues. And even if I found them, what would I say? How could I face them?"

Her mouth went dry and she swallowed. "I abandoned my family and entered a blood oath with Lucien. Just like everyone else who wound up in Gehenna. And when I was desperate, there was no one who would intercede for me. I entered Gehenna totally broken. The last person I tried to help . . ." Her mind flashed to Delilah, the stunning redhead who had ridden in the carriage with her. "It didn't go well." Acadia shook her head. "I tried to help a young woman on the way to Gehenna. She betrayed me and I lost my red gemstone necklace, the last connection I had to my family."

Arnion brushed a hand through her hair. Acadia turned and pressed her head into the crook of his shoulder. "I wish it could always be like this. Just you and me. When I'm with you, I don't feel like I need anything else." Arnion's hand froze on her back. Acadia laughed and pulled back. "That's silly, isn't it? We can't run away and abandon the whole world."

Arnion gently tilted her chin so that she met his serious gaze. "Would that make you happy?" His voice was raw.

She looked away, slipping from his grasp. "Of course not." She hugged herself, suddenly cold. "It would be impossible anyway. You can't abandon Eiren."

As he watched her, echoes of emotion flickered across his face. Arnion was good at hiding his feelings, but Acadia was also trained in the subtle shifts that signaled emotional cues. How a shift in breathing patterns indicated anxiety. The inability to hold another's gaze signaled guilt. The slight parting of lips suggested attraction.

She detected traces of concern, love, and possibly fear. With Arnion, it was hard to be sure, but Acadia's gut told her the slight tensing of his shoulder muscles wasn't her imagination. But what would Arnion have to be afraid of?

Worry gnawed at her thoughts.

He cleared his throat. "It's getting late. We should probably head back."

"Of course." Acadia dipped her head in agreement. Arnion carried the burdens of an entire kingdom on his shoulders. It was no surprise he was stressed. The last thing he needed was to worry about her too. She wanted to make life easier for him, not harder. She looped her arm through his and beamed at him. "Lead on, my prince."

His answering smile was affectionate, but sad.

It felt like there was a clock ticking in her chest, counting down to disaster. Wearily, Acadia wondered how much time she had left before her luck finally ran out.

Later that night, Acadia couldn't sleep. She tossed and turned so much, her spallo gel mattress deactivated the magnetic sleep field. A robotic voice from her bedside table asked if she would like a sleeping draught.

"No, thank you." Her voice was groggy as she rolled over and turned off the automated message.

Her thoughts were consumed by memories of a rundown Kifan farmhouse. Of children's laughter. Of the sharp scent of jarl wheat ripening in the sun. She had pushed all the memories of her family deep down, to a place where she barely felt the pain. If she could contact them, what would she say? How would they react after she'd abandoned them all those years ago? Would they even want to see her?

They must hate me after what I've done.

<That's a lie, Acadia.>

Acadia shot up from the bed, tripping over her thermal blanket. <Who said that?> Questing tendrils shot from her spirit, casting her awareness like a net around herself. She tried to pull on the dwindling thread of spirit energy, but it evaporated from her mind as quickly as it had appeared.

Weird.

Acadia rubbed the back of her neck, unnerved by the unusual spir-com. The voice had been rich and melodic, like nothing she'd ever heard before. She glanced at her arm and frowned. It was covered in goosebumps.

After a few more minutes of scanning the area with her spirit, Acadia gave up and sank back onto her bed. She was probably overtired. What with Petra recognizing her and the chaos in the marketplace, the day had been an emotional rollercoaster. Just hearing the name Sapphyre set her teeth on edge. How was she ever supposed to tell Arnion the truth?

She hadn't been lying to Rhys when she said she wanted more time. It was one of many thorns piercing her heart. Every second spent with Arnion was precious. She didn't want to ruin it by dredging up her awful past. But if she didn't tell him . . . if he found out some other way . . .

Acadia buried her face into the pillow. Once Arnion knew the truth, there was a strong possibility he'd reject her. She pictured his handsome face, his disgust of Lucien's cruelty. Arnion had made it clear that Lucien wasn't just an enemy of Eiren. He was the enemy of Arnion's family, a creature of darkness beyond hope or compassion, even for someone as forgiving as the prince. What would he think when he found out how closely she and Lucien had worked together in Beulah?

Acadia slunk down and pulled the blanket over her, wishing she could shut out the world. If only she could wipe out her past, erase all memory of it from anyone's minds. If only she never had to deal with it ever again.

She wanted to take Arnion and run, as far as they could go, to the ends of Elorah. Where no one had ever heard of Lucien, or Sapphyre, or even Eiren.

No more kingdom.

No more meetings.

No more rules.

Acadia smiled to herself. That would be a dream come true.

A buzz tickled the back of her neck, and Acadia felt Arnion's spirit reaching out to her. <Good night, Acadia. Sweet dreams,> he whispered.

<Good night, my prince,> she sent back. Her message trailed off into purple-and-green butterflies.

She had to tell him. Soon. Once the Separatists calmed down and the idea of a security escort was irrelevant. When the issues between Kifu and Avathys were settled. Then, she would ask Arnion to make some time for them to talk. She had to tell him the truth, before he found out from someone else. If the people in Eiren wanted to crucify her for her past, like the Dardaki had with Onyx, at least it wouldn't catch Arnion by surprise.

She had thought escaping Gehenna would be the end of her problems. But now it felt like they were dealing with the political affairs of the entire planet. There was bickering between countries, Lucien was still at large, and people were protesting within Eiren. All of Elorah wanted a piece of Arnion.

Despite Acadia's exhaustion, worries swirled through her mind, keeping her awake. She needed sleep. Being overtired would only make things worse. There was a solution to every one of her problems, and she would find it. She always did.

Relax, Acadia. You have time. You have all the time in the world.

But it didn't feel that way.

If there was one lesson she had learned in Gehenna, it was that everything could change in the blink of an eye.

Chapter 6

SUNLIGHT SPARKLED ALONG THE turquoise sea, reminding Kaya of a gemstone. The little white sailboat she and Ellio sat in rocked gently on the waves. Kaya held up a hand to shield her eyes from the glare and admired the rugged cliffs along the shoreline. Even she had to admit Avathys was a beautiful country, with miles of pristine coastline and orchards sprawling stadion after stadion in the lush inland soil. What a difference from Kifu, the neighboring country, where even the hardiest crops struggled to grow. Normally she wasn't one to notice scenery, but she always enjoyed people-watching.

Kaya shifted her gaze from the coastline to the blue-haired young man beside her. Watching Ellio never bored her. Her handsome Kifan mechanic was currently leaning over the side of their boat, causing it to list to one side. Warmth pooled in her belly. He was too cute. Kaya mentally shook her head. She used to think attachments made people weak, but Ellio had taught her the value of friendship.

Kaya and Ellio were an unlikely pair. He'd grown up in the Downs, the worst district in the sprawling metropolis of Beulah. Kaya was a nomad, raised by her grandfather, Dragul, to follow in his footsteps as a spirit warrior of Eiren. After a falling out with Dragul, Kaya had found herself alone and angry in Beulah—never a good combination. A series of bad choices landed her in the clutches of the city's notorious guild boss. It was there, at one of the lowest points in her life, that she'd met Ellio. His kindness broke down the walls around her heart, and they formed a strong friendship that soon blossomed into love. Working together, they'd been able to free Kaya from the guild boss and escape the city.

"Kaya!" Ellio turned back to her, a wide smile on his suntanned face. Her heart careened against her ribs. "The water is so clear; you can see all the way to the bottom," he said. "It must be at least eighty fathoms! Come look!"

Kaya snorted but resisted the urge to point out they'd been enjoying the crystal waters for almost a year. They had found Dragul, her grandfather, ten months ago and had been living with him on the Avathysian coast ever since.

The ocean had done wonders for Ellio. He'd lost his pale complexion and the dark circles under his eyes, earned by years of surviving in the Downs. Kaya barely recognized the young man before her now, with sun-kissed skin and dark-brown eyes that always crinkled at the corners when he was excited. Sparks skittered through her stomach as he focused those eyes on her and patted the space beside him. Kaya covered her embarrassment with a grunt but joined him. She bumped her shoulder against his and peered into the water.

Up close, the ocean was so clear, it was almost a mirror, and she could indeed see the sandy ocean floor below, dotted with a network of nubby coral. The reef was her target, where the rare bluebell oyster liked to hide amid the fluorescent sea flora.

"You ready?" Ellio asked.

Kaya donned her flippers then tucked her dark bangs into her diving hood and pulled down her mask. She slid onto the ledge of the deck, her back to the water, and gave him a two-fingered salute. Ellio grinned and returned it, his blue hair shining beneath the morning sun. Kaya flipped backward off the edge of the boat before he could notice her blush. Kicking her fins up over her head, she somersaulted into the water. Even in the summer months, diving to the depth of the reef would have felt chilly if not for her wetsuit.

Kaya scissor-kicked, pushing herself deeper. A speckled sea turtle darted out of her path as she made her way toward hazy white sand below. A trio of silver fish flitted by, and she pumped her legs, bringing her closer to the bottom. She circled a bed of blue-and-yellow speckled coral, searching for the telltale shape of a bluebell oyster.

There!

Her fingers brushed over the ribbed shell. Kaya slipped her diving knife into her hand and pried the oyster loose, dropping it into a pouch on her belt. She swam further around the coral bed, eyes scanning.

Another one!

Kaya would have smiled if her mouth wasn't molded around the rebreather. Bluebell oysters fetched a good price at market. While fishing was part of their cover story, she'd found she truly enjoyed being out on the water.

Her grandfather was currently on an undercover assignment posing as a fisherman in Avathys. It was amazing how much information he was able to gather hanging around other crusty sailors at the docks. Of course, he needed fish and crustaceans to sell whenever he went to the local market. Too bad he didn't actually enjoy fishing. So, although he wasn't thrilled when his granddaughter showed up for training with a handsome Beulan man in tow, he allowed Ellio to stay, provided they took over the fishing.

Dragul let them keep any profits he made from selling their wares. Kaya figured his Eirenian stipend must be very generous, and she didn't need much. She was content to train and have a safe place for Ellio to stay. The market sales were an unexpected perk. She was helping Ellio save up for a new maglev coupler for his jetbike. He'd promised it would take them higher and faster than ever before.

Her fingers tugged on the second bluebell oyster. Its shell was stuck tight to the coral. She chipped away at its base then slipped her knife underneath and pried it loose. She reached to drop it into her pocket when a shadow fell across her eyes. Something large was swimming overhead.

Kaya jerked her head up. A large, sinuous shape twined above her. A spiny eel! The creature's mottled body blended into the sunlight filtering through the water. If not for its shadow, she would have missed it. The eel circled above, watching her with its six yellow eyes. The jagged spines running along its back rippled through the water. Kaya gritted her teeth. Of course it had to be a male eel and a large one, too. It was at least three times as long as she was.

<Ellio?> Kaya sent a spir-com up to him. Ellio wasn't naturally gifted with spirit abilities, but he'd learned enough to send and receive spir-coms when she was nearby. It had come in handy on multiple occasions.

<I see it. Can you get clear so I can use the harpoon gun?> Ellio's voice was strained.

<An eel that big could capsize the boat. Then we'd both be in the water.>

<Not if I hit the soft spot in its skull.>

Kaya rolled her eyes, not that Ellio could appreciate it. <No offense, Ellio, but that shot is one in a million.>

She clenched her fists. That stupid eel had to show up and ruin her day. This was the best spot near their home to collect bluebell oysters. But if a spiny eel staked out a territorial claim, she and Ellio would have to find new fishing grounds. The eels were notoriously violent. They killed even when they weren't hungry, often destroying entire reef ecosystems before moving on to terrorize a new area. Annoyance blossomed into full-blown anger in her chest. That wasn't happening today, not if she could help it.

<I can handle it.> Her spir-com thrummed with determination.

<Dragul warned us to leave them alone. Don't they hunt in packs? Where are the rest of them?> Ellio's spir-com was laced with purple streaks. He was worried.

Kaya scanned the waters around her in a slow circle so as not to attract attention. <There's only one. Must be a rogue.>

<At least let me *try* to harpoon it,> Ellio pleaded.

<I said, I've got this.> Kaya severed the spir-com abruptly. She cinched her oyster pouch shut and changed her grip on her dagger. Spiny eels were a menace to the ecosystem, and she'd grown attached to this reef. There was no way she was going to let one stupid eel desecrate it. She took a deep breath through her rebreather and called on her spirit. Blue flames trickled down her arms, unaffected by the water. She gave the eel a disdainful glare. With her spirit abilities, that pest didn't stand a chance.

Kaya directed a burst of power in her legs and shot upward. Then, gathering her spirit in her left hand, she forced the flames to dance along the edge of the blade. The spiny eel broke from its circle pattern to face her head on. It thrashed its tail and opened a maw with hundreds of jagged teeth. Then, the eel charged.

Icy fingers of fear clamped around Kaya's throat. She forced herself to focus. Her timing needed to be precise; there was no room for error. The eel unhinged its mouth, jaw stretching wide enough to swallow her whole. As the creature streaked toward her, she took a slow breath. Its eyes narrowed in gleeful anticipation.

At the last second, Kaya twisted to the right. The eel snapped its jaws, missing her by a hair's breadth. As it charged past, Kaya slammed her knife through its largest eye.

The spiny eel jerked away. Blue ichor gushed from the wound and streamed behind it in the water. The eel gnashed its teeth, swimming erratically for a moment, then it found its center and swung back toward her. Its movements were unsteady, swerving back and forth. Kaya wouldn't be able to evade it a second time. She gripped her knife and breathed deeply, channeling her spirit once more. The eel sped toward her.

She flung the knife, infusing it with the blue flames of her spirit. It shot forward like a javelin, straight into the spiny eel's gaping mouth and embedding itself deep into the brainstem at the back of its throat. The eel shuddered. Blood streamed from the wound in a dark-blue ribbon. It opened and closed its mouth once, twice, still swimming toward Kaya. Five yellow eyes dimmed, and it bumped past her, no longer seeing as it sank to the sandy floor.

Kaya patted her sheath, mourning the loss of her diving knife. But at least she was still in one piece. <Told you,> she sent to Ellio. Smugness coated her words a light green.

<Uh, Kaya?> Panic reverberated through Ellio's spir-com. <Get back to the ship! Now!>

Kaya looked over her shoulder. Terror froze her heart and stole her breath. A herd of spiny eels were hurtling toward her. Their fins sliced through the water, spines angled to attack. She did a quick mental count, heart racing. There were at least twenty.

Her stomach clenched. With blood in the water, spiny eels became deranged. One frenzied eel with bloodlust was difficult to kill, but twenty would be impossible, especially for one diver, and she had lost her knife.

<Kaya! Come up! Now!> Ellio fired a harpoon into the water. One eel spasmed and started sinking, but the rest surged forward, a seething, chomping mass of rage. Their mouths snapped open and closed, eager to rip her to bloody shreds.

Dragul's presence rippled nearby, and Kaya took a shaky breath. <Shields, Kaya,> her grandfather's spirit urged.

Kaya flinched and brought her hands in front of her, but nothing happened. The eels were almost upon her. She tried to imagine the spirit shield forming around her, but all she could see were hordes of gleaming yellow eyes. Her spirit would not respond to fear. Kaya froze, heart hammering in her chest. The eels were so close now, she could see bits of flesh caught between their teeth. One eel pushed ahead of the pack. It unhinged its jaw and leaned forward.

Kaya flinched.

Blam!

The eel slammed into something three hands in front of her and ricocheted backward. It careened into the charging pack and the tight formation broke. One lashed out at its companion, tearing off a tail fin. Blue blood spiraled in the water. Three of the eels wrenched around and tore into the wounded fish, but the rest of the pack refocused on Kaya. They circled back together, like a flock of birds, and charged, only to be rebuffed at the last second by an invisible force.

Kaya hovered in the water, uncertainty gnawing at her. She swam forward, held up a hand, and bumped against something invisible but rock hard. She blinked and activated her spirit vision. A giant golden wall coalesced between her and the eels, extending from the water's surface to the sea floor.

Wonder and envy spiraled through her. It was Dragul. It had to be. Her grandfather had activated a spirit shield of this size and strength from the shore, reminding her once again that he had earned his title as a master of the Eirenian warrior class. His skill both annoyed and awed her. He didn't even need to have her in his line of sight; his spirit was so strong, he could project it to where she was.

<Home. Now,> Dragul commanded.

Shame spiraled through Kaya. She'd been unable to form her spirit shield when she needed it most, and she'd disobeyed Dragul's order about not attacking the spiny eel to begin with. Her shoulders drooped. She was going to get an earful. Crestfallen, she kicked her way back up to the ship, and Ellio helped haul her aboard.

She yanked off her mask and rebreather and gulped in the fresh air.

"Kaya!" Ellio's hands traced down her arms, checking for injuries.

She managed one disgruntled snort before he crushed her against him. His fingers trembled as he threaded them through her short, wet hair.

"I'm fine." She hated how her voice came out shaky.

"Don't ever scare me like that again." His breath tickled her ear. "It took years off my life. Next time put up a shield in the first place."

Kaya went rigid. "It wasn't me," she mumbled into his shoulder. "I tried to shield, but I couldn't. Dragul put it up."

Ellio's head dropped to her shoulder, and he let out a shaky breath. "Dragul?" He jerked his head up and fixed her with a blazing glare. Resolution settled over his face. "I'm never letting you take a risk like that again. When I saw those spiny eels charging, my heart stopped." His voice was hoarse.

Kaya huffed, and he shook her shoulders. "I mean it, Kaya. You need to start listening to him."

She brushed his hand away. "Stop mothering me, Ellio."

Hurt flashed in his eyes, but he swallowed and firmed his jaw. "I'm not going to apologize for worrying about your safety. You take too many risks."

"No one said you have to come with me."

Ellio threw up his hands. "That'd be even worse. What if no one had known you were out here?"

Kaya looked away. "I'd have figured something out."

He groaned and ran his fingers through his blue hair. "You're maddening sometimes. You know that, right?"

She punched him on the arm. "One of the many reasons you love me."

Ellio rolled his eyes and slung an arm over her shoulders. "You're freezing!" He let go to pull out a rumpled emergency blanket and tucked it around her shoulders. "Let's head back. You need to get out of those wet clothes."

"And hear another lecture from the old man?" Kaya crossed her arms over her chest. "Not interested."

"C'mon, Kaya. Dragul's your family. Do you know what I'd give for one more day with my pops?"

Guilt swelled in Kaya's throat. All of Ellio's family were dead. If not for her, he'd be completely alone. At least she had found her grandfather—even if he was a shriveled old prune with the personality of a dried moj fish. She grunted and laid her head on Ellio's shoulder. "Sorry," she mumbled.

"All I'm saying is try to lighten up around Dragul." Ellio rubbed her back in a soothing circle, and Kaya knew he'd chosen to let her thoughtlessness slide. "You said it yourself; he's a master. There's a lot you can learn from him. Especially that shielding technique. It could save your life one day."

Kaya snorted. "I'm an offensive fighter. I don't hide behind some giant glowing wall."

"Well, maybe it'll help save someone else. You never know." Ellio grinned at her, and Kaya felt her anger melt away. He was so cute when he was hopelessly optimistic.

She tweaked his nose.

Ellio laughed and pressed his forehead against hers. Then he leaned back and fixed her with a serious look. "Were you scared?"

Kaya stiffened, but then let out a breath. Her hand wandered from the blanket to clutch the fabric of Ellio's shirt. "A little."

He kissed the top of her head. "I was terrified."

"Reckless, insolent, and foolhardy! Do you listen to a word I say? Or are you deliberately disobeying every rule I've set in place?" Dragul paced back and forth, his voice growing louder with every word.

The sun gleamed across his bald head, sweat dripping in rivulets from his wrinkled brow. He wore a pair of gray overalls over a white shirt, yellowed with age and crusted with salt. Wiry muscles twined up his arms like rope as he gripped the buckets of yellowtail he had been carrying up from the shore. His glare molded into a look of disappointment that shredded Kaya's heart, and he shook his head. "Every time I try to give you a hint of responsibility, you prove to me again you're still a child!"

Kaya bristled. "You never said we couldn't go fishing on the reef."

"I didn't think you could be so senseless. Provoking a spiny eel! What were you thinking? I've told you they hunt in packs. Did you even check the area before diving?"

Ellio cleared his throat. "I was with her, sir. We scanned the area but didn't pick up any pings for hazardous wildlife."

Dragul's gaze slid over Ellio dismissively, and rage churned in Kaya's gut. The old fossil turned back to her. His eyes narrowed. "What if I hadn't been here? We'd be scraping bits of your carcass off the seafloor."

Kaya sneered. "And that'd be such a hassle for you. You'd have to find another apprentice and start training all over again."

Dragul took a step toward her and flung open his hands. "Don't be ridiculous. It's not about being my apprentice. You're my granddaughter. My flesh and blood. I don't want any harm to come to you. But you have to learn to grow up."

Kaya's pulse roared in her ears. Darkness wavered at the edge of her vision. She closed her eyes and took a deep breath. Then her eyes flew open. "Tell that to my parents," she said coldly, clenching her fists. "Oh right, you can't. They're dead!" She stormed across the sand, ignoring Ellio's plea for her to come back.

Chapter 7

APPREHENSION SNARLED IN ARNION'S chest. He paused on the palace steps and tugged the zipper of his fibro jacket up to his chin. Dawn had not yet broken. Yellow and purple streaks painted the sky, like a bruise. Once the summer sun came up, he'd probably regret the jacket, but right now, he stuffed his hands into the side pockets, thankful for the extra warmth.

His feet crunched across the gravel walkway, and he directed his steps to the southern side of the palace, toward the vehicle bay. The large domed structure mushroomed out behind the residential buildings. There was a subterranean passageway for royal use, but today he couldn't stomach the thought of being confined underground.

Arnion strode past the large bay doors to the smaller pedestrian entrance. He pressed his palm against the security lock. The scanner hummed, tickling his hand like a warm feather, and the door slid open with a swish. Corridor lights winked on ahead of him, lighting a path. Arnion took a deep breath. The scents of rubber, grease, and electrostatic energy soothed him. He made his way toward the collection of vehicles designated for royal use.

The fugas hummed in their charging ports, hovering a hand's breadth above the ground. Electric blue, fluorescent yellow, and a dozen other glossy metallic-paint schemes glimmered under the xenon lights. Short fiberoptic wings jutted out from either side of the vehicles, like the fins of a manta ray. Underneath their lightweight bodies, twin jet thrusters peeked out, their apertures closed like sleeping eyes. The aerodynamic design of the fugas was ideal for aerial racing and acrobatic tricks. A shiver of anticipation stirred along Arnion's nerves. He had always loved flying.

Rhys was already there, unplugging the charging ports on a bright green fuga. When he caught sight of Arnion, he dropped the cable and stepped from behind the vehicle. His broad shoulders brushed a wingtip as he passed. "Arnion! You made it!" Rhys clasped his friend's forearms in an enthusiastic greeting.

Worry melted off Arnion's shoulders at the sight of Rhys's familiar grin. He'd been looking forward to this ride. The meeting with the churlish Kifan emissary was hard enough, but the violence in the marketplace had left him shaken. When he thought about how Acadia had been targeted, cold fingers of dread cinched around his throat, and he forgot to breathe.

Flying would help. It always calmed his mind. Helped him see more clearly. And Rhys was a good sounding board. His bubbly personality was like a fountain of effervescent positivity and sage advice. As an ambassadorial advisor, Rhys prepared agents for worst-case scenarios. More than one ambassador claimed his safe return was because of Rhys's wisdom. But right now, Rhys looked more like a schoolboy than a renowned Eirenian advisor. He bounced on his toes, dark curls swaying. A ruddy flush colored his cheeks, and his eyes shone.

Rhys's excitement was contagious.

Arnion grinned. "I'm here. Thanks for waiting."

"Are you kidding? It isn't every day I'm invited to an early-morning flight with His Royal Highness. I've been looking forward to it." He handed Arnion the magnetic fob that would activate his light shield. "Here. I'm guessing you wanted blue."

"You know me." Arnion pressed it to his right temple. The light shield slid across his head and the upper portion of his face. For a moment, the world was washed in a blue grid, then sensors calibrated for optimal visual acuity within the hanger. A battery readout flashed. Ninety-eight percent. More than enough for their morning ride. He checked the zippers on his fibro jacket and slung a leg over the fuga. "It's been a while." He revved the handle.

Rhys slipped onto his own vehicle and activated a yellow light shield. "Race you around the grand hall."

Arnion gave a thumbs up. "You're on." He gripped the flexi handles and reached for his spirit. White energy crackled along his arms and spiraled down his fingertips, seeping into the receptor pads embedded in the grips. The fuga hummed, rose higher in the air, then spluttered.

Not again!

His spiritual energy winked out like a snuffed candleflame, and the fuga began to sink. Arnion took a shaky breath and tried to focus his thoughts. Worries clamored for his attention, like hawkers in a Beulan market. He glanced up to see if Rhys had noticed. His friend had flown ahead to the entrance and was craning his head over one shoulder.

"Everything all right?" Rhys called out.

Arnion gave him a wave and clenched his fists. He closed his eyes and remembered the first time he took Acadia to his favorite meadow. The scene unfurled in his mind. Beautiful windswept fields nestled under a cerulean sky. He remembered the feeling of her hand in his and how she took off her shoes to walk barefoot in the grass.

The peaceful memory soothed his spirit, and he reached for its energy once more. White sparks traced down his arms. This time, the fuga didn't short out. He flew to Rhys, who was eyeing him curiously.

"Mechanical trouble?" Rhys asked.

"No." Arnion shook his head. "The fuga's fine. Just taking a moment to gather my thoughts."

Rhys hummed thoughtfully. "You sure?"

"Yes," Arnion said with assurance. He twisted the throttle, revving the engine. "Let's fly."

The two friends zoomed out of the garage and flew upward. Pink clouds scored with streaks of purple and amber canvassed the sky, undergirded by the golden light of the fresh morning sun. Arnion and Rhys raced through the air, dipping and swirling. Contrails of moisture twisted behind them. After doing a few laps around the palace, they raced to the bend in the river that curled around Capital City. They spiraled around each other and landed in a field. It was their secret meeting spot; a place they had discovered as teenagers.

Flowering trees blossomed along the riverbed. The mossy banks provided a comfortable place to rest, and the peaceful murmuring of the stream was soothing. It was the ideal place for sharing a heartfelt talk.

Rhys threw himself down on a clump of moss. "I almost had you that time."

Arnion laughed and sat down beside him. "Almost."

Wind rippled across the water, dusting them with flower petals. Rhys plucked one out of his hair and sent it spinning through the water. A contented smile lit his face. "It's always a pleasure flying with you."

"Even when I'm scaling canyon walls?" Arnion teased. The flower petal had reminded him of the time they'd been racing through Katsavra

Canyon, and he'd leaped from his fuga mid-flight. Rhys had been furious.

His friend pressed a hand against his heart in mock distress, but his toothy grin ruined the effect. "Even then." His expression sobered as he studied Arnion's face. "What's troubling you? It looks like you have the weight of the world on your shoulders."

Arnion ran his hands through his hair. "Do you want the whole list or just the highlights?" Rhys gave an encouraging nod and Arnion took a deep breath. "The Separatist movement is growing. They're at every council meeting, demanding we deport the Gehennians." He picked up a small gray stone and set it beside him. "There was an outbreak of violence yesterday, and Acadia was targeted." Arnion added a white stone streaked with black on top of the first. "The Gehennian culture integration committee is constantly asking for more funding to set up scholarships and small business loans. Kifu has sent another diplomat clamoring for us to leverage pressure against Avathys. And Lucien is still missing." For each worry, he added another stone, creating a precariously balanced tower. "We all know his defeat in Gehenna was just a setback. I'm not foolish enough to think we've stopped him for good. He's vanished and been able to hide his presence, along with at least a thousand followers." Arnion added a jet-black pebble on top and the whole structure tumbled apart.

Rhys's eyebrows furrowed. "It sounds like a lot, but you never let politics weigh on you like this before."

"I died, Rhys. I went to the underworld and came back. I experienced an incredible influx of spirit power. I held a sword in my hand that could cut through space and time. And yet now, when those abilities would be of great use, they're gone."

"Gone?" Rhys's voice cracked. He stared at Arnion with wide eyes..

Arnion opened his hand and gestured as if tossing a flower into the wind. "Gone. I've never been able to replicate it. In fact, all my spirit abilities seem weaker. I feel as though I can't control my spirit the way I used to."

Rhys drew his knees up to his chin. "Do you think it's because you died? That you weakened your spirit in some way?"

Arnion leaned back and sprawled on the ground, interlacing his fingers behind his head. "I'm not sure. I feel . . . unsettled. Like I was broken apart and stitched back together, but the thread's gone crooked. It doesn't line up like it should. I have doubts that I never had before. It feels like Acadia is slipping away. She's not thriving in Eiren, and I don't know why. It rips me in two. She's my chimad, you know. The thought of not spending my life with her is like someone is tearing my heart from my chest, sticking it full of arrows, and then trampling on it."

"Ouch." Rhys flinched and rubbed his chest. "That bad, huh?"

"Worse." Arnion closed his eyes briefly. He clasped a hand over the back of his neck and let out a deep sigh. "I want to protect Acadia with my whole life. I want to make her dreams come true. But I also need to serve Eiren. I'm the crown prince. I have duties to my country that no one else can fulfill. And my fear . . ." His heart shuddered and his mouth went dry. Arnion swallowed. "My greatest fear is that Acadia will decide she wants no part of it." His sight blurred with unshed tears.

"Oh, come on." Rhys nudged him.

Arnion propped himself up on an elbow. "What if she won't accept the title and responsibilities that come with marrying me? With being a queen someday? Acadia would have to love Eiren, not just tolerate it for my sake. She has to choose. And if she decides to leave, it's going to shatter me. I don't know how I could go on without her. But forcing her to stay . . ." He pressed his lips together and shook his head. "It isn't even an option. That's not love." He picked a blade of grass and twirled it in his hand. "I never thought I could love anything more than Eiren, but if I had to choose between my country and Acadia . . ." He flicked the grass away.

Rhys let out a low whistle. "I think I'm starting to get it. You think your spirit's out of whack because it's torn between Acadia and Eiren."

Arnion nodded. "And I'm not sure what I can do about it, other than wait it out."

"Waiting can be painful." Rhys clapped a sympathetic hand on his shoulder.

"Excruciating," Arnion agreed. "But the choice is ultimately Acadia's. I can't force her hand. And I'm afraid if I push too hard, if I put too much pressure on her, it'll make her run away that much faster."

Rhys lay down next to Arnion and put his hands behind his head. "Today's a new day, Your Highness. Rather than worry about all the things you can't control, why not worry about the things you can? Spend time with Acadia. Get to know her better. Allow her to get to know you. Show her what you love about Eiren."

Arnion sat up and rested his elbows on his knees. "That's good advice. If only there was time for it all."

"Make the time," Rhys urged. "You need to make time for what's important. Always. If Acadia has your heart, you need to carve out time for her. Show her that you love her, and give her opportunities to grow and do the same."

Arnion drummed his fingers against his shins.

Lately, Acadia looked so sad and lost.

Maybe he was just imagining things. But his gut told him otherwise, and he'd always had good instincts. The trouble with his spirit also unnerved him. Like he'd lost a vital part of himself. Spirit abilities had always come easily to him. Instinctively, like breathing.

So why now?

Why the struggle with Acadia, with his spirit, and with Lucien all at once? It was the perfect trifecta of problems to crush him. His chest tightened, like his heart was being shoved through a rusty sieve and sliced into wet, pulpy ribbons.

Arnion wanted to shake the eerie feeling that had been haunting him lately. The feeling that Acadia wasn't being honest with him. She hid it behind smiles and jokes, but the tilt of her lips, the way the skin around her eyes tightened—not with laughter, but anxiety.

She was hiding something from him.

And for the life of him, he couldn't understand why.

What was she scared of? After everything they'd been through together in Gehenna, what was left?

If only he could do something to help her see how far she'd come. He knew she wanted to spend more time with him. It was no secret, even if every moment they spent together lately, he was consumed with how she was drifting further away. Like she was locking her heart inside a vault, rather than opening up to him. Dread clung to her like a thunderhead, and Arnion didn't know what would happen when the storm finally broke.

Rhys cleared his throat. "Maybe she's lonely. I see her by herself a lot. Has she been able to make any friends?"

Arnion clenched his fist. "There's been some . . . objections to having a former Gehennian in a leadership position at court. You've seen the drama. She visits with Has and Eril from time to time, but female friends have proven . . . elusive."

"Petty jealousy," Rhys grumbled, sitting up. "You'd think the women of Eiren would be above such things."

Lonely? Of course, Rhys was right. Acadia must be terribly lonely.

Arnion remembered sitting in a classroom full of empty desks, the room so quiet, he could hear the scratching of his instructor's stylus from across the room. He never wanted Acadia to feel that pain.

She needed to know how much he loved her. If she doubted him and his intentions, he needed to persevere, not throw himself into his work. It might mask his anxiety, but it was probably the worst thing he could do.

And that's exactly what I've been doing.

Arnion swallowed and brushed sweaty palms against his leg. He knew what it was like to feel isolated and alone. If it wasn't for Rhys, wasn't for his father . . .

That's it!

The thought lit up Arnion's brain like a klepton reactor. He smacked a palm against his forehead. Why hadn't he thought of it earlier?

"Rhys!" He clasped his friend's arm. Excitement zinged through his veins. "You're a genius! You've given me a brilliant idea!"

Rhys blinked at him in amazement. "I have?"

"Yes! I know the perfect way to cheer Acadia up. And it's all thanks to you." Arnion beamed at him. He hopped up, brushing the grass from his legs. "Let's head back. I've got a lot of work to do if I'm going to make this plan work."

Chapter 8

SUNLIGHT STREAMED THROUGH THE window in golden bars. Dust twirled through the brilliant morning light. Acadia sat up with a yawn. She raised her arms over her head and stretched. It had been a few days since the incident in the marketplace, and she'd woken feeling strangely hopeful.

Maybe the enforcers had quelled the Separatists for good? At least no one else had brought up the idea of a security escort.

The door chimed, announcing a visitor.

Who could that be this early?

Acadia shuffled out of bed, feet sinking into the soft rug. She walked to the door panel and pushed the button to open it.

Arnion stood there, dressed in tan calf-length breeches and a white lace-up shirt—a simple traveling outfit. He leaned into the doorway, smiling down at her. "Good morning, Acadia."

"What are you doing here?" She shrank back, mortified that he'd caught her before she'd even had a chance to brush her hair. She had thought it was one of the maids coming in with breakfast.

Arnion rocked back on his heels, and she noticed he was bursting with energy. He was trying to hide it, but she could tell he wanted to dance around the room. His eyes twinkled and he bounced up and down on his toes.

"Did something happen?" she asked.

"Why do you say that?"

"I don't normally get to see you this early in the morning. Don't you have meetings and committees to attend?"

His grin widened. "I cancelled them."

Acadia blinked. "All of them?"

"All of them." He nodded somberly, and leaned against the door-frame. Acadia didn't think he looked sorry in the least. In fact, he looked positively ecstatic.

She studied him, suspicious. "Why?" she asked slowly.

"It's a surprise." He straightened and held out a hand. "Are you up for an adventure?"

A sudden, inexplicable urge to flee surged up her throat.

What was he planning?

Acadia looked at his palm—the palm that had reached out to her so many times, offering her water, friendship, healing. She reached out, brushing her fingertips over his hand before clasping it. No matter how difficult it was, she wanted to stay by his side. "All right."

Arnion squeezed her hand, drew it to his face, and kissed her knuckles. "Thank you." He released her hand. "I'll meet you in the vehicle bay."

"Vehicle bay?" she echoed, surprised. His answering grin stole her breath away.

"Wear something comfortable. We're going to fly."

Acadia gaped at the aircraft Arnion stood beside. When she'd met him at the vehicle bay, she expected him to lead her to a two-person fuga.

Instead, he'd walked right past those, brought her to a large, multi-pas-senger aircraft, and gestured at it with a flourish.

"Your chariot awaits, my lady."

Warning trilled along her nerves. This was no pleasure cruiser. This was built for long-distance flight. The aerodynamic curves of its body and wings reminded her of a shark, but one that swam through air rather than water. The muted gray paint scheme, with orange pinstriping, furthered the illusion. "We're flying in *this*?" She pointed at the aircraft. "This is the size of a transport shuttle." Disbelief cracked her voice.

Arnion tilted his head to consider the craft and patted its hull. "Not quite. It can only fit eight people comfortably."

"Eight?" Acadia fought to keep the shock from her expression. "How many people are coming with us?"

Arnion turned back to her, a boyish grin on his face. "Just the two of us."

"Then why the . . ." Acadia waved at the aircraft.

"Halcyon," Arnion answered. Energy buzzed through his posture like electricity, and Acadia realized he was barely able to contain his glee. "We have a long distance to travel and only a short amount of time to do it." He strode toward her and took her hands in his. A slight blush stained his cheeks. "I also thought this might be your first chance to ride in one. They're one of our fastest vehicles. And you did say you were up for an adventure."

Acadia bit her lip. Old habits were hard to break. Gehenna had woven suspicion along her nerves. Her gut told her to be wary, but she couldn't stand to douse Arnion's enthusiasm. Why was she worried? It wasn't as if Arnion was going to lead her into harm. She needed to relax. This was clearly important to him, and he thought she'd enjoy it.

She squeezed his hands, her pulse fluttering in her throat. "I did." Acadia focused on Arnion. She trusted him and she used that trust to heave all her concerns to the far corner of her mind. "Let's go!"

Acadia had flown with Arnion a few times on a two-person fuga. The first time he'd launched them into the air, the experience of flight took her breath away. The speed as they rocketed upward, the wind tugging at her hair, the view as they burst above the clouds—it was magical. Her heart had ached at the beauty of it all. It was only at the end of the flight that Acadia realized her face was wet with tears.

Flying in the halcyon was a whole new world. When Acadia sank into the bucket seat beside Arnion, web-like bands of a light harness slipped around her. After her ride in the Eirenian transport shuttle when leaving Gehenna, Acadia knew not to panic as the soft warm light brushed over her. The light harness auto-adjusted to body size, making her comfortably snug. At first, she was disappointed by the thick bubble of glass that sealed off the cockpit from the outside world. One of her favorite things about flying on a fuga was the wind whipping by her face. But once Arnion had maneuvered the halcyon into the open air, she understood the need for a sealed cockpit. The aircraft hurtled along at speeds that would tear a person apart, light harness or not.

Acadia watched the sprawling expanse of Capital City fade to a mere speck in the distance. Green fields streaked below them—the farmlands of Eiren. Later, the verdant scenery faded to browns and pinks. A great chasm cracked the earth beneath them, like a giant puckered scar.

"That's Katsavra Canyon," Arnion said. "Rhys and I like to race fugas through there sometimes."

Acadia peered down. The canyon snaked across the landscape, cutting a path toward a distant mountain range off to their right. Beyond the canyon spread an expanse of bleached yellow.

The Cursed Barrens.

Apprehension tickled the base of her skull. The Cursed Barrens were on the border of Kifu, her home country. She recognized the Meyhorn Mountains rising on their left, another of the borders between Eiren and Kifu. The rocky mountain crags stood out like skeletal fingers, reaching toward the sky.

Arnion banked the halcyon to the left, skirting the edge of the mountains.

Acadia's knuckles itched. She pressed her hands against her thighs to stop herself from scratching. "Are we going into Kifu?" She tried to keep her voice light, like she didn't care either way.

"Yes." Arnion toggled one of the controls then flipped a switch on the nav consol. "Is that okay?"

"Why wouldn't it be?" Acadia laughed, but it sounded forced, even to her ears. "I'm just surprised. They're on the brink of war with Avathys. Do they really want foreign jets in their airspace?"

"Eiren and Kifu are allies," Arnion reminded her. "And I got the proper clearance permissions ahead of time."

Acadia realized she'd wriggled to the edge of her seat with shoulders hunched forward to stare at the ground. She willed herself to sit back, take a deep breath, and relax her shoulders. When scraggly fields of jarl wheat unfolded beneath the halcyon, Acadia pressed her hand against the glass. She remembered toiling alongside her brothers, battling the rocky soil and dry winds to bring in a meager crop each year. Kifans joked that their farmers harvested more dust than crops.

Nostalgia sawed through her heart like a knife. Her throat felt dry, and her eyes pricked with tears. Questions darted through her mind like minnows, too slippery to grasp for more than an instant. Would they pass over the village where she'd grown up? Would she even recognize it from the air? Why was Arnion bringing her to Kifu? Did he need to attend a diplomatic meeting?

About an hour later, they set down outside a small merchant town nestled at the base of the mountains. "Cobasso," Acadia read on the flickering sign. "Do you have business here?"

He powered down the halcyon and helped her climb out. "*We* have business here."

"We? I've never even heard of Cobasso before."

He took her shoulders and squeezed gently. "Acadia, your family is here."

"W-what?" Her strength gave out, as if her bones had crumbled to dust. She would have collapsed if Arnion hadn't caught her.

He held her close to his chest and brushed a hand through her hair. "It's going to be all right. I'll stay by your side, whatever happens."

Acadia's eyes stung, and her throat pinched shut. She burrowed into Arnion's shoulder. One question dominated her thoughts. "How?" she whispered.

Arnion rubbed soothing circles on her back. "I asked Naileah to help."

"Naileah?" Acadia hated how weak her voice sounded. Her mind conjured up an image of a young woman with russet skin and burnished bronze hair. They'd met a few times during palace debriefings. "The analyst?"

"That's right. After Gehenna, my father introduced us. She was the Lead Analyst during my mission and her calculations were spot on. I figured if anyone could help us crack the mystery of your family's disappearance, it would be her. She was honored to help and worked for hours, combing through data to find them."

Acadia let out a chuckle that sounded more like the croak of a dying frog. "That sounds like her." Even though they didn't know each other well, she liked Naileah. For an analyst, she was downright friendly. Acadia could picture her giving the shirt off her back if someone asked. And, like others in her chosen profession, Naileah seemed possessed by a determination to root out the truth. If Arnion had asked for her help, Naileah would have found a way to make the impossible happen.

A flash of resentment stabbed Acadia's chest at the thought of Arnion and Naileah huddled together planning this secret trip. No one had consulted her about it. Did she even want to see her family? As quickly as it came, the emotion fled, replaced by a deep wave of shame. Of course, she did. Hadn't she just told Arnion the other day how much she missed them? That's what probably gave him the idea.

But now, faced with an imminent and unplanned reunion, fear pierced her heart like a rusted nail. Her pulse throbbed behind her temples and sweat gathered on her palms. "What if they don't want to see me?" Her greatest fear slipped out. Was it too much to hope they wouldn't be at home? She started to pace, wringing her hands. Panic frazzled her thoughts, and more words slipped out. "I can't do this."

"You won't be alone," Arnion assured her.

Acadia took a shaky breath. A part of her wanted to bolt. A part of her wanted to tear her hands through her hair and scream. Another part thought it would be best to sit in the dust and cry. Instead, she fixed her eyes on Arnion's face and gazed into the love and acceptance she found there. She stopped pacing. Could she do this? By herself it was impossible, but with Arnion . . .

Acadia reached for him and instantly he swept her into his arms. She trembled in his embrace, trying to calm her ragged breathing. Acadia listened to his heartbeat and remembered the open tomb. He had cleaved through the gates of death to return to her. If he was with her, maybe she would see another impossible victory.

"All right," she whispered against his shirt. "I'll try talking to them. Just don't leave my side."

"I promise." Arnion's voice was husky, choked with emotion. He pressed a kiss into the palm of her hand. "I'll never leave you."

The sincerity in his voice brought tears to her eyes. Acadia wove her fingers through his. "Then lead on, my prince."

Chapter 9

ACADIA FOUND HERSELF STANDING in front of a small black door along a row of houses in town. The dwelling was medium sized, not impoverished but also not lavishly wealthy. There was a mercantile store-front on the ground floor. As they passed by the shop window, she'd glimpsed all kinds of trade goods—bolts of cloth, foreign spices, maglev coils, zip runners, and xenon burners. Everything a growing frontier town needed.

Acadia's stomach churned. Arnion must have sensed her trepidation because he squeezed her hand. Her feet were rocks, cemented into the ground by inertia, fear, and doubt.

How can I face Ma after what I've done?

Acadia took a deep breath through her nose and stepped up to the threshold. She pressed the buzzer before she could think better of it. Footsteps thumped toward her, and panic licked down her spine. If it wasn't for Arnion holding her in place like a gravitational field, she would have fled.

The door slid open and a young man with dark hair and piercing blue eyes stood before her.

"T-Talon?"

He'd gotten so big!

The last time she'd seen her younger brother, he'd been a scrawny kid. Now a young man stood before her. His shoulders had broadened, and he'd shot up in height. He was taller than her. Acadia did some quick mental math. Three years working for Lucien, fifteen months in Gehenna, and then nine months living in Eiren. That made it five years since she had seen her brother. But it was Talon; she was sure of it.

Talon stumbled back a step. His mouth gaped like a moj fish. "Acadia? Is it really you?"

Acadia nodded, too choked with emotion for her tongue to form words.

Talon laughed and stumbled forward, then clasped her arms. "Acadia! I can't believe it . . . we thought we'd lost you." He let go of her to rub his eyes. Tears glistened on his lashes. "I still can't believe it." He reached out and pinched her.

"Ouch!" Acadia stepped back and rubbed her arm. "What was that for?"

"I'm making sure this isn't a dream."

"Aren't you supposed to pinch yourself in that case?"

"Oh, right." Talon laughed. "Sorry, sis. It's . . ." He swallowed and swiped at his eyes with his sleeve.

Acadia almost sobbed at the familiar gesture. How many times had Ma scolded them for wiping their eyes and noses on their sleeves as kids?

It looked like Talon had never grown out of it.

"Wait 'til Ma and Dren see you!" Talon smacked a palm against his head. "Here I am making you wait outside. Come in." He waved his hand and then seemed to realize Arnion was standing there. "And your friend too, of course. Welcome to our home, Mr . . ."

"Arnion. Just Arnion is fine."

"Welcome, Arnion, to our humble home!" Talon clasped his forearm and pulled him into a bear hug. Acadia slipped in beside them, and Talon led them down the hall. Her brother clapped Arnion on the back as they walked. "Am I right in guessing we have you to thank for restoring my sister to us?"

"It was my pleasure to help her find her family." Arnion's voice was heavy with emotion, and Acadia was surprised to see his eyes were red.

Old softie.

"Ma! Dren!" Talon called out. "You won't believe it! Look who appeared on our doorstep. It's Acadia, back from the grave."

Acadia heard a crash as they approached the kitchen.

"Ma!" Talon rushed into the room; Acadia and Arnion hurried after him.

The kitchen was warm with sunshine. A hand-embroidered lace cloth covered a table in the center. The walls had pale-blue wallpaper with a diamond design. A gridscreen was softly playing a classical quartet in the corner.

There was broken glass on the floor. Water pooled by Ma's feet, soaking into her slippers, but she ignored it. She appeared frozen in place, hands clenched in front of her chest, knuckles white. Talon dashed over to check she was all right, then he grabbed a broom, swept up the broken glass, and dumped it into the trash receptacle.

Ma stared at Acadia in shock. "Acadia?" Her voice was broken and hoarse, but Acadia would recognize it anywhere.

Acadia hesitated in the doorway, and her mother rushed forward with a shriek. Trembling hands came up and stroked her face, pushing her bangs back from her forehead. "Sweetheart, is it really you?" Her mother's black hair was heavily streaked with gray. Wrinkles gathered at the corners of her eyes and around her mouth, and her collarbone, thin and bird-like, stood out against her soft woven shift.

Acadia let out a hiccup that was half a laugh and half a sob. "It's me, Ma." She collapsed into her mother's waiting embrace, hugging her tightly. Unshed tears stung her eyes, and Acadia blinked. Her heart pummeled her ribs, and a healing warmth seeped through her limbs. "I'm home."

"Acadia, my darling little girl," her mother whispered over and over. Her palms cupped her daughter's face. "How I've missed you." She fingered the short ends of Acadia's hair. "What happened to your beautiful hair? You always said you'd rather die than have it cut short."

Acadia laughed through her tears. Had she really been so young and foolish once? She cleared her throat, trying to gather her self-composure. "It's a long story, Ma."

Her mother pressed Acadia's hands between hers. "I want to hear it. I want to hear everything."

Acadia's heart spluttered, like a failing xenon light. "I—"

"What's going on in here?" a deep male voice cut in. "What was Talon shouting about?" Footsteps stomped into the room and the voice turned sharp. "Ma! Ma, what's wrong? What have they done to you?" A rough arm jerked Acadia away.

Angry brown eyes met hers under dark brows furrowed in confusion. Acadia recognized her middle brother Dren. He still had an expressive face, although his ragged mop of unruly black hair was now cut military short. Dren dropped her arm and stumbled backward, bumping into one of the chairs by the table. "Acadia!" His expression darkened like a thundercloud, his eyes hard. "We thought you were dead."

Acadia hugged her arms across her chest. "In a way, I was."

"Sit down, Acadia." Ma bustled up beside her. "You and your handsome friend." She dabbed at her eyes with a handkerchief and flashed a watery smile. "Let me make you something to eat."

Acadia bit back a sob. Ma always loved to feed people. Hospitality and cooking were two of her greatest gifts. After all this time, some things hadn't changed. Acadia's heart warmed at the thought. She stumbled toward the table, and Arnion pulled out a chair for her. She flopped into it, grateful to rest her trembling legs.

Talon sat across from her and reached forward to place his hand on top of hers. "I still can't believe you're really here. It's a miracle, isn't it, Dren?"

"It's something," Dren replied, shaking his head. He sat stiffly in the seat next to his brother and Arnion slipped into the chair on Acadia's right.

Talon bounced up and down in his chair. "Wait 'til Kep hears about this!"

"Kep?" Acadia asked.

Dren glared at her. Even Talon's bubbly energy seemed to dissipate a little.

"Oh, right. You don't know," Talon said. He shook his head, his eyes sad. "Kep is Ma's new husband."

Acadia flinched.

Dren tapped the table. "What did you expect? After you disappeared and Da died, we were destitute. The creditors descended on us like ravenous ungalors. They took the house, the fields, and then some." His voice sliced through her heart, sharp as a blade.

"I didn't know," Acadia said in a small voice. "I had no idea."

"But we ended up all right in the end." Talon nudged Dren's shoulder. "We sold the rest of our belongings and left town, looking for a place to stay. Along the way, Kep found us. He's a merchant who travels throughout Kifu. At first, he was helping Ma out of pity, but they fell in love. Ma takes care of his home, and Kep raised us like his own sons. Dren's doing well too, even if he's a stodgy old grump most of the time. He's interning at the medical center in town."

"That's amazing, Dren." Acadia's voice was bright. Dren had always been clever. She turned toward him, pride welling in her chest. Her brother scowled and looked away.

"Don't mind him," Talon insisted. "He's like that with everyone."

Acadia was sure Talon was just trying to encourage her. She remembered Dren had always been quiet as a boy, but never bitter and suspicious like he was acting now. How much damage had her betrayal caused her family? Were the relationships broken beyond repair?

Ma came over to the table with mugs of sugar cider and glazed lemon cake. She sat on Acadia's left and placed a trembling hand on top of Talon's. "I still remember the day I sent you into Beulah to sell the sagrins. You disappeared without a trace. After so much time passed, we all feared the worst." Her throat bobbed. "What happened to you?"

There it was. The question Acadia had been dreading since the moment Arnion had told her why they'd come to Cobasso. How could she tell them? Her palms were clammy. The bitter taste of fear rose in her throat. She swallowed and frantically thought of what she could say. How could she spin it to lessen the blow of what she had done?

"I was robbed and thrown into Gehenna."

It was a stretch, but Lucien *had* tricked her. And she *had* been thrown into Gehenna . . . eventually.

"Oh, my baby," Ma reached across the table to clutch Acadia's hands.

Arnion shifted beside her and cleared his throat. Acadia refused to meet his gaze. Couldn't she just let them think she'd been the victim?

What good would the truth do after all these years? It would only hurt them. She'd finally found her family again. Did Arnion expect her to sabotage their relationship the moment she'd got it back?

<*Tell your mother the truth, Acadia.*>

That voice!

She sent a questing tendril of spirit energy toward Arnion. He stared back at her, frowning. One night, when they had been trapped by a sandstorm in Gehenna, she'd confessed to Arnion what she'd done. How she'd betrayed her family for fine clothes and flattery. Was this strange new voice coming from him?

Arnion's spirit flickered with disapproval, but he was silent. The threads of power emanating from the firm, chastising voice strayed far beyond her prince. Could he hear the voice too? It didn't appear so. She glanced across the table at Talon and Dren, a question forming on her lips. Talon was hanging on her every word, while Dren glared at the wall beyond her, his jaw clenched. Could it be . . .

No, none of her family were radiating any kind of spiritual energy.

Where was it coming from?

Acadia trembled. Who was this stranger? She couldn't sense anyone else's spirit nearby, and they were thousands of stadia from Eiren. Who could be powerful enough to project over such a distance? Acadia's thoughts roiled. Arnion had been able to send spir-coms from Gehenna to Eiren, but he was a prodigy. There was no one else alive who could do what he did. And Acadia was willing to bet Cobasso was even farther from Eiren than Gehenna. Was someone using Eirenian tech to enhance their spirit power and conceal their presence?

<*The truth, Acadia!*> the voice insisted. Power resounded in each word. A heaviness built up inside her, like a boulder crushing her chest. She couldn't breathe.

The wall of lies and excuses Acadia had built around herself crumbled. The truth carved through her. It flayed the hardened layers around her heart until she could see the awful ugliness at its core.

What have I done?

Acadia had felt moments of guilt in the past, but nothing like this. Remorse flooded through her. Pressure throbbed behind her eyes, and she knew tears weren't far behind. The conviction of how deeply she had wronged her family seared her heart like a branding iron. The pain was unbearable. Waves of fire washed over her; there was only one thing she could do.

"No." Her voice was little more than a choked sob.

"No?" her mother echoed.

Shame scorched her. She fought against the tears building behind her lashes by scrunching her eyes shut. The truth of what she'd done was so horrible. How could she ever find the words to explain? She scratched her knuckles until they burned. Her body shook, and she realized she'd been shaking her head furiously. "That's not what happened," she whispered.

"Why don't you tell us what *really* happened, Acadia?" She could hear the sneer in Dren's voice.

Acadia opened her eyes and looked toward Arnion. She expected to see his mouth curled in disgust. Instead, she met eyes brimming with compassion. He reached over and covered her hand with his.

"It's okay, Acadia. I'm not going anywhere," Arnion said in a gentle but firm tone.

Hope fluttered in her stomach, as fragile as newborn bird, and Acadia dared to believe. Arnion knew the truth, and he hadn't forsaken her. Maybe her family could forgive her too? Another wave of guilt rocked through her, and she bit back a moan. The truth surged up her throat and pressed against the back of her teeth, like floodwaters about to break free. Even if her family rejected her, she had to tell them.

"I stole the money." The words burst from her lips.

Talon recoiled, as if she'd slapped him. Ma's face twisted in anguish, and Dren watched her, malice glittering in his eyes. Acadia wanted to pull back, to qualify her answer, but found that once she'd started, she couldn't stop. The ugly truth poured from her like a torrent of putrid water. "I used the money to buy expensive clothes and start a new life for myself in Beulah. I hired a broker to help me, and when you came looking, I hid. I convinced people to turn you away because I was ashamed—ashamed of our poverty, ashamed of our farm, and, most of all, ashamed of what I'd done."

"I knew it." Dren's mouth curled in an unkind smile. "All this time, I knew it."

Sweat dripped down Acadia's back. Her thoughts dissolved into static, like a broken gridscreen. How could she be so stupid? Her family could never forgive her for this. She pressed her trembling hands on the table. "Now you know the truth, I'm sure you'll never want to see my face again." She tried to rise, but Ma snatched up her hands in a vice grip.

"Acadia, why?" Ma's voice broke.

Why had she done it? Whenever her thoughts drifted in that direction, she found something to distract herself. Acadia never wanted to consider what had driven her to betray her family in their time of need. She'd spent the last few years furiously burying the shame of her actions, never stopping to let herself think about it.

"Why?" Tears streamed down Ma's wrinkled face.

I don't know.

Acadia wanted to tear out her hair. She would never be able to forget the heartbreak etched on her mother's face. Or how Talon's admiration had crumpled into disbelief and shock. This was what the truth got her. Pain and suffering and tears. What answer could she give? What on Elorah could ever excuse her behavior?

"How could you do that to us?" Talon seemed to curl into himself. He stared at the center of the table, glassy-eyed. "You knew we needed that money after Da was injured."

Acadia opened her mouth, but no words came out. She hunched her shoulders, wishing she could disappear. Their expressions would haunt her dreams for years to come.

<*You were selfish.*> The voice tingled through her spirit.

"I was," Acadia agreed out loud. At her mother's puzzled look, she cleared her throat. "I was selfish. Utterly selfish. And I'm very, very sorry." Tears dripped down her chin and onto the tablecloth. Acadia watched them form dark circles against the fabric, lost in the barrage of emotions that cascaded over her. "I'm so sorry," she sobbed. She would have slid to the floor, but Ma caught her and hugged her to her chest.

"Acadia, my beautiful girl." Ma patted the top of her head. "I'm so glad you've come home to us."

"What?" Dren jerked out of his seat, eyes blazing. "How can you say that after what she's done?" His voice seethed with fury.

"I never stopped hoping," Ma said, brushing her fingers through Acadia's hair. "I never stopped searching. I've been reunited with my daughter, Dren. I'm not going to let the past stop me from celebrating this miracle. My baby girl has come home. She's here, and she's sorry. That's enough."

Dren slammed his fists onto the table. "But she—"

"That's enough, Dren." Ma's eyes flashed a warning.

Dren scoffed and turned away, jaw clenched.

Acadia knew she must be a sight. Tears soaked her cheeks and mucus dripped from her nose. Frantically, she swiped at her face. Then Talon was shoving a handkerchief at her.

"Here. Ma would kill us if you used your sleeve."

His words broke the tension that hovered over them, like a ray of sunlight piercing through the clouds. Ma started chuckling, low at first but then louder, until she let out a deep belly laugh. Acadia reached up to take the handkerchief and saw that Talon's shoulders were shaking with mirth.

He threw his arms around her. "I'm so glad you found us," he said, laughing.

Dren eyed their soggy huddle. He snorted and shook his head. "I think you're all crazy." He turned and gave Arnion an assessing look. "And what's your story? How are you connected to any of this?"

Arnion had been watching Acadia and her mother, a tender expression on his face. At Dren's question, his eyes snapped up to her brother, and he extended a hand in greeting. "I'm Arnion. Acadia and I are courting."

A flash of heat swept across Acadia's cheeks. She knew Arnion was pursuing her with an intent toward marriage. They talked about it occasionally during their walks. But this was the first time she'd heard him speak of it to others—to her family, no less!

"Acadia, that's wonderful!" her mother gushed, drawing her into another hug.

Acadia squirmed. "It's still early," she stammered. "There's nothing officially announced yet." She risked a glance at Arnion and caught a flicker of hurt play across his features. Guilt twinged her stomach. "But we are courting," she said firmly and tried to convey an apology to Arnion with her eyes. "I really was sent to Gehenna. That's where we met. Arnion rescued me . . ." Emotion choked off her words as she remembered the price he had paid. She blinked back tears, forcing the terrible memory away. "And afterward, I was invited to his home, to live with him and his father." Her words still warbled a little, but she was able to get them out. "I searched for you, but only came up with dead ends, and then Arnion, he . . ."

A surge of gratitude overwhelmed her as she considered what Arnion had done. Not only had he died for her, he'd spent hours with Naileah pouring over data to find her family. Despite all his other responsibilities, he'd thought of her. How much kindness was one person capable of? Arnion's love felt like an ocean. She could swim through it forever and never find the end. The thought made her dizzy.

What had she done to deserve such love?

Nothing.

Unworthiness cinched around Acadia's ribs, a vice grip that stole her breath. Arnion was bound to realize it sooner or later. Could she find a way to earn his love before that day came? Some way to atone for her past and prove an invaluable asset for the future. She had to be perfect. Acadia had failed as Sapphyre, but she wouldn't fail this time. She had sworn to herself, with all the intensity of a blood oath.

Acadia realized her family were still hanging on her words. She snapped a lid over her doubts and refocused on the people before her. "Arnion is the reason I was able to find you." *And I love him with all my heart.* The words caught in her throat like thorns. Someday, she would earn the right to speak her deepest feelings out loud, but for now, she repressed them.

Talon turned to Arnion and clasped his hand in thanks. "Thank you for returning my sister to us." His bright eyes turned to Acadia. "Now that you're back, we can—"

"I can't stay." Acadia hesitated. "I do want to be a part of your lives again—if you'll let me—but my home is with Arnion."

Talon's face fell. "But you'll come and visit us again?" he asked hopefully.

Acadia nodded. Tears slipped down her cheeks. "Many, many times."

Talon mulled over her words. "Then I guess it's all right," he declared, puffing out his chest.

Dren rolled his eyes. "Great."

"You'll stay for dinner." Ma's words were a statement, not a question. She stood from the table and brushed her hands down her maroon shift.

"We wouldn't dream of leaving before then," Arnion assured Ma. Acadia glanced at him. His eyes twinkled with amusement.

The rest of the afternoon passed in a blur. Ma put them all to work in the kitchen, peeling potatoes, chopping vegetables, or making a glaze for the roast. More tears were shed, especially by Talon, who was tasked with dicing the onions. Her brothers competed, trying to find the most outlandish and embarrassing childhood stories to share with Arnion. Dren, in particular, relished dredging up these old memories. Acadia was mortified at first, but Talon's good humor was contagious. Soon, she was laughing along with them, remembering their childhood misadventures. A pervasive contentment settled over the room, and Acadia realized she was happy. She had thought reconciling with her family was impossible, but here she was, welcomed into Ma's kitchen.

It's all thanks to Arnion.

Joy fizzed through her veins, dissolving the sorrow and shame that had calcified around her heart for the past five years. Ma cooked a feast fit for a king, even if she didn't realize she was entertaining royalty. A large crown roast dominated the table, stuffed with fruit, nuts, raisins, and spices. There was a heaped pyramid of baked potatoes, still steaming and ready to be slathered with butter. Acadia admired the colorful platter of roasted vegetables, lightly charred on the outside, but she knew each bite would be perfectly soft and moist within, seasoned with Ma's special citrine herb infusion. A tantalizing aroma wafted from the oven, and Acadia's mouth watered. Ma had made her famous shabba bread. Normally, that recipe was reserved for one night a year, during the winter solstice festival. Her mother was treating her homecoming as one of the highest Kifan celebrations.

Kep arrived home just as they had finished setting the table. At first, Acadia was taken aback by the slender, wiry man, with a neatly trimmed beard and laugh lines stretching around his eyes. He was so different from her father. Da had come from a long line of farmers, evident by his stout, muscular build. She remembered her father's untamed beard and scarred hands, nothing like the polished stranger before her. When Kep shook her hand, his palm was smooth and dry. The hands of a merchant. But not even Acadia could doubt his enthusiasm once he realized who she was. Kep's eyes grew wide, like a child at a toy shop on his birthday. He took Acadia's hands in his and danced a jig around the table, laughing with delight.

As Acadia watched Kep celebrate her arrival, and the tender way he greeted her mother and ruffled Dren's hair, the sliver of resentment in her heart dissolved. He wasn't Da, but it was clear he loved her family deeply and had saved them when she had faltered. She owed him a debt of gratitude and told him so.

Kep drew an arm around Ma's shoulder. "I was more tumbleweed than man when I met your Ma. Roaming from place to place, never a home to settle in or a family to call my own. There's not a day goes by I don't thank my lucky stars that she had pity on this poor old bachelor."

Ma clucked her tongue. "You were just skin and bones when we first met." She poked him in the side, a rosy blush coloring her cheeks.

"And now look at me." Kep patted his stomach. "How's a man supposed to stay fit when he's married to the best cook in Kifu?"

"You don't have to worry, Kep," Dren said. Acadia noticed the unguarded smile that played across his face—the first she'd seen all day. "With all your travels, you're in great shape."

"Well, thank you, Dren." Kep clapped him on the shoulder. "I know you're a man of your word. I trust you wouldn't stuff my ears with empty flattery."

Dren straightened his shoulders and raised his chin, clearly pleased by the compliment.

"You got that right, Kep," Talon agreed. "Dren's such a sour sport; a compliment from him is worth its weight in gold."

Acadia repressed a chuckle, disguising it as a cough. Dren's nostrils flared and his face flushed. He drew in a sharp breath.

Kep rubbed his hands together. "Well, now." His voice was jovial, if a tad louder than necessary. "We don't want this delicious meal your Ma prepared to get cold. Let's eat."

Dren muttered but refrained from further comment.

Ma had outdone herself with the cooking. For a few minutes the table was silent, aside from the sound of scraping forks and contented chewing as they savored the delicious flavors. After a while, the conversation resumed. Talon persuaded Kep to share some of his traveling stories. Kep was a wonderful storyteller, and they all listened in rapt attention.

The evening progressed pleasantly. By the end of the meal, even Dren's icy demeanor began to defrost a little. Acadia and Arnion said their goodbyes, with promises to meet again soon.

Walking back to the halcyon, a wave of exhaustion swept over Acadia. Arnion helped her into the cockpit, and she slipped into the passenger seat beside him. When Arnion pressed the ignition, her harness activated automatically. The yellow bands of electric light snapped into place, securing her tight. She tilted her bucket seat back and dropped into the deepest sleep she'd had in years.

"Something's wrong."

The concern in Arnion's voice jostled her awake more than his words. Acadia blinked bleary eyes. Waking up felt like swimming through water. She pressed her fingers into her cheeks, trying to rouse herself. "What?" Her voice was groggy.

"Something's wrong." Arnion's gaze was fixed straight ahead, his jaw tight.

Acadia turned to see what he was staring at. They were in the halcyon, on an easy descent toward Capital City. She could make out the spires of the palace in the distance. "Something's wrong with the halcyon?" she asked.

"No, something's wrong in Eiren. I started getting the messages a moment ago."

The back of Acadia's neck itched. Spir-coms buzzed through the air like a swarm of angry hornets. Goosebumps raised on her arms, and she shivered.

Arnion flexed his fingers around the flight controls, his knuckles white. He breathed in sharply before glancing at her. Tension carved a worried furrow between his brows. "They're going to meet us when we land, and I wanted you to be ready."

"Who's going to meet us?"

Arnion was silent for a moment. His gaze moved back to the palace, and he let out a defeated sigh. "Everyone."

Chapter 10

ADVISORS AND PALACE STAFF swarmed the halcyon the moment it touched down. They crowded around the vehicle so closely, Arnion could barely open the exit hatch. He had to open the window and gesture for them to move back before he and Acadia could disembark.

A frazzled attendant pushed his way to the front. "Your Majesty, where have you been?" he asked, wringing his hands.

Arnion wrapped an arm around Acadia, keeping her close to him in the press of the crowd. "Acadia and I had personal business to attend to."

"But you could have at least taken a communicator," another advisor said in a pleading voice. "King Elyon is not pleased."

Arnion's expression fell. "My father is upset?"

"Yes!" The advisor nodded. "This morning there was an incident. A village in Kifu was attacked, and they're blaming Avathys. The Kifans are preparing to declare war. Emissary Narhast has been demanding to speak to you all day. He's threatening to break our alliance and leave if Eiren doesn't take immediate action, but the king and his council don't want to make a decision without your input. Everyone's been looking for you."

Arnion held out his hand. "Prepare a conference room immediately. Summon Emissary Narhast. You can brief me on the way."

Acadia's thoughts churned at the whirlwind of events. Reconciling with her family after five years and now two countries at war. Spots swam before her eyes, and she stumbled.

Arnion caught her elbow. He waved over a man wearing light blue palace livery. "Please see Lady Acadia safely to her room and send up a tray of food. She's had an exhausting day." He turned and pressed a kiss to her forehead. "I'm sorry I can't stay with you."

She shook her head vigorously. "Go. I'll be all right."

His eyes were troubled as he turned away. Acadia's heart twisted in her chest. They'd only left Eiren for one day, and calamity had descended upon the city. Was Arnion's presence so critical that his absence made the world implode?

War.

The word sucked the air from her lungs. There had always been tension between Avathys and Kifu. Political maneuverings, occasional shots fired across the border. But there seemed to be an unwritten agreement that neither nation wanted a full-scale conflict.

Why would Avathys escalate things? What drove their aggression?

The advisors had mentioned something about an attack. Were Ma and her family all right? She'd only left them a few hours ago to fly back to Eiren. The advisors had said the attack happened in the morning. Or did they? Acadia couldn't remember. She swayed on her feet, and the servant took her arm.

"Come along, Lady Acadia. Let me help you to your room. You look in dire need of rest."

"Thank you," Acadia mumbled and allowed herself to be led down the hall. When she entered her room, she barely managed to shuck off her shoes before collapsing onto the bed. She threw an arm over her flushed face. Tears dripped warm tracks down her cheeks.

Had the world gone mad?

Acadia grabbed her data pad and tapped out a quick message to Talon, asking if everyone in Cobasso was all right. His quick assurance of their safety lightened the tension in her neck. She let out a long, slow breath. Thank goodness. At least her family was safe. Her fingers trembled as she set her data pad in the charging port beside her bed.

If Kifu and Avathys were about to go to war, maybe she could convince her family to move to Eiren. She was sure Arnion and King Elyon would welcome them.

Arnion's face flashed in Acadia's mind, and she remembered the tautness around his mouth as he'd kissed her goodbye. It was her fault he hadn't been where he was supposed to be. She hoped he wouldn't be in too much trouble because of it. Surely no one could blame him for failing to predict Avathys would break their age-old posturing and initiate a war today. Her thoughts writhed like a tangle of serpents before weariness dragged her into a restless sleep.

The door chime buzzed, and Acadia groaned. She sat up and combed her fingers through her hair. What time was it? A cold plate of food sat on the golden yeulwood table in the center of the room. She must have slept through the night. Sunlight streamed through the large picture window that opened onto a balcony above the palace gardens. Acadia held up a hand against the brightness, squinting at the dust motes that danced in the sunbeams. Judging by the angle of the light, it was past midday.

The tinkling chime resounded through the room again.

Acadia picked at the crust in the corner of her eye with a fingernail, then reached over to press the control panel by her nightstand. The door slid open.

"Pardon the intrusion, my lady." Tifa, her handmaiden, curtsied in the entrance. Behind her stood another maid, a petite teenage girl with black-rimmed glasses and auburn hair. Tifa gestured to her companion. "This is Silvie, my lady. She's a maid in training. We're here to help you get ready for the ball this evening."

Acadia waved them inside. She smothered the urge to frown, pressing her lips into a smile instead. "Just 'Acadia,' please."

No matter how many times she asked the palace staff to call her Acadia without all the honorifics, the habit persisted. Eirenians valued formal manners so much, trying to change their habits was like smacking her forehead against a brick wall. Acadia pressed her fingers against her temples and drew little circles. Her head throbbed. Exhaustion gripped her mind with steel claws, and she struggled to focus her thoughts.

The maids bustled into the room and headed for her wardrobe. Silvie bounced on her toes, taking in the splendor of Acadia's suite with wide eyes. "What marvelous rooms you have, my lady. These must be some of the finest in all the palace."

"Thank you." Acadia tried to summon a flicker of enthusiasm, but her energy was sapped. She walked to her dining table and picked at the cluster of wilted grapes beside her neglected dinner. "Can you remind me what ball we're talking about?" There were so many; it was impossible to keep track of them all. Eirenians had no shortage of reasons for celebrating.

Silvie clasped her hands together. "The Starlight Memorial Ball, ma'am. It's one of our most honored traditions. Every year we gather to remember those who have passed from this life with a grand ball, full of feasting and dancing. Though it may seem strange to celebrate our deceased with music and dancing, we believe a grand ball is the best way to honor their memory." Her voice took on the tone of a schoolteacher reciting lessons. "We give thanks for their lives by living life to the fullest. At the peak of the festivities, the roof of the grand ballroom retracts, and under the glorious summer sky, we release paper lanterns. They drift into the firmament like stars to commemorate the passing of our loved ones." She raised an arm as if releasing an imaginary lantern. "Dignitaries attend from all over Elorah to pay their respects. When the lanterns take flight, the heavens are filled with the golden glow of our memories."

"That's tonight?" Acadia sank into the chair beside her table. Her finger traced along the lines of the wood grain. "I'd completely forgotten." Pain pounded against her skull. She groaned and rested her cheek on the table's glossy surface. All she wanted to do was curl up in bed and sleep for a week straight. Forget dancing. Another day of completely undisturbed slumber was what she needed. That would be heavenly.

"Do I have to go?" Acadia hated the whine that slipped into her voice. She pressed her forehead into the table, letting her hair cover her face like a petulant child.

"It's a great honor to attend," Tifa said. "I'm sure Prince Arnion is looking forward to your presence."

Acadia sat up straight, wincing as her head protested the sudden movement. *Poor Arnion. He must be exhausted.*

Their journey had left her drained, physically and emotionally. Even with Arnion's incredible stamina, he must be tired. He had been working with Naileah late into the night to find her family—and flown to Cobasso and back in a single day.

If anyone had earned a moment's rest, it was Arnion. But with all the demands on him, Acadia doubted he'd slept at all. A diplomatic crisis had welcomed him home.

War.

The events from the night before coalesced in Acadia's brain, and a bitter taste coated her tongue.

Avathys and Kifu were preparing for war!

Acadia sprang up, her chair screeching across the marble floor. She whirled toward the maids, throwing out her hands. "What do you mean there's a ball tonight? How can there be a ball when Avathys and Kifu are about to start a war?" Her voice was shrill, tinged with hysteria. She must have been quite a sight, because both maids gaped at her. Acadia imagined her disheveled hair, chapped lips, and shrieking voice would startle anyone.

They couldn't possibly expect her to flounce around, batting her eyelashes at the nobility, while her homeland was at war. When the advisors had surrounded Arnion yesterday, she'd heard one of them say a village had been attacked. How many Kifans were injured, or worse? Acadia's stomach clenched. She stared at the maids, waiting for them to tell her they were kidding, that it was all a ridiculous joke. Eiren couldn't expect her to pretend everything was normal.

Tifa recovered first, her face transitioning from shock to concern. "It's all right, my lady. Prince Arnion is working with the Kifan emissary to de-escalate the conflict. I'm not privy to the details, of course, but there's nothing for you to worry about."

Silvie pursed her lips. Puzzlement scrawled across her youthful face. "What do Avathys and Kifu have to do with it? The Starlight Memorial Ball is a cherished Eirenian tradition. We can't cancel it. That would be scandalous." Silvie shook her head and brushed her fingers down her apron, as if the very thought could stain her clothes. "Besides," she said cheerfully, "the other countries of Elorah are always fighting about something. We can't always be worrying about their problems."

Disbelief chilled Acadia's blood. Could Eirenians really be so callous? Acadia remembered the starving people of Gehenna, fighting over scraps of moldy bread. Emaciated children lying in the dust with skin stretched so taut over their bones, it was nearly translucent. She remembered the feeling of going to bed hungry, night after night, her gums bleeding, lice gnawing at her skin. But worst of all was the despair, knowing she was forgotten by the world.

Meanwhile, in Eiren, they were feasting and dancing. Acadia knew tonight there would be tables overflowing with more food and drink than the attendees could eat in three lifetimes. Of all the wasteful, foolish, pointless things.

"Pointless?" Silvie echoed. Her face flushed and she puffed out her cheeks, clearly offended.

Acadia cringed. What an amateur move. She'd got so lost in her emotions, she'd started muttering out loud.

Silvie's jaw tightened. "How can you say that?" she demanded, crossing her arms over her chest. "Don't Gehennians honor their dead?"

"I've seen more dead than you could possibly imagine," Acadia said quietly. "There's no point in giving honor to a rotting corpse. The person they were before is gone."

"Oh!" Silvie shuddered. She clamped a hand over her mouth and took a step back, bumping into the open wardrobe door.

Tifa cleared her throat. "Lady Acadia is still new to our culture. She can't be expected to value it as we do."

Acadia swallowed back her retort, biting her tongue until she tasted blood.

Silvie nibbled her bottom lip and nodded at Tifa. "You're right." She gave Acadia a wavering smile. "This is truly a special night for our country. Please allow us to help you get ready, my lady. It's an honor for me to be able to participate. I've been looking forward to it for weeks."

Guilt suffocated the anger stirring in Acadia's chest. Silvie was young, barely more than a child. Acadia couldn't expect her to understand. Eiren was so insulated from the rest of the world; the maids probably had no concept of war or the suffering it brought. Arnion and his father might be empathetic, but that didn't mean everyone in Eiren shared their feelings.

Besides, why should Silvie empathize with Kifu? It wasn't like Eiren and Kifu were on the best of terms. Lucien had been torturing people in Gehenna for years while Kifu did nothing. It was a miracle that Arnion had been willing to intercede for her homeland.

Acadia pinched the bridge of her nose and drew in a slow breath. "Okay." She pressed her hands together and took a deep breath. "Let's start over. Tonight is the Starlight Memorial Ball." She gestured at the wardrobe and tried to muster up some semblance of polite interest. "If I remember correctly, a gown was commissioned months ago. It should be in there, but I've forgotten what it looks like. You'll have to search for it."

Silvie instantly perked up. She pivoted back to the wardrobe and ran her fingers along the hangers, cooing over the dresses. "This is like a dream. You're like a princess in a fairy tale, Lady Acadia."

Tifa swept a lavender jacket out of the wardrobe with a flourish. "This shoalskin jacket is lovely. Even at this time of year, the nights can still get chilly."

"That's not it." Acadia frowned. "It should be labeled."

"Look at this silk gown! It's the exact shade of a summer rosebud," Silvie squealed and held up an elegant fishtail dress with capped sleeves.

Acadia dug her nails into her palm. A sharp, throbbing tension pulsed behind her eyes as she watched the maids air out her dresses and hold them up to the light. She didn't want this. She didn't want any of it. In Beulah, she'd had enough pomp and circumstance to last a lifetime. All it did was leave her broken and full of guilt.

What was Arnion doing while she was here playing dress-up? Was he still meeting with Emissary Narhast? Or was he being lectured by the king? The prince had dropped everything to help find her family, but they'd only been gone one day. Surely, King Elyon couldn't stay upset with Arnion for long, but Acadia knew that disappointing his father would hurt the prince deeply.

Acadia twined her fingers together and squeezed, fighting the urge to scratch her knuckles. If she could go around in rags with dust on her head, she would. Even if she walked barefoot up Ilyon mountain, it would never be enough. Arnion had helped her, and now he was suffering for it.

"This must be it!" Tifa pulled out a gown of royal blue, embroidered with silver thread and studded with diamonds. The slim waist flared out into an elegant bell shape that grazed the floor, and gauzy fabric draped from the sleeves and bodice in rippling waves. "It had a note pinned to the hanger."

"It's perfect!" Silvie agreed. "It looks like starlight."

The maids held the dress out to her, beaming.

Silvie clasped her hands together. "What about your hair, Lady Acadia? We could weave in extensions. You'd look radiant with tresses down your back."

A memory flashed in Acadia's mind. She was Sapphyre, seated like a queen, wearing a blood-red dress, glossy hair cascading down her shoulders in an ebony waterfall. She had been Lucien's precious Jewel, working tirelessly to stretch his dark influence over the city of Beulah. Her obsidian hair had been her pride and joy. "Hair as black as her heart," people used to whisper behind her back.

No!

She'd never be like that again.

Silvie reached for Acadia's jagged, chin-length hair, and Acadia slapped her hand away. "My hair is perfectly fine as it is. Don't be ridiculous." Her scathing tone was sharper than a surgeon's scalpel, slicing neatly through the atmosphere of comradery and leaving a trail of destruction in its wake.

Silvie jerked backwards. Her lower lip trembled. "Begging your pardon, my lady. I meant no offense."

"No, I apologize," Acadia said hastily. "I overreacted."

Why was she so bad at this? She'd never had trouble building relationships before. Eiren seemed to bring out the worst in her. Arnion assured her that in Eiren she could be herself. No more putting on an emotional mask or calculated persona to please others. But every time the real Acadia slipped out, someone got hurt. She stepped forward and reached for Silvie's hands. "I'm very sorry."

Silvie flinched away. Fear shuttered her features, and Acadia knew the damage had been done.

Why do I always ruin everything?

Acadia pushed down the self-loathing smothering her. It fell like a poisonous stone settling in her stomach. She cleared her throat. "I fear I'm not myself today. I feel a bit unwell. Perhaps it's best if I prepare for the ball myself."

Tifa blinked and Silvie moved to hover behind her, as if using the older maid as a shield.

Acadia firmed up her resolve. "Please. I'm honored by your assistance, but I think it's best if you leave."

The two maids curtsied wordlessly and headed for the door. Acadia heard a distinct sniffle as they passed.

Dral. I made Silvie cry.

Acadia wished she could tear out her hair. Or maybe shave it all off again. Would that be enough repentance for bullying her maids? She didn't belong in Eiren. Once they found out—

No.

Acadia wouldn't let that happen. She had to try harder. Learn quicker. Stop lashing out. She wouldn't give them a reason to go poking around her past. She'd be perfect. A model citizen of Eiren. She'd stop moping and whining and making Arnion worry. It was just a matter of willpower. Then no one would ever need to know how she'd worked for Lucien as Sapphyre. How she'd risen to be the shining star among all his Jewels through sheer ruthlessness. Acadia didn't know the number of souls she had condemned to Gehenna, but her nights were haunted by the memory of their screams.

Acadia opened the door, intent on following the maids to apologize again. Tifa had an arm wrapped around Silvie as they hurried away, the younger maid's shoulders shaking. The words dried up in Acadia's throat. She hesitated in her doorway.

A whisper slithered through the air. ". . . not cut out to be a princess."

Acadia jerked her head to the left and saw two servants, heads bent together. One held a hand over her mouth, but the words carried. "Maybe the Separatists are right."

Fear punched Acadia in the gut, and she sucked in a panicked breath.

The servants darted a glance and her and hurried away, hiding their faces.

"Acadia!" a cheerful voice called out.

Acadia whirled around and saw Rhys striding down the hallway toward her. Never had she been more grateful for a friendly face.

Her distress must have shown because Rhys leaned in and patted her on the shoulder. "I heard about your rough reception last night." He took in her expression, and concern tightened his features. "Hey, are you all right?"

Anxiety pressed against her teeth, leaving a sour taste behind. If she started voicing her fears, she might never be able to stop. Instead, she settled for shaking her head and burying her face against Rhys's shoulder, knocking him off balance.

"Whoa!" Rhys stumbled. "I guess that's a no."

Acadia sniffed. Rhys smelled like lavender and citrine. He'd probably been making more of his famous herbal tea. Word must have already spread about her exhaustion yesterday and her propensity for emotional outbursts. Rhys was here to do damage control.

She needed to get it together.

"Never mind me." Acadia tightened her grip on the sleeve of his robe before forcing her fingers to relax. She lifted her head, determined to get some answers. "I heard there was an attack on Kifu."

Rhys held a finger to his lips and scanned the hall. His expression was wary. "Let's go into your receiving room. Then we can talk."

"Okay." Acadia held out her hand for him to enter.

Rhys nodded back toward the hallway. "By the way, did something happen? Silvie looked like she'd been crying."

Of course, Rhys knew every maid by name. Even the trainees.

Acadia bit her lip to keep a hysterical laugh from escaping. If only he knew the truth. She firmed up her resolve and allowed the self-reproach to show through. "I'm sorry, Rhys. I snapped at them." She walked into her suite and grimaced at the gown draped across her bed. "Sometimes the balls, the pageants, the political agendas . . . it all seems so shallow to me. I started feeling overwhelmed and . . ." She threw up her hands in defeat. "I don't know what's wrong with me. And I'm worried about Arnion. What happened in Kifu?"

Rhys rubbed the back of his neck. "Honestly, we don't even know if it's an attack yet."

Acadia leaned back against the dining table and waited.

He blew out a breath, stirring his curly bangs, then pulled out a chair and sat down heavily. His shoulders slumped. "A village along the Vosna River was found empty yesterday."

"Empty?" Acadia echoed. Her mind puzzled over the strange word choice.

Rhys nodded. "All the inhabitants are gone."

Acadia's stomach fluttered. She slid into the chair across from her friend. "Maybe they relocated?"

Rhys shook his head. "All their belongings are still there. Clothes, food, means of transport. Only the people and animals are missing."

"Maybe there was a sickness? Could they have been fleeing a plague?"

Rhys leaned forward and rested his elbows on the table. "But there were no bodies. No graves. Nothing disturbed. No sign of a struggle, except that every living creature in the town of Reditona has vanished without a trace."

A chill crept down the back of Acadia's neck. She shook her head and pressed her palms into the table. "But if there's no sign of a struggle, how can the Kifans blame Avathys?"

Rhys sighed and cradled his head in his palms. "That's where the history between Kifu and Avathys is to blame. The Kifans are claiming that Avathys always wanted full control of the Vosna River. That this is a deliberate attack to pressure them to surrender the territory along the riverbank."

Acadia chewed her lower lip. "As a child, I remember hearing that Avathys once led raiding parties across the river. But that was ages ago. Long before my time or even my parents' time. Why would Avathys change tactics now?"

"That's what the Avathysian delegates are saying. They claim their country has had no part in this strange occurrence and that Kifans are blaming them without any proof."

"And this all happened yesterday while Arnion and I were gone?" Acadia asked.

"Unfortunately, yes. Arnion's been getting an earful from just about everyone. Even King Elyon lectured him about his responsibilities to the kingdom. I've never heard Arnion get in trouble before. He's always been above reproach."

"And he still is." Acadia wanted to slam her hands on the table. Guilt clawed at her throat, making it hard to breathe. All of this was her fault. "Arnion was just trying to take care of me. We were too far away to do any good, even if he had brought communicators. How is any of this his fault? There was no way he could have known what would happen."

Rhys sighed. "Arnion was aware that the tension between Kifu and Avathys was reaching boiling point. Some say he never should have left Eiren when such an important political issue was at stake."

Indignation surged through Acadia at the thought of small-minded people criticizing Arnion's every move. Bureaucrats who sat comfortably behind a desk all day could never understand the hardships he had endured to set her and the other Gehennians free. She was also partly to blame. If she had been doing better integrating into Eiren, Arnion wouldn't have felt the need to take a whole day off to help her. The more she thought about it, the angrier she became.

"It's not his responsibility to save the world!" Acadia's voice was sharp. "Hasn't he done enough?" At Rhys's hurt expression, she pulled back. "I'm sorry, Rhys. It's not your fault. I hate that Arnion is in trouble for helping me." She covered her face with her hands. "No matter where I go, I always hurt the people who love me."

<*That's a lie,*> the strange voice said to her spirit.

Acadia looked up. "Did you hear that?"

"Hear what?"

"That voice. That strange voice. It said, 'That's a lie.'"

Rhys blinked. "I didn't hear anything, but I agree. You're too hard on yourself."

"But the voice—"

"Maybe it was your subconscious, trying to talk some sense into you." Rhys smiled and patted her arm. "You've been under a lot of stress too. And I'm sure that a welcoming committee of panicked advisors yesterday didn't help anything."

Acadia forced herself to chuckle. Maybe the stress of so many secrets had caused something in her brain to rattle loose. She was grateful to Rhys for trying to cheer her up. Then she remembered the gossiping servants in the hall. The Eirenians were worried about her relationship with Arnion. "Rhys, why does everyone assume I'm going to be a princess?" As soon as the words passed her lips, she wished she could take them back.

Rhys leaned back with a smile. "That's easy. Because Arnion has named you his chimad."

Acadia twiddled her fingers, looking down. "What exactly is chimad?"

"You mean Arnion hasn't told you?" The words exploded out of Rhys in a rush. He jumped out of his chair and began pacing the carpet. "Of all the stubborn, foolhardy nonsense! No wonder you're so confused."

Acadia scratched her knuckles, her stomach twisting in knots. It was as she suspected. Chimad meant something important. She was missing something big. It reminded her of her early days in the Eirenian palace, when she kept getting lost. Then, Rhys had taught her the secret code. Using the embroidered patterns that swirled along the carpet's edges, she could easily find her way to the great hall, the dining room, the kitchens, even the throne room. Eirenians were marvelously efficient, working little hints and patterns into the carpet, showing the palace staff, residents, and ambassadors a map hidden in plain sight. Maybe there was some unwritten rule about chimad that she was missing, like the patterns in the carpet?

When Arnion called her by that name, she couldn't help but notice the knowing looks it garnered. But Arnion hadn't explained it to her.

Why not?

It wasn't that he was being dishonest. Arnion would never lie. But it was painful to think he was keeping something from her, withholding information he didn't believe she was ready to hear.

Acadia's heart jerked painfully in her chest. She forced her voice to remain steady. "Rhys, calm down. I'm sure Arnion has his reasons." But what could they be? What was Arnion hiding from her?

Rhys continued walking around the room. "I can't believe he hasn't explained it," he muttered to himself.

"What is it?"

He paused and gaped at her, a flush spreading across his face. "It's, well, it's a very important aspect of Eirenian culture. A sort of bond."

He shifted from foot to foot, biting his lower lip. "It really should . . . it's best if it comes from him."

Acadia was not going to let him evade her questions, not when she was so close to the truth. For months, this secret had been hovering over her head and she wanted it out. Now.

She strode to her friend and blocked his path. "Rhys, you're not leaving this room until you tell me exactly what chimad means." She pinned him with her most imperious glare. A glare that Sapphyre had used to bring kings and courtesans to their knees.

Rhys sighed, his shoulders sagging in defeat. "It means 'beloved.' According to Eirenian tradition, each spirit has its perfect match somewhere in Elorah. A soulmate. The person you're destined to be with. In openly calling you his chimad, Arnion has declared you are his one true love."

Acadia's heart lurched, and for a moment she forgot how to breathe. Warmth curled up her toes and pooled in her belly like molten honey.

Soulmate?

Her legs wobbled and she sank to the carpet. "But that's . . . how can he be sure?" Her voice cracked on the last word.

Rhys sat down beside her. "You're kidding, right? This is Arnion we're talking about. He never does anything in half measures. If he says he's sure, he is."

Acadia pressed a hand to her mouth. That certainly explained some things. "But what if the other person doesn't agree? Surely, chimad isn't one-sided. What if the other person is attracted to someone else?"

"It can happen." Rhys shrugged. "But it's rare. Unconditional, all-encompassing love has a lot of sticking power. Most chimad pairs are mutual from the beginning."

Acadia's stomach roiled, and she feared she was going to be sick. "But there's so much he still doesn't know about me. What if he changes his mind?"

"He won't." Rhys spoke with so much certainty, it made her pause.

"And what if I don't accept?" Acadia asked quietly. "What if I can't handle being a princess of Eiren?"

"Arnion would never force you," Rhys assured her. "He would let you go, if that's what you truly wanted."

"And he'd marry someone else?" The words needled her heart as they came out.

"No." Rhys shook his head. "I suspect he would remain alone. When chimad isn't returned, most people don't choose to marry someone else. Not everyone finds their chimad, but those who do claim it would be almost unbearable to settle for someone else."

"But he's a prince," Acadia stammered.

Rhys tapped his nose. "A stubborn prince." He waggled his eyebrows, wringing a chuckle out of her.

Acadia leaned back. "I guess you're right." But inside, she was troubled. Arnion had already sacrificed so much for her. She needed to tell him about her past with Lucien, and soon, before he entangled himself too much in his feelings and couldn't let her go if he needed to. The clock chimed, making her flinch. "It's already late. And I've still got to get dressed."

"I'll leave you to it." Rhys walked to the door and looked back. "Don't worry so much. Things will work out, you'll see."

She waved him out with a smile that fell as soon as the door slid shut. Acadia leaned against the door, pressing her forehead against the cool metal surface.

One true love.

Fire blossomed in her belly at the thought.

Arnion loved her, but would he still feel the same once he knew the truth about her past?

Acadia wanted to believe he would. She loved him, so much that it was painful. The thought of losing him cut through her flesh and bone, twisting like a knife in her spirit. How far could she expect his love to extend? Could he really forgive her for working hand in hand with his mortal enemy?

Acadia shuffled to the wardrobe and brushed her fingers over the royal-blue ball gown. The silky fabric rippled under her touch. Diamonds embedded in the bodice twinkled, catching the light. Acadia sighed. It was a beautiful dress. When she slipped it on, the silk clung to her body, enhancing her slender frame with flattering curves. It flared out at her waist, pools of glittering fabric brushing the floor. She'd need to wear heels to keep the gown from dragging. She peered into the wardrobe and saw a matching set of shoes, the perfect height to keep her hem from brushing the ground.

She walked to her standing mirror and ran her fingers through the short ends of her hair. As Sapphyre, she had obsessed over her ebony locks. Hours were spent on expensive treatments and elaborate hairstyles. She had bedecked herself with jewels and expensive silks fit for a queen. Now, the thought of long hair was another painful reminder of a past she was trying desperately to leave behind. Acadia didn't want to draw attention to her appearance. She settled for brushing the tangles from her hair and clipping it to one side with a porcelain barrette shaped like a chiksa blossom.

Acadia glanced at her dresser, at the pots of kohl and rouge, the glass perfume decanters, and tiny gold tins of lip tint. A ringing sound filled her ears. It all reminded her of Beulah. She flung out an arm and swept the delicate jars and bottles over the edge. They crashed to the ground and shattered. A fragrance of flowers and musk drifted up as the spilt cosmetics and perfumes mingled together.

Why had she done that?

She was never going to use it, but she could have at least given it to somebody else. Most of them were gifts. Her mouth twisted in a wry smile. *Knowing my luck, I'd have probably given it back to the same person who gave it to me.* Agitation tore through her as she stared at the mess on the floor. She ran her hands through her hair, disheveling it, then stomped to her closet and grabbed a broom. After the mess was cleaned up, the room still smelled like a perfume explosion, but the evidence had gone.

Acadia peered in the mirror and smoothed down her hair. She slipped on the matching shoes and took a couple of practice steps. Good. She hadn't forgotten how to move in heels. It had been a while, and Arnion was certain to ask for a dance. She wanted to be sure she wouldn't fall flat on her face.

She straightened her shoulders and steeled herself for a night surrounded by people she didn't know, hemmed in by foreign customs and pinned under the stares of a thousand judgmental eyes, analyzing her every move. Acadia smoothed the agitation from her face and pressed on a smile. Her bedroom door slid shut behind her. The soft click of the lock was a reminder that she was no longer in the safety and privacy of her suite.

Lost in her thoughts, Acadia slipped down the stairs and followed the ornately embroidered carpet to the great hall, accompanied by the soft rustling of her silk gown with every step. After Arnion's resurrection, Acadia had become a de facto member of the palace staff. She was on an advisory board for the former Gehennians and spearheaded the emotional welfare committee, where the idea for home visits had originated. She also met with analysts from time to time, providing consulting advice on Lucien and his activities in Gehenna.

Acadia had expertise in dealing with people and a working knowledge of Lucien's activities as the Heartless King, but the real reason she held such sway in the palace was because of her relationship with Arnion. Everyone knew it. Elyon and Arnion accepted Acadia as if she were family, and the good manners and customs of Eiren dictated that others should follow suit. Before the Separatists, no one had openly questioned her right to be here. Now the hallways bristled with hostile stares and barely concealed whispers. If her past was revealed and Arnion chose to stand by her, it would tear Eiren apart.

Acadia had to find a way to mitigate the damage her work with Lucien might cause. The last thing she'd want was to hurt Arnion. If only there was some way for her to prove her worth to the Eirenians.

Unlikely.

Lately, she was having trouble finding a sliver of worth in herself.

Acadia's steps brought her closer to the ballroom. Orchestral music tickled her ears. The melodic hum of strings and lutes wove together in perfect harmony, tempting listeners to the polished marble dance floor. Her body itched to dip and sway to the familiar rhythm. She walked up to the arched entryway. Butlers on either side bowed to her and moved toward the gigantic carved doors.

Acadia knew what she would find inside. This entrance led to the top of the grand crystal staircase. Below, couples would already be swirling around the dance floor. Guests would be in elaborate costumes, privately comparing themselves to everyone else to see where they fitted into the hierarchy. White-gloved waiters would be gliding through the crowd, unobtrusively serving hors d'oeuvres and sparkling beverages in fluted crystal glasses. The splendor of Eiren would be on full display, an opulence beyond imagination. Meanwhile, an entire village in Kifu had disappeared, and the world was plunging into war.

Acadia's heart seized and her steps faltered. It was all a lie, a façade of peace while the outside world suffered. The Eirenians seemed adamant to ignore the chaos around them. But who was she to judge? She was the biggest liar of them all. Her relationship with Arnion and her life in Capital City balanced precariously on a pedestal of hypocrisy and half-truths. All it would take was one wrong move for everything to shatter.

Chapter 11

ARNION FOUGHT THE URGE to glance at the ballroom entrance again. Uneasiness tugged at the base of his scalp. The ball was already in full swing, and there was no sign of Acadia. After the emotional whirlwind yesterday, he wanted to make sure she was okay. Concern wrestled against twenty-seven years of princely etiquette training. He knew he should be mingling with his guests, not hovering by the entryway, but his heart rooted him to the spot.

Where is she?

Arnion's gaze flicked to the entrance involuntarily. The glittering crystal staircase dominated one side of the ballroom. It provided access to two levels of balconies and arcades above the ballroom floor. Guests flowed up and down the luminous steps, bedecked in all manner of evening wear, from traditional Eirenian dress to the most outlandish fashions. Arnion tracked a woman in emerald-green feathers as she made her way to the second floor. He scanned the balconies on the east side of the room.

Had Acadia slipped in and made her way upstairs to avoid the crowd?

The upper levels were swarming with people. Guests peered over railings to take in the grand scene. Each balcony was bordered by pearlescent marble columns and crowned with elaborate stonework. Colorful frescoes above the third-floor archway depicted key moments in Eirenian history. Arnion tilted his neck to admire the translucent glass roof that would retract later in the evening for guests to cast their lanterns into the night sky.

His father, King Elyon, sat on a canopied dais across the room. Swathes of blue silk, embroidered with the royal crest, draped between the golden pillars of the raised platform. Along the wall, a line of guests had formed, each waiting to pay their respects to the king. Arnion knew his father would not leave the dais until he had greeted each one.

Elyon sat on a carved yeulwood chair, leaning forward as he listened to a woman telling a story with animated hand gestures. The king's craggy face was surrounded by a mane of silver-gray hair, his wide jaw hidden beneath a matching beard. His strong, weather-hardened features could have been intimidating if not for the tenderness that shone clearly in his golden eyes. Fortunately for the rest of Elorah, King Elyon's compassion extended beyond his borders. He was deeply concerned about the disappearances in Kifu, convinced that Lucien was involved.

Arnion clenched his fist at the beratement he had received earlier. The advisors were panicked. The strange circumstances in Kifu had spooked them. There were already rumors that Lucien had spirited away the people of Reditona. Arnion shook his head. Without proof, the best any of them could do was guess.

The worst part was the disappointment in his father's eyes. Arnion had thought he was doing the right thing, helping Acadia connect with her family, but doubt crept in. When his father had asked what his priorities were, he'd struggled for an answer. Was he always supposed to put Eiren first, even at the cost of his own happiness? Before meeting Acadia, Arnion had never considered anything else; now the thought pierced him like a jagged splinter in his lungs.

A diplomat from Ulekrew interrupted Arnion's brooding to introduce himself. "It's an honor to make your acquaintance, Prince Arnion." The man was tall and tan-skinned. His long black hair was pulled back in a warrior's braid, typical of Ulekrew. He extended a calloused hand in greeting.

Arnion exchanged pleasantries with the Ulekren, but his half-hearted attempts at conversation petered out when he noticed Acadia appear at the top of the staircase. His pulse skyrocketed and a wave of heat swept across his face. Stars, she was beautiful. His mouth went dry and he swallowed, cutting off his words mid-sentence. The other man cleared his throat and Arnion apologized.

Making a polite excuse, Arnion slipped away. He navigated through the crowd, his dress boots clicking on the marble floor. Guests tried to waylay him, but Arnion nimbly avoided being entrapped in conversation.

He only had eyes for Acadia.

When he thought about his chimad, the woman he'd risked everything to set free, a tingling warmth zinged along his nerves. He wanted to know her completely, all her little secrets and habits. Why she skipped over cracks in the pavement, and why she avoided the paneled mirrors in the hall. Why she sighed with longing sometimes when she passed the kitchen. Why she always picked the raisins out of her toast and lined them up in a row on her plate, only to eat them at the end. What the look on her face last night meant as he'd walked away.

There was still so much he didn't know, but he wanted to learn it all. Just as he wanted to tell her all his secrets, all his hopes and dreams that he'd never shared with a soul, not even Rhys. Things he barely dared to put into thought, let alone words that would fall from his lips and solidify into something real. If he spoke about what he really wanted, he risked losing it.

When he was a boy, Arnion had learned the people of Eiren desired the image of a prince more than the person beneath it. So, he'd tucked his truest self away, hiding it in the depths of his heart. The isolation he'd felt since he was a boy was the price that came with his crown. What had started as a childish habit had grown into a pattern of keeping himself aloof. Eiren wanted a perfect prince, and he did his best to comply. For years, he had done so without a second thought. But on meeting Acadia, something in Arnion's heart had awoken. He never let anyone in completely, but with Acadia he wanted to. For the first time in a long while, he wanted someone to really know the man beneath the crown.

His chimad was making her way down the staircase, trying to be as unobtrusive as possible. She looked radiant, but truth be told, he was a little concerned. Acadia had been pulling away from him lately. Most of the Gehennians had settled happily into their new lives in Eiren, but he sensed her struggle. She was turning more and more inward. Even the gregarious Rhys hadn't been able to wring her secrets from her. Arnion knew she wanted them to spend more time together, and he was determined to make that happen. Somehow, he'd find a way to balance running his kingdom with her needs.

Arnion leaned against a marble pillar and waited for Acadia to descend. She hovered uncertainly at the bottom of the stairs, then made a beeline for the wall. He stepped out to meet her. "You look beautiful, Acadia. That color suits you."

"Arnion!" Relief washed over her features. Her sapphire eyes brightened as they met his, and Arnion's heart careened wildly against his ribs. "I was looking for you." She reached for him.

Arnion lifted her hand to his lips and kissed it. "You found me."

Acadia fidgeted, flashing him a nervous smile before looking away.

He stepped closer, alarmed to see the glisten of tears in her eyes. "What—"

"Nothing. It's silly," she sniffed. "I behaved badly with Tifa and Silvie, the new maid. I wanted to tell you before you heard it from someone else."

He tugged her into an alcove that afforded them a modicum of privacy. Acadia bit the corner of her lip and studied the decorative molding along the wall, avoiding his gaze.

Arnion gently turned her toward him, his fingers brushing away a tear on her cheek. "Will you tell me about it?"

Acadia picked at a seam on her sleeve, relaying the story in an embarrassed rush. When she had finished, he pulled her in for a hug. "I think you're making more out of it than the offense merits. You made a mistake; you apologized. Tifa and Silvie will let it go."

Her arms wrapped around his neck, fingers tracing the embroidered thread on his collar. "What happens when I make a mistake that's too big to fix?"

Arnion pressed a kiss to her forehead. "Then we'll tackle it together. Tell me, what's the biggest thing bothering you right now?"

She laughed bitterly. "You expect me to choose one?"

Arnion's heart twisted at the anxiety threaded between her words. It sounded eerily similar to his conversation with Rhys. He and Acadia were under an increasing amount of pressure, but as a prince he was accustomed to it. She was not. He had carried the responsibilities of the crown his whole life and had a built-in support network. Acadia had been cast into the raging sea of Eirenian politics without a raft. He wanted to reach out and rescue her from the turbulent waters, but she had to be willing to take his hand.

Arnion rubbed a slow circle against her back. "Let's start with the first one that comes to mind. Once we solve that, we can move to the next."

Acadia reached to scratch at her knuckles, and he wove his fingers through hers to stop her.

"Well, there's—"

"Your Highness," a butler said at his elbow. "Pardon the intrusion, but Emissary Narhast requests your presence."

Arnion suppressed a groan. His father and the Eirenian advisors had made it clear he must make Narhast and the international relations with Kifu a priority. He squeezed Acadia's fingers and leaned in to whisper in her ear, "Hold that thought. I'll be right back; I promise."

Chapter 12

FRUSTRATION SMOLDERED IN ACADIA'S chest as the butler led Arnion away. She desperately wanted to talk with him, but someone else always seemed to need him more. There was a whole kingdom in line ahead of her. She closed her eyes and took a deep breath, rolling her shoulders back. Arnion would return as soon as he was able.

In the meantime, Acadia grabbed a fluted glass from a passing butler and took a sip. A delicious strawberry flavor fizzed on her tongue. She turned, searching for someone to engage in conversation while she waited for Arnion. A group of women standing nearby met her approach with hostile stares. Another man actively moved away from her as she walked toward him. Acadia frowned. Maybe a stranger wasn't the best option. She wasn't in the Eirenians' good graces at the moment. Even the waitstaff seemed distant. Had news of her mishap with the maids traveled so fast?

Acadia reached to scratch her knuckles and caught herself at the last moment, rubbing her hands together instead. There was no point in getting worked up about it. That would only make things worse. Even if the Eirenian courtiers were shunning her, she still had allies. Rhys was her stalwart friend, regardless of the palace gossip. She scanned the room, looking for his familiar silhouette, a head above the crowd crowned with a mess of dark curls. Instead, she caught sight of an unlikely duo—a broad-shouldered elder and a slender young man with dark hair.

Has and Eril!

Two of Arnion's first allies from Gehenna. They had met the prince even before Acadia had. Has was muscular for a man pushing sixty. The Eirenian diet certainly agreed with him, as he no longer had the emaciated look of a prisoner. Soft tufts of white hair curled above his ears on an otherwise bald head, and his good-natured smile wasn't diminished by the fact he was missing quite a few teeth.

Next to Has's sturdy frame, Eril looked slim and waif-like, even though he was a young man of twenty-six. Eril had a head full of jet-black hair, meticulously slicked back. His bright green eyes shone with amusement. He bounced back and forth on his feet, unable to keep completely still, though he'd lost the manic energy that defined him in Gehenna.

As former Gehennians, Has and Eril didn't have the same affectations as the Eirenian court. Maybe she could ask their advice about improving relations in the palace. They seemed to be doing all right for themselves. The two men were in a group of young people, and Eril was clearly telling a funny story. His wide eyes and exaggerated gestures held his audience enraptured. As Acadia approached, the whole group burst into laughter.

A shard of ice twisted in her heart. Why couldn't she connect with the Eirenians like that? As Sapphyre, she always had a group of followers, but now Acadia wondered whether any of it was real, or if their obsequious laughter was as artificial as Sapphyre had been.

Acadia stepped around a cluster of young women, each dressed in a stylized form of Eloran wildlife, when an arm snaked around her elbow.

"Lady Acadia," a young woman purred. Her makeup imitated the black-rimmed eyes of a kryet desert cat, and her long painted nails were filed like claws. "Please join us. We were just talking about you." Her tone was light, but her eyes shone with malice. "Tell us about your ordeal in the marketplace. You must have been terrified."

Acadia pried off the other woman's grip. "Thank you for your concern, but the reports were exaggerated. It was a simple protest."

"That's not what I heard," another woman said. She had black-and-red hawk feathers woven into her hair. "My servants told me the Separatists were attacking Gehennians and destroying their stalls in the market."

"I heard the Separatists were violent," a woman dressed in silver scales chimed in. "And if the enforcers hadn't intervened, they would have rounded up the Gehennians and forcibly ejected them from Eiren."

"Maybe that would have been for the best," another voice muttered.

Outwardly, Acadia maintained a placid expression, but inside she raged. How dare they criticize Arnion's policies within the very walls of his palace, all the while helping themselves to his abundant hospitality?

The kryet woman drummed her nails against her forearm. She looked at Acadia as if she were something to be scraped off the bottom of a shoe. "It's a shame we have these Separatists at all. Eiren was a unified country before our prince's priorities became confused."

White-hot anger seethed through Acadia. She opened her mouth to shred the little chit to ribbons, when a tinkling laugh cut her off. It sounded oddly familiar.

"Causing a scene, Analise?" Espina stepped up beside Acadia with her hands on her hips. "Isn't that your father I see with a girl younger than you glued to his arm? I don't know how you stomach being in the same room with such a vulgar display."

Analise spluttered. Her knuckles whitened around the stem of her glass.

Acadia sucked in a breath. Had an Eirenian just stood up for her? She stared at Espina. The analyst had forgone the traditional robes of her office in honor of the ball. She wore a silky white dress that draped asymmetrically off one shoulder. Her midnight-purple hair was pinned in an elaborate updo. Espina must have sensed her staring, because she met Acadia's gaze out of the corner of her eye and winked. Relief bubbled up Acadia's throat, and she choked back a laugh. She could have almost hugged the quirky analyst.

"Furthermore," Espina continued, "if you'd studied Eirenian history rather than flirting with Joash Silban all through school, you would know that the Separatists have existed for years, although their membership and platform varies depending on the decade. The faction ebbs and flows. Gehenna is just their most recent touchpoint."

Analise had recovered enough to roll her eyes. "Dear Espina, only you would ruin a party dredging up dusty old history."

Espina's answering smile reminded Acadia of an ungalor cornering its prey. "And only a fool would overlook history, blindly repeating the same mistakes. It's no wonder your family has never landed a seat on the council."

Analise drew herself up, shoulders bristling. "I didn't come here to be insulted by the likes of you. Come, ladies, let's seek out more refined company." Chin held high, she turned away.

Espina stuck out her tongue behind Analise's back. Mischief danced in her eyes and she smirked at Acadia. "I think that went well."

Acadia tapped a finger to her lips. "To be honest, it seemed a little unfair."

"That's what I was thinking! "Espina exclaimed. "They outnumbered you five to one."

Acadia shook her head. "No, unfair to them. To be so ill-matched in a battle of wits."

Espina threw her head back and laughed. "I guess I shouldn't be surprised, considering everything in your file. You sized them up quickly."

"I could've handled it." Acadia crossed her arms. "You didn't have to interfere."

"The less commotion you cause, the better. You're under enough heat as it is. Besides"—Espina proudly jerked a thumb toward herself—"I'm known as something of a nonconformist."

"Really?" Acadia let the sarcasm leak into her voice. "I'd never have guessed."

"Acadia!" Has's gruff voice spoke up behind her as he engulfed her in a hug. After a hearty squeeze, the older man stepped back and nodded in approval. "Ye clean up well, lass. Eril nearly choked on his drink when he caught sight of ye."

"Yes, well, that is to say . . ." A red-faced Eril coughed into his hand. "We're all a far cry from Gehenna now. It still surprises me sometimes."

Relief washed over Acadia. So, she wasn't the only one who still struggled. She patted Eril on the arm. "Me too," she said gratefully.

Espina dug her fingers into Acadia's arm. "Is that really Has and Eril? In the flesh?" Her voice was strangely high-pitched.

"Have we met?" Eril raised his eyebrows. A panicked look flashed across his face. "I apologize; I don't remember your name."

"Our prince's first allies, heroes of Gehenna." Espina's voice came out in a rush. "I've read all about you!" She clasped her hands together, stars in her eyes.

Acadia assessed the analyst beside her. Espina's enthusiasm for Gehennians seemed boundless. The analyst had obviously studied Arnion's mission thoroughly. Acadia watched a blushing Eril form the

Eirenian gesture for greeting. Espina squealed, clearly delighted, before mimicking the sign back to him.

Espina's reactions to Gehennians were so different from her country-folk. It was as if she viewed them as heroes or celebrities. Acadia wasn't sure what to make of it but couldn't deny it was a refreshing change from the frigid rejection she'd been receiving lately.

Non-conformist indeed.

Chapter 13

ARNION BIT BACK A groan of annoyance. Fifteen minutes of conversation with Narhast and he had nothing to show for it. The Kifan's stormy blue eyes glared at the prince from below bushy gray eyebrows, his thin lips twisted in a scowl below his hawk-like nose. Narhast stomped his cane on the marble floor to emphasize each word. The two of them were going around and around in circles. Arion tried to ignore Narhast's open hostility, which only seemed to infuriate the older man.

"Your Majesty"—Narhast spat the title like an insult—"Please remind me why I am wasting time with this frippery when my people are being snatched from their beds by murderous Avathysian scum."

Arnion held up his hands. "We have no proof that Avathys was involved in the disappearances."

"And nothing to disprove it either," Narhast grunted. "We came to Eiren for help, but so far, all you've done is waste our time. I expected more from the prince of the Glittering City."

Arnion frowned. "You know that we're assembling a team to investigate what happened. They're preparing as we speak."

"I don't want a team of screen-fried pencil pushers! Do you honestly expect a trembling analyst to be able to call the nation of Avathys to account? If so, you're sorely mistaken."

"What do you suggest, Narhast?" Arnion asked.

"I want you." Narhast jabbed a bony finger at Arnion. "If half the rumors about you are true, you're the only one capable of bringing Avathys to its knees."

Arnion struggled to keep his expression neutral. He held out a placating hand. "I'm not going to destroy any nation. Especially not without irrefutable evidence."

"Then get it," Narhast snorted. "Come to Reditona and look for yourself. Those Avathysian vermin must have left traces behind. Surely someone of your *illustrious* reputation is up to the task." His words oozed disdain.

Arnion knew Narhast was trying to bait him and deliberately kept his face calm. "Interesting suggestion, Emissary. I'll make sure to share it with our advisory board first thing in the morning. In the meantime, I suggest you enjoy the Starlight Memorial Ball, before any diplomatic misunderstandings can occur."

Narhast choked back an enraged cough, but Arnion had had enough. Throughout their conversation, he'd been keeping a subtle eye on Acadia. She looked . . . haunted. He'd thought the trip to reconcile with her family would help things, but it appeared to have made things worse. Why had she become so upset with the maids about her hair? That wasn't like her.

Arnion remembered Acadia's story about her life in Beulah. She used to love fine clothes and hair accessories. But here in Eiren, she shied away from those things like the plague. Of course, her time in Gehenna would have changed her, but it almost seemed like she wanted to punish herself by withholding things she might enjoy.

Concern gnawed at Arnion. He wanted Acadia to be comfortable in Eiren, for it to truly be her home. But what if that wasn't what she wanted? Arnion's heart was bursting with plans. He wanted to sweep

Acadia away on a starry night and whisper in her ear what it meant when he called her "chimad." To pull out the matching armbands he had forged and ask her to share her life with him, to be his betrothed. But if Arnion was honest with himself, he had growing doubts Acadia wanted that. He had hoped she would settle in easily and learn to love Eiren. Almost all the former Gehennians were thriving, though there were a few who chose to leave. A small stream trickling out. But it had been months since the last one.

What if Acadia secretly wanted to leave too?

He knew she didn't like conflict. Was that why she was avoiding him? Because she was working up the nerve to say goodbye?

Foreboding seized Arnion followed by an immense desire to be by Acadia's side. He needed to squeeze her hand and remind himself that she hadn't fled yet; he still had time to win her heart. Beside him, Narhast was still sputtering with outrage. Arnion held up a hand. "I have listened to your requests and provided my answer. Now there is something I must see to." The emissary's cane shot out to detain him, but Arnion nimbly avoided it. "Good evening." The prince's words contained a finality that made Narhast's mouth snap shut.

Good. Narhast had ruined enough of Arnion's evening. He strode toward Acadia with swift, decisive steps. A strange buzzing filled the air and every light in the ballroom cut out.

Chapter 14

Panicked voices rose. Glass shattered. A woman shrieked.

Adrenaline surged through Arnion, accelerating his pulse and sharpening his thoughts. He strained to see through the darkness. *What was going on?*

The roof groaned, and a beam of moonlight sliced across the ballroom floor.

The ceiling was retracting!

Arnion's thoughts whirled. Was this part of the evening's events? But they always gave a warning before dousing the lights and, even then, some of the sconces were merely dimmed. The ballroom was never left in complete darkness, especially with this many guests. And the ceremony to retract the ceiling was always accompanied by a joyous fanfare of trumpets. Instead, an eerie silence reigned.

Arnion pushed forward in the crowd, letting the silvery moonlight guide his steps as the ceiling retracted further. He remembered where Acadia had been standing. As long as she waited for him, he knew he could reach her.

"Look up!" someone gasped.

Arnion turned his head skyward, along with a thousand other guests. Lights twinkled in the sky, but they weren't stars. He squinted. It looked like a military-grade hovercraft, but that was impossible. How could it have got past the palace's air-defense system?

A flame blazed along the sides of the vehicle, burning away part of the paint to reveal a blood-red handprint.

Separatists!

So, this was a political stunt. Anger swept through Arnion at the brazen nature of the protest. Was respect for the crown so low that people felt they could stage a pseudo-attack on the palace? They must have sympathizers within the household staff who deactivated alarms and shared security codes. That was the only explanation.

Why go to these lengths? The Eirenian crown welcomed dialogue with its citizens. Sharing opposing views was always encouraged, but this was far beyond what he and his father could tolerate.

Arnion's thoughts were interrupted as a bright blue light burst from the hovercraft, projecting an enormous shrouded figure in the air. A hooded cowl hid the Separatist's face above black riot armor, emblazoned with a red palm print. The figure raised gloved hands.

"People of Eiren," a gravelly voice crackled through the air. The hovercraft amplified his voice for all to hear.

Arnion reached into his spirit. <Security!> he demanded.

The response was immediate. <We're on it, Your Majesty. Somehow they bypassed our scanners. We're working to shut them down, but they've got an Adept technician on board. They've been blocking our attempts, but it's only a matter of time.>

Arnion frowned. An Adept skilled enough to throw off the security staff had to be registered. That meant he or she could be traced. It might take time, but whoever it was knew they would get caught. Did they expect to gain sympathy by being imprisoned?

"Do you know why we're here?" the holographic voice boomed. "On this night, it is tradition to light candles for every Eirenian life snuffed out by pointless conflicts beyond our borders. But I'm here to tell you"—The man's voice thrummed with intensity—"There is nothing out there worth One. Single. Eirenian. Life."

Arnion reached for his spirit, but it resisted him, buzzing against his skin and sending goosebumps prickling up his arms. His spirit pulled inward, retracting into a recalcitrant little ball. It would not help him. The prince gritted his teeth. Of all the times for his spirit to fail!

Above him, the Separatist was clearly warming to his topic. His words fell faster and louder. "We are here to cleanse the corruption from our lands. To wipe away the filth that has invaded our borders."

Agitation seared through Arnion, and he straightened his shoulders. Even without his spirit, he wasn't powerless. "That's enough." The intensity in his tone caused the people around him to wince. Arnion stepped forward, spreading his arms. "We cannot tolerate the excessive nature of your protests. First in the marketplace and now this. You will no longer be allowed to flout Eiren's laws. My father and I have welcomed the people of Gehenna who chose to abandon Lucien's manipulations. I will not tolerate you denigrating them."

The Separatist laughed, a high-pitched sound that grated against Arnion's nerves. "Young prince, that woman has bewitched you. She has stolen away your good judgment with her siren tongue."

"You forget yourself." Arnion cast out his hand. His spirit would answer him. It *had* to. He couldn't allow this to continue. The Separatists had taken their protests too far. Someone could get hurt. He took a deep breath, mentally preparing to break through their shield.

"Do you not know what she truly is, my lord?" The holographic projection peered down at him and shook its head incredulously. "*Lady*

Acadia's gowns are steeped in blood that will never be washed away." A spotlight blazed from the hovercraft. The white light sheared through the crowd until it came to rest on one woman, standing alone.

Acadia.

She was in danger. Dread sliced through Arnion's gut. He pushed forward through the crowd, but she was still so far away.

Shielding her eyes from the glare of the light with one hand, Acadia peered up at the hovercraft. Light refracted from her gown, skittering reflections across the faces around her. It wasn't fear Arnion read in the set of her jaw, but cold resignation. She accepted his people's rejection and hatred as if she deserved it.

What had she been hiding from him? He shouldered through the people around him who had frozen like statues, eyes riveted on the spectacle above.

Disgruntled murmurs rippled through the partygoers as the Separatist leader jabbed a holographic finger toward Acadia. "Do you know how many have suffered and died at her behest? How many souls she condemned to Gehenna?" With each word, the man's voice grew louder and sharper. "The first and most vile of all Lucien's Jewels, the painted harlot who sat at the Heartless King's right hand—Mistress Sapphyre herself."

Arnion stopped short. Acadia was one of Lucien's Jewels? His heart twisted painfully. *Why didn't she tell me?*

Around him, people gaped at Acadia with revulsion. There was a beat of silence before angry mutters rose in the air like a swarm of bees.

The Separatist on the hovercraft laughed. "It's time to show the world your true colors, girl." The hologram raised his arms over his head.

Then Arnion saw it. Two acolytes in the hovercraft heaving a bucket over the lip of the vehicle. His blood froze in his veins. Acadia was right beneath them!

Arnion reached for his spirit. <Protect Acadia,> he commanded, but his spirit wavered, refusing to heed him.

The acolytes tipped the bucket over. Blood and offal rained down on Acadia, drenching her in red. She screamed, clawing at her dress, trying to wipe off the filth. The train of her gown clung to her legs. She tripped and crashed to the floor. Acadia sat up, her eyes wide and dark. Her mouth hung open. She looked down at her stained hands as blood pooled around her.

Ringing filled Arnion's ears, and he mouthed one word.

<No.>

A wave of energy blasted outward from his spirit, sending rippling shockwaves across the ballroom floor. It shattered the shield around the protestors, but it was beyond his control. The rush of his spirit knocked down guests, blew the food off tables, cracked the marble floor, and blasted out all the windows in the ballroom.

Shattered glass showered everyone in a vicious, stinging rain. The air was filled with frightened screams and sobbing. Arnion could feel the terror rising in the people around him. Spotlights shone on the Separatist hovercraft. The palace security forces had arrived. They surrounded the vehicle, shooting electric tethers into its sides. The ballroom lights flickered back on.

Arnion watched the chaos, detached, as if floating outside his body. The security team towed away the hovercraft. Other palace staff rallied, calling out instructions, coming in with blankets and first-aid supplies. The crowd was separated into groups. No one seemed seriously hurt, but there were minor injuries from the glass shards.

Arnion looked down at his hand as it clenched and unclenched. He'd never lost control of his spirit before. What if he'd hurt someone? What was wrong with him? He shook his head. He could untangle these thoughts later. For now, he needed to get to Acadia.

Their eyes met for a second across the cracked ballroom floor. She gathered her blood-drenched skirts, kicked off her shoes, and fled.

Arnion replayed the words of the Separatist leader in his mind. Was it true? Had Acadia really worked hand in hand with Lucien? How could she have kept that hidden from him? She knew he—

Self-loathing swallowed Arnion's train of thought. Acadia expected it. She knew she'd be rejected after her past was revealed. Worst of all, she believed it was what she deserved. He'd seen it written across her face just before she and the ballroom were splattered in blood.

Arnion's chest loosened, and warmth flushed across his face. He loved Acadia. Her past didn't matter. But when his chimad needed him the most, he couldn't protect her. The failure settled like an ache in his bones, overridden temporarily by the all-consuming need to go to Acadia. He raced after her, following the trail of blood smeared along the ballroom floor.

Arnion finally caught up with her by the fountain. She had waded into the water and was furiously scrubbing her arms.

"Acadia, stop." He stepped into the stone basin, barely aware of the water soaking his uniform. The agony in her eyes tore a hole in his soul. He rushed to her and clutched her hands in his to stop her from scraping her skin off. "I'm sorry. I'm so sorry, Acadia," he whispered over and over.

She tried to yank her arms free, and he held her fast. Acadia looked up at him and her face crumpled. A sob tore from her throat. She pressed herself into his chest.

"It's my fault," Arnion whispered. "I should have protected you."

She looked at him with glassy eyes, and it felt like the world was crumbling beneath his feet. How could he have let this happen?

They sank down until they were sitting on the tile floor. The water lapped against their chests.

"Here, lean back." Arnion turned Acadia gently. "Let me wash your hair."

A muscle ticked in Acadia's jaw, but she acquiesced silently. Arnion cradled her neck in the crook of his elbow and tilted her back. With deft fingers, he picked the bits of offal from her hair then rubbed the crust of drying blood from her scalp with his thumbs. Acadia took a shuddering breath and closed her eyes. Every few moments she shivered, her body wracked with noiseless sobs.

Arnion vowed he would not let this cowardly act go unanswered. After he had cleaned every trace of blood, he helped Acadia back to her room and tucked her into bed. When he bent to kiss her good night, she turned away and buried her face in the pillow.

She hadn't spoken a word.

Chapter 15

KAYA SLAMMED INTO THE bone-white dune. Her left shoulder screamed from the impact and sand lodged up her nose. She sat up, spluttering, and spat out a clump of grit.

Dragul stood to the side, the sun barely cresting the ocean horizon at his back. A lone gull warbled in the sky and a gentle breeze scented the air with salt and palm. Kaya used to dream about the beauty of the sea, but she couldn't appreciate it when Dragul's dawn training sessions always ended so poorly.

Her grandfather and mentor tapped his foot on the ground, his mouth a grim line of disapproval. He had evaded another one of her attacks. Kaya clenched her teeth. Dragul's training robe was still impeccably white; hers was caked with sweat and grime. Worse, her breath sawed in ragged gasps while the old man's chest barely rose and fell.

"Again," Dragul demanded in his raspy baritone.

Kaya growled. That stinking old fossil never let up. She got to her feet, hiding a wince. Her calves ached, and stiffness was spreading up her legs. She brushed herself off.

"Don't tell me you're tired," Dragul taunted. "I'm three times your age and I'm still waiting for you to start fighting."

Kaya launched herself at him, fist swallowed in blue spirit flame.

Dragul knocked it neatly aside. "You're still letting your emotions control you."

Kaya darted forward. She feinted a left hook, then crouched, swinging a leg out to trip him.

Dragul leaped nimbly backward. "Better. But. Still. Too. Slow." He punctuated his words with a devastating flurry of punches and kicks that sent Kaya reeling.

Frustration curdled in Kaya's gut. Dragul was going easy on her. If he'd wanted to, he could have knocked her flat. She couldn't even land one hit.

"I thought you learned something in our time apart," Dragul chided. "You're still relying on your anger for strength."

Kaya's chest heaved. She staggered to her feet and leaned forward, hands on her knees. "My anger"—*pant*—"is"—*pant*—"my strength." She leaped forward again, and this time Dragul stepped into her kick. He grabbed her leg and flung her away.

Kaya faceplanted in the dune. Sand wedged under her lashes and her eyes burned. She coughed and swiped at her eyes with the back of her hand. Her knuckles were bloody. "I'll get you for that, you old fossil!"

"No, you won't." Dragul crossed his arms and fixed her with a dismissive glare. "At the rate you're going, you'll never lay a finger on me."

Kaya roared, and blue flames danced down both shoulders, tickling her arms and flicking out from her body in little forked tongues. Numbness spread up her limbs. Her spirit curled back into her, and the flames winked out. A dull buzz droned through her skull as she sank to her knees.

"You've exhausted yourself again." Dragul walked forward and flung a towel over her head. "Time for a break."

"I can still . . ." Kaya stood and wobbled.

Dragul caught her, brushing her bangs back from her forehead. "That's enough for now. Rest. Resting is also a part of training."

Kaya's face warmed and irritation shot through her. She'd failed yet again, and Dragul had the audacity to tell her to rest. She shoved herself off him. "I don't see how sitting around is going to make me stronger." She stomped away from their training area in the dunes, sand spraying behind her.

Gravel crunched under her feet as she approached the series of domed structures that made up Dragul's home. The bright orange walls—caused by the heavy concentration of shells in the local limestone—normally amused her, but not today. Kaya skirted the house and headed around back where Ellio liked to tinker with his jetbike. That machine was his pride and joy. Whenever he had a spare moment, he was out in the yard modding parts or polishing its electric-green aero panels.

Ellio must have heard her coming, because as she rounded the corner, he peeked out from behind the three-wheeled vehicle. He had swapped out the sleek street tires of Beulah for chunky all-terrain mods. Sometimes they blasted over the dunes together or raced along the shoreline, and Kaya would cinch her arms around his waist—more tightly than she truly needed to—and breathe in his scent. Bergamot and sandalwood with just a hint of engine grease.

Her mechanic pushed his goggles into his dark-blue hair and grinned. "How's the training going?"

Kaya glared at him. How could he be so cheerful this early in the morning?

Ellio scratched his nose, smudging it with grease. "That good, huh?"

She crossed her arms and leaned against the orange stucco wall. "It's that stinking old man." She lowered her voice in a mocking impression of her grandfather. "'Don't get angry, Kaya. Don't lose your temper, Kaya.'"

A weak smile flickered across Ellio's face before he turned away to pick up his torque wrench. Kaya watched his hands as he carefully fitted a bolt and began tightening it. Click. Click. Click.

"You know," Ellio said, still looking down, "I wouldn't totally disregard his advice." He glanced up, caught sight of the annoyance building on her face, and ducked back down. "Age has its wisdom," he said with a shrug.

Kaya groaned. "Not you too. Don't tell me you're on his side."

Ellio must have finished what he was working on, because he stood up, dusted off his coveralls, and stepped around the bike toward her. He was at least two heads taller than her, but he slouched against the wall so that they were shoulder to shoulder. "Do you regret coming?" he asked seriously. "If you're really unhappy, we could leave."

Kaya combed the sand out of her hair. She probed her sore lip with the tip of her tongue. "No," she said slowly. "I don't want to leave. Not yet."

Tension visibly left Ellio, and guilt twinged Kaya's conscience. Ellio had no family left in the world; of course he'd want her to reconcile with her grandfather. She ground her teeth and huffed. "If anything, I'm not going to leave until I figure out how he's so dratted quick."

Ellio's brows quirked in confusion.

Kaya rolled her eyes. "That geezer is one slippery old fox. I couldn't even lay a finger on him today."

"Or any day," Ellio teased. At her frown, he relented, bumping her with his shoulder. "I think there's a lot you can learn from him. Try to think of things from his perspective." She opened her mouth to argue, but he spoke louder, effectively smothering her protest. "I know it's not your style, but think of it like . . . like adapting to a new enemy." His speech quickened as he warmed to the idea. He slapped his fist in his palm. "Like he's a villain you have to defeat. But to defeat him, you need to think like him."

Amusement bubbled up inside Kaya at his enthusiasm. She raised an eyebrow. "So, Dragul's a villain now?"

Ellio gave her an exasperated look. "You know what I mean," he grumbled, toying with the end of his torque wrench. "I don't mean Dragul's an actual villain, but to defeat him you have to know where he's coming from. Anticipate his attacks and defenses."

Kaya nudged the toe of her boot in the gravel. The old geezer was always telling her to let go of her anger and be self-controlled. If she could anticipate his defenses, maybe she'd find a weak spot. And if she could finally land a blow, maybe he'd give up correcting her and let her train the way she wanted.

Kaya let out a snicker. Beat the old man at his own game. That would be fun. She knocked Ellio on the arm. "Maybe you're onto something."

He laughed, eyes sparkling. All at once, they both seemed to realize how close their faces were. Ellio choked on his laugh, eyes tracking to her lips.

Kaya could feel her face warming.

For Dral's sake!

She stood on tiptoe and pressed her lips to Ellio's. His mouth was warm, lips a little dry from always working outdoors. His arms wrapped around her waist, drawing her closer.

A loud cough sounded behind her.

Ellio sprang back as if he'd been hit with a buzz baton. His face was burning red.

"I'll thank you to keep your hands off my granddaughter," Dragul said with a scowl.

"Dragul!" Kaya whirled around to face him. Heat warmed her face, and white-hot fury churned her stomach. "H-how dare you!" The fact that she stuttered made her even more incensed.

"I laid down the rules when you arrived. Ellio gave me his word. Or does that mean nothing to you, young man?"

"Of course it does, sir." Ellio fumbled with his jumpsuit, shoving his hands in his pockets. "I'm sorry."

Kaya read his distress in the slump of his shoulders. Rage blistered her nerves raw. "It was just a kiss!" she shouted. "What's wrong with you? Why did you make Ellio say that stupid vow in the first place?"

"In Eiren, relationships mean something. You don't just throw yourself away on the first person you meet."

"Newsflash! I'm not Eirenian. I'm some kind of mongrel half-breed left for dead by my mother and her oh-so-great nation."

"Kaya!" Ellio took her hand and squeezed it. "That's enough. No one forced me into anything. I want to respect your grandfather's rules. That's all."

She jerked her hand away. "Of course you're on his side. Like always." She turned on her heel and stormed away.

Men.

They're either spineless, ridiculous, old-fashioned, or some combination of the three.

Kaya kicked at a clump of sea grass. She stormed down the path to the little pond that bordered their property and stomped around to the far side. She picked up a rock and flung it into the water. This made her feel mildly better, so she picked up a larger rock and hurled it in. The splash sent frogs and skaklops scrambling for cover. There was a boulder she and Ellio had sat on before. Kaya focused her spirit through her arms, blue flames forming along her skin and rushing from her shoulders to her fingertips. She gripped the boulder and tugged. It was stuck fast. She breathed in through her nose and tugged harder. It gave a little.

Harder.

Her spirit rushed out of her like a living flame as, muscles bulging, she heaved the rock out of the ground and hurled it into the pond. Water exploded upwards, waves careening across the pond and splattering her with salt weed and pond scum.

Yuck.

Kaya plucked at a weed that had lodged in her hair. A chuckle sounded behind her.

Ellio had followed her. His eyes crinkled, as if he was suppressing a grin. "Better?" he asked.

She nudged a stone with her foot. "A little," she admitted.

"You look like a drowned rat."

She harumphed her displeasure, and he held up a small paper bag and waved it in front of her. "I brought you something. A peace offering."

Kaya sniffed. A heavenly sweet scent emanated from the bag. "Is that . . . melon pan?" A weaker woman would have squealed with excitement. Not Kaya.

"I made it earlier today while you were training."

She beamed. "I didn't know you could make melon pan."

Ellio turned red and scratched his nose. "Well, I know it's your favorite, so . . ." He trailed off with a sheepish grin.

Kaya's pulse fluttered. "Ellio . . ." She couldn't get the words out, couldn't get her tongue to shape the feelings in her heart into words. That he made her feel safe, made her feel loved, even when she was behaving like a spoiled rotten brat.

How did he always manage to see the bright side of things?

Rather than figuring out what to say, she took a bite of the melon bread, and a smile stretched from ear to ear. "Hey," she mumbled with her mouth full, "this is pretty good." She managed to fit in another bite and chewed. The melon pan was crunchy on the outside but soft inside, and in the middle was a delicious sugar-melon jam. "It's *really* good."

As she watched Ellio's face light up, a tingle ran through the tips of her toes to the top of her head. He was so good. She'd do anything to protect him. No one was ever going to steal anything precious from her ever again. Kaya wouldn't let that happen. She was stronger now, and she'd fight tooth and nail to protect what she loved. Not Lucien, not Eiren, not even Dragul would stand in her way.

Kaya polished off the roll and licked her fingertips. "How'd you learn to make those?"

"I bribed the baker in town to share her recipe."

Jealousy rose like a lump in her throat. Kaya put a hand on her hip. "Bribed how, exactly?"

Ellio rubbed his chin. "I guess traded would be a better word. One of the ovens in her kitchen was acting up, so I fixed it in exchange for the melon pan recipe. But she swore me to secrecy." His eyes were sparkling now, devious. "So, I can't ever reveal the details. Not even to you." He bopped her on the nose.

Kaya waggled her fingers at him. "Not even if I tickle you within an inch of your life?"

Ellio shuddered and crossed his arms over his chest. "Not even then." He pouted. "Plus, I'll be less likely to make it again if you do that."

Kaya snorted. "It was a joke. I'd never force you to go back on your word."

He turned to her, his expression serious. "I know you wouldn't."

She found herself leaning toward him, drawn by a magnetic pull that buzzed like electricity in her chest and sizzled along her veins.

Ellio leaned back and cupped his neck with his hand. "Let's not." He looked around. "Dragul's been clear about his expectations, and he's letting me stay here even though I'm not family and not even a part of his mission. I want to try and respect that. Besides, I think he wanted to talk once you'd calmed down."

Kaya eyed him coolly. "He's what got me upset in the first place."

Ellio took her hands in his and squeezed. "You should try to reconcile, Kaya. He seems to know what he's doing and training with him is helping you get stronger."

Kaya looked away. "It doesn't feel like it."

"Are you kidding?" Ellio's tone was incredulous. "I just watched you hurl an enormous boulder into the pond. You never could have done that before."

Maybe Ellio was right. She was able to draw upon her spirit a lot more since training with Dragul. Before that, she'd only been able to use it once, when she and Ellio were in a life-or-death situation in Beulah. But accessing her spirit was becoming more normal. It was now a common presence in the back of her mind, like an extension of herself.

"All right, all right." Kaya slipped her hand in his. "I'll go and make nice with the old man. Will that make you happy?"

He smiled at her, and Kaya's insides turned to jelly. It should be a crime to look that cute. She could melt into a puddle whenever Ellio smiled at her like that.

How ridiculous.

She wasn't the type to swoon over a handsome guy. But Ellio was different. He saw something in her that she could barely believe herself. A good Kaya. Someone who was strong but kind; smart but compassionate. Ellio never pushed her. He just seemed to draw the best parts out of her, like a magnet pulling gold coins from the ocean floor. Like he saw her potential and helped her start making it a reality. As crazy as it sounded, she wanted to be that better version of herself that he believed in. For him.

But no swooning. No matter how darn cute he was.

They wandered back to Dragul's home, and Ellio slipped inside. Kaya hovered in the doorway. Where had the old man got to? She sent out a questioning tendril with her spirit.

There! At the sagrin pen. Dragul keep a pair of the six-legged equine species to pull his cart into the local fish market in town.

Kaya headed over to confront him.

No, wait. Not confrontation. Just talk. She'd promised Ellio she would try to work things out with Dragul. But the old fossil had to stop interfering in her love life.

That was nonnegotiable.

"Dragul," she called out. "Ellio said you wanted to talk."

Her grandfather was pouring oats into the feed trough. After he finished emptying the bag, he patted the sagrin, a female with a splotched purple hide. The creature snorted and chuffed him with her long, prehensile snout. Dragul walked out of the pen and shut the latch behind him.

He gave Kaya a sidelong look. "That boy's a stabilizing influence on you." His voice was begrudging.

Kaya snorted. "No thanks to you. Ellio's so worried about winning your approval."

"Really?" Dragul's sharp eyes gleamed in the morning light. "You could have fooled me."

Kaya balled her hands into fists. "What do you have against him, anyway? Just because he's not from Eiren—"

"He's a stranger you picked up in Beulah who helped you destroy half the city."

"Not half. Not even one third." Kaya rounded on him, anger sharpening her words. "Why do you even care? Beulah is a cesspool! Elorah would be better if we'd torn the whole place down."

"Maybe so," Dragul conceded. "But it was reckless. You could have both been killed."

"You're one to talk. You abandoned me there."

Dragul narrowed his eyes. "I hadn't considered the depth of trouble you would wander into in my absence, that's true." His voice was low.

Kaya planted her hands on her hips and jutted out her chin. "Now you know what I'm capable of."

Dragul let out an exasperated breath. "That's just the problem, Kaya. You don't realize it yourself." He held out his hands. "You're capable of so much more. But without self-control, you'll never realize your full potential."

Kaya's stomach roiled. Why didn't he get it? "I'm strong. Stronger than almost anyone I've ever met."

"You have no idea of the forces you're going to be up against." Dragul paused, briefly closed his eyes, and took a deep breath. Then, he fixed her with a withering glare. "Lucien and his warriors are unlike anything you've ever seen. You think I'm tough to beat? You can't conceive of the power Lucien will be capable of when he uses trividium. That Beulan guild boss was just a taste. A pion. He had the tiniest infusion of trividium in his spirit, and it took crushing him with a three-ton stadium to take him down. Do you really think your little temper tantrums and paltry skills could stop someone with trividium embedded inside them?

When they're crazed beyond all reason and will kill anything in sight?"
Dragul leaned in close. "You. Have. No. Idea." He thumped his palm
against her forehead to emphasize each word.

Kaya swatted him away. Fury burned hot across her face. "I never will
if you keep flitting around like a butterfly and don't train me. Teach
me to fight! Train me to be stronger! Stop with all this nonsense about
self-control, and just get on with it!" she shouted.

"I'm trying, you foolish girl!" Dragul roared back, his face reddening.
"When are you going to learn?"

"When you stop spouting nonsense and start making sense!" Kaya
screamed in his face.

Dragul's hand jerked up, like he wanted to slap her. He restrained
himself. Barely.

Kaya's pulse throbbed, and rage blurred her vision. "Where's your
precious self-control now, old man?" she seethed. "Where was your precious Eiren when my mother was slaughtered on the plains of Alsehir?
Where were you then?" Kaya shoved him. Her breathing was ragged.
Furious tears pricked the corners of her eyes.

Dragul watched her. His throat bobbed, but he remained silent.

Kaya snorted in disgust and shouldered past him.

So much for talking.

Chapter 16

WHEN THE MORNING SUN warmed her cheek, Acadia turned and burrowed deeper into her pillow. She never wanted to wake up again. All of Eiren knew her secret now. Had Petra told the Separatists who she was? Or had another person recognized her?

More importantly, what did Arnion think? A part of her desperately wanted to know and a part never wanted to find out. She hunched under her covers and scratched her knuckles until they bled.

The door chimed, and chills rode up her arms. She couldn't bear to face anyone. It would be better to die than see the disgust written on every Eirenian face after the spectacle last night. Acadia double-checked the door was locked and jammed her pillow over her head.

<Acadia, it's me.> Arnion's voice spoke quietly to her spirit. <Please let me in.>

Adrenaline shot through Acadia's body. Her heart hammered against her ribcage with murderous intensity. She sat up, frantic. This was the moment she had been dreading.

<They told me you're not eating. Please let me in; I need to talk to you.>

She pressed a button to open the door. She was still in her nightshift, but she didn't care. What was the point in worrying about appearances? Arnion was probably here to tell her to pack her bags. She heard him step into the room, but she didn't dare look up. If this was her last moment with him, she couldn't bear to see his face twisted in disgust at the sight of her.

"Acadia!"

She kept her eyes downcast, but she heard him cross the room in great bounding steps. His arms swept her into a hug, and she squeaked in surprise.

Why wasn't he berating her? Didn't he care that she had humiliated him in front of his entire kingdom?

"I'm so sorry." Arnion was shaking. "How can I ever apologize for such behavior from my people?"

Her chest tightened. Arnion was crying, she realized in shock.

"I failed you." His voice broke on the last word. "I couldn't protect you and what those Separatists did . . ."

Acadia felt a tear land on her cheek and roll down her chin.

"I'm so sorry, Acadia. Can you ever forgive me?"

Slowly, she raised her trembling arms until they encircled Arnion's waist. "It wasn't your fault," she said in a hoarse whisper. "It was mine. I wanted to tell you so many times, but I was terrified."

Arnion took a shuddering breath and relaxed his hold just enough to look at her face. His fingers traced along her jaw with a featherlight touch. "Are you . . ."

"No." She dug her fingers into the fabric of his shirt. "I'm not all right. Don't you hate me?" She looked up at him, tears streaming down her face. "Now you know who I was?"

"Acadia." His breath ghosted across her lips, and he rested his forehead against hers. "Of course I don't hate you. I've told you before that your past doesn't matter. It's who you are now that I care about."

She ducked her head under his chin. Could he really forgive her that easily? Even if Arnion could, what about the people of Eiren? What would they think? How could they possibly accept her as their future queen now?

Arnion rubbed soothing circles along her back. "I can't believe the Separatists took their protests this far. We've met with them. I knew their leaders weren't satisfied, but this . . ." His hands stopped their tracing, and he pulled her tighter against him. "I should have known they were targeting you. But how did they find out about your past?"

Acadia let out a shaky breath. "It was bound to happen. Sapphyre was notorious, and she had a lot of enemies." She picked at a loose thread on his collar. "What will happen to them?"

"The Separatists involved in yesterday's attack have been arrested. At least, all the ones we've discovered so far. The palace guards caught the aerial protestors and some of the collaborators in the crowd. We'll question them to find out how they were able to breach our security." Arnion's breath warmed her neck as he spoke. "Our security team believes the Separatists have powerful sympathizers within the system. Someone provided them with high-level security codes. Otherwise, they never would have made it so far. It will take some digging, but they'll be caught. Once we've learned all we can from them, they will be prosecuted to the full extent of the law."

Acadia nodded and studied his face. Arnion's jaw was clenched, his eyes tight as if in pain. She pressed her palm against his cheek, wishing she could smooth away his burdens. Things like this weren't supposed to happen in Eiren. The fact she was bringing this chaos to his doorstep wrenched her heart. Still, maybe she wasn't the sole factor responsible. "Do you think . . ."

Arnion seemed to read her thoughts. "Lucien may be involved."

"That stunt with the glass had his name written all over it."

Arnion stiffened. "Actually, that was me."

"What?" Acadia couldn't hide the surprise in her voice.

"I saw them in the hovercraft above you and realized . . ." Arnion swallowed. "I reached out with my spirit to shield you, but something went wrong. Nothing happened. And then, when they . . ." His voice was rough, and he paused for a moment, flexing his fists. "After they attacked you, I lost control. I only wanted to break through their protective shield and make sure they were taken into custody. But when I tried to disband it, I used too much force. There was fallout."

"*You* had trouble with your spirit?" Acadia gaped at him. "How is that possible?"

Arnion rested his forehead against her shoulder. He sighed, and she felt the weight of his burden, the weight of the world, in the rush of his breath. "It's been happening for a while now. Ever since I died."

Acadia stiffened. "Why are you only telling me this now?" she demanded.

"I didn't want to worry you. I'll figure it out."

Acadia's pulse ratcheted. She didn't need to say it, but they were both thinking the same thing. Arnion was a powerhouse of spirit abilities. Why was his control fluctuating now? She tilted her neck to study Arnion's face. Dark circles shadowed his eyes, and his pulse ticked rapidly in his throat. Maybe he didn't know what made him lose control, but Acadia suspected he had a theory. She knew Arnion wouldn't lie to her, but he wasn't always forthcoming with his thoughts. Why did he always feel the need to bear everything alone?

"What will happen to the ballroom?" she asked.

Arnion cleared his throat. "Maintenance is cleaning it up. All the guests were evacuated. Thankfully no one was seriously injured. When

I stopped by this morning, the palace glazier was already taking measurements. She'll recast the glass and repair the windows as quickly as possible. Honestly, I'm more worried about you."

Acadia's cheeks burned. Her lower lip trembled, and she looked away. "I'm fine." Stubborn pride jangled through her words.

"Anyone would be upset after what happened."

"I'm not upset."

Arnion raised an eyebrow. "Really? Because you seem . . . agitated."

"I'm not." She crossed her arms.

"Acadia." The chiding tone of his voice made her flush with irritation.

"What? Why are you looking at me like that? They're right. I do have blood on my hands. I don't even know how many people I sent to Gehenna, how many lives I destroyed while working for Lucien. I deserve their hatred and yours. You have so many other things to worry about and all I do is cause trouble for you!" She pulled away and stalked across the room. "I'm trying my best not to be selfish. So why won't you let me—"

Arnion reached out and grabbed her hand. She glared at him, and he met her gaze with a look of longing that broke her heart. "I don't want to let you go." Arnion squeezed her hand. "I don't want you to suffer alone. I want to stay by your side, no matter what." Resolve settled over his face, his eyes burning with intensity. "I love you, Acadia. I want to marry you and spend the rest of my life with you."

The world tilted on its axis. How could he say that after what she'd done? "Why?" her voice croaked. "Why do you love me?"

"Because you're beautiful and kind."

Acadia turned away, wrapping her arms around herself. An uncomfortable heat bloomed on her cheeks. "What if I were hideous? What if I were a selfish monster? Would you still love me?" Her voice rose in challenge.

Arnion stepped beside her. "Of course."

She glared at him, bangs falling across her face. "So, why do you love me?"

"Acadia." He sighed. "What do you want me to say? I don't think there's a reason I can give that you'll be satisfied with. I can tell you I love you for eternity, but you have to choose whether or not to accept it. Whatever happened in your past is over. I love you. That's it. And there's nothing you can do or say that will ever cause me to take it away."

"I don't deserve your love," Acadia said. "I don't know if I ever will, no matter how much good I do. I keep waiting for this dreamworld to shatter. For me to finally screw up badly enough for you to realize the truth—that you don't love me, and you never will. That you can't. That I am unlovable."

Arnion sighed. "I've never told you what 'chimad' means."

Acadia lowered her gaze and stared at the carpet. "Rhys explained the gist of it," she said softly.

"Did he?" Arnion ran a hand through his hair. "Well, let me tell you what it means to me. You are my great delight. The one I've been waiting for. The one I want to share my life with. When I call you 'chimad,' it means you are precious to me, the other half of my heart."

Heat seared through Acadia. Joy, peace, and contentment lodged in her throat like stones, choking her words. Tears pooled behind her lashes, and she blinked, trying to hold them at bay. "It's like a dream to hear you say that." She cleared her throat. "After you died, I didn't think I would ever smile again. It felt like my heart had shattered within me. I realized I loved you more than I ever thought possible."

Arnion smiled at her, but Acadia could read pain in the tightening of his jaw. "Why do I feel like a 'but' is coming?"

"There are things from my past I need to atone for. Things that may never be fixed."

Arnion took her hands in his. "Then we'll fix them together." The pleading in his voice broke her heart.

"I don't know if that's possible." Acadia shook her head. "I need time."

"Time." Sadness stole across Arnion's expression. "That reminds me of the other reason I came to talk with you." He looked away. "The council has decided to send me to Reditona, to investigate the disappearances."

"What?" Acadia felt the world dropping away beneath her feet. Arnion was her rock. She wouldn't survive Eiren without him. "When?"

"Tomorrow morning. The situation in Kifu is unstable. If I don't leave with Narhast tomorrow, the Kifans will send a declaration of war against Avathys. They're giving Eiren the courtesy of being a part of the investigation in the hope we'll turn up something they missed."

Panic froze Acadia's heart. Arnion was leaving? Tomorrow?

"Acadia, what's wrong?" Arnion stepped toward her, brows pinched in concern.

She shuddered, her limbs trembling uncontrollably. Ringing filled her ears. She stumbled, but Arnion caught her. "You can't leave me!" Terror warped her voice.

"This is a dangerous mission. I wouldn't be surprised if Lucien is involved. I can't jeopardize your safety—"

"You can't leave me here!" Acadia sobbed "Please, don't leave me in Eiren alone. I can't bear it." She knew she was being hysterical, but she'd given up caring. The icy fear that Arnion would leave her alone, surrounded by people who despised her, was more than she could bear.

Maybe this was her chance. If she helped Arnion prevent a war, perhaps it would prove to the Eirenians that she was worthy of his love. A chance to atone.

"Please, take me with you," Acadia begged. "I-I could help. I grew up in Kifu." She clutched his shirt, desperate. "I want to earn my place at your side. How can I show my face around the city after what happened yesterday? All of Eiren will hate me. I need to prove I'm worthy of you. Worthy of your love. Worthy of Eiren." Arnion tried to interrupt, and she pressed a hand over his mouth. "Maybe I'll notice something that you miss. Give me the chance to do something, to make a difference. Don't leave me here, please."

"Acadia," Arnion mumbled against her hand. He pressed a kiss into her palm and then took her hand in his, rubbing the inside of her palm with his thumb. "You don't have to *do* anything to earn my love." He rubbed his chin and sighed. "I'm afraid. After what happened yesterday with my spirit . . . What if I can't protect you?"

Acadia brushed her thumb across his cheek. "Then *I'll* protect *you*."

He took her face in his hands. "Do you realize what you're asking? We could be playing right into Lucien's hands. I'm going into a potential war zone. Are you prepared for that?"

"Yes." She nodded. "Please, let me go too. You don't have to save the world alone."

Arnion leaned forward and rested his forehead against hers. When he exhaled, his warm breath tickled her nose.

"You'll need to pack light," he whispered. "This is an ambassadorial mission, and I suspect the living conditions will be a little rough."

Hope fluttered in Acadia's chest. She nuzzled her nose against his. "After living in Gehenna, it'll probably feel like a vacation."

Acadia laid out her final traveling outfit and nodded. A week's worth of clothes should be enough. She could recycle the pants multiple times, but she'd take five days' worth of shirts and undergarments. As she folded them into her traveling pack, her thoughts turned back to her conversation earlier today.

Arnion said he wanted to marry her.

But what if the Eirenians refused to recognize her as an eligible candidate?

Did she even want to be a princess? A part of her dreamed of living a quiet life somewhere with Arnion, just the two of them. No kingdom, no politics, no diplomatic protocols dogging their every step.

Would he choose her over his country?

She could never ask him to abandon Eiren. It would be the most selfish thing she could do.

Acadia sat on the edge of the bed and looked at her hands. The Separatists were right, she did have blood on them. How many people had she sent to Gehenna? She could remember some of their faces, sobbing, pleading, screaming. But there were countless others. How could she even begin to atone for her past if she didn't even know the extent of the damage she'd caused? She'd begun reconciling with her family, and that had been terrifying. There was no way she could personally help every person she'd hurt before. Some of them were probably dead.

People died because of me.

If she could help Arnion stop a war between Kifu and Avathys, she would be saving lives. It would be a way to offset the balance of her past actions.

Not that it could fix everything I've done. Acadia dug her fingernails into her palms. *But it's a start.*

Maybe this would even sway some Eirenians to her side. Stopping a war could prove that she wouldn't be such a disaster as queen. It might help them see she was a different person now. Sapphyre was dead. She had died in Gehenna. And Arnion had brought Acadia back to life.

Acadia zipped her podpack and placed it on the side table by the door. She would make this mission a success. She would help Arnion keep his dream of peace. This was the way to start proving to herself and the world that she was worthy of Arnion's love after all.

She brushed her teeth, finished her ablutions, and was reaching over to turn on her spallo mattress when she heard a knock.

Acadia paused, puzzled. *A knock? Not the door chime?*

She pressed the door release, but there was no one there.

The knock sounded again.

Acadia whirled around. It was coming from her window. She threw open the curtains and stumbled back in shock. Espina's face was pressed against the glass. She was floating in midair! The analyst gave her a cheeky wave.

Acadia yanked the window open. "Espina!" she hissed. "What are you doing here?" Then curiosity got the better of her. "How are you doing that?"

Espina raised her arms and did a little twirl. "Antigrav boots. They use reverse polarization emissions to counteract Elorah's gravitational pull." She swept forward until she almost bumped Acadia on the nose. "Can I come in? It defeats the purpose if someone sees me out here."

Why any Eirenian would want to see her after the disaster at the ball was a mystery. Acadia could only imagine the vicious comments swirling around the palace rumor mill. But Espina didn't seem fazed. If anything, the analyst appeared eager to speak to her. Acadia stepped back and held the curtain aside. "Come in then, but be quick. I still have packing to do."

Espina flexed her fingers and drifted lightly into the room. Her heavy black boots hummed, propelling her through the air. The analyst drifted to the floor with a light thud.

Unease scorched the base of Acadia's scalp. Something strange was going on. "I've never seen that Eirenian tech before."

"There's a lot of Eiren you haven't seen." Espina gave her a conspiratorial wink. "I wanted to avoid any unnecessary surveillance, so I had to resort to a more *creative* entry. These antigrav boots open up a lot of possibilities."

Acadia crossed her arms. "You were at the ball. You know my past. What could you possibly want from me?"

Espina clasped Acadia's hands between her palms. "It was so awful. How are you holding up?" Her face flushed. "We heard reports of possible Separatist activity, but to launch a direct incursion." She shook her head, brows furrowed. "It was a statistical deviation we failed to account for."

Annoyance nipped at Acadia. She pulled her hands free and turned back to the travel pack sprawled open on her bed. If Espina thought she could reduce the suffering and humiliation she'd experienced last night to a series of numbers, she was sorely mistaken. "I don't want to talk about it," Acadia said curtly. She wadded up a shirt and shoved it into the bag.

Espina stepped up beside her and fished in the sleeve of her robe. She pulled out a small metallic sphere, about the size of an apricot, and held it in her palm. Acadia clenched her jaw, refusing to ask what the device was, even when the sphere emitted a series of chirps and began to hover in midair. A blue light pulsed from the orb three times, then it emitted a cheerful beep and plopped back into the analyst's hand.

Espina caught her staring and smiled sheepishly. "It's a scanner. I was checking for incongruent radon frequencies, nonlinear junctions, anomalous nanocrystal flares—"

"You think someone's spying on me?" The edge in Acadia's voice could have sliced through reinforced steel.

Espina gave her an approving nod. "After what happened yesterday, I don't want to take any chances. It's clear the palace security is compromised."

Acadia looked pointedly at Espina's antigrav boots and then at the open window. "Clearly." She crossed her arms and glared at the analyst. "So, let me ask you again: why are you here?" The accusation threaded through her tone, like honey laced with snake venom.

Espina slipped the orb back into her sleeve. She picked a loose thread from her robe and flicked it away. "What if I told you there was a way you could make it up to the crown prince?"

Acadia froze. A bead of sweat dripped down her spine, and she shivered. "What did you say?"

Espina traced a finger along the stitching of Acadia's pack. "I work for military intelligence, remember?"

The apprehension coiling around Acadia's throat slid down to clench her stomach. She flexed her fingers to keep from scratching. "So? I would think Eirenian military intelligence would want nothing to do with a former Jewel."

"On the contrary. Your past makes you an ideal candidate. You have all kinds of skills we can use."

Acadia flinched. Those *skills* caused untold suffering. The thought of Sapphyre's cruel smile opened a hollow feeling in her gut. Acadia swallowed back the bile gathering in her throat. "Sapphyre died in Gehenna," she said angrily. "Go find someone else."

Espina blinked. Then an embarrassed blush spread across her face. "We're not asking you to seduce anyone." She fluttered her hands frantically. "I apologize. That came out wrong. But you are highly trained in persuasion, infiltration, manipulation, and coercion. All these things could tip the balance. Help us put the right pressure on Avathys to avoid a war."

Acadia stopped packing and gaped at her. "That's Lucien's way of solving problems. How can Eiren stoop to tactics like that?"

Espina shook her head. "The source may be bad, but we can still use the skills. Why let all that training go to waste? You would be an incredibly valuable asset to us. To the prince."

"Arnion knows about this?" Dread wormed through Acadia's heart. Would he really ask her to do something like this? She clutched a pair of socks to keep her hands from shaking.

Espina chuckled. "Of course the prince doesn't know. Do you think he knows every military operation that's run in Eiren? All he needs to know are the results. If we stop the planet from descending into war, what difference does it make how?"

Acadia frowned. She wadded the socks into her bag. "I doubt Arnion would agree with that logic."

"Royalty can afford to be high and mighty." Espina sniffed. "They're constantly in the public eye, but you of all people should know sometimes you have to get your hands dirty to see results."

Acadia's hands curled into fists. "My hands are dirty enough! I won't be Sapphyre again."

"No one's asking you to be Sapphyre. But you can read people, manipulate them, direct their thoughts where we want them."

Acadia grabbed a pair of pants and refolded them. "I think you're giving me too much credit."

Espina leaned forward, pressing both palms into the mattress. "The woman called Sapphyre brought kingdoms to their knees. She had kings and princes eating out of her hand. She could make people smile as she cut out their hearts." The sheer admiration in Espina's voice was unnerving.

"It's not something to be proud of!" Acadia's voice blazed with rage. "I can't even count all the people I hurt with my recklessness." Her hands trembled. How dare Espina ask this of her after what happened yesterday? Sapphyre was *hated*.

"People are going to get hurt either way. At least this way we can minimize the damage," Espina protested. "If you get us information on Kifu and Avathys, we can have a complete picture—find out what's really going on and use it to our advantage."

Acadia dropped the clothes she was holding and turned to the analyst. "You want me to be a spy?"

Espina took Acadia's hands and pressed her warm palms against them. "Acadia, yesterday's disaster should be a wakeup call. Eiren will never allow you to marry Arnion as it stands now. This is your chance to prove to all the stuffy aristocrats that you truly belong. To show them how amazing you are. I see it, but most of my nation is blind." She shook her head derisively. "Forget them. I know you can do it. You could prevent two nations from going to war and prove to the world just how powerful an intelligent woman can be."

Passion warmed Espina's words, and Acadia realized the analyst may have more in common with her than she first guessed. Espina was unconventional. Maybe she also struggled with Eiren's rigid social structure.

Espina flapped her hands, excitement building with each word. "Military intelligence thought I was crazy for suggesting it, but I knew—"

"Arnion would never allow it."

Even if Espina could relate to her, there was no point entertaining this idea any further. Not when she knew Arnion would disapprove.

Espina raised her eyebrows, surprised. "The prince can never know. For this plan to work, it must be absolutely secret. Lucien has ears, even within Eiren. The crown can't know we're getting intel this way; it breaks diplomatic treaties, international laws, all the bureaucratic processes that caused these problems in the first place."

Acadia agreed that the political maneuverings between the nations were ridiculous. And she had to admit, the thought of being able to help Arnion was tempting. Sapphyre had been powerful. People listened to her, even if they didn't always like her. Right now, Acadia had nothing. The people of Eiren hated her, no matter what she did. But what if she helped avert a crisis? The Eirenians couldn't reject her then.

The thought of donning Sapphyre's persona again made the hollow pit in her stomach grow. There was a darkness to the Jewel that consumed everything she touched. And she would have to keep more secrets from Arnion, but it would be for his own protection. Acadia could work to save lives without him ever knowing. Arnion already carried so many burdens. If it lessened the weight on his shoulders, was it worth the cost?

More secrets, more lies . . . An empty chasm cleaved through Acadia's heart, numbing the pain. Alone in the darkness, as she had been before Arnion found her. The prince had so graciously forgiven her past, but what if he discovered she was lying to him again? Guilt welled in her stomach.

"What happens if I'm discovered?"

"That's the beauty of it." Espina swung her arms behind her head in a stretch. "We negotiate to get you out. If the prince was involved, Eiren would never recover. But you're a free agent. You're not bound by Eirenian laws. You can do something to help the crown prince that would be impossible for the rest of us." She dropped her arms and scooted closer to nudge Acadia's shoulder. "Plus, the sooner this conflict between Avathys and Kifu is resolved, the sooner you two can be together. There will be nothing left to stand in your way. And the prince can get some much-needed rest." Pity bled into her expression, and she bit her lip. "I've never seen him so exhausted."

The concern in Espina's voice needled Acadia's heart. If Arnion was suffering, how could she say no? He'd given his life to save her, and here she was hesitating over some scruples. Lucien may have intended her training for evil purposes, but she could use it for good. If she had to use deceit and coercion to help her prince, she would do it.

"All right," Acadia said. "I'll help you." Espina opened her mouth, but Acadia held up her hand. "But it's going to be on my terms. You tell me the information you need, and I'll choose what means I use to get it to you." Acadia thrust out her chin defiantly. This was nonnegotiable. "Trust me; I can be creative."

Espina's eyes twinkled. "Then we have a deal." She held out her hand, and Acadia took it.

Chapter 17

FRIGID SILENCE REIGNED IN the passenger compartment of the halcyon. Acadia flexed her fingers, tapping them against her thigh. Across from her, Emissary Narhast scowled, his lips an angry pucker of disdain. She stopped tapping and inclined her head toward the emissary, before fixing her gaze out the window once more.

Since time was of the essence, Eiren had offered high-speed transport to Reditona. The halcyon was faster than any Kifan vehicle, but Arnion was the only one in their group who knew how to fly it. This meant Acadia was relegated to the passenger section with the recalcitrant emissary.

Narhast had told them the journey to the impromptu military camp outside Reditona would take about nine hours, even with the halcyon's speed. He glared at Arnion, as if the prince was personally responsible for every minute of delay. Annoyance prickled the base of Acadia's scalp. She knew her prince was under immense pressure to improve Eiren's relationship with Kifu. Still, Narhast could at least be grateful Eiren was willing to get involved. Without Arnion acting as a mediator, Avathys could grind Kifu into the dust.

A sharp pang tweaked Acadia's stomach. She'd been too anxious to eat breakfast this morning and it was catching up with her, but she didn't want to be the reason for further delay. Narhast was already giving her scathing looks. If she asked for a break before their designated refueling stop, he would be even more insufferable, making things harder for Arnion. She shifted in her seat, trying to make herself more comfortable.

<Everything okay back there?> Arnion's spirit resounded in her mind.

Acadia jumped and glanced guiltily at Narhast, but the emissary had fallen asleep, a line of drool dribbling down his chin. Gross. <A spir-com? Now? Don't you think it's risky?> Acadia asked back.

<Spir-coms can be useful when traveling in mixed company. I don't sense any spirit energy coming from Narhast, and he seems to be asleep, so I think we're safe.>

The amusement was clear in his tone. Acadia could imagine him winking at her. She repressed a groan. <Everything's fine if you overlook the fact that I'm sitting in the most pained silence I've ever experienced in my life.>

Arnion's syna twinkled in her mind, expressing sympathy and mild amusement. <Thank you for sitting with him. I know it doesn't feel like it, but even your mere presence is a form of emotional support.>

Acadia cringed. <The last thing I think Narhast wants is emotional support.>

<You'd be surprised,> Arnion replied. <These days, there are more desperate, isolated people than you could ever imagine.>

Acadia hummed and thought back to the debriefing early that morning. Narhast had lashed out at everyone. Whether it was fear, insecurity, or simply a cantankerous personality, the Kifan advisor provoked people and alienated himself.

"What is there to talk about? Avathys declared war when they blockaded our only seaport!" Narhast had thundered. Veins bulged at his temples. Scarlet splotches spread across his nose and cheeks. "It's clear Avathys intends to swallow Kifu completely. They want us paying tribute for the use of their canals. Let me be clear—we will die before we allow that to happen!" He slammed his walking stick across the tabletop, smashing the data screen of the analyst unfortunate enough to be seated next to him. "Avathys has grown fat and arrogant, like a cow ready to be slaughtered. Once they've finished with us, who will be next? Dardak? Eiren?" He jabbed his cane toward the head of the table, where Arnion and King Elyon sat. "It is time for you to descend from your glittering towers and fight for Elorah once more."

Mutters of disgust swept up the table, and Acadia rubbed her temples. Narhast had no idea how many Eirenian protocols he had just violated with his little speech. The analyst next to him was still mournfully collecting shards of his broken data pad.

Advisor Maulki stood and spread his large, calloused hands. His ocher tunic identified him as the head of the agricultural department. "Surely you are not suggesting we go to war against an unsuspecting ally?" His deep voice was incredulous.

Next to him, Advisor Genoas scoffed, his aquiline nostrils flaring. "Avathys is no ally of ours! Where were they when our prince was being tortured in Gehenna? We don't need allies who hide inside their walls when trouble comes."

"Didn't all this start because of a dispute over some mud?" Advisor Ayam piped up. Her beringed fingers fluttered over the collar of her tunic, as if the mere thought of getting dirty agitated her.

Advisor Arsk took off his spectacles and wiped them with a cloth. "Birano mud, my dear lady, is a highly valuable resource, known to have many curative properties. Our medical department is still finding new uses for it. Though you are correct that Kifu and Avathys have disputed the ownership of Birano for centuries." He placed his spectacles back on his nose and sniffed. "But the real problem is that Kifu has a limited area of usable coastline. With Avathys blockading Kifu's only viable seaport, they are choking off the income stream of the entire nation."

"Kifan agriculture doesn't yield enough crops to support their population. The soil's barren in most places." Advisor Maulki tapped on his data pad and a holographic map of Kifu unfurled above the table. "They have swaths of heavy-metal deposits, which make the soil inadequate for farming. Look at the map; I'll show you." Red lines traced along large sections of Kifu's surface, and Narhast grunted. Maulki acknowledged him with a nod. "But Kifans are survivors. Metal ores have become their primary source of income, allowing them to purchase the produce they need from other nations. Without the free flow of trade, Kifans will starve."

"That's unconscionable." Ayam's face flushed. "I didn't realize . . ."

Arsk cleared his throat. "There is some historical precedence to support Avathys's claims—"

"Ridiculous!" Narhast spat on the floor. "If you're talking about those moth-eaten documents that Avathys likes to trot out every hundred years to justify attacking us, they're not even legible. Probably used as toilet paper to wipe some old Avathysian king's arse."

Advisor Arsk sniffed disapprovingly. "Instigating war is out of the question. We must endeavor to find a diplomatic solution."

Narhast's lips curled up in a snarl. "Avathysians don't understand honor." His voice seethed with hatred. "Nothing but greedy little liars and schemers, waiting to stab you in the back."

Arnion stood. "I am not undertaking this mission under the assumption that Avathys is involved in the disappearances at Reditona. We are going there to investigate, not make wild accusations."

"And while you play at being a detective, our people starve," Narhast roared. Flecks of spittle flew from his mouth and dotted the table.

Arnion held out a calming hand. "Eiren will send aid in the interim. Your people will not go hungry. Once we uncover the truth of what happened, I'm sure we can avoid war."

King Elyon nodded. "We have suspicions that Lucien is involved. His mark is often written underneath conflict in Elorah. My son will investigate his involvement as well."

Narhast pounded a fist against the table. "Your young prince will not be able to stop a war between our countries if Avathys refuses to move those ships. For every hungry belly in Kifu, we will make Avathys suffer."

The room erupted into shouting. Some advisors nearly resorted to fisticuffs.

Acadia blinked back the memory. So much was riding on this mission and tensions were already high. Failure was not an option. Only Eiren stood in the gap to stop a world war from igniting.

Correction. Acadia's thoughts turned bitter as she remembered the tightness around Arnion's jaw when he accepted the assignment. *Only Arnion stood in the gap. If he couldn't resolve this conflict, the world would blame him. It was ridiculous to put so much pressure on one man.*

Her fingers slid down her right forearm to the slight bump under her skin, about the size of a copper coin. Espina had embedded an Eirenian data crystal there. This marvel of Eirenian tech would allow Acadia to communicate with the analyst across distances that would be impossible with a spir-com, along with a host of other impressive abilities, like a navigation system, an electromagnetic frequency detector, and short-range tech jamming.

She resisted the urge to pat her pocket, where another gift from Espina nestled. The bacillus port was a crucial piece of equipment. With it, she would be able to access foreign intelligence data and share it with Espina.

With enough data, the analyst assured her Eirenian military intelligence could avert the war.

Arnion didn't have to do this mission alone. Acadia would make sure he succeeded, even if he never realized the full extent of her help. Her stomach rumbled, and she pressed a hand to her belly. She was starting to regret skipping breakfast.

When they finally stopped to refuel, Acadia was faint with hunger. As Arnion helped her down from the halcyon, she nearly slipped off. "Acadia!" Arnion caught her. His eyes scanned her for injuries. "Are you hurt?"

"No. I didn't get a chance to eat breakfast today, so I think I'm just a little hungry."

"We've been flying for hours. Why didn't you say anything?" His eyebrows drew together, and he fixed her with a look of reproach.

Acadia stepped out from his embrace, wrapping her hands around her shoulders. "I'm fine. I didn't want to be the first one to call for a break. It's not like I'm dying."

"This isn't a game, Acadia. We're on a mission as representatives from the sovereign nation of Eiren. We need to be alert and communicate with each other. How can I focus on our mission if I'm worried you're hiding things from me?" His stern tone grated on her nerves.

Annoyance soured Acadia's tongue. She was tired and hungry, and she wanted Arnion to appreciate her sacrifice, not badger her over it. "Don't you think you're overreacting? It's nothing to get worked up about." Her words came out sharper than she intended.

Hurt flickered over Arnion's face. "If you're hungry or hurt, you need to tell me. Otherwise, how can I fix it?"

"Who said you need to fix it?" Acadia crossed her arms over her chest. Why didn't he understand? "I'm not a child. I don't need you to take care of me all the time. It's suffocating."

Arnion's mouth snapped shut. A muscle feathered in his jaw. Then he let out a slow breath. "I'll keep that in mind." He turned and walked to the refueling station.

Acadia dragged a hand down her face. *That went well.* Her first mission with Arnion was off to a great start.

When they arrived at the Kifan outpost, things were still tense between Acadia and Arnion. Neither had been particularly chatty for the remainder of the flight. Acadia knew things were off, but she was exhausted. All she wanted was to curl up in her bedroll and go to sleep. Even Narhast had dark circles under his eyes, and he'd slept most of the trip.

A squad of Kifan soldiers met them at the edge of the landing pad in drab military fatigues. Acadia noticed their curious looks as they took in Arnion and her.

"These are the Eirenian ambassadors." Narhast gestured toward Arnion and Acadia. "They've come to help us with our investigation. You are to afford them every courtesy. Understood?"

"Yes, sir!" The soldiers saluted.

Acadia blinked in surprise. She thought Narhast was retired, but it was clear he still commanded respect among the soldiers. Given his military background, his brusque attitude and propensity for giving orders started to make a little more sense.

One of the soldiers stepped forward. "Sir, we've prepared a short debriefing."

"Excellent." Narhast clapped him on the shoulder. "Let's go."

Acadia took in the military camp as they walked. It was set up in a grid pattern. Beige tents were staked in neat rows, their color blending seamlessly into the dusty countryside. Boxes of supplies were draped with camo nets and armed guards patrolled. Soldiers hurried back and forth. Exhaustion clung to them. They marched with slumped shoulders, haggard lines tracing their eyes. Acadia wondered if they hadn't slept since the disappearances occurred three days ago.

They approached a large tent with two guards stationed outside. The men saluted Narhast and allowed the group entry. Their escort waved them toward a table with a large gridscreen at one end. Arnion nodded at her, and she took a seat next to him.

As they were settling in, a tall, gangly soldier brought them each a steaming mug of coffee. "Here you are, Ambassador." He smiled at Acadia, and she realized how young he was, still on the cusp of adulthood.

"Thank you"—Acadia read the name stitched on his uniform—"Riggs."

Riggs blushed and scratched his nose. "You're welcome."

Narhast cleared his throat, and Riggs ducked his head, moving down the line and continuing to hand out coffee.

Once he was done, a female officer—Acadia recognized her rank by the eagle emblem on her shoulders—stepped alongside the gridscreen and activated it with a button on her wrist. She had dark hair pulled into a tight knot at the base of her neck and piercing green eyes. "Major Tascom reporting, sir. We've set up a perimeter around Reditona. Last census put the population at roughly ten thousand."

"And they've all vanished?" Arnion asked.

Tascom nodded. "Preliminary reports estimate the disappearances happened sometime between eighteen hundred the previous evening and zero eight hundred hours the next morning. We have witness reports from one man who left that evening and a band of traders who arrived the next day and found the town deserted. We've sent a file summary to you, sir."

Narhast flicked on his data pad and tapped it. He swiped through the report with his stylus. "What evidence have you gathered?"

Major Tascom straightened her shoulders and fixed her eyes at a point beyond them. Her ears turned pink. "We've conducted a sweep of every house and the surrounding area, but there's nothing." Desperation hovered at the edge of her words.

"What do you mean nothing?" Narhast pounded his fist on the table. "Ten thousand people don't just vanish without a trace."

"Yes, sir. We must have missed something. We plan to go out with thermal scanners in the morning. See if there's anything outside our visual spectrum that could be a clue."

Narhast sighed and rubbed his temples. "What about relatives? Have you contacted their next of kin? Do any of them have a clue about what happened here?"

Major Tascom wilted a little bit. "We didn't want . . ." She swallowed. "We decided it would be best to wait, at least for another day or two, to see if we could gather more intel before sharing the incident with the public and risking a panic."

Narhast nodded and leaned back in his chair. "Very well." He looked at his watch. "It's late. The best we can do tonight is get a good night's sleep and start fresh at first light."

Acadia sagged in relief at his words. Without adequate lighting, it was likely they would miss or even potentially damage any clues that remained. They headed to bed in the military tents with the plan to rise early, have a brief breakfast, and head into Reditona to investigate the disappearances.

She glanced at Arnion out of the corner of her eye. He still looked fresh and energized. *How does he do it?* In Gehenna, and again here, when by all rights he should be exhausted, Arnion somehow found the strength to go on. Seeing him inspired her. It was one of the things she loved about him. Acadia squared her shoulders. She'd give it her best too. Not just for Eiren, but to help the Kifans. Seeing the anxious looks of the troops firmed her resolve.

Riggs led her to the female barracks where eight cots were set up. Five had small duffle bags laid alongside them, and two were occupied by sleeping soldiers.

"I'm sorry we don't have more sophisticated facilities for you here, ma'am," Riggs said, pointing at the free cot.

Acadia shook her head. After such a long day, just looking at the cot filled her with relief. "This is fine. Thank you, Riggs." She smiled at him.

He blushed and scratched his neck again. "We operate on twelve-hour shifts, so someone will always be on duty. If you need anything, just ask one of the soldiers." She thanked him again, and Riggs slipped out of the tent.

Acadia stretched out on her bedroll with a grateful sigh. She didn't mind a simple military tent setup. This was nothing compared to the pile of rags she used to sleep on in Gehenna. Besides, she was so drained, she probably could have lain on a bed of sharp rocks and fallen asleep. Just as she was drifting off to sleep, she felt a pulse in her right forearm. Acadia flinched. It vibrated again, and she pressed her left index finger on the data crystal Espina had embedded there.

Black letters wrote themselves across her skin. Acadia panicked. She jerked the blanket over her arm and looked around. No one had seemed to notice. Espina had assured her the data crystal would encrypt messages so they were only visible to her optic nerve, but it seemed too incredible to believe.

Acadia peered at the text on her arm.

I have your first assignment.

Chapter 18

ACADIA SLIPPED THE BACILLUS port out of her pocket. Espina had instructed her to place it in the military's central data hub. From there, Espina would be able to hack into the system, scanning all their data and monitoring the Kifan communications.

Eiren needed to anticipate Kifu's every move and stamp out conflict before it happened. Acadia used to think it was almost magical how Eiren seemed to know things before they happened. She'd thought it was the power of the analysts, but maybe all this time they were spying and infiltrating other countries' security networks.

Acadia's chest tightened.

Was this really the way Arnion and King Elyon wanted her to operate? Was all the beauty and perfection of Eiren just a shallow veneer covering up the same fraud and corruption that permeated the rest of Elorah? Acadia pinched her lips together and shook her head.

No. There was no way Arnion was like that.

Acadia remembered Arnion's smashed and broken face as he died for her and all the other prisoners in Gehenna. Arnion was all good.

But that didn't mean everyone in Eiren was the same. Acadia had been naive to assume it, but growing up, she'd heard stories of Eiren that described it like a fairy tale. She had met so many good people in Eiren: King Elyon, Rhys, Arnion, even Espina. But there were bound to be nasty people as well. People like the Separatists who hated Gehennians and manipulated circumstances to blame them for everything. Lady Sapphyre had been a queen of manipulation. Witnessing the antics of the Separatists was uncomfortably close to holding up a mirror and seeing Sapphyre smirking back at her. Acadia wondered how long she would be haunted by the former Jewel's shadow. She scratched her knuckles.

The thought of helping Espina hack into the Kifan military database left Acadia conflicted, but maybe Eiren would find something they had missed. Major Tascom admitted earlier that they've found no evidence of what had caused the disappearance of Reditona's populace. Maybe with Espina and the Eirenian intelligence working on it as well, they'd uncover a clue. After all, Kifu had requested Eiren's help. Wasn't sharing data a part of that?

Espina had warned her that she'd have to insert the bacillus covertly. Even if it was all for the greater good, Kifu wouldn't take kindly to Eiren sifting through their data. The analyst assured her they would only be accessing the files on Reditona, but it was up to Acadia to find a way into the tactical operations tent and plug in the bacillus. If Acadia was caught, there was a chance she could be executed.

Acadia rubbed the slender, matte-gray data port. The metal was cool beneath her touch. Espina told her that it could take a few minutes for the port to complete its scan. While working, the port would flash a blinking red light. Once it had completed its scan, the light would change to solid green.

Acadia needed an excuse to enter the tent and plug the port into one of the data hubs, then stall for time until it finished loading. But how? Looking at the earrings she'd placed in her shoe before lying down, she smiled.

She tucked one of the dangly earrings into her pocket and pinched the other one back on her ear. Then she pulled on her jumpsuit and poked her head out of the tent. This late at night, the camp was quiet, but just like Riggs said, there were a couple of soldiers patrolling, and the operations tent was still guarded.

Acadia slipped out of her tent, molding her face into an expression of concern. As she approached the operations tent, the guards straightened.

"Ambassador?" one of them asked.

"I'm sorry." Acadia made her voice quiver. "I woke up to get some water and realized one of my earrings is missing."

The guards shared a look between them. Good—they thought she was a foolish consort. Not a threat to be concerned about.

Acadia wrung her hands. "I've checked everywhere; the only place left I can think of is this tent. Would it be okay if I had a look around?"

One of the guards practically rolled his eyes at her. "We're not supposed to—"

"Lady Acadia." Riggs stepped up from behind her. "What are you doing out so late?"

Acadia let out a grateful breath and turned to clutch his arm. "Oh, Riggs, please help me. I've misplaced one of my earrings. It was a present from the prince. I don't want him to find out I've lost it." She made her lower lip tremble, and tears formed in the corners of her eyes.

Riggs blushed and looked at the two guards. "It should be all right if I accompany her inside. I can help her look around the area where we were sitting."

Acadia fixed the guards with her best helpless look. One of the men cleared his throat. "All right, but make it quick."

Riggs led her inside. "Where do you think you lost it?" he asked gently.

Acadia sniffled. "I'm not sure. Do you mind if I look around the conference table?"

"Of course not!" Riggs beamed at her. "I'll help too. I'm really good at finding things. I have three younger sisters, and they're always losing bits of jewelry."

Acadia gave him a wavering smile, but guilt pricked her chest. Riggs seemed genuinely concerned over her distress. She regretted deceiving him, but the ends justified the means. If she could take some of the burden off Arnion's shoulders, she'd do it gladly. Though she might have overplayed the damsel-in-distress act. How was she supposed to plug in the bacillus port if Riggs shadowed her every move? In any case, she had to find an access point first.

Acadia dropped to her hands and knees, patting the floor. While her hands skimmed over the packed dirt, she subtly glanced around. There was a tech station a few paces to her right that was unmanned. The operations personnel were probably only running on limited strength at this hour of the night. Acadia slowly began making her way toward it as unobtrusively as possible.

Riggs crawled around beside her, patting the ground around the table legs and underneath the chairs. He was so diligent and earnest, biting his lip as he searched for her earring. Acadia didn't want to get him in trouble, but she needed him out of the way.

"Any luck over there, Lady Acadia?"

Acadia took a shuddering breath and let a tear slip down her cheek. "No." Her voice trembled, and she covered her mouth with a hand.

"Aw, don't give up yet, ma'am. We'll keep looking for a few more minutes. It's bound to turn up," Riggs assured her with a friendly pat on the shoulder.

Acadia hiccupped as if restraining a sob, and she dabbed at her face. "I'm sorry, Riggs. Do you think you could . . ." She held a trembling hand to her face. "Could you bring me a tissue, please?" She forced out the words in a breathless quiver.

Compassion shone in Riggs's eyes. His younger sisters must adore him; he was the best kind of big brother. "Of course, Lady Acadia. I'll find something." He stood and brushed the dirt from his knees.

The moment he turned away, Acadia leaned forward and shoved the bacillus into the port of the tech station. The light flashed red. Acadia sat back down and pretended to look forlorn, occasionally swiping away tears with her fingertips. In reality, she was keeping an eye on Riggs as he earnestly searched the operations tent for something resembling a tissue. The poor guy. Luckily the military didn't seem to have an abundance of tissues for weepy ambassadors on hand.

Riggs was still frantically hunting down a tissue when Acadia noticed another soldier enter the tent. He was broad-shouldered with short dark hair cropped in a military cut, although he still managed to have a cowlick on the right-hand side. He rubbed sleep from his eyes and greeted the other soldiers.

One of the women working at a tech station on the other side of the room looked up. "Galston, you're on night shift tonight?"

Galston yawned. "Yeah, I switched with Jennich yesterday."

"Hmm. There's an open tech station over there." She pointed in Acadia's direction.

Acadia's heart seized so tight, for a moment she forgot how to breathe. The bacillus was still flashing red.

"Thanks." Galston gave the technician a sleepy smile and headed toward Acadia.

Nausea surged up Acadia's throat. Sweat coated her palms. Galston was coming closer.

The light on the bacillus blinked red once, twice, then switched to solid green.

Galston was only a few steps away.

Acadia needed to distract him somehow. He hadn't seen her yet, sitting on the floor beside the station. His eyes were on the login panel.

As Galston took another step forward, Acadia threw herself under his feet, screaming, "I found it!"

Galston's sleepy eyes widened. He tumbled over her with a shout of surprise, and they both went sprawling. In the confusion, Acadia snatched up the bacillus port and tucked it into her sleeve. "I'm so sorry," she cried. "Are you all right?"

"Lady Acadia!" Riggs hurried over and helped her up. "What happened?"

Acadia reached out to brush Galston's shoulder. "I was looking for my missing earring, and then I saw it shining, right under that desk, and I just reached for it. I didn't mean to trip you."

Galston rubbed his chin and gave her a puzzled look. "No harm done. But how'd you get in here unsupervised, miss?"

Riggs blanched, and remorse twisted in Acadia's chest. She needed to talk their way out of this. "That's my fault. I was crying so much, I asked Riggs to find me a tissue."

Galston frowned. Acadia could see him connecting the dots in his mind. "But he really shouldn't have—"

"I'm so grateful for all of your help!" Acadia gushed, fluttering her eyelashes in a way she knew melted men's hearts. "I'll be sure to tell Prince Arnion how kind you all were to me. These earrings were a special gift, you see. But I've caused you all enough trouble for one night. Could someone please kindly escort me to my sleeping quarters?"

Galston cleared his throat. "Riggs, see the lady back to her barracks."

"Thank you for your kindness," Acadia said in a breathy voice. Then she turned and flashed her most charming smile. "I can see why you all are the pride of Kifu. Good night." She swept an elegant curtsey and took Riggs's arm. He was quiet as they walked back, mouth in a firm line. His eyes looked tired and strained.

Regret wriggled down her spine. At the entrance to her tent, Acadia tugged on his sleeve. "I'm sorry for getting you in trouble."

His gaze snapped to hers, and he gave her a small smile. "That's all right, ma'am. No harm done."

Acadia nodded and let go. "Good night, Riggs."

He tipped his patrol cap at her. "Good night, Lady Acadia."

Acadia snuggled into her bedroll and curled up on her side. It took a long time for her heart to stop racing. That had been a close call! If she hadn't tripped up Galston, he might have seen the bacillus in the tech station's port, and she might be sleeping in a jail cell rather than this cot. Acadia shivered, cold in spite of the balmy summer weather.

It's done, she traced the words along her forearm and the data crystal transcribed them in a message to Espina.

The cursor flashed for a moment. Then *Good work* wrote itself along her arm.

Acadia breathed a sigh of relief. She didn't want to betray Kifu, but Eiren could be trusted to monitor their communications. Espina and the military intelligence were doing it for the safety of Elorah.

No one else needed to know.

Besides, if Kifu was doing nothing wrong, what did they have to hide?

Acadia had almost convinced herself by the time she drifted off to sleep.

Chapter 19

The Avathysian catacombs were not an ideal location to set up a laboratory, but Lucien had found a way to make it work. Water dripped through cracks in the stone ceiling. Gelatinous orange mold slicked the walls. Sensitive medical equipment was sprawled across wooden crates and rusted metal tables. Power cables snaked along the floor in thick, grimy coils. It would be a safety inspector's nightmare, but fortunately Lucien wasn't bound by such paltry regulations.

Before settling on this location, he had kept his laboratory mobile to avoid detection. The Eirenians pursued him with diligence, but he was always three steps ahead. Lucien brushed a fleck of dust from his sleeve. There was no call to get slovenly, even if he was working in substandard conditions. That was something those rule-loving Eirenians would never understand. They were so focused on conforming to their regulations, they lacked the flexibility to handle problems outside the box. Their prince, on the other hand—

A muffled shriek rose from the metal containment vessel in the center of the room. The guards beside him flinched. Lucien curled his lip. If they tried to cover their ears again, he would thrash them within an inch of their lives. He adjusted the glasses he was wearing, protection against the ultraviolet light radiating from inside the containment pod.

Lucien glanced at the series of dials, gauges, and spectrometry coun-ters arrayed on the table before him. A gridscreen displayed an erratic heartbeat, flashing with red warning lights. He gestured to the pudgy scientist beside him in a stained lab coat. "Increase the output. Maximize ultraviolet absorption."

"But, sire," the scientist said, wiping his goggles with a dirty handker-chief, "the subject will—"

"Do it!" Lucien screamed. "We're this close!" He held up his thumb and index finger a hair's breadth apart.

The scientist turned a small white knob on the control panel. Blue light flooded the laboratory, and a piercing howl rose from within the pod. The heartbeat monitor spiked and then flatlined.

The scientist's shoulders slumped. "We've lost another one, sire."

Lucien threw his clipboard across the room. "I can see that, you idiot." He jabbed a finger at the guards. "Get that pod cleaned out and bring in the next one." The guards staggered past him, dragging the smoking corpse, and Lucien lashed out with his foot, kicking one behind the knee. "Be quick about it! I don't have all day."

Lucien turned back to the scientist. The shorter man was sweating profusely. Beads of perspiration dotted his thinning hairline. Repulsive. Why was good help so hard to find? He flicked his fingers toward the little man but avoided touching him. "Get me the results of the last twenty-five tests."

The scientist fumbled for a data pad and tapped hastily through the reports. He handed it to Lucien with shaking fingers. The disgusting little man had left dirty fingerprints on the screen. Lucien considered gouging out his eye with the stylus, but then he'd have to train somebody else. That was getting tedious. Even semi-competent workers were in

short supply in this intellectually barren landscape. Lucien closed his
eyes, took a deep breath, and focused on the lab results instead.

Subject 295: Dead.

Subject 296: Dead.

Subject 297: Dead.

Whenever he tried to increase the amount of trividium, the results
were always the same. A brief influx of power, then death. The human
body seemed to reject more than the bare minimum of the dark mineral
substance. It caused complete cellular collapse, as if the subject's body
craved a tremendous amount of energy and ate itself alive in the process.

Lucien had experimented with a multitude of different ways to sur-
pass the body's limitations and increase tolerance to trividium. Minerals.
Chemical stimulants. Different wavelengths of electromagnetic radia-
tion.

"You scientists are worthless." Lucien stalked across the floor, thinking. Maybe light wasn't the key after all. Maybe it was temperature. What
if he forced the body into a reactive, feverish state? Then trividium might
be able to pass through the cell membrane. If he could find a way to bond
the substance with the human body at a cellular level . . . Lucien rubbed
his hands together. That was when the real fun would start.

Ever since he'd realized trividium could counteract effects of the spirit,
Lucien knew he'd hit a gold mine. Eiren was only powerful because of
its knowledge of the spirit. Without that advantage, they were weak.
But when he'd brought this problem to Elyon's attention, the pathetic
monarch had forbidden him from experimenting further. That bleeding
heart was too afraid to take risks, to do what must be done to maintain
power. Lucien would have shared his knowledge with all of Eiren; they
could have ruled Elorah like gods.

Instead, Elyon had exiled him. That short-sighted fool.

Every knee on Elorah would bow to Lucien. He would make sure of it. Then he'd swipe Elyon's head clean off his shoulders and put it on a pike.

As for that conniving little prince who had foiled his plans in Gehenna . . .

Fury swelled in Lucien's chest. He clenched his jaw to smother a scream of frustration.

There would be no resurrection this time; Lucien would make sure of it. He would tear out the princeling's heart and preserve it in a crystal box where he could admire it for all time.

Lucien had been hiding in this festering crypt long enough. His day was coming. He was going to build an army. Then he would finally have his revenge on Eiren.

But first, Lucien needed to figure out the key to unlocking trividium's potential. He traced a finger along the edge of the data pad. Heat was promising. It just might initiate the metabolic reaction he was looking for.

Lucien strode over to the scientist. The little man stank of sweat and fear. He was so absorbed scanning the research documents that he didn't notice Lucien's approach. Lucien tapped him on the shoulder, and the man nearly jumped out of his skin.

Pleasure welled in Lucien's chest. His lips curled into a vicious smirk. "For the next one, let's try something different. How hot can we make it in the absorption pod?"

"H-hot?" the man stammered. "That's n-not . . . w-well . . ."

Lucien clapped him on the shoulder and squeezed hard. "I want to increase the temperature in there. Add pressure, steam, radon coils—whatever it takes. I want you and your team working on it non-stop. Tomorrow morning, we'll start new trials. My pod had better be ready, or heads will roll. Literally. Starting with you." Lucien swiped a finger through the air. "Do. Not. Disappoint. Me. Is that clear?"

"Y-yes, sire," the scientist stammered.

Lucien smiled. Tomorrow would be a good day. He could feel it.

Lucien walked out of the lab, passing row upon row of containment cells. People wailed and cried, begging for mercy. Dirty hands stretched out beyond the cage bars, but he stepped neatly out of the way. "Start with cell eight tomorrow," Lucien ordered the guards and strode down the hall.

Four hundred people had followed him after the collapse of Gehenna, but Lucien was running out of test subjects. He needed more bodies. They would have to find somewhere discreet, where there would be less of an outcry when people went missing.

Lucien arrived at his personal quarters. A guard held the door open for him, and he snapped his fingers. "Send for Trask. We're going to organize a raiding party. He has knowledge of remote Kifan villages. Tell him to bring the maps with him."

The guard saluted and hurried away.

Lucien rubbed his hands together.

He was going to need a lot more test subjects.

Chapter 20

ACADIA STRAPPED A FLUX sword to her right hip. Narhast had arranged a military escort for Arnion and her into Reditona. Because it was a military operation, all participants were required to be armed. Arnion had a photon pistol holstered at his side, and she had her blade.

The village nestled along a gentle curve of the Vosna River. Simple earthen houses with thatched roofs dotted the landscape. A few of them had garden patches with scraggly crops. The rest were peppered with reedy clumps of crabgrass. The town center had the essentials, an animal-feed store, and a sundry goods merchant. A rusted sign declaring *Barber Shop* creaked as it swayed in the light breeze. Other than that, there was no movement.

Narhast hadn't been exaggerating. It was a town of ghosts.

They divided into pairs to do a sweep of the town. Arnion and Acadia entered a home with wobbly purple butterflies painted on the window. The owner must have let their children help decorate. Inside, the family's belongings were still there. Plates, bowls, and cups sat on tables waiting for the evening meal. Toys were scattered in bedrooms. A book lay open, resting on the arm of a faded leather chair, waiting for its reader to come and pick it up again. The air was stale, and a pervading feeling of emptiness, of *wrongness*, saturated the dwelling.

Where could they have all gone?

Acadia looked over at Arnion. He had closed his eyes and was doing a careful search with his spirit.

After a few minutes, Acadia cleared her throat. "Do you sense anything?"

Arnion let out a breath and opened his eyes. "No." His voice was troubled. Dark circles rimmed his eyes. Sweat glistened on his forehead and dripped down his neck, staining his collar.

"Hey, are you feeling okay?" Acadia asked.

Arnion winced and rubbed his temples. "Just a headache. I don't sense anything amiss here. It was as Narhast reported. Everything looks normal except for the fact that Reditona is missing all its people."

They walked down the main street of the little trading town and headed toward the riverbank. Suddenly Arnion doubled over, clutching his head.

"Arnion!" Acadia gasped. She bent to help him up.

"I'm all right," he gasped. "The headache is getting worse, that's all."

His skin was feverish to her touch. "You don't look well," Acadia said. "Maybe you should sit down for a bit."

"That's not a bad idea." Arnion groaned. He stumbled to a large ruewood tree and slumped beside it. "I think I'll rest in the shade for a moment."

Acadia sat next to him. Concern nibbled at the base of her scalp. It wasn't like Arnion to feel sick. Maybe the exhaustion was finally catching up with him. She ripped up a wad of crabgrass, picking out individual blades of grass and flicking them into the wind. The breeze carried strands of grass downhill, and Acadia took a moment to admire the scenery. She could just make out the curve of the river at the bottom of the hill. Sunlight sparkled on the crystal-clear water. A gentle wind rustled the foliage above them.

"It's so peaceful." Acadia leaned against Arnion's shoulder. "Hard to imagine anything terrible happening here."

Arnion gave a gentle hum of agreement. He had closed his eyes and was resting his head against the tree trunk. Sweat soaked his shirt. His breath rasped.

Acadia bit her lip. Was Arnion getting sick? She looked away and spied something gleaming in the grass. Acadia walked over and picked it up. It was a small metal box that smelled faintly of photon powder. She recognized it as a spent energy cartridge from a pistol. It had a strange marking etched across its surface—a triangle intersected by two wavy lines.

"Arnion, I found something." Acadia brought it over to show him. "It's an energy cartridge, but I don't recognize the symbol."

Arnion took the cartridge, his brows creased with worry. "I do. It's a Melican manufacturing company."

Acadia's jaw fell open. "Melica is the capital of Avathys. So, that means Avathys really was involved." Her words came out a breathless whisper.

"Or someone was using weapons purchased there." Arnion clenched the metal cartridge in his hand. "This isn't definite proof that Avathys was involved, but there does appear to be some connection. But if we show this to Narhast and the Kifan military, they're bound to assume the worst."

"So, you think we should keep this from them?" Acadia bit her lip. Did Arnion want to withhold information from the Kifans too? Maybe Espina really was operating in line with his wishes. The thought settled like lead in her stomach.

Arnion pulled himself up, using the tree for support. "I think we should wait until we know exactly how Avathys and this incident are connected. We still don't know who was using the weapon, and whether they were acting independently or with the sanction of the Avathysian government."

"And how can we possibly know that?" Acadia asked.

As Arnion opened his mouth to reply, a rustling sound rose from the riverbank. He paused, and they both listened. Acadia's pulse thundered in her ears.

A muted cry rose from the same direction.

Arnion's eyes widened. "Did you hear that?"

Acadia nodded. "Do you think . . . could it be . . ."—her mouth went dry, and she licked her lips—". . . a survivor?"

Chapter 21

ARNION STAGGERED AWAY FROM the ruewood tree, and Acadia reached out to steady him.

"Thank you." He squeezed her forearm. "Let's go. It could be someone who needs our help."

They rushed down the hill toward the river. A figure was thrashing in the center, caught against a broken tree branch lodged between the stones.

"Hurry!" Arnion cried. He was still sweating, and Acadia felt him shiver as she looped her arm through his to help him down the embankment.

The man's back was facing them. His short blond hair stuck out in matted clumps, and he wore a tattered gray shirt. Blood dripped from his fingers as he clawed frantically at the branch pinning him.

"Sir! We're here to help!" Arnion called out. He gripped Acadia's hand as they waded into the water.

At the sound of Arnion's voice, the man jerked his head around. Black veins protruded from his skin. His eyes were dark pits, and a dribble of black saliva trailed down his chin. His jaw stretched open, impossibly wide, and he let out an eerie shriek.

Arnion grabbed Acadia's arm and thrust her behind him. "Get back!"

Fear crushed Acadia's heart between icy fingers. Her spirit writhed under her skin. The man continued to thrash against the branch, tearing at himself with his nails and teeth. His movements were jerky, unnatural. The hair on Acadia's neck stood up as she watched in horrified fascination.

Arnion dragged her toward the riverbank, but she couldn't look away. "Acadia!" Arnion's voice was desperate. He shook her. "We have to—"

The tree branch cracked and gave way. The man sprang at them with a snarl. He lurched through the water, stumbling over the stones. Black sludge dripped from his eyes and nose. He snapped his teeth. A wicked smile curled over his chapped lips.

Arnion fired his photon pistol. The energy blast shot through the man's chest, just below his collarbone, but he didn't stop. The prince managed another shot that grazed the man's cheek. A black, tar-like substance oozed from the wound. The man lunged at Arnion, digging bloodied fingernails into his shoulder. Arnion smashed an elbow into his jaw. The other man snarled. He craned his neck and tore into Arnion's forearm with his teeth. Arnion bashed his head with the butt of his pistol. An inhuman screech tore from the man's throat. He grabbed the prince's free arm and the photon pistol sailed into the water.

Blood dripped from Arnion's torn sleeve. He grappled with his assailant, the two of them thrashing in the shallows. The strange man howled, clawing at Arnion. His blackened teeth inched closer and closer to Arnion's neck.

Acadia's hand whipped to her the flux sword strapped to her side, but a large blade was too risky. The two men were locked in a violent embrace. She needed to put more distance between them first. Acadia slipped out her multipurpose dagger and leaped forward, swiping at the man's bicep. She scored a clean slice through his deltoid muscle and his right arm fell limp.

Arnion seized the opportunity and slammed a palm into his nose. There was a sickening crunch. The man reeled backward. Black blood poured from his nose.

Acadia drew her flux sword. "Stay back!" Her shout was hoarse. The weapon hummed beneath her fingers, energy gathering along the blade.

The man tilted back his head and laughed. The sound was something out of her darkest nightmares—a chilling shriek of mirth and insanity. He charged at her, impaling himself through the stomach. The stench of burning flesh and oil seared Acadia's nostrils.

Horror froze the blood in her veins. The man was still reaching for her, writhing around her blade. He gnashed his teeth, mottled black and green against rotting gums. A gust of his fetid breath made her gag. His hands curled around her shoulders in a cruel parody of an embrace. A blast tore through the air. Ringing filled her ears as the man's head jerked backwards. His body slammed into the water and remained still.

Terror dulled Acadia's senses, like she was in a tunnel that warped all sights and sounds. Arnion was in front of her, touching her face. Someone was shouting in the distance, but it was overwhelmed by a buzzing that rattled inside her skull.

Riggs was calling out to them. Acadia watched him barrel down the hill, gripping his photon pistol.

Arnion pulled her to face him. His fingers tugged at her jaw, drawing her gaze up to his. His lips moved, and the sounds around her slowly coalesced into recognizable words. "—cadia! Did he hurt you?"

Mutely, she shook her head.

Arnion crushed her to him. His arms were shaking.

"How?" Her voice cracked. Acadia swallowed against the dryness building in her mouth. "How could he keep fighting with those injuries?"

"Trividium," Arnion said softly. "He had been driven mad by it."

Acadia shivered. She burrowed into his embrace.

Narhast and a squad of soldiers followed in Riggs's wake.

Riggs splashed toward them in the river. "We heard shots and came running. Then I saw you being attacked." Riggs's voice was breathless. He glanced at the man lying unmoving in the water and holstered his pistol. Then his face wrinkled, and he clamped a hand over his nose. "Dral! What is that stench?"

"He didn't stop." Acadia's voice trembled. "Even after he had run himself through."

"What is going on here?" Narhast had reached the riverbank and was taking in the scene. Anger gathered across his brow like thunderclouds before a storm. "Someone had better start explaining. Now."

Arnion wrapped an arm around Acadia's shoulders and tugged her toward the shore. "We were attacked. The man was driven mad by trividium." He helped Acadia out of the water, tiny river pebbles crunching under their feet. "They don't stop; they can't. Not until they're dead."

Narhast's nostrils flared and his eyes blazed. "So, you killed the man? We could have interrogated him and discovered what happened here."

"I was the one who took the shot, sir." Riggs stood ramrod straight, hands at his sides. "When I saw the ambassadors in imminent peril, I didn't hesitate." His eyes widened, taking in the blood dripping down Arnion's arm. "Ambassador, you've been hurt!"

"It's nothing serious." Arnion tried to deflect but Riggs was already waving over a med tech.

The med tech cut the torn sleeve off Arnion's forearm and checked the wound. The skin puckered around two bloody crescent-shaped gashes.

Acadia took in a sharp breath.

Arnion met her gaze and raised his eyebrows playfully. "I'll be fine."

"He bit you?" the med tech asked. At Arnion's nod, she turned his arm slightly, checking the other side. "Can you still move your fingers?"

"Yes." Arnion wiggled his fingers obligingly.

"Good. It looks like a superficial injury. I'll disinfect and seal it to prevent infection, but you should still get it checked out at a medical center when possible." The med tech pulled a steel cylinder out of her side pouch. "Sanovex. This spray will sterilize the wound and encourage skin regrowth. There's a numbing agent, so you won't feel a thing."

"Thank you." Arnion smiled at her. The med tech blushed and looked down. She shook the sanovex and carefully sprayed it over his arm.

"Fantastic." Narhast growled. "More time wasted."

Acadia shot him a poisonous glare.

Sorrow swept across Arnion's face. "You wouldn't have gained anything from him. That man was already dead. All that was left was rage and darkness."

A muscle worked in Narhast's jaw. "So, you're still trying to shift the blame to Lucien." He stabbed a finger toward the corpse. "That man was clearly Avathysian."

"He was from Gehenna," Acadia mumbled. "I remember him." Regret tore a hole through her heart. No one should have to suffer like that.

Narhast scoffed. "And I should just take your word for it? When all signs point to our traitorous neighbor?" His fist clenched the knob of his walking stick, knuckles white. "This was our first real clue, and you executed him. How convenient that you claim he attacked you before anyone else could witness it."

Arnion straightened. The fiery look in his eye reminded Acadia that he was crown prince of Eiren, the greatest nation on the planet. Even Narhast looked cowed. "If Riggs hadn't shot him, he would have killed everyone in your camp."

Narhast scowled and turned to his soldiers. "Get that man out of the water! There may still be some evidence we can use." The soldiers shuffled around him, surreptitiously covering their noses as they dragged the body from the river. A horrible odor rose up, like burnt hair and rotten meat. One of the soldiers gagged.

"Look," Riggs cried. "He had compound fractures in both his legs. He shouldn't even have been able to walk, let alone attack anyone." Some of the soldiers shuddered and crossed themselves.

"Quiet!" Narhast snapped. "Get that body back to base so we can analyze it. Whatever happened here, we are going to get to the bottom of it." The soldiers fell silent.

As they trudged back to base camp, Acadia sent Arnion a spir-com. <Are you okay?>

<Yes. It looks worse than it is, I promise.>

<But he had a high concentration of trividium in his body, right? Could he have infected you?>

<It doesn't work like that. Trividium can't be passed from person to person.>

Acadia's shoulders relaxed. The knot of fear that had been building in her chest loosened. <Is that why you felt sick earlier? Because you were close to trividium?>

<Must be.> Arnion flashed her a troubled look. He cleared his throat and spoke out loud to Narhast. "Assemble your staff. There's more I need to share with you."

Tension reigned in the command tent. Acadia sat silently beside Arnion, her thoughts a jumble. The chief Kifan medical technician had conducted an initial analysis on the corrupted man and was presenting his findings. "It's like nothing I've ever seen before." He rubbed the back of his neck. "Unprecedented muscle growth, severe brain damage. The man shouldn't have even been conscious."

Narhast scowled as he scrolled through the medical data.

Arnion stood and spread his hands across the tabletop. "If Lucien is experimenting with trividium again, this is bigger than Kifu and Avathys. This is a threat to all of Elorah."

Major Tascom cleared her throat. "What exactly is trividium?"

Arnion tapped a data pad, displaying a holographic image of trividium ore above the table. "Our analysts believe it is a mineral originating from the planet's core. It has . . . unusual properties that make further study dangerous."

"Turns people into monsters," someone muttered.

Acadia wove her fingers together under the table to stop herself from scratching her knuckles. Soldiers around her shifted in their seats. The sergeant sitting opposite her twisted the wedding band around his wrist over and over.

"What do you mean 'dangerous'?" Narhast demanded. "Does this mean Eiren is responsible for that abomination?"

"Lucien is responsible," Arnion corrected. "His experiments nearly destroyed Eiren and led to a massive civil war. He was exiled forever."

Narhast grunted. "Eiren doesn't clean up its mistakes very well, does it?"

A muscle ticked in Arnion's jaw, but he remained silent.

"Do you know anything about trividium's effect on the human body?" The chief medical officer wrung his hands. "Any research Eiren would be willing to share? Is there a cure?"

"I'll put in a request to send over the data we have," Arnion replied. "But I can tell you that trividium destroys its host, one way or another. There is no cure. A person can accept it as it burrows into their veins and corrupts them. They gain unnatural strength but lose all reason. They become a mindless killing machine."

"A berserker," someone whispered.

Arnion nodded.

"And what if they reject it?" Major Tascom asked.

Arnion's eyes were tight. "They die," he said in a dull voice. Murmurs broke out across the room, and Arnion sat back down.

Acadia's heart ached for him. This was his worst nightmare come to life. Lucien hurting people again, and Arnion being powerless to stop him. She sent him a syna of a single purple orchid. Hope. <Are you going to tell them about trividium's effects on the spirit?> she asked.

Arnion's eyes flicked to hers. <Not yet. Most Kifans aren't spirit users. It would only complicate things further.>

It was eventually agreed that the Kifan military would retain custody of the 'Berserker,' as the soldiers had dubbed him. Narhast wanted a full autopsy and samples sent back to their official military lab. Arnion conceded there was a strong implication of Avathysian involvement, although he was adamant they could not assume it was government sanctioned. He vowed to personally travel to Melica and intercede for the blockade's removal. Once there, he and Acadia would continue investigating the disappearances and their connection to Avathys. Lucien's name hung heavy in the air. Arnion didn't speak it out loud, but Acadia knew stopping the Heartless King was another weight added to her already overburdened prince.

Despair bled into the room as the debriefing concluded. Soldiers stared vacantly into space, their shoulders slumped. There was still no concrete evidence of what had happened to Reditona's citizens, but now everyone feared the worst.

Arnion contacted Eiren immediately afterwards from a teleport in the communications tent, requesting an emergency advisory session. "I need you to connect me to our best operative in Melica."

"That would be Dragul, Your Majesty," Advisor Ayam replied. "He's been maintaining cover as a fisherman outside the capital to train his young protégée."

Advisor Arsk spoke up. "She isn't ready, from all reports. The girl is still having trouble with basic spirit forms."

"But Dragul says she shows great promise," Advisor Ayam countered.

"Being his granddaughter might have something to do with it," Advisor Genoas muttered.

Advisor Maulki frowned and cleared his throat. "Even if the girl isn't ready, Dragul is one of our top agents. He's a veteran skilled in diplomacy and infiltration. He has a variety of talents that would be useful to us."

Arnion nodded. "Acadia and I will meet Dragul and continue to the Melican palace. We must convince them of the true threat and get them to remove this blockade."

Ayam twisted a stylus between her beringed fingers. "You should enter Avathys under the radar, Your Majesty. Lucien has agents everywhere. The more we can conceal your movements, the better."

Advisor Arsk agreed. "We advise you to keep a low profile. Fly the halcyon to a city near Dragul's safe house. Birano would be ideal. Lay low. He can contact you and arrange discreet transport into Melica."

"That's a good idea," Arnion agreed. "Send Dragul the coordinates and arrange for our meeting. Acadia and I will fly out first thing in the morning.

They took their leave of Narhast and the Kifan military at daybreak the next day. It was nothing like the joyous farewells of Eiren. Acadia watched Narhast's rigid form grow smaller and smaller as the halcyon sailed into the sky.

Acadia swiveled in the copilot's seat. It was just her and Arnion in the halcyon, so she could sit up front with him. The navigation system pinged and Arnion turned the steering yoke slightly to the left.

The advisors had directed them to fly to the outskirts of Birano. Arnion was to stay in Kifan airspace, following the flow of the Vosna River. Their Eirenian contact, Dragul, would meet them at a tavern called the Speckled Sagrin. After debriefing Dragul, they would secure entry into Melica and continue their investigation together in Avathys. The journey was significantly shorter than the flight to Reditona, but they would still have a few hours of air travel.

Acadia ran her finger over the cushioning on her armrest. "Who is Dragul? Can you tell me anything about him?" This was the first time she'd heard of an Eirenian spy. Maybe Espina's plans weren't so extreme after all.

"I've never met him personally, but he's one of the best, currently on a long-term undercover assignment in Avathys. He's stationed on the outskirts of Melica. Military intelligence set him up with a fake identity as a fisherman that he uses to gather information. One of his chief purposes is to track potential intel on Lucien. He also has an apprentice, but the training has been a challenge. The girl, or young woman, I should say, is stubborn. She has a hard time using her spirit the way Eirenians are accustomed to."

Acadia could understand. Using her spirit didn't come naturally to her either. Maybe she and this woman could be allies. It would be nice to have a friend who could relate to her struggles. But then again, Acadia had never been very good at friendships with other girls. She picked at a loose thread in the armrest.

"Everything okay?" Arnion asked.

Acadia looked up. Arnion was watching her. She shifted in her seat, avoiding his gaze by looking out the window. The halcyon had a canopy window that molded over the cockpit, providing a fantastic view as they flew. The Vosna River twined beneath them, rippling through the grasslands like a glittering silver snake. A warm, feathery feeling tickled her chest. She grinned at Arnion. "I always wanted to travel the world, but I never thought I'd get the chance. Since meeting you, I've been to Eiren, home to my family in Kifu, and now I'm going to Avathys." She reached over and squeezed his hand. "You fill my life with adventure."

Arnion's lips parted. Then he gave her his glorious chimad grin that sent her heart careening against her ribcage. "It's my pleasure. I hope we'll have many more adventures together." His smoldering gaze softened into something more mischievous. "I've been meaning to ask—how much do you know about flying?"

Acadia glanced at the complex flight-control system in front of her, filled with lights and dials. She recognized the navigation system, at least. Acadia bit her lip. "Not much."

Arnion raised an eyebrow, grinning. "Would you like to learn?"

As they flew, Arnion explained each of the gauges in the cockpit, along with some piloting basics. The halcyon also had an autonav AI installed in the flight computer. Most of the systems could be automated in the event of an emergency, even takeoff and landing. A white-knuckled Acadia gripped the copilot's steering yoke for about five minutes, while Arnion let her pilot the craft. She hadn't anticipated the rush of adrenaline that surged along her nerves. Flying was definitely something she wanted to practice more. Of course, having Arnion's warm hands slide over hers to guide her steering didn't hurt either.

When Acadia's stomach rumbled, she told Arnion she was hungry. He was happy to stop for a break and landed the halcyon beside a traveler's lodge. Arnion taught Acadia how to plug in the thick galvanic cables to recharge the halcyon's fuel cells. Once everything was connected, they entered the lodge. The owners were a married couple with an adorable toddler named Finn. The meal was a simple but satisfying butterchuck stew with root vegetables and oat rolls. During the meal, Finn reached for a second roll, but his mother moved the basket beyond his reach.

"Mama, why can't I have two? I always have two." Finn rubbed a pudgy cheek with his fist.

"We need to save it, luvvie," his mother replied. The corners of her mouth pinched in anxiety. "There might not be more bread for a while."

Acadia stiffened. This family was already feeling the effects of the Avathysian blockade. Arnion met her eyes across the table, his expression troubled. He gave her a slight nod, and with that, Acadia knew he would appoint someone to discreetly send aid to this family. Acadia's nails dug into her palms. Helping this one family wasn't enough. The whole nation of Kifu was suffering. Her resolve hardened; she would make sure Espina got all the information she needed to stop Avathys's nonsense. They couldn't get to Melica fast enough.

Finn stared at his mother curiously. "But why?" he asked.

"Hush," his mother chided and ruffled his hair. "Be thankful for what you have in front of you."

The toddler pouted, stirring his stew with an aggrieved air.

After the meal, Arnion and Acadia went outside to check on the halcyon. The energy gauge showed they still needed about twenty more minutes to recharge. There was nothing to do but wait. They found a small picnic area with a chipped wooden table and chairs. Acadia pulled two chairs to the side to have a better view of the grasslands, and they sat down. Acadia couldn't stop fidgeting. It felt like ants were racing underneath her skin. She wanted to get to Avathys as soon as possible and convince them to remove their ridiculous blockade. Waiting was painful. She spared a glance at Arnion to see how he was faring. The prince's eyes were closed, and he had leaned back, resting his head against the chair. His skin was sallow and dark circles ringed his eyes. There was a tightness in the set of his jaw that hinted at exhaustion.

Acadia's gut clenched. Arnion carried the burden of two kingdoms now, and it looked like the strain was consuming him from the inside out. Being injured by that trividium-infused berserker had only made it worse. There must be a way she could help him. Acadia tapped a finger against her lips. Then, she had an idea.

She stood and walked behind Arnion's chair. When she brushed her fingertips along his shoulders, he cracked an eye open to look up at her. She tilted her head and gave him a soft smile. "Can I rub your shoulders while we wait?"

"Sure. That would be nice." Arnion closed his eyes once more.

Acadia brushed her palms over Arnion's shoulders in a gentle sweep. When she felt him relax, she switched to a kneading technique, rolling her fingers along the trapezius muscle that connected his neck and shoulders. When she found a knot, she would switch to a circular motion with her thumb and fingers to loosen it.

Her prince sighed. His head turned, dark hair falling over his eyes, and he nuzzled her arm. Heat swept across Acadia's face, and she stilled. His handsome features were peaceful, eyes still closed. She reached to brush a lock of curly hair from his forehead and his fingers curled around her wrist.

Electricity danced along her nerves at his touch. Arnion opened his eyes, his gaze like molten gold.

"Thank you." His voice was low and rough. "For coming with me. I've never . . ." He swallowed. "I've never had someone accompany me before. It's nice to not be alone."

Acadia's heart grew wings and fluttered up her throat. She knelt beside him and rested her forehead against his. "You'll never be alone again if I can help it." She kissed him, pouring herself into it like she'd never done before. All the words that tangled in her chest, that she never allowed herself to speak out loud—*I love you; I'm with you; I never want us to be apart*—seared across her lips in an unspoken vow.

Soon she would find the courage to speak the words aloud.

Once she'd stopped Avathys.

Once she'd earned it.

Chapter 22

"Here?" Acadia eyed the tavern with distaste. The Speckled Sagrin was more of a hovel than an eating establishment. The sun-bleached words on the sign above the door were barely legible. The slate roof sagged over patched stone walls, crusted with lichen. Men with whiskery faces and patched cloaks slouched against the wall smoking kelta pipes.

Arnion stepped closer beside her. His hand hovered by the photon pistol holstered at his side. "We did ask for somewhere discreet."

Acadia clicked her tongue. "Discreet I understand, but this place should be condemned."

He chuckled. "Sometimes these are the places with the best food. Has to be a reason it's still around, right?" He bumped his shoulder against hers.

"Hmm." She eyed him skeptically. The old wooden threshold was worn down by the passage of hundreds of feet. Maybe Arnion wasn't far off.

Inside the tavern, the atmosphere was better, if no cleaner. A boisterous group of men crowded around the counter, hassling a frazzled bar matron. Arnion and Acadia wound their way to a table at the back of the room. Acadia brushed crumbs off the top with the edge of her sleeve. A few of the men flashed her curious looks, but she brushed her fingers along the hilt of her flux sword, and they quickly lost interest.

Arnion ventured to the counter and managed to return with a plate of cured sausage, a thick wedge of cheese, a loaf of crusty bread, and two mugs of chilled citrine cider.

Then they settled in to wait.

A rainstorm blew in from the sea, and Acadia watched as droplets pelted the windows. One corner of the ceiling dripped murky water on an unfortunate patron. He quickly relocated amid raucous laughter from the group at the bar.

Wind rattled the building, howling down the empty chimney, when the door burst open. Two hooded figures entered, sopping wet. They left a trail of muddy footprints to their table. After briefly conferring with one another, the taller one headed toward the bar.

The shorter one took off her coat and draped it on a peg in the wall. She was a young woman, with cropped black hair and long jagged bangs. She was short, much shorter than her companion, and dressed in black leather.

It didn't take long for the other men around the tavern to notice. Acadia watched the glances go from surreptitious to full-on staring. They were practically licking their lips. Acadia shifted in her seat. The woman seemed so young and small. Acadia started to stand, but Arnion put a hand on her arm and shook his head slightly.

"Arnion?" Heat curled in her belly at his touch, and her breath hitched.

"Give it a moment." Arnion watched the pair with interest but not concern. Acadia stifled a groan. He knew more than he was saying.

Three men from the bar approached the woman. They sauntered over, speaking in low, husky tones. Acadia was too far away to hear the words, but her imagination supplied the gist.

The woman shrugged them off. She looked bored, elbow propped on the table, cheek in her palm. But the men wouldn't take no for an answer. They pulled three chairs around her and closed in like vultures. One man leaned forward and reached for her face. Like lightning, the woman struck. She grabbed his forearm and twisted viciously.

Crack.

The tavern grew silent, except for the man's screams. His companions sprang up and launched themselves at her, cursing.

The young woman smiled, all teeth.

Acadia cringed. She'd read the situation in reverse. Those men weren't the predators; they were the prey.

One man lunged. He threw a right hook at her jaw. She blocked with the side of her forearm, ducked, and slammed a fist in his gut. The man doubled over. Vomit spewed from his mouth. The third man tried to grab her from behind, but she twisted and lashed out with her elbow.

Crunch.

Blood gushed from his shattered nose.

A ferocious grin unfurled across the woman's lips. She rolled her shoulders back and tossed her head, flicking the bangs out of her eyes. "Finished already?" She sounded disappointed.

"You witch!" The first man rose, his left arm cradled against his chest. He raised his right hand, a photon pistol gripped between trembling fingers. The barrel wavered precariously at her face.

Acadia stiffened. At that range, the woman had little hope. Why hadn't Arnion let her intervene?

A buzz chittered through the air, and the man's body jerked. His eyes rolled back, moon-white behind fluttering lids. He swayed, then pitched forward and crashed to the floor.

Behind him stood the woman's companion, hood thrown back to reveal a disapproving scowl fringed by dripping blue hair. He was handsome in a youthful way and very tall. In one hand, he held two mugs of citrine cider. A stunner crackled in the other. He set the mugs on the table and glared at his companion. "I can't leave you alone for a minute."

Acadia sighed in relief.

Arnion released his hold on her arm and nodded toward the young pair. "Now, you can go and meet Dragul's protégée."

Chapter 23

KAYA IGNORED THE GROANING men at her feet. The Speckled Sagrin was known for having a rough crowd, but these clowns were a joke. She jutted out her chin at Ellio's rebuke. "Lighten up. I knew you had my back."

Ellio groaned and dragged a hand down his face. "You shouldn't take risks like that! What if I'd been delayed? What if I wasn't paying attention?"

Kaya scoffed. "You're always paying attention. You can't take your eyes off me." She was pleased to watch a blush bloom on his face.

Ellio spluttered. "Th-that's . . . I mean . . . C'mon, Kaya! Gimme a break."

Kaya slugged him in the arm. "Relax, Ellio." She slouched in her chair and hefted her muddy combat boots onto the table, crossing her ankles. "You worry too much."

Ellio blustered around for a moment more. He nudged the last fallen man away from the table with his foot, pulled out his chair, and sat down. "Seriously, Kaya, you need to be more careful. Dragul sent us here to meet someone. We're supposed to be inconspicuous, not drawing attention to ourselves."

"They're over there." Kaya pointed to the table where two cloaked strangers were just standing up. "They've been here since we arrived."

Ellio fumbled with his mug, craning his head around. "What? If you knew that, why didn't you say anything?"

"I wasn't sure at first. It took me a moment. And then these guys approached me. I thought it'd be a good opportunity to let off some steam." Kaya tilted her head to the side and cracked her neck. "It helped, a little. I'd rather have cracked Dragul's skull, but—"

Ellio dragged a hand across his face. "C'mon. Be serious."

"Relax." Kaya spread her arms over the back of the chair. "Our guests are coming over."

Ellio sighed and put his cup on the table.

The newcomers approached. One was a handsome young man—athletic with dark curly hair and golden eyes. Eirenian. Kaya could sense his spiritual energy from across the room. It didn't surprise her this man was involved with her grandfather. He must also be in the spirit warrior class. Maybe she could talk him into some sparring sessions? Anything to get that old fossil off her back.

His companion was a woman, about a hand shorter, with an upturned nose, straight black hair, and the bluest eyes Kaya had ever seen. She was beautiful in the classic sort of way, not that Kaya cared about anything like that. But the woman looked uptight, with eyes narrowed in disapproval.

She's probably a big priss. Kaya jutted out her bottom lip. *Probably doesn't approve of women fighting.*

"Pardon the intrusion," the young man said. "We're looking for a man. We're supposed to meet him here."

Kaya took a swig of her cider and set the mug down. "What a coincidence. We're here to meet someone too. My grandfather sent us. He was called away on sudden business, but he said to meet some of his friends who'd be coming into town today."

The woman stepped up beside her companion. "Is your grandfather Dragul? We were told he would be discreet." Her voice had a sharp edge of disapproval.

Kaya frowned and picked at her teeth with her pinky. "Might be."

"Kaya, be nice," Ellio chided. He stood and gestured at the pair to sit. "Dragul sent us. I'm Ellio." He thumbed at his chest. "And this is Kaya. Sorry about the rough introduction."

The young man smiled and held out a hand. "I'm Arnion. Nice to meet you."

Ellio smiled and shook it. The woman extended her hand toward Ellio, and he blushed. Kaya frowned.

"I'm Acadia," the woman said. Now she was all sweetness.

Kaya's scowl deepened. She didn't like that goofy smile plastered on Ellio's face. "Acadia," Kaya said. "You're not Eirenian, are you? I can hardly feel any spirit presence in you."

"Kaya!" Ellio's voice was mortified. "Cut it out! What is *wrong* with you today?"

"I'm always like this." She puffed out her chest.

Acadia waved her hand. "It's all right." She smiled at Ellio, and Kaya wanted to wipe that patient look off her face. "You're right, Kaya. I'm not Eirenian by birth. I'm from Kifu originally but was trapped in Gehenna until Arnion rescued me."

Ellio gaped like a fish out of water. "Then, Arnion, you're the prince of Eiren? The resurrected prince?" He leaned forward in his chair, rubbing his chin. "I-I didn't realize." His eyes were as wide as dinner plates, and he beamed at their new companions in awe.

Even Kaya struggled to mask her interest. She'd heard about the Eirenian prince who died to settle Lucien's blood oath, and of his miraculous resurrection, but it was a hard story to swallow. She'd wondered how much was fact and how much was embellishment.

She took a swig of her cider. "Did you really die?" she asked.

Acadia frowned at her, shoulders bristling. "Of course he did. Are you questioning the Eirenian crown prince?"

Kaya waved her hand. "There's a lot of stories going around. Stories about Lucien lurking in the shadows, stories about an undead prince. Rumors of whole towns disappearing. It's hard to know what's real without seeing it with my own eyes." Kaya smirked. It was easy to get Kifans riled up. Acadia wasn't a tough nut to crack at all.

Arnion gave her a tempered look. "Yes, Kaya. I took on the blood oaths for all of Gehenna, and Lucien extracted the price with my life."

"If that's true, then pardon my asking, but how are you here now, sitting right in front of us?" Kaya asked.

"Listen, you little—" Acadia began.

"In the realm of the dead," Arnion quickly said, "I found myself filled with an influx of the spirit. Stronger than anything I've ever known. I was able to generate a sword that cut through the fabric of space and time, and I returned here to Elorah."

Ellio was staring at him with stars in his eyes. Even Kaya had to snap her mouth shut. She hadn't expected the prince to be so direct. Judging from the pinched expression on Ms. Priss's face, neither had she. If what Arnion said was true, it really was a miracle. Kaya leaned forward, resting her elbows on the table. "So, why don't you use this spirit sword and take out Lucien once and for all?"

Arnion clenched his fist. A muscle in his jaw tightened. "Replicating it has proven difficult. We're not sure what triggers it. Does it only appear in life-and-death situations? Was it a gift that could only be used once? Or is it like any other spirit skill that I can cultivate and improve over time? Unfortunately, with the spirit, many things are a mystery. And this spirit sword even more than most. No one has ever achieved it before. No one has ever heard of it. No one other than me has even seen it. And the situation in which it was activated was unique, to say the least."

Kaya could concede that point. She knew how hard spirit training was. And that was with a mentor who knew what he was doing to help her train. Well, at least Dragul claimed to know what he was doing. Even if his methods seemed ridiculously tedious and impossible to her. They also failed to get the results either of them wanted.

"So, you're a prince without your primary weapon?"

Arnion smiled at her. "You could say that." He flashed her a smile that would have turned a weaker woman into a quivering puddle of goo.

Kaya cleared her throat. "Let's get you back to Dragul's place. We have two jetbikes parked out back. You can secure the halcyon here. Taking it to the fishing village would destroy Dragul's cover."

Kaya and Ellio rode together on one jetbike while Arnion and Acadia followed behind on the other. When Acadia saw Dragul's dwelling, she exclaimed over the orange color and interconnected domes. "What an amazing house! And such a bright color." She patted the stone exterior.

Ellio nodded enthusiastically. "Avathysian architecture is so vivid. I'm from Kifu too, and I'd never seen anything like this before. Kaya and I also love the bright colors."

Kaya grunted.

Ellio smacked a fist into his palm. "Are you hungry? I could make something."

"Don't go to any trouble for us," Acadia said. "We ate at the tavern while we were waiting to meet you."

Kaya smirked. "Well, that's good, cuz all Ellio can cook is burned beans and watery soup."

Ellio drew himself up to his considerable full height and scowled down at Kaya. "What's with you today? Maybe that was true at first, but I'm getting better. You even told me yesterday I'd improved. Keep this up, and I'm going to stop making melon pan for you."

Kaya flinched. "Okay, okay. I'm sorry. Jeesh."

Arnion sat at the dining table. "When will Dragul be home?"

Kaya pulled up a chair across from him. "Later this evening or early in the morning, depending on how his rendezvous goes. He's out gathering final bits of intel to prepare you for your trip to the capital."

"Have either of you ever been to Melica?" Acadia asked.

"Of course we have." Kaya cast her a disdainful glance. "It's only half a day's journey from here. What? Do you think because we work as fishermen that we're a bunch of country bumpkins?"

"No." Acadia frowned. "I grew up on a farm doing manual labor myself. It's honest work . . ." Her voice trailed off and a tragic look came over her face. "In a lot of ways, I miss it. I have precious memories of our farm. Of playing with my two younger brothers, Talon and Dren. They're practically all grown up now."

"So, you come from a big family, Acadia?" Ellio asked.

"Medium-sized," Acadia said. "My parents, my two younger brothers, and me."

A look of sadness washed over Ellio. "You must have lost touch when you went to Gehenna. I'm sorry."

"No." Acadia fiddled with her hands, scratching at her knuckles. At a look from Arnion, she stopped and clasped her fingers together. "We lost touch before that. It's a long story. But Arnion helped us reconnect." Tears pricked the corners of her eyes. Her throat itched, and she coughed. "Things aren't easy, but it's a start. And I'm thankful for that."

"I'm sorry for prying!" Ellio waved his hands in front of him, as if to ward off his awkward questions.

Arnion rested a hand on Acadia's shoulder. "You look tired. Would you like to get some rest?" At her nod, he turned to their companions. "We've been traveling all day. Is there a place we could sleep for the night? We'll talk to Dragul in the morning. I'm sure once he arrives, he'll desire a good night's rest as well, before he debriefs us."

"Of course." Ellio sprang up.

Kaya clenched her teeth. Did he have to be so enthusiastic?

"It's right this way." Ellio gestured. "I'll show you where the bath and water pumps are as well. That way, if you need them . . ." He trailed off with an awkward laugh. "It couldn't hurt to know, right?"

Acadia smiled back at him, and Kaya felt like she'd been sucker-punched in the gut. Who did Ms. Priss think she was, smiling at Ellio like that? Kaya's blood boiled.

That princess—a farmer? Who did she think she was fooling?

Acadia was one of those ladies who looked glamorous without even trying. The kind who had men eating out of her palm. Women like her didn't seek out hard labor. They avoided it, or better yet, found some poor sap to do it for them. *Probably ditched her family in Beulah.* Kaya didn't trust her, whether the prince vouched for her or not.

Chapter 24

ACADIA BOLTED UPRIGHT FROM her sleep. She glanced outside. It was still dark; the twin moons were like glowing silver coins. She combed her hair back from her face, tucking her bangs behind her ear. The data crystal on her forearm was pulsing. She pressed it, and a message scrawled along her arm.

Requesting status update.

Acadia bit her bottom lip. The beginnings of a headache pounded behind her right eye. She sighed and laid back down on her cot, fingers tracing over the message. Espina kept in frequent contact. Military intelligence wanted every little detail of their journey, whom they spoke to, where they stopped, even a detailed breakdown of the conversation Arnion had with the council advisors. Lucien's spies were in the Eirenian network, and every piece of information Acadia could provide got them one step closer to unmasking them.

The Eirenian military intelligence should have known most of the information already, but maybe it got tangled in bureaucratic knots and never made it to the proper channels. Or maybe Espina was testing her to make sure she could provide accurate intel.

Acadia's head throbbed, and she threw an arm over her face. Sometimes Espina's relentless comms annoyed her, but then she remembered the exhaustion etched in Arnion's face. She was helping him, even if he didn't realize it. Once they caught Lucien's spies, Eiren would be safer for everyone and Arnion would have one less thing to worry about.

Acadia gathered her thoughts into a coherent summary of their last two days. Her fingers traced the message along her skin where the data crystal would transmit it to Espina.

We were attacked by a trividium-corrupted person in Reditona. The Kifan military eliminated him and is retaining the body for further study. Diplomatic tensions are still high. We found evidence of Avathysian involvement at Reditona. We've connected with an undercover agent in Avathys to help us with our investigation.

The cursor paused. Then a response feathered across her arm.

Information on that subject is highly classified. It's above my clearance. Are you sure it was trividium?

A shiver slid down Acadia's spine as she remembered the man's gaping black eyes and cruel snarl. She wrapped her arms around herself, chilled.

Yes. Arnion confirmed it.

How did you manage to kill it?

Acadia could sense Espina's burning curiosity, even across the distance. She grimaced. There were some things better left alone. Lucien's twisted experiments were proof of that. A knot of sorrow lodged in her throat. That man had been a normal person once, with people who loved him. Seeing him reduced to that mindless creature . . . Acadia slapped her palms against her cheeks. Knowing how to effectively stop a berserker was critical knowledge. It could save lives. Her finger swirled against her forearm. *A Kifan soldier shot him in the head.*

Noted. What did you find that implicated Avathys?

Acadia traced out her response. *The corrupted was Avathysian, but I'm certain he was a former Gehennian. We also found a photon pistol casing. Arnion recognized the insignia as a Melican weapons manufacturer.*

The cursor blinked for close to a minute.

Did you inform the Kifans about the discovery of the casing?

No, Acadia sent back.

Good call. We can't trust the Kifans to act rationally under these circumstances.

Acadia bristled. She was Kifan too. Any nation would be upset if a whole town's population vanished without a trace and Avathys's blockade was trying to starve them out. But even Arnion had wanted to keep quiet about the metal casing until they knew more. He worried the Kifans would readily blame Avathys, even if there was another explanation.

Acadia took a deep breath and relaxed her shoulders. Between Arnion's reticence and their rendezvous with Dragul, she was learning more about how Eiren operated in the shadows. Espina might be a little more cynical of the other nations, but her actions were still understandable, even if Acadia didn't particularly like them.

Agent's name and status?

Acadia frowned. Shouldn't military intelligence know this already? Or was this another test?

Dragul and mentee, Kaya. Long-standing undercover agents of Eiren stationed just outside Melica. Currently ensconced as fishermen in a village outside the capital.

Next move? came Espina's reply.

We're meeting with Dragul tomorrow morning to begin planning our investigation of the Melican weapon casing. Dragul will also help us get an audience with the royal family in Melica.

Excellent. Proceed according to plan.

The lights on the data crystal winked out. Acadia stroked the fingernail-sized bump under her skin. Espina told her the bacillus port had been successful at hacking into the Kifan database. Now Eiren could monitor their military chatter and determine the best course of action. Espina assured her that every piece of information was crucial if they wanted to stop a war.

Acadia laid her forearm across her eyes. Was she making any difference? Haggardness still clung to Arnion. Their visit to Reditona had only seemed to make it worse. But she remembered the light in his eyes as he thanked her for accompanying him. Maybe she was doing some good after all. She just wished Espina and the Eirenian military would help lift some of the burden off their prince's shoulders.

So far, Acadia had done everything the Eirenians requested. Her heart ached for the Kifans who were suffering from the Avathysian blockade. And the people of Reditona . . .

A cold sweat broke out on her skin. If Lucien was experimenting on them like that man . . . Fear clenched her heart with icy fingers.

They had to stop him.

The berserker was an empty husk. Trividium had carved out his humanity and left a monster in its wake. She wondered if deep inside his mind was still in there somewhere, a prisoner in his own body.

Resolve tightened in her chest. She wouldn't let Lucien win.

The discovery of the energy casing had been lucky. Other than that and a berserker corpse, they didn't have any concrete leads about the disappearances. And they had made no progress toward a peaceful solution between Avathys and Kifu.

Acadia slapped her face. Worry settled like a two-ton weight across her chest. At least she hadn't heard that strange spirit voice lately. She had finally relented and asked Arnion, but he had never heard it. At least he didn't think she was crazy. He just patted her shoulder and said many things about the spirit were still shrouded in mystery.

Acadia's fingers skimmed over her knuckles, but she resisted the urge to scratch. Somehow she'd managed to rub Kaya the wrong way. She needed to find a way to get on the girl's good side. It wouldn't do for Arnion, and the rest of Eiren, to think she was incompetent because she couldn't play nice with others. Acadia would make herself indispensable. Then no one would be able to challenge her relationship with Arnion. She absolutely must not let this mission fail. If that meant putting up with Espina's micromanaging and Kaya's immaturity, she would do it.

A restless energy coiled through Acadia's limbs. She stretched and got out of bed. There was no way she'd be able to fall back to sleep, and other people would start stirring soon. Maybe she could sneak in a quick training kata. That always helped clear her mind.

Acadia went out to the water pump and splashed water on her face. The icy cold stung her skin and chased away her dark thoughts, at least for the moment.

"Sorry there's no hot water, princess," Kaya said from behind her.

Acadia raised an eyebrow. "I'm not a princess, and I don't care about hot water. I lived through Gehenna, remember?" She eyed the young woman. Kaya wore a black athletic outfit accented by jagged streaks of purple. Fitting for someone who could be so combative first thing in the morning. "What are you doing up this early?"

Kaya stuck up her nose. "I'm always up at this time. To train."

Acadia relaxed her shoulders. She wasn't going to let Kaya's attitude get to her. "Is Dragul back, then?"

"Not yet, but I'm fine training on my own."

That's not what I heard. Acadia had to bite her lip to keep from lashing out. The last thing she needed to do was become enemies with an Eirenian protégée. But Kaya was certainly being difficult. Maybe if she met Kaya on the right battlefield, she could overcome the younger girl's hostility.

"Mind if I join you?" Acadia asked innocently. "I've missed my last few sparring sessions."

"You *fight*?"

Acadia didn't know if she was more insulted by the derogatory tone or the blatant look of disbelief in Kaya's eyes. She shrugged. Let Kaya think what she wanted. People had underestimated Acadia all her life, and she used it to her advantage. She hunched her shoulders and twined her fingers together, playing to Kaya's perception of her insecurity. "I'm still learning. My weapon is the flux sword. You?"

"Staff." Kaya frowned, considering Acadia once more.

She's trying to decide how much she can pummel me without getting into trouble.

There was a calculating look in Kaya's eyes. Her thoughts were obvious. Someone needed to teach the girl some subtlety if she was going to be an Eirenian agent.

Annoyance shredded Acadia's self-restraint. Kaya's arrogance was a liability she could exploit. She was certain she could land a few hits on the girl. At the very least, it would teach her not to underestimate an opponent. And she'd finally get a good sparring session in. Kaya wouldn't go easy on her like Arnion did. It was obvious the girl didn't do things in half measures.

When they agreed not to use spirit abilities, Kaya gave a snotty little laugh. "Otherwise, I'd decimate you."

Acadia gave her a bland smile, deliberately feeding into Kaya's misperception. Her muscles tensed, and adrenaline surged through her. She was going to teach that brat a lesson.

She borrowed one of Dragul's training swords and bowed to Kaya across the sparring ring.

"First one knocked out of the circle or unable to continue?" Kaya twirled her staff.

Acadia hefted her sword. "Fine by me."

They lunged at each other, sword and staff connecting with teeth-rattling force. Kaya swung at her, but Acadia leaped backward then charged. Kaya was ready. The staff landed a glancing blow on Acadia's shoulder. But Acadia retaliated, switching her sword grip and executing a left-handed strike that nicked Kaya's side.

Sweat dripped off Acadia's chin as they battled across the ring. Neither of them was holding back. Kaya lashed at Acadia with her staff, while Acadia retaliated with thrusts and parries.

Kaya was good. Better than Acadia had expected. So, there was some legitimate skill behind her enormous ego.

Acadia was being pushed closer and closer to the edge of the ring. If she didn't do something soon, she'd lose. Lucky for her, Kaya was young and wore her emotions like a flashing xenon sign. Time for Acadia's secret weapon. "That Ellio's pretty handsome." She smirked at Kaya. "I wonder if he's a good kisser."

Kaya's jaw dropped, and she tripped over her feet. That was the opening Acadia needed to hook the staff around her hilt. A quick twist, and the weapon jerked from Kaya's hands. Acadia sent it spiraling through the air. It landed at least ten hands beyond the boundaries of the outer ring. She leveled her sword at Kaya's throat. "I win."

Kaya's eyes narrowed. "Cute trick."

A flush of victory warmed Acadia's cheeks. She smiled, tucking a strand of sweaty hair behind her ear.

Applause rose from the sidelines, and Acadia realized they had an audience. Arnion, Ellio, and an older man she assumed was Dragul stood watching from beside the house.

"Why didn't you say anything?" Kaya whispered in a harsh voice to Ellio.

"I didn't want to disrupt your concentration." Ellio ruffled her hair. "You both looked so focused."

Kaya crossed her arms over her chest and mumbled, "She cheated."

Acadia laughed. "It's not my fault you're so easily distracted."

"Kaya," Ellio chided. "Be polite. Lady Acadia might be your leader one day. If she and Arnion get married." He blushed.

"Just 'Acadia,' please," Acadia said. "Especially among friends."

Ellio beamed at her.

Kaya snorted. "Princes, princesses, la-di-da. I didn't know you were so interested in Eirenian royalty, Ellio."

"They're right under the same roof as us. And they're so nice and down to earth. Nothing like the rulers of Beulah," Ellio protested. "Aren't you the least bit interested?"

Kaya narrowed her eyes, but Dragul cut her off. "Breakfast is waiting. I'm sure you've both worked up an appetite."

They seated themselves around a wooden table in the kitchen, and Dragul served heaping plates of potato mash, hot rolls, fried eggs, and sausage links.

"No Melty O's." Kaya pouted. Acadia was surprised she knew about the sugary Kifan breakfast porridge.

"Cheer up, Kaya." Ellio bumped his shoulder against hers. "I'll make you melon pan later today."

"You're the best!" Kaya wrapped her arms around his neck and kissed his cheek.

After they had finished eating, Dragul cleared his throat. "It's an honor to have you here, Your Majesty. I only wish it were under better circumstances. The dispute over ownership of the Birano coast has been brewing for years. Frankly, I'm surprised they haven't gone to war before now."

"But Avathys has stadia of coastline. Surely, they could concede this small section to Kifu," Ellio said.

Dragul crossed his arms and leaned back in his chair, flashing Ellio a stern look. "Avathys isn't known for its benevolence, young man. They're known for shrewdness. Closing off Kifu's trade routes eliminates a potential rival and forces the weaker nation to go through Avathysian channels, paying tribute. It would effectively put Kifu in servitude to Avathys."

"Sounds right up Lucien's alley," Acadia muttered.

Dragul folded his hands together and rested them on the table. "The Heartless King is keeping his plans quiet. There's been no distinguishable spirit influence throughout the conflict. I've been keeping watch."

Acadia shifted in her chair. She clasped her hands under the table. "What about the berserker?" His face still haunted her nightmares.

Kaya leaned forward, interest sparking in her eyes. "Berserker?"

"A trividium-corrupted human," Arnion replied. "We found him half-drowned near Reditona."

Ellio looked between Kaya and Dragul, his brow furrowed in confusion. Kaya patted his arm and mouthed, *I'll explain later.*

Concern lit Dragul's face. "Are you certain?"

Arnion nodded. "The Kifans retained the body for further testing, but there was no doubt. My spirit and strength were both affected. I was injured, but the wound is healing nicely." At his words, Dragul jerked to his feet, but Arnion waved him back down. "I'm fine. Truly." His pained gaze swept across the table. "I think we can assume Lucien has been using this time to experiment on his followers with trividium. He unearthed a large deposit shortly before his defeat in Gehenna. The berserker shows that he's been at least partially successful. He could have hundreds of soldiers at this point."

"Hundreds?" Ellio gulped, eyes wide.

Kaya drummed her fingers on the table, looking unimpressed. Acadia could tell she wasn't concerned about fighting trividium-corrupted. But Kaya hadn't seen the man and the ferocious madness that consumed him.

"These aren't normal soldiers." Acadia gave Kaya a withering look. "It took everything we had to take one down. They don't stop, even when they're dying."

Dragul brushed a hand over his forehead. "That might explain why we lost contact with some of our informants in Melica. People who start digging disappear."

More people missing? Acadia pressed her hands against her thighs to keep from scratching her knuckles. They had to find Lucien and stop him. Every delay meant more lives would be lost.

Arnion caught Acadia's eye, his face weary. "We'll need to go in and meet with King Atta of Avathys on an official diplomatic visit."

Dragul rubbed his whiskery chin. "All the pomp and circumstance."

Arnion ran a hand through his curly hair. "As much as I dislike it, I don't think we'll be taken seriously at the negotiating table otherwise. Avathys is starving Kifu. We don't have time to play games, but from what I remember of Avathysian protocols, we're likely to make little progress without putting on a bit of a show as we enter."

"Your Majesty is correct," Dragul agreed. "Which is why I've taken the liberty of collecting suitable clothing for you all upon entering the city. Please change. I'll send a wave that an Eirenian diplomatic party is requesting entrance."

"Kaya, Ellio, and Acadia will aid me in keeping all the eyes of Melica distracted by a royal visit from Eiren," Arnion said." Meanwhile, Dragul can slip out and investigate the connection between the weapons casing we found and the disappearances in Reditona."

"Weapons casing?" Dragul cocked his head. Arnion held it out to him, and the older man took it and examined it between his fingers. "An energy charge from a photon pistol. Melican military grade. You found this in Reditona?"

Arnion put his arm around Acadia's shoulders. "Acadia found it with her sharp eyes. We need to know whether it's connected to the disappearances in Reditona."

Dragul bowed his head slightly. "Of course, Your Highness. I would be honored to investigate this for you."

Arnion looked grave. "With all these disappearances, it's clear Lucien also has agents in play. We have to assume they have some knowledge of our plans. Let's use that to our advantage and try to throw them off by playing up the superficiality of this diplomatic visit. Pack what you need and change your clothes. We'll leave for the capital city of Melica within the hour."

Acadia changed into a gauzy white dress with a heavy golden collar. Ellio and Arnion wore loose linen pants. Their shirts were embroidered with waves of blue and gold thread along the collar and sleeves. Kaya wore her black fighting leathers with her collapsible staff tucked into her belt. She clipped her bangs back with silver rings, accenting her violet eyes with smoky eyeshadow. Although Kaya was the only one overtly dressed for it, they were all ready for a fight.

Chapter 25

A SHORT TIME LATER, Dragul returned with Melica's response to Arnion's request for a diplomatic visit. "King Atta wants to send an envoy to escort us into the city."

"Did you refuse?" Arnion asked.

"I've tried to stall them," Dragul replied. "I apologize, Your Majesty, but Avathysians are quite insistent on their protocols. They request that we land the halcyon in the palace shuttleport and wait for an official escort."

Arnion ran a hand through his hair. "Dissuade them, if possible. I'd like to observe the city fortifications. We might be able to sense if there is something amiss if we enter more discreetly."

"Yes, Your Majesty." Dragul thumped his fist over his heart.

When the halcyon landed, a trumpet fanfare rocked the shuttleport. Multicolored petals showered over the airship, and banners unfurled with the Eirenian and Avathysian flags. A parade of Avathysian diplomats marched into the hangar, their tall white hats embellished with plumes and ribbons.

Acadia dug her nails into her palms. The extravagance reminded her of Sapphyre. Espina would undoubtedly have more tasks for her in Avathys. But it would be harder to complete them when Avathys was giving them so much attention.

"Prince Arnion." A noble with a golden mustache performed a sweeping bow. "If only you had provided us more notice of your coming, we would not have provided such an inadequate greeting."

Inadequate?

Kaya and Acadia's eyes met.

This lavish parade was the most elaborate thing Acadia had seen in a while. The politicians of Avathys had managed to put it together in less than an hour. They clearly valued ostentatious displays. Acadia's stomach churned. From the look on Kaya's face, she wasn't enjoying it either.

At least we have one thing in common.

Acadia peeked at Arnion. He smiled pleasantly, but a muscle ticked in his jaw. Empathy twinged her heart. As a prince, he must get this sort of treatment all the time. But Acadia knew it was another burden. Arnion preferred to avoid extravagant displays, but since it helped their cover story, he had to play along.

The procession led them along pristine cobbled streets to a spired palace overlooking the sea. The beauty of it stole Acadia's breath away. White marble archways led to the multi-tiered complex of towers and a large building capped with a periwinkle dome. The walls were encrusted with golden carvings, and Avathysian flags fluttered from hundreds of windows.

Although the architecture was impressive, Acadia found herself longing for the more simple, organic buildings of Eiren. In Capital City, the decorations were functional *and* beautiful. Melica used embellishments for embellishments' sake. The level of opulence was stifling. Acadia knew Avathys was a wealthy nation, but this went far beyond anything she'd imagined.

From what Acadia could see, Avathysian fashion followed the same trend. Men and women wore long belted kaftans covered in tassels, buttons, and embroidery. They all wore silken slippers with pointed toes, the fabric twisting in curlicues above their feet.

"Doesn't that make it hard to walk?" Kaya asked, eying a particularly daring pair of shoes with decorative curls extending at least two hands outward.

"Beauty is pain, my lady," one of the noblemen answered.

Kaya gawked at him until Ellio pinched her.

The parade entered a grand hall, following the rich blue carpet spread across the floor, and stopped at the base of an immense crystallum staircase. Colorful schools of fish darted among the steps, and sea fans fluttered along its base. A giant orange octopus crouched on the left-hand side, tentacles pressed against the glass, and a red-tipped shark circled above the fray.

"An aquatic staircase," Ellio whispered, eyes wide. He took a step forward, but Kaya snagged his hand and jerked him back into line. She inclined her head toward the golden-haired figure waiting at the top of the stairs.

The young woman's hair fell across her shoulders in soft waves, pinned back from her face with a headband of aquamarine brindle stars and pearls. Her gown had an embroidered golden bodice, and flowing white sleeves. She gave an elegant sweep with her hand, and from that gesture alone, Acadia realized she must be royalty. The nobles around Arnion and his team bowed deeply before retreating to the sides of the room.

The young royal descended the staircase, two handmaidens trailing behind to carry the train of her gown. She had a petite upturned nose and long lashes. A hint of mischief flickered at the corner of her mouth as she approached.

"Prince Arnion, I bid you welcome to our fair kingdom." She swept into a low curtsey, the handmaidens at her side flawlessly following her cue. "My father has sent me to greet you in his name." The princess rose and held out a hand decorated with long, bejeweled fingernails.

Arnion smiled warmly and reciprocated with an elegant bow. "I thank you, Princess Zeliaris. The last time I saw you, you were still a young child."

Zeliaris swept her hair over her shoulder, releasing a sultry waft of perfume. She stepped closer to Arnion, eyes bright. "We used to build sandcastles by the sea, and I would cry when the other princes knocked them down." She stepped forward and squeezed his hands. "You were always kind, promising to help me build another one." She leaned in closer to whisper in Arnion's ear. "I think you'll find I've grown in many ways since then."

Jealous seared Acadia's throat even as Arnion pulled away. "You'll always be that precocious little girl in my eyes," he said firmly. "My little sister, covered in sand with seashells in her hair."

Zeliaris clicked her tongue. "Same old Arnion. You never did fall for any of my pranks. I used to torment the other princes who visited." She waved a hand at her maids. Silently, they moved forward and clipped the train of her gown into a bustle. Zeliaris hooked her elbow around Arnion's arm and tugged on him. "Let's walk to the docks like we used to."

Arnion remained standing in place. "I'm afraid this isn't a simple social call. I trust your father is aware of the reason for our visit."

"Some tedious diplomatic issue, I'm sure." Zeliaris's tone was dismissive. She pressed against Arnion's side and fluttered her lashes. "I do hope you're able to have some fun while you're here." She gave the other members of his party a sidelong glance. "Let me guess whom you've chosen to accompany you." The princess pointed to Kaya, Ellio, and Dragul. "Bodyguard, technician, and . . . advisor? You travel very lightly, even for a surprise visit." Zeliaris's voice twinkled with amusement. Then her eyes fell on Acadia. She snapped her fingers. "You there, why are you dawdling? Get the prince's bags and bring them to his suite."

"Excuse me?" Acadia arched a brow.

Kaya snorted.

Arnion held out his hand protectively in front of Acadia. His quick defense mollified her annoyance, and she relaxed her shoulders. "She's not my servant; she's my . . ." He cleared his throat. "She's with me."

"Oh dear." Zeliaris held a jeweled fingertip against her lips, her words dripping with artificial sweetness. "I apologize. I meant no insult." Her eyes met Acadia's with a blaze of disdain. "I must have missed the royal crest on your garments." She turned to Arnion with a pout. "I didn't realize you were betrothed, Arnion. Such joyous news hasn't reached us here, I'm afraid."

The smile fell from Arnion's face.

"We're not betrothed." Acadia hesitated. "At least, not yet. It's . . ." The words stuck in her throat.

"Complicated," Arnion finished.

"I see." Zeliaris's expression turned calculating. "A thousand apologies, Agadia. One would never expect the crown prince of Eiren to have such"—she flicked a dismissive hand in Acadia's direction—"humble tastes."

Acadia fought to hide the tension twining up her spine. "It's Acadia," she said.

"Agadia. That's what I said." Zeliaris gave her a patronizing smile.

Ellio started to interrupt, and Kaya smacked a hand over his mouth. "Shh," she stage-whispered. "Ms. Princess can handle it."

Zeliaris led them out through a side door from the grand hall into a gallery. Ornate frames lined the walls with oil paintings of the sea, Avathysian orchards, and historic sea battles. The walls were adorned with white-and-gold wainscoting, accented with gilded carvings of flowers and fruit, a nod to Avathys's agricultural prosperity. Magnificent frescoes on the ceiling depicted key moments in Avathysian history.

Ellio looked around, wide-eyed. "It's like art, encased in art, covered by art."

Zeliaris giggled, and Kaya smacked him in the arm. "Try not to look so impressed," she whispered.

"Oh, right." Ellio ducked his head, an embarrassed flush creeping up his neck. Acadia could understand his awe. The wealth of Beulah was nothing compared to the prosperity of a seafaring nation like Avathys.

"I'd like to meet with your father as soon as possible," Arnion said. "This is a matter of urgency."

"Father never has meetings after three o'clock," Zeliaris said petulantly. "He says it hinders the digestion."

Acadia scoffed. "Is he going to slight the crown prince of Eiren?"

"There's no slight." Zeliaris gave Acadia a patronizing smile, then tossed her mane of golden hair. "Perhaps a person of your station cannot comprehend. My father wishes to show Prince Arnion the respect he's due. That requires a banquet with music and dancing. One simply doesn't barge into a neighboring kingdom and shove a bunch of diplomatic treaties under another sovereign's nose. That would be quite unseemly, don't you think?"

The threat underlying Zeliaris's words was obvious. Acadia frowned. She glanced at Arnion and could read from his expression that he'd picked up on the same thing. The king of Avathys wouldn't give them the time of day until they played along with his little games. Flattery, niceties, and meaningless formalities while the people of Kifu starved.

White-hot indignation flared inside Acadia, a thousand scathing insults burning her tongue. How could Avathys be so callous? She flexed her fingers and pressed them against her thighs to prevent herself from snapping at the princess.

Zeliaris had made her stance clear. If they tried to push the issue, they'd get nowhere. In fact, she'd implied that trying to rush the process might alienate the Avathysian king entirely. No sovereign wanted to feel threatened or coerced by another foreign power. If Arnion, and by de facto, Eiren, pushed too hard, the alliance they had maintained with Avathys could crumble.

The princess led Arnion and his team to a suite of prepared rooms. There was a bedroom for visiting royalty with an attached bathroom styled in exquisite black marble and gold, a receiving room, a kitchenette, and rooms for accompanying noblemen and palatial staff. Acadia noticed Zeliaris stuck her in the smallest quarters, a half-room relegated for handmaidens and lower-level servants.

Acadia plopped on the squeaky cot and sighed. The joke was on Zeliaris. She'd slept on much worse while surviving in Gehenna. A servant's bed didn't faze her at all. That banquet, on the other hand . . .

Dancing, fripperies, and meaningless conversation here we come.

She remembered Finn, the toddler from the travelers' lodge, with his wide-eyed innocence, oblivious to the political games being played with his food supply. Arnion would make sure that family received aid. But what about all the other Kifan families in need? How could Eiren possibly support them all? And how long could Kifu hold out while Avathys maintained this contemptible blockade?

Did Avathys intend to fight a war of attrition, deliberately drawing things out until Kifu was too weak to fight back? They could starve out their enemies and achieve their goals without firing a single shot.

Was that Avathys's plan?

Chapter 26

TRUE TO AVATHYSIAN FORM, King Atta prepared a lavish banquet that night to welcome Prince Arnion and his Eirenian entourage. Whole-shell crabs glistened in their fire-roasted shells. Steam curled above glass-hewn bowls of savory fish stew. There were platters heaped with dumplings, breaded fish cakes, and coconut rice. Giant purple lobsters sizzled on beds of coals, their shells cracked open, and the shiny white flesh sprinkled with purple petals. The crowning glory of the banquet was an enormous red-tipped shark that must have weighed two tons. Four servants bustled between the creature and the tables, serving up seared shark steaks with a pineapple-honey glaze.

The dining hall was arranged in rows of long wooden tables. At the head of the room was a curved marble dais reserved for King Atta and his family. Arnion and his team were seated at the table to the immediate right of the royal family, a place of high honor.

The king of Avathys was a barrel-chested man with a long curling beard that reminded Acadia of a lion's mane. He had the look of a man who had been muscular in his youth, but age and ease of living were starting to settle around his jowls and gut.

Acadia picked at her food, guilt tight in her chest. Avathys was feasting while Kifu suffered. Tension radiated off Arnion sitting beside her. Ellio's shoulders slumped as he swirled a spoon through his stew. Even

Kaya was subdued as she munched on the fish dumplings, her face contemplative.

Acadia speared a shrimp with her fork and swirled it in the jade-green sauce that decorated the platter. When she popped it into her mouth, flavors of fresh lime and honey burst on her tongue. She couldn't stop herself from exclaiming, "Wow!" Kaya and Ellio glanced at her curiously. Acadia shrugged. "The shrimp are amazing. It doesn't make me any less angry with Avathys, but . . ."

Arnion shifted in his seat beside her. "We're going to convince King Atta to lift the blockade," he said. "And in the meantime, Eiren will provide aid to Kifu. No one is going to starve." He glanced up at the head table where King Atta roared with laughter. "I know we can get through to him."

The gloom surrounding their team dissipated, and Acadia was amused to watch Kaya and Ellio dig into the meal with relish. She stabbed another shrimp and took a bite.

Arnion leaned toward her. His breath tickled her ear. "Can I try it?" he whispered.

Acadia's pulse spiked, heart battering against her ribs. "O-of course!" She held out her half-eaten shrimp, and Arnion bent toward her. His lips brushed her palm as he took a bite. Heat rushed to her face, and Acadia cleared her throat. "So, what do you think?"

"Delicious," Arnion agreed. "We'll have to ask if their kitchen staff would be willing to share the recipe. Perhaps we can prepare them in Eiren."

Acadia assumed he would ask the royal chef to make them, but she was already analyzing the sauce in her mind, guessing at its components. She wished that she was allowed to cook in the royal kitchens. Sadness pinched her heart, but she squelched it. Arnion was only trying to be kind. She reached over and squeezed his arm. "I would love that."

Arnion covered her hand with his. "I want Eiren to feel like home. For you to be comfortable there. There's nothing I wouldn't do to make that happen."

Warmth flooded her chest. She leaned closer to Arnion, brushing her nose against his. A loud cough sounded behind them, and they jerked apart.

"Look at you two lovebirds." Zeliaris fluttered her long lashes at them. She was wearing an aquamarine gown that mimicked the ocean waves, with thousands of tiny pearls stitched along the crests to form whitecaps. "How sweet," she cooed, managing to make it sound like an insult. "Father's asking for you, Arnie. He wants to welcome you personally."

"Arnie?" Acadia echoed.

Arnion cleared his throat. "Arnion, please."

"Whatever you say, Arnie." Zeliaris wound her arm through his and tugged him toward the throne. "You can wait here, Agadior. There's no need for you to come along."

Acadia fumed. Zeliaris had been deliberately mispronouncing her name all night, no matter how many times she and Arnion corrected her. She dug her nails into her palms and choked down the insults scalding her throat. *That uppity little blueblood. Zeliaris isn't clueless; she just pretends to be.*

Acadia reminded herself for the thousandth time she was here to support Arnion. Humiliating a foreign princess with barbed insults would be counterproductive. She couldn't let Zeliaris get under her skin, no matter how petty the young princess behaved. But Acadia didn't have to like it.

Arnion tugged his hand free of Zeliaris's grip and turned back to Acadia. "Please join us." He held out his hand. Acadia smiled and took it.

Zeliaris's mask of innocence slipped for a moment, and she scowled. Acadia maintained a demure expression, but inwardly she preened. Arnion was trying to avoid making a scene, and she would have stayed at the table if that's what he had wanted. But it felt nice that he continually pried himself free of Zeliaris's grasp and returned to her side.

Zeliaris led them to the dais, skipping up to the king. "Father," she said happily, stretching out her hands.

"Zellie!" King Atta beamed. "My beautiful girl! Have you been taking good care of our guests?"

"Of course, Papa," Zeliaris said with pouted lips.

What an actress!

Zeliaris clearly had King Atta wrapped around her finger. The princess swept into an elegant curtsey, then rose and gestured toward Arnion. "May I present Arnion, the crown prince of Eiren, and Agidiot, his servant."

Acadia clenched her jaw, a brittle smile frozen on her lips.

Arnion stepped forward and inclined his head toward the king. "Thank you for hosting us, King Atta." He turned and took Acadia's hand, drawing her forward. "But Zeliaris is mistaken. Acadia is not a servant. She is the other half of my heart."

King Atta stroked his beard, a playful glint in his eye. "You have some competition, Zellie. However, I can't help noticing what you didn't say, young prince. Your heart is missing an engagement band around her left arm."

Mortification washed over Acadia and her face burned. Arnion squeezed her hand. <Don't let them get to you,> his voice whispered in her mind. <It's all a game to them.> He turned his focus back to the king. "What keen eyes you have, King Atta. But my heart is settled and will have no other."

Acadia's breath caught in her throat. Arnion defended her, even when her indecision made others deride him. His love was so immense, it overwhelmed her. She blinked back tears. What had she done to deserve such love?

King Atta tipped his head back and roared with laughter. "You Eirenians are always so poetic. But let me tell you something, young man." He leaned in close. "Royalty comes with responsibility. Your heart is well and good, but your people want stability. They want heirs and a queen they can put on a pedestal and adore." King Atta reached for his daughter's hand and brought her forward. "Like my little Zellie, beloved by all of Avathys."

A table of knights seated to the right cheered in agreement. "To Princess Zeliaris!" they shouted, raising their glasses. "The most beautiful woman in Elorah!"

Acadia wished she could pound some humility into Zeliaris in the sparring ring. But a princess like her would never willingly set foot on rough turf or grip a practice sword. She might crack one of her long, bejeweled fingernails.

The nobleman seated to King Atta's right whispered in his ear. He was a wiry man, with a thinning hairline and a large hooked nose. King Atta guffawed and slapped the man on the shoulder. Then the king turned back to his guests. "Allow me to introduce our trade minister, Tramak Hadril. His genius devised the secret trade routes that have increased the wealth of Avathys tenfold."

Hadril held up a hand in protest. "Your Majesty is too kind," he said in a nasally voice. "I merely analyzed the most efficient routes of travel and coordinated them with the most recent trends in commerce." He gave an oily smile that made Acadia's skin crawl.

"You're too modest, Hadril." King Atta lifted his golden wine goblet and twirled it between his fingers. "Your predictions have never failed." He winked at Arnion. "If Eiren is looking to augment their trade, perhaps Hadril could consult for you. If he could stomach the flight." King Atta cupped a hand to the side of his lips and mouthed *airsick* with a grin.

Hadril wiped the corner of his mouth with a napkin. "I could never leave my beloved Avathys."

A quartet of musicians began playing in the background, and Acadia recognized the tune as "Amantes Duellum," lover's duel. It was a traditional Avathysian dance, famous for its complex choreography and challenging footwork. Acadia knew it flawlessly. As Sapphyre, she had used it to steal many hearts.

Zeliaris tapped her foot to the beat.

So, the princess liked to dance, did she?

A reckless plan took hold of Acadia's mind. She knew it was childish, but she was tired of Zeliaris's antics. It was time for a little payback. "Arnion, do you know this song?" she asked, louder than was necessary. "It's one of my favorites."

Zeliaris took the bait. Her lips curved in a disdainful smirk. "How quaint. A peasant has heard of "Amantes Duellum." But do you know the story behind it?"

Acadia molded her face into a picture of naive innocence. Zeliaris already thought she was a country bumpkin, and Acadia preyed on her expectations. "What story might that be, Your Highness?"

Arnion shot her a questioning look. 'What are you up to?' his expression asked.

Acadia avoided his gaze, focusing her attention on the princess.

Zeliaris flipped her hair over her shoulders with a derisive laugh. She looked at Acadia through hooded eyes, like a serpent sizing up its next meal. "'Amantes Duellum' is the story of two women who vied for the affections of the same man. After months of fighting, they finally came to an agreement. They would compete for his love with a dance. The more skilled dancer would win an engagement; the other would withdraw her pursuit in defeat."

"How thrilling." Acadia pressed her fingers to her lips with false modesty.

Arnion cleared his throat. "It doesn't seem very fair to the man in question. In fact, it ignores his feelings entirely."

Acadia squeezed Arnion's arm gently. "Unless his heart was swayed by the dance."

"You think his love so shallow?" Arnion gave her a warning look, which she pointedly ignored.

King Atta tugged on his golden beard. "You young people are always so energetic. You think your first love will be your only love." He tilted his head, considering Arnion.

Anger flared down Acadia's spine. How dare he belittle Arnion's feelings? It was bad enough that he and Zeliaris were treating him like a prize sagrin at auction. Acadia straightened her shoulders and shot a challenging look at Zeliaris. "Would Your Majesty care to try it?"

For a moment, Acadia thought she might have lost her quarry. Zeliaris hesitated, drumming her fingernails on her armrest. Then the princess stood. "Why not? But don't expect any mercy. I don't do anything half-heartedly."

"I wouldn't dream of it," Acadia said.

Adrenaline sparked along her nerves. Zeliaris was puerile and petty; she didn't have a chance against a true seductress like Sapphyre. A part of Acadia knew she shouldn't stoop to the princess's level, but it felt good to enter a challenge she knew she could win.

Arnion crossed his arms, and a muscle in his jaw ticked. "You do realize this isn't going to change my affections in the slightest," he pointed out, his voice sharp.

Zeliaris laughed. "Of course not, Your Highness. 'Tis but an antiquated custom. All in good fun." She smiled daggers at Acadia.

The princess gestured to the musicians, and the music cut off abruptly, sending the crowd on the dance floor scattering. Acadia and Zeliaris made their way to the center of the room and curtsied to each other. Silence washed over the crowd. Zeliaris spun her finger in an elegant circle, and the orchestra began playing the opening notes for "Amantes Duellum" again.

Acadia and the princess began to dance. It was a mirror game, really. One person would create a six-step pass, the other would imitate it, adding embellishments—sultry little movements like hip rolls, undulating arms, and mincing steps. And then it passed to the next person. It was a test of memory, improvisation, and seduction rolled into one.

Acadia struggled to keep the grin from stretching across her face. Those were all things she excelled at.

The two women started with easy traditional steps and standard arm movements. But little by little, the dance became more complicated. Zeliaris arched her back, extending into an elegant walkover that melded into a split. She rolled gracefully to her feet and bounced on her toes. Acadia tilted her head in acknowledgment. Zeliaris was good, but she was better.

As the song reached its crescendo, Acadia allowed herself to be completely free. Her feet flew across the floor, leaping and spinning as if she were weightless. She dipped backward, arching her spine so far, there was a collective gasp from the audience. Acadia barely heard it; she was so consumed by the music. She rolled her hips, curving back up into a spin, and lifted one slippered foot in the air. Then she undulated her body in a sensual wave that rippled to the floor in a split.

Acadia had always enjoyed dancing. When she'd lived as Sapphyre, it was one of the few things that brought her joy. She was naturally flexible, and her sword training with Arnion had given her more strength in her core and upper body. Acadia rolled back up, wriggling her shoulders, her hands twining around her body like twin serpents.

For the first time since she'd escaped Gehenna, Acadia missed her long hair. It would have spiraled out behind her when she turned. She missed the weight of it on her shoulders, and the way she could scent it with a musky perfume that cocooned around her while she danced.

For a brief moment, Acadia even forgot about the competition, moving to the rhythm of the music with pure, unadulterated joy in her heart.

There was a gentle tap on her shoulder. Arnion stood before her, holding out his hand. "May I have this dance?"

Acadia nodded, slipping her hand in his. He led her into a beautiful spin, and then a dip so passionate, it sent her heart racing.

"Amantes Duellum" was not a couple's dance, but Arnion seemed to anticipate her movements. With each leap or spin, he drew her closer, matching each of her graceful steps with an elegant counterstep. His touch on her waist was electric. Heat seared through Acadia. When he lifted her, a heady weightlessness consumed her. She felt like she could fly.

Arnion had taken a lovers' rivalry and turned it into a passionate declaration of his own. *I love you. I only have eyes for you.* Each movement,
each look, each touch declared his feelings clearly for all to see. He spun
her around and dipped her, bending his head to brush his nose against
hers. Acadia heard applause erupting around her, but her focus was on
Arnion, his face flushed as he panted slightly. His eyes glittered with a
tenderness that made her knees weak. She was thankful he was holding
her up. Out of the corner of her eye, she noticed Zeliaris storm off the
dance floor. Acadia bit her lip.

So much for diplomatic relations.

Arnion would probably make Acadia apologize later, but the radiant
smile on his face right now extinguished her guilt. She didn't know he
was such a good dancer. Why had they never danced together like this
before? Maybe because she was always holding back a part of herself,
trying to be what she thought the Eirenians wanted.

Arnion scooped her up, twirled her out into a spin, then drew her
close to his chest. He held her as if she were the most precious treasure
in the world. "I've always known you loved to dance," he whispered, his
voice breathless. "But I've never seen you dance so freely. It brings me
great joy to see you happy." He brushed a lock of her hair behind her
ear. "I only wish it didn't come at Zeliaris's expense. You shouldn't tease
her."

Acadia blew her bangs out of her eyes. "She started it."

Arnion spun her around and caught her back up against his chest. He
dipped her backwards. "And you finished it."

The music entered its final bars, and he used his wrist to twirl her a
pace away. He bowed to her, and she curtsied slowly, trying to analyze
his expression. How upset was he? Zeliaris had been picking at her since
they'd arrived, and she'd been holding up admirably until now.

Acadia frowned. She was used to smaller-scale negotiations than this. This was two whole countries at stake. Publicly embarrassing Zeliaris probably wouldn't sit well with King Atta either. Acadia didn't think she'd jeopardized the mission, but she had allowed her pride to hinder it.

Dral!

Arnion expected more from her than to give into petty jealousy. *I guess where Arnion's concerned, I'm still lacking.* She brushed her fingers across her knuckles but managed not to scratch. This mission had to succeed for her relationship with Arnion to move forward. If she aided him in brokering peace between Avathys and Kifu, it would legitimize her as a worthy princess-apparent.

How would she ever prove herself capable if she let a pest like Zeliaris get under her skin? If she could be provoked into losing her composure over something so small, what would she do against a real threat? A threat like Lucien.

Acadia repressed a shiver.

Thankfully, the rest of the ball proceeded without incident.

Acadia settled onto her squeaky cot that evening. Her pillow was so thin, she folded it over on itself to block out the feeling of the bars underneath her mattress. A cynical laugh escaped her lips. Zeliaris probably thought it was an insult to relegate Acadia to the shabby servant's quarters, but after living in Gehenna, even this flimsy bed was a paradise.

Chapter 27

THE DATA CRYSTAL PULSED under Acadia's skin, wrenching her from sleep. She pressed a fingertip against the crystal and activated it.

Espina's message flickered across her arm. *We need to access the server room in Melica's palace.*

How? Acadia sent back.

There's an abandoned access tunnel at the back of the gardens. I'm sending a map point to your data crystal. It will guide you. Get to the server room and insert the bacillus. It will do the rest.

Acadia tapped her fingers along her arm. Allowing Eiren to hack into Avathys's data was a breach of many diplomatic laws, but . . . She thought about the people in Kifu with their dwindling food supply while Avathys feasted. King Atta had a callous disregard for the suffering they were inflicting on their neighbor. Maybe with more data, Eiren could force Avathys to the negotiating table. Acadia pressed her lips together.

Nope, she didn't feel guilty at all.

Acadia slipped on a pair of dark pants and a loose-fitting shirt. She tucked her hair away from her face with a series of matte black clips. Abandoned access tunnels sounded dirty, so she tugged on a pair of athletic shoes with soft rubber soles.

She inched open the door and crept into the hall. The palace was quiet, and the lights had been dimmed for the night. Relief swept through her.

Most of the palace staff were probably already asleep. Servants had to rise early to prepare the palace before the royal family awoke, so it made sense they went to bed early.

She'd glimpsed the gardens earlier as she and the others were being led to Arnion's suite. Luckily, she'd been paying attention. Acadia had always loved gardens, and the thought of escaping there to avoid Zeliaris's incessant yammering had already crossed her mind. She retraced her steps and found herself standing in front of an illuminated fountain.

Even in the middle of the night, the colored lights shone, and water was splashing merrily down the sides. Acadia activated the data crystal and swiped through the options. Espina's map point popped up and she pressed on it. The data crystal projected a holographic view a few inches above her forearm. Acadia tested it, turning her arm over. The map stayed activated. When she closed her fist, it shrank back into the crystal, but if she reopened her hand, it sprang back out.

Acadia smiled. It wasn't every day she got to play with spy tech. Anticipation skittered down her spine. She wiped her hands on her pants and proceeded to follow the map to a leafy green wall at the back of the gardens. Thick vines of ivy covered the wall, but when Acadia brushed them aside, she found a rusted metal door. Dirt clogged the seams, and the metal was pockmarked with corrosion. Espina was right, it looked like this door hadn't been used in a long time.

Acadia felt around with her fingers until she found the latch and tugged.

Dral! Locked.

She bent down and brushed the lock with her fingers. It was a simple cam lock. She tugged two of her hairpins free and bent them open. Lock-picking was one of her gifts from Lucien's training, a skill she'd used multiple times when she was one of his Jewels. Breaking in and uncovered leverage on people was all part of the job. After winding up in Gehenna, Acadia had never thought she'd use this skill again. She inserted the two metal edges and adjusted them until she felt the lock click.

Still got it!

The thought brought a smirk to her lips. Then Acadia caught herself. *What am I smiling about? Arnion would be furious if he knew I was breaking into the palace while King Atta has welcomed us as guests.*

Acadia scratched at her knuckles. She was doing this for Arnion. Even if he was angry initially, he'd forgive her once he realized it was for a good cause. If this helped stop Kifans from starving, skirting around diplomatic niceties was worth it.

The door creaked open, and she sucked in a breath. There'd be time for explanations afterward. Right now, she had a job to do, and she wanted to finish it and return to bed before anyone could become suspicious. She bent the hairpins back into shape and used them to tuck her bangs to the side.

Acadia entered the access tunnel. She plucked a small rock from the garden and wedged it in the door hinge. Then she tested the door handle to make sure it didn't close all the way. She didn't want to get trapped down here.

The tunnel was dusty. A dry, musky smell told her there hadn't been fresh air inside for a long time. Cobwebs brushed along her arms and face as she walked. She swept them away, hoping any spiders had moved on long ago. The tunnel was as empty as a tomb and her steps echoed down the metal floor, no matter how softly she trod.

Acadia followed the map point down twists and turns. Thank goodness for the data crystal. She tried to take note of each turn, just in case, but it was a relief to see the map point left a green beacon at the door to the garden, so she'd be able to find her way back.

When Acadia reached the red dot on the map, she looked up and found a large metal door. There was a dusty plaque on the wall beside it. She dusted it off and read *M.A.D.S.* in black letters.

That's an odd name for the server room. Acadia hummed. *Maybe Melica is trying to be inconspicuous.*

The metal door had an access panel next to it. No more cam locks. Acadia sighed. Electronic locks meant higher security. She took a moment to scan the area for surveillance cameras. Nothing caught her eye, but they could be microscopic.

Acadia activated the data crystal and did a scan. It didn't pick up any surveillance equipment outside the room, but a red light flashed, warning her there was a motion sensor and surveillance camera inside. She set the data crystal to emit a jamming frequency. Then she stepped up to the control panel.

A handprint scanner flickered to life at her approach.

That wouldn't be too hard to bypass.

She toggled the data crystal and held her palm over the scanner, a few millimeters above the surface. The data crystal scanned the control panel, cycling through thousands of finger and palmprint combinations. One by one, it narrowed down each finger. When the data crystal flashed green, the scanner chirped. A warm, ticklish sensation slid across her hand as the sensor swept over it and the metal doors slid open.

The temperature inside the room was cool, with a slightly electric scent, like ozone. Acadia stared at all the server towers, impressed. So, this was Melica's main server room. Everything from the lights in her bedroom to the palace gates was controlled here. Where was she supposed to insert the bacillus? Acadia circled one of the server towers, but she couldn't see a connection point. Then she glimpsed a tech station at the rear of the room.

That's probably a control hub for the servers. I'll bet it has an access point.

Sure enough, she found one in the tech station and inserted it. The bacillus flashed red. Acadia tapped her fingers, waiting for it to finish.

Speakers crackled to life above her head, and a robot voice blared, "Unauthorized access detected in M.A.D.S. Security dispatched." Whirring filled the air. A metal panel in the wall slid open, and a familiar whirring filled the air.

Dral.

A sentry bot wheeled toward Acadia. A red targeting light shot from its bulbous head and fixed on her chest. Heavy metallic sheets of reactive armor coated the robot's protective shell. Even the weakness in the neck joint was covered. This was a newer model than the bot she had faced in her spirit exams. There would be no sawing through the power cable with this one.

The robot thrummed—an angry metallic sound. "Intruder detected. Lethal force authorized," a deep voice recording played from its chest cavity. Twin laser rifles unfolded from its arms. The targeting light moved up Acadia's chest to her forehead.

"Not even a warning," she muttered. She took a defensive stance and called upon her spirit. <Shield.>A golden shield coalesced around her body. This machine was lethal. She wouldn't get a second chance. All those practice sessions had better come in handy, or she was dead.

The robot beeped, its laser rifles glowing red. Acadia firmed up her stance, throwing out her hands to hold up the shield, but the blast from the weapon still blew her backward, smashing her into the wall.

Acadia groaned. If she took a direct hit, she'd be obliterated. The bot emitted a low thrum, as if frustrated she was still alive. Metal treads clacked against the tiled floor as it rolled toward her.

She dove out of the way as another blast aimed at where she'd been standing seconds before. Her shield had worked, sort of, but she wouldn't be able to keep it up for long. She had to find a way to take out that bot, and quickly. Acadia ran between the servers, hoping the bot had protocols in place that prevented it from damaging the towering stacks of Melican tech.

A blast shot through the server stack next to her, spraying bits of wire and circuit boards everywhere.

Maybe not.

Was the bot malfunctioning? That'd be just her luck.

The sentry bot turned the corner, leveling its lasers at her.

Panic shot through Acadia. Black spots danced in her vision. <Shield!> she screamed.

The blast ricocheted off her shield and bounced into another server stack. It exploded. Debris pelted her shield and the stench of melted plastic filled the air. Live wires snapped, sending electricity crackling across the floor. She was thankful she was wearing her rubber-soled shoes. The defense bot wheeled toward her, its treads crunching over the remnants of the server tower.

In a split second, Acadia made her decision. She wouldn't last much longer against this bot. Not without any kind of weapon. There was only one thing she could think of, and it was crazy. She was probably going to get herself killed, but her adrenaline-fueled brain seized on the chance of success. The red tracking beam centered once more on her chest, and Acadia stepped up close to the bot, less than a foot away, her spirit shield blazing to life.

The blast blew her backward again. She blinked, bleary-eyed, and pressed a hand against her forehead. Her ears were ringing, and when she ran her tongue over her teeth, she tasted blood. She patted her arms; she was dusty and banged up, but still alive.

Acadia jerked her head up, searching for the bot. The recoil from shooting its laser rifles so close to her shield had smashed it into the wall. It was crumpled in a heap on the floor. Oil leaked from its cracked carapace. Its infrared sensor sparked.

Acadia wiped her mouth with the back of her hand. The sentry bot was out of commission.

"That's what you get, you heaping bucket of bolts." Acadia kicked its mangled tread. She took a shaky breath, willing her hands to stop trembling, but it was no use. It would take a while to calm down after this.

Blasted Espina! Her bacillus was supposed to block auto-defense protocols in the system as it hacked.

The sentry defense bot was still sparking. And now it had started to give off acrid black smoke.

Acadia took in the damage to the server room. Maybe the dumb thing really was defective, causing all this damage to the servers. She brushed off her shoulder and walked back to the tech station—mercifully still intact. The bacillus blinked a solid green at her. She was good to go. After all the racket and destruction, human security forces wouldn't be far behind. Acadia yanked out the bacillus port and tucked it into her pocket.

An alarm signal blared, and red lights flashed from the ceiling. "Fire alert! Emergency lockdown initiated."

Flames engulfed the defense bot and were spreading across the oil slick on the floor. They traveled through the puddle into the wires of a nearby server stack, and the whole electronic tower erupted into flames.

The metal panels of the door were closing. Acadia raced forward, but she wasn't fast enough. The doors snicked shut as she approached.

She pounded her fist against the door, but the riveted metal didn't budge. It was like being trapped inside a steel vault. Her heart sputtered. Heat pressed against her back, and she looked over her shoulder to see flames broiling through half the room. She ran to the control panel on the side of the door and typed furiously.

"Emergency lockdown in place," a computer voice chimed at her.

"Dral!" Acadia screamed. She pounded her fist against the panel.

There was a sound like rushing wind, and Acadia looked up. A cloudy gray gas was pouring in through the ventilation grates. She coughed and clawed at her throat. Her eyes teared up, and she fell to her knees. Despite her great gasping breaths, she couldn't get enough air.

Terror gnawed at her heart, and she looked up at the gas again with a sudden realization. The control system was trying to put out an electrical fire. It was pumping in a chemical compound to extinguish the flames and sucking the oxygen out of the room.

While she was still inside.

Chapter 28

ACADIA'S VISION BLURRED. PANIC numbed her limbs. She flopped on the floor as if boneless. Darkness rimmed her vision. Stomach heaving, she crawled toward the control panel.

There had to be a way. An emergency security override.

Her thoughts slid away like slick stones.

Why does everything hurt?

She lay her head on the cool floor.

Maybe I'll just rest for a moment.

<—cadia! Get up!>

Who was that? Why were they bothering her? She just wanted to take a little nap.

<Acadia! Wake up!>

She blinked and stared at her surroundings, confused.

Where am I? Why is it so smoky?

Acadia wrinkled her nose. Her throat burned. She looked at the flames licking up the sides of the server towers. Then it came back to her.

She tried to take a rasping breath, and a fit of coughing consumed her.

<Go to the security panel.>

"I've tried that." Her voice came out in a hoarse whisper. "I can't . . ." The words slipped from her mind. Why was it so hard to focus? She doubled over, coughing again. All she wanted to do was curl up in a little ball and sleep.

<The security panel. Now!>

The voice in her head was so bossy. Acadia wanted it to be quiet. Maybe if she did what it said, it would leave her alone, and then she could sleep. She crawled on wobbly knees toward the panel and stared up at it. It loomed above her—an impossible distance. "I can't . . ." she wheezed.

<Lean against the wall and push yourself up.>

Acadia grumbled but did as the bossy voice suggested. She pushed herself up along the wall and stared at the panel. The glowing blue lights were so pretty.

<Press your hand against the panel.>

"Won't work," Acadia muttered but pressed her hand against it, nonetheless. A surge of spirit energy surged through her. Brilliant white sparks crawled along her skin and sunk into the panel. The lights on the interface flickered, flashing red then green then white. The metal doors began to creak open.

<Now, Acadia! Get outside!>

As the doors opened, a rush of air brushed past her face. Acadia gasped. Air had never tasted so sweet. Behind her, the flames roared with the influx of oxygen. She crawled toward the door, sucking in a deep breath.

<Hurry!> the voice shouted.

The metal doors began closing. Sweat dribbled down her back. Each movement tore screaming waves of agony down her arms. Her fingers brushed against the grooved metal of the door sill. She clutched it and heaved her torso across the threshold.

The doors were coming closer. A metallic screech tore through the air as they inched toward her.

Acadia hunched her shoulders, tucked in her head, and tumbled forward in a somersault. She landed in a heap as the doors snicked shut behind her. Acadia rolled onto her back and flung her arms out. Hysterical laughter wound its way up her throat and out her mouth. She laughed and coughed and cried. Tears streamed down her cheeks.

She had almost died, multiple times, in the span of an hour.

"Blasted Espina! Blasted bacillus!" Acadia clenched her fists. The sentry bot should never have been activated. Why had the bacillus failed to stop the security protocols? When she got back to her room, she and Espina were going to have words. She couldn't complete her mission if Eiren had her relying on faulty tech. But she had to get to safety first.

Acadia hauled herself up. A cramp sliced through her side, and she pressed a hand against it, hissing.

I need to move! It's a miracle this place isn't swarming with guards and the fire corps already.

She stumbled back through the tunnel, using the map point from her data crystal to guide her to the garden entrance. Thankfully, no one was in the garden to take in her disheveled appearance. The outside air was sweet, perfumed with blossoming plants. It felt like heaven after the musty air inside the tunnel.

She wished she could sit by the fountain and gather her thoughts, but she knew she had to get as far away from the server room and the fire as possible. She crept back down the hall to Arnion's suite of rooms and cracked the door open. No one was in sight. Acadia slipped inside on tiptoe and locked herself in the bathroom. Her pulse hammered in her ears, and she pressed a hand to her chest. Her legs trembled uncontrollably, and she sank to the floor.

That had been one of the most terrifying experiences of her life. She'd almost died, nearly suffocated by the server's fire lockdown program. She pressed her fingers to her throat, it was scratchy and raw. Each breath sawed through her chest. It had been dangerous, but she was still alive. A fierce pride bloomed in her chest.

She stepped into the shower, careful to wash away every sooty smudge and purge the smell of smoke from her hair. She soaked her clothes in soapy water in the sink and hung them to dry on the towel rack. Then she wrapped herself in a soft robe and stepped out.

"Acadia." Arnion greeted her from the table in their kitchenette.

A bitter mix of guilt and terror corkscrewed up Acadia's throat. She flinched, a hand pressed to her chest. "You startled me."

"I thought I heard someone else up." Concern tightened around his eyes as he took in her appearance. "I'm sorry for frightening you."

"N-no worries." Acadia didn't have to pretend to stutter. Her tongue felt heavy and clumsy in her mouth. "I couldn't sleep." She rubbed her arm, feeling self-conscious. "I thought a hot shower might help."

His smile made her stomach twist uncomfortably. He pointed at his temple. "I don't think I've seen you wear your hair like that before. It looks nice."

Acadia reached up and fingered the clips she'd used to pick the lock. "These old things? I just wanted to keep my bangs out of my eyes while I washed my face." She looked away.

"Are you upset about Zeliaris?" Arnion asked. "I can speak to her directly; tell her to stop the teasing. She's not a bad girl, just young and a little spoiled."

Acadia dug her fingernails into her palm. "Don't do that. Zeliaris is a challenge, but I realize I need to be more diplomatic with her. If we marry, I'll have to face much more intimidating people than a pampered princess. I just felt uncomfortable sleeping in a strange new place, but

I'm tired now." She yawned ostentatiously. "I'm going to head to bed. We have an early day tomorrow."

Arnion nodded. He walked over to her, brushing a lock of hair behind her ear. "Don't let her get to you. I only have eyes for you." Arnion pressed a kiss against her forehead and Acadia folded herself into his embrace.

"Thank you." Tears stung her eyes. Guilt tugged at her, making her skin feel too tight. She didn't want to lie to him, but this was for his protection. Arnion couldn't know about her mission, or it could jeopardize Eiren's integrity on the world stage. Acadia slipped from his embrace and walked back to her room before she made a mistake and said something she'd regret.

She lay in bed, staring at the ceiling. Arnion had looked so sad just now. Like he had the weight of the world on his shoulders. Should she tell him about Espina and the work she was doing? He certainly wouldn't approve.

This work was dangerous. If the bacillus was malfunctioning, she could be put in even more dangerous situations. How many times did Eiren expect her to risk her life?

Her stomach twisted.

But that's what Arnion had done for all of them in Gehenna. He'd paid the ultimate sacrifice to free them.

Was her one life worth more than all the good that would come from stopping the conflict between Kifu and Avathys?

The thought chilled her blood. This was for the greater good. If Espina and the Eirenian military intelligence had the data they needed, it would help them prevent a war. Even if they had to sacrifice some of Kifu and Avathys's security to do it.

Espina needed her. Acadia was the only one who could complete this mission, and she wouldn't let them down.

Everyone was relying on Arnion, but Acadia could help lift his burdens from the shadows. Even if he didn't approve of her methods, he'd understand once he saw the results. And then they'd be able to move forward.

Once Acadia had earned it, once she was worthy of him, she could accept his marriage proposal. Once the people of Eiren saw she had helped prevent a world war from breaking out, they'd accept her. The Separatists would have to admit that something good had come out of taking in the former Gehennians.

When Acadia remembered how Arnion hadn't even flinched when he'd learned she was a Jewel, it brought tears to her eyes. He accepted her past and allowed her to move forward. And here she was, still keeping secrets from him. Bile soured her mouth at the thought.

After this mission, she would never keep secrets from Arnion again. Hiding Espina's mission from him turned her stomach, but it was necessary. She carried this burden so he didn't have to.

Once they stopped Avathys from trying to starve out Kifu, she'd come clean. She'd share with him what she'd done. He would probably be mad at her, but he'd forgive her, like he always did.

Acadia would finally know she'd earned the right to his love, and she'd never keep secrets from him again.

Sleep wrapped her in its comforting embrace.

Then the nightmare took hold.

Chapter 29

Pipes hissed, and water dripped from a duct curling around the corner of the ceiling. The laboratory was not hygienic, but it didn't need to be. Screams echoed down the halls, but all Lucien's attention was on the hyperbaric chamber in front of him. It was a pressurized metal cylinder, welded together with thick bolts and seams. Steam hissed. Needles danced on the gauges beside him.

The scientist next to him fiddled with a clipboard.

"Increase the dose to six hundred milligrams," Lucien ordered.

"But, sire—"

Lucien slid his gaze down to the shorter man, a sneer curling his lip. "Do you presume to question me?"

"N-no, sire." The man's hands holding the clipboard trembled. He nodded to his lab assistant who stood behind a desk monitoring the gridscreen that displayed the test subject's vitals. "I-increase the dose."

The other man ducked his head, depressing a syringe full of dark liquid into a series of plastic tubing. "Increasing the dosage to six hundred milligrams."

Lucien watched the black fluid wind through the tubing into the chamber. A screech echoed from within. "Increase internal heat in the chamber to assist absorption rate."

"Y-yes, m'lord," the scientist whispered.

The screams continued. Harsh, piercing cries, more animal than human. The walls of the chamber shook. The pressure gauges flicked into the red zone.

"Ignore it," Lucien commanded. "We're almost there."

Howls of pain tore through the room, transforming into gibbering yowls that were no longer words, just raw terror. Gray smoke swirled through the viewport. Inside, one final guttural scream reverberated through the canister and then nothing, except an eerie silence.

The lab assistant let out a breath.

Lucien clapped his hand on the man's shoulder, just to see him nearly jump out of his skin. "How's she looking?"

The assistant behind the monitor pushed his glasses further up his nose. "Her heart rate is stabilizing."

"Good, good." Lucien rubbed his hands together. "How are the absorption rates?"

The lab assistant leaned forward to peer at a gauge on the gridscreen. Relief washed over his face. "It's reporting one hundred percent trividium absorption." He tapped the screen, pulling up a series of data points and charts. "Cerebral activity looks normal. No hemorrhaging. Heart rate continuing to stabilize. Metabolic activity increasing. Sire, I think we've done it."

"*I've* done it," Lucien corrected. "You sniveling fools would have gotten nowhere without my explicit involvement."

"O-of course, my lord." The scientist bowed.

Steam hissed from the pipes.

Lucien grinned. "I had a good feeling about this one. She was determined." He could barely contain his glee. After all these months of study, he'd finally done it; he'd finally achieved a one hundred percent trividium absorption rate in the bloodstream while maintaining a spiritual tie on the test subject. She'd have superhuman strength, and yet be completely subservient to his power.

"Vent the chamber," Lucien ordered.

"Right away, sire." The scientist snapped his feet together. His assistant behind the desk pressed a large red button. Gears cranked, machinery whined around them, and a series of fans activated. Rushing air pumped into the canister. Smoke swirled through the dirty yellow pipes and outside the lab. Where it went from there, Lucien couldn't care less.

He licked his lips. "Open it."

"Yes, my lord." The scientist nodded to his assistant. "Do it."

The chamber door slid open with a hiss.   ·

Lucien drummed his fingers along his arm. Excitement surged through him. He was about to see the fruits of all his months of hard labor. His new creation. A human who had absorbed trividium throughout her body and hadn't been driven mad. Once he had replicated the results on his army, all of Elorah would be his for the taking. Lucien snickered. *Elyon, you simpering fool. You and all your kingdom have no idea what's coming.*

Smoke billowed from the chamber and curled across the laboratory floor. The stench of burnt hair filled the room. Ragged breathing emanated from the chamber.

"Release the restraints," Lucien commanded.

"S-sire?" the scientist asked, lips quivering.

One look from Lucien silenced the pitiful worm. "Yes, my lord."

Metallic restraints snapped and retracted, cracking through the air. One bare foot appeared in the doorway, and then the other. A slender young woman stepped out of the hyperbaric chamber. Black veins crawled up her legs until they were hidden by a tattered hospital gown.

Lucien activated his spirit vision to study her further. A dark purple aura, almost black, flickered around her, absorbing the light. The stench of rotting meat and sewage filled the room.

The two scientists gagged and flinched backward. Lucien tipped his head back and laughed.

Success, at long last.

"Step forward," he commanded the woman. She nodded and obeyed. He pranced up to her, taking in her physical form. Haggard, but no permanent damage. He lifted one of her arms, examining the broken fingernails. She must have been clawing at the metal wall during the experiment. "You are a beauty," Lucien crooned.

"My . . . lord," she rasped, slinking into a sultry curtesy. Her voice was hoarse, probably from all the hours of screaming. Red hair hung in matted clumps from her scalp. She swayed on her feet for a moment, drew a breath, and straightened her shoulders. She closed her yellow, slit-pupiled eyes and tilted her head up, scenting the air. Then she shuddered, a vicious smile curving over her lips. Black sludge dripped from her mouth and elongated canines flashed in the dull light.

"Welcome to the new world, Delilah."

Acadia sat bolt upright and pressed both hands over her eyes. Sweat-slicked hair stuck to her neck. Shivers wracked her body, and she wrapped her arms around herself. What a horrible nightmare! Why had she dreamed about Delilah after all this time?

She and Delilah had been sent to Gehenna on the same day. They'd ridden in the same collection wagon. Acadia thought they could be friends, but Delilah betrayed her during in-processing, revealing the pendant Acadia had smuggled past the observers. Acadia was beaten into unconsciousness and woke up in her cell. She had never seen Delilah again.

Could Delilah have survived Gehenna and still chosen to follow Lucien after Arnion had set them free? Acadia shook her head. What was wrong with her? Her mind must be twisted if her subconscious could cook up such a horrific nightmare.

<*It wasn't a nightmare,*> the strange voice resounded in her spirit. <*It was an echo.*>

<What are echoes?> Acadia asked, not expecting an answer. No matter how much she tried talking to the voice, it never acknowledged her questions. There were just these strange blips into her spirit from time to time.

Acadia didn't know what to make of it. She was so far from Eiren, only Arnion, Dragul, or Kaya should be able to reach her with spir-coms. But this strange voice seemed to read her thoughts—her very dreams—and followed her wherever she went.

Maybe I'm finally losing it.

<*You're finally starting to see.*>

There it was again! Acadia yanked on the trailing thread of the message.

<Who are you?> she demanded.

<*Ruah.*> The voice waned, its volume fading in and out like a poor radio signal.

<Who are you? I don't know anyone named Ruah.>

The voice pulsed. <*Not much time . . . You must—*> The spir-com severed, winking out without a trace, like a snuffed candle.

<Ruah, who are you? Where are you? Are you Eirenian?> Acadia's spirit called into the darkness.

But there was no reply.

Chapter 30

FRUSTRATION CHURNED IN ARNION's gut. They had been in Avathys for over a week, and he still hadn't been able to speak with King Atta. Something was off with Acadia too. Her shoulders were always tight, like she was constantly tensing to flee, and she wouldn't look him in the eye. She was uneasy around him, and he didn't understand why. What had changed? Arnion couldn't shake the feeling something was deeply wrong. But with so many pressures mounting on his shoulders, he couldn't pinpoint the cause of her distress. He rested his elbows on the table and propped his chin on his thumbs.

Dragul's entrance into the suite disrupted his line of thought. The older man moved quietly into the room, and Arnion was reminded that, despite his age, Dragul was one of Eiren's top agents.

Dragul had been probing his contacts at the docks. There were whispers of weapons being smuggled, but no one could share anything concrete. Older fishermen complained of a black dye leaching from the sewers, causing the fish to frenzy and tear each other apart. One supplyman hinted at discontentment in the government. Division ministers were tired of yielding to King Atta's whims.

So many loose threads, but so far they hadn't been able to pull them together into a coherent picture. Maybe today Dragul would have some good news.

"Any luck in your investigation?" Arnion asked.

The Eirenian agent slipped into a chair across from the prince. "I was able to track the origin of the weapons cartridge. But you're not going to like the answer. The ammunition was part of a large weapons purchase made months ago by Tramak Hadril."

Arnion sat up. "The trade minister?"

Dragul nodded. "The very one."

"But why would he be purchasing weapons? Shouldn't that fall under the Ministry of Defense?" Arnion asked.

"The paperwork was difficult to trace." Dragul spread his hands on the table. "A lot of dead ends and fake names. Hadril went to a lot of trouble to conceal his involvement. That in itself is suspicious."

"There's more?" Arnion leaned forward.

"Yes." Dragul's voice sounded dry, and he licked his chapped lips. "No one seems to know where the weapons disappeared to. They were left on pallets in the warehouse and vanished overnight. But there's been no official investigation, not even a complaint lodged."

"If Hadril paid for the weapons, it would stand to reason he would complain when they went missing."

"Unless he had some reason for keeping it quiet." Dragul nodded. "Something strange is going on in Avathys, and Hadril is in the thick of it." He turned questioning eyes on the prince. "Do you plan on sharing this information with King Atta?"

Arnion shook his head. "Not yet. We don't know if he's involved. If he is, we've tipped our hand. If he isn't, revealing the information prematurely could put his life in danger." Was King Atta complicit in Lucien's experiments? Or was Hadril working behind his back?

"There's more." Dragul rested his hands on the table. "Suspicious activity in the Melican security systems. They're claiming a sentry bot malfunctioned and destroyed a couple of their server towers before self-combusting. But something about it feels off. My sources tell me their military people suspect sabotage, and with our visit occurring around the same time, it looks suspicious at best."

Arnion pinched the bridge of his nose. One more worry to add to his plate. Acadia was acting strangely. Kaya and Ellio were easily distracted. Dragul was steadfast but inscrutable. King Atta was playing games, and Zeliaris was throwing herself at him every chance she got. Bumping into him in the halls. Stumbling into his arms when they went for a walk in the gardens. She was even so brazen as to knock on his door one night and offer to read together. Arnion politely rebuffed her advances and asked repeatedly when he could speak to her father, but he could never get a straight answer.

He was getting tired.

Tired of trying to hold this broken team together. Tired of Atta's games. Tired of the confusion he felt in his spirit.

As his team stumbled out of their rooms to join him for breakfast, an idea popped into Arnion's head. The thought made him smile. Maybe he could do something about at least one of his problems. He had been thinking of ways to help Acadia and Kaya get to know each other better. Arnion had a feeling the two women would get along well if Kaya could see past her mistaken first impressions.

"Do you have a moment?" Arnion beckoned toward the two women. "I need your help with something."

Chapter 31

ACADIA STIFLED A GROAN as she followed a sulking Kaya around the marketplace.

"I can't believe I got stuck going shopping," Kaya griped. "Who does Prince Arnion take me for? I'm a warrior, not an errand girl." She stuck her hands behind her head as she walked.

"Arnion has a lot on his plate right now," Acadia said. "It's only natural that we help out if we can."

Kaya glared at her out of the corner of her eye. "I still don't see why Ellio couldn't come," she mumbled under her breath.

Acadia smiled. *So predictable.* For such a great prodigy, Kaya could be a spoiled brat. When Arnion had told Kaya that Ellio needed to stay behind to help him with fine tuning the halcyon, she had nearly refused. Only at Ellio's gentle insistence did Kaya concede to go with Acadia to the market.

"Let's make this quick, princess. I hate shopping."

Acadia rolled her eyes. She wasn't sure what she'd done to get on Kaya's bad side, but the young fighter had been hostile toward her since day one. As they browsed the stalls, checking off the items on Arnion's list, she had to wonder. Had Arnion sent them out here for female bonding time? If only it were that easy. Kaya was closed up tighter than a clam.

Their first stop was a merchant selling leather goods. Arnion had claimed he needed a new strap for his pack. The man at the counter tried to overcharge Kaya. Acadia watched the younger woman tense up. She knew that look. Kaya was preparing some scathing remark.

Acadia put a hand on her arm. "Allow me." She batted her eyelids at the store clerk. By the time she was done, he'd practically paid *them* to buy his supplies and had given them each a free leather bracelet decorated with silver beads.

As they stepped out of the shop, Kaya huffed. She twisted the bracelet on her wrist, a smile sneaking across her face before she caught herself and smothered it. "Not bad," she admitted gruffly.

Acadia shrugged. "I'm good at reading people. Some people respond to threats. That one responded to flattery." She leaned in close to give Kaya a conspiratorial whisper. "No matter how empty."

The awkwardness between them lessened as they continued through the market. They started with small talk, both pleasantly surprised to learn that they had a lot in common. Kaya was gruff but genuine. In a world of masks, Acadia was relieved to find someone real. Kaya didn't pretend to be someone else for others to like her. In fact, she seemed to delight in pushing people away.

I've been around worse company, Acadia mused as they entered the fruit section.

A servant girl carrying a basket laden with apples scooted by her. "Steady there," Acadia said. She helped the girl navigate around a seller's wares spread out in front of his booth. "You can hardly see with that huge basket. Do you need some help?"

"I'm all right, ma'am." The servant bobbed and hurried on her way. As she turned a corner, she ran smack into someone. Apples tumbled everywhere.

"You stupid fool! Watch where you're going. You nearly took my head off," a nasally female voice screeched.

Acadia helped the girl to her feet. "Are you all right?"

"Is *she* all right? What about me?" Acadia turned to see a spidery-thin woman in courtier's robes. The woman frowned with painted lips and fanned herself. "That ridiculous servant assaulted me. Who do you work for? I'm going to find your employer and tell them what a silly and incompetent wretch you are."

The servant burst into tears.

Anger sizzled up Acadia's throat. "There's no need for idle threats. I witnessed the incident, and you were equally at fault."

"Of all the impudent rubbish. How dare you talk back to me? Don't you know who I am?"

"Is there a problem here, *Lady* Acadia?" Kaya puffed up her chest and stormed to Acadia's side, glaring at the courtier. "Should I tell His Royal Highness you were threatened in the marketplace? Eiren can skip the negotiations if this is a representation of Avathysian courtesy."

"E-Eiren?" The courtier licked her lips. "I didn't realize you were part of Prince Arnion's retinue. Perhaps I've been too hasty. It might have been an honest mistake."

"I can assure you it was." Acadia raised a brow in what she knew was a perfect, imperious stare. "Don't let it happen again."

Kaya flashed the edge of her staff, capped with the Eirenian royal crest. "Very gracious of you, my lady."

The older woman flounced off with her nose in the air.

Acadia shook her head and helped the servant girl dust herself off. "I'm sorry about your apples," she said. "Can I help you replace them?"

The servant's eyes were as wide as saucers. "You . . . you're . . . you're really from Eiren?"

"Got that right." Kaya beamed at her. "Running errands for the prince himself. Seems His Majesty was craving some fresh fruit from the market stalls."

Acadia and Kaya helped the servant girl restock her supplies and carry them to her destination. "You're too kind," the girl protested, but at their insistence, she relented. With a grateful bow, she hurried inside.

Kaya fixed Acadia with an appraising stare. "That was . . . kind of you."

Acadia shrugged. "I know what it's like to be in her shoes. It was the least I could do." Kaya hummed and continued down the street. Acadia smiled after her. Maybe Kaya's heart was beginning to thaw a little.

They finished up Arnion's shopping list and were preparing to head back when Kaya stopped to peer into a market stall. She seemed fascinated by the dizzying array of spices on display. Bright green, orange, and hot pepper red.

"Do you like spicy food?" Acadia asked.

Kaya scoffed. "Hate it."

Acadia tilted her head, examining the younger woman. "Then why are you so fixated on the spices?"

Kaya clicked her tongue and scuffed the ground with her shoe. "Ellio likes it," she mumbled.

Acadia grinned and elbowed the younger girl. "You want to cook him something?"

Kaya's head whipped up, and Acadia could see the panic in her eyes. After a moment, the wild look faded, replaced by resignation. She looked away. "I have no idea how to cook," she admitted. "My mom started to teach me, but then she died." She studied the ground.

Acadia bit down a smile. This was her chance! She cleared her throat. "I could teach you?" Kaya's head popped up, and Acadia continued hastily, waving her hands. "Only if you want. I did a lot of the cooking growing up on a farm, helping my mom in the kitchen every day. I can still remember our family recipe for spicy beef dumplings."

"Ellio loves dumplings." Kaya stared at her with something akin to awe. "Could you really teach me?"

Acadia grinned. "Of course. They say the way to a man's heart is through his stomach." She tapped a finger against her lips. "We'll need to go to the palace kitchens. The little reheater in our kitchenette won't cut it. We need a full heating filament to cook them correctly."

Kaya beamed.

When the two women arrived home, they dropped Arnion's bags in their suite and waved goodbye to the boys.

"We're heading to the kitchens," Acadia declared. "Come by in about an hour, and we'll give you a treat."

Arnion and Ellio stared at them dumbfounded.

Kaya shook a finger. "And don't you *dare* come early and ruin the surprise. Got it?"

Ellio nodded vigorously. Kaya smiled. Acadia hooked her elbow through Kaya's and they sauntered off.

Kaya stared at the rotating kitchen door as if it were a formidable enemy. "You really don't think they'll mind if we're in here?"

"We're their guests. If Avathysian hospitality is as good as they say, they should accommodate a request from the delegates of Eiren." Acadia leaned closer to whisper, "No matter how strange it may be."

Acadia was able to finagle them a space in the kitchen, much to the bewilderment of the palace staff. She showed Kaya how to chop up the onions and mix them with ground beef, raw egg, and a spoonful of hot pepper paste. Kaya watched in rapt attention. Then Acadia taught her how to measure out the flour, mix it with egg, water, and a sprinkling of leavening powder. They rolled out the dough onto the thick butcher-board kitchen table and traced circles with a knife.

"Then you take a spoonful and wrap it in the dough, like this." Acadia demonstrated how to swaddle the meat in a little dough circle, pinching the edges shut to form a cute half-moon shape.

Or, at least, it was supposed to be cute. Kaya's brows furrowed as she attempted to imitate Acadia. The dough stuck to her fingers, tearing little holes in her dumplings.

"When your fingers start to stick, rub them with a little flour, like this."

Kaya studied the dough, like she was sizing up an opponent in the sparing ring. The intensity of her focus was endearing. She must really care about Ellio. Acadia envied the simple but heartfelt charm of the younger girl's romantic pursuit. Kaya may lack subtlety but at least she was honest. It was a refreshing change from the Eirenian court. Watching Kaya and Ellio's gentle romance unfold reminded Acadia that there was still innocence in the world.

"You really love him, don't you?"

Kaya flinched and a mangled dumpling tumbled out of her hands. "What?"

"Ellio, you really love him."

A flush spread across Kaya's face and she picked at the dough stuck between her fingers. "Yeah." Her voice was small, but then she jerked her head up, eyes defiant. "What of it? Are you going to lecture me too?"

"Would I be in the kitchen helping you make dumplings for your chimad if I didn't support you?" Acadia propped a hand on her hip and raised an eyebrow.

Kaya spluttered. "You know about chimad?"

"I'm courting the crown prince of Eiren. It's come up." Kaya gaped at her. Acadia picked up the discarded dumpling and began reshaping it. "I just wanted to say, I can relate to the challenges you and Ellio are facing. Many Eirenians don't approve of me because I'm Kifan." She set the restored dumpling on the tray and met Kaya's gaze with a soft smile. "If you ever want to talk—"

"I'm good, princess." Kaya grabbed another dough circle and plopped a spoonful of meat onto it. "But thanks," she said, still looking down.

"Of course." Acadia relaxed her shoulders. Contentment settled over her heart like a warm blanket. Finally, a breakthrough with Kaya. She would have to thank Arnion later for his contrived list of errands.

After about thirty minutes, they were done prepping and stuffing the dumplings. Next, Acadia taught Kaya how to fry them in hot sesame oil, using long chopsticks to turn the them over until they were a beautiful golden brown on all sides. A delicious aroma of spicy fried meat filled the kitchen. They piled the dumplings on a serving platter, with smaller plates and chopstick settings around the table. Acadia also set out a bottle of shoyu and another of white vinegar.

Kaya looked doubtful. "Vinegar?"

"People in Kifu love it." At Kaya's incredulous look, Acadia crossed her arms over her chest. "Don't knock it 'til you've tried it. Speaking of which . . ." She snatched up a dumpling with her chopsticks and nodded at Kaya. "Chef's privilege. We have to make sure they came out all right."

"Nice!" Kaya picked up a dumpling, hesitated, then with a smile dipped it in the vinegar sauce. She blew on it, switching the piping hot dumpling between her fingers, and then took a bite. "Oh yeah, this is good," she exclaimed with her mouth full. Then her eyes widened, and she started to fan her mouth. "Hot! Hot! Hot!"

Acadia burst out laughing. "You said he likes spicy food." Kaya glared at her, and Acadia held up a hand. "Let me get you some milk."

Kaya gripped the cup of milk like it was her last hope. She chugged it down and wiped her mouth with the back of her hand. "Phew, that burns." She smiled at Acadia. "Ellio's gonna love 'em!"

Acadia resisted the urge to pat Kaya's head. She didn't want to push her miraculous luck breaking through Kaya's shell by going too far.

Arnion, Ellio, and Dragul arrived a few minutes later. Arnion flashed Acadia a bright smile, clearly pleased that she and Kaya were getting along better.

"Something smells amazing!" Ellio took in a deep breath and beamed.

"You two were cooking together?" Dragul asked. He gaped at Kaya in shock.

"Yes." Acadia nodded. "Kaya said Ellio likes spicy food, so I decided to teach her an old Dannon family recipe. Spicy beef dumplings."

Ellio flushed. "You went to all this effort for me? Thank you!" Kaya had a smattering of flour on her nose, and Ellio wiped it off with his thumb.

Dragul grunted, and Ellio stepped back, holding up his hands. Acadia watched the interaction quietly. The tension between grandfather and would-be suitor was clear. Kaya and Ellio were in love. Equally obvious, Dragul didn't fully approve.

Everyone pulled up stools around one of the long kitchen prep tables.

Some of the dumplings were misshapen, but they all tasted amazing. The crew settled down to eat, laughing and joking. Each team member bravely tried the vinegar and found out they actually liked it.

"Acadia, I didn't know you were such a great cook." Arnion slid an arm around her shoulder. "Thank you for this."

Acadia shifted in her chair, twining her fingers together under the table. "I've always liked cooking. But in Eiren . . . at the palace . . ." She fidgeted with her hands. "It always felt like someone else was already taking care of it. There didn't seem to be a need for me to cook."

Arnion waved a morsel in the air with his chopsticks. "These dumplings are incredible! We don't have anything like this in Eiren. If you enjoy cooking, you can cook any time you want at the palace. It's your home. Besides"—he popped another dumpling in his mouth and chewed happily—"if this is any indication of your cooking abilities, you'll have no lack of friends in Eiren."

Acadia's face warmed, pressure building behind her eyes. It *had* been uncomfortable at the palace. Like she was always a visitor walking on tiptoes. Maybe being welcome in the kitchen to cook from time to time would help. She should have asked, but it felt so silly. The princess-apparent cooking her own meals. She hadn't cooked for a group this large since she'd lived on the farm.

Sitting around the table with Arnion, Kaya, Dragul, and Ellio, she felt like she *belonged*. A lump formed in her throat and she swallowed. "It almost feels like we're a family eating together." Acadia chuckled to mask the emotions running riot through her heart.

Arnion reached over and squeezed her hand. "We *are* family."

"I feel the same." Ellio leaned forward, a blush dusting his face. "Like you're the big sister I never had." He rolled his chopsticks between his fingers. "When you trust someone enough to let them into your heart, they become family, even if you're not related."

"Blood isn't everything," Kaya agreed, talking with her mouth full.

Dragul shifted in his chair, an inscrutable look on his face.

Ellio glanced at Dragul and fumbled with his chopsticks, dropping one onto his plate. "That is, I mean..."

The air of camaraderie evaporated, replaced by a thick, stinging tension.

Arnion cleared his throat. "Traveling with you all, eating like this. It's a first for me." His voice tensed with emotion.

"But you're a prince," Ellio protested. "You're around people all the time."

"People, yes." Arnion gestured around the table. "Friends, no. It's been a long time since I've been around people I could call my friends." His expression grew distant. "When I was a child, I used to attend lessons with the other palace children. One day, after a big rainstorm, we all snuck out and played in the mud. It was glorious! We trudged back to class filthy and sopping wet, trailing water down the marble halls."

Kaya snickered. "You mean princes can get dirty?"

Arnion's eyes dimmed. "But when their parents saw them . . ." His hands fisted on the table. "They were angry, embarrassed. I can still remember the children's cries as they were dragged away. The harsh adult voices. 'What were you thinking? You can't play in the mud with the crown prince!'

"The next day, none of the children showed up to lessons. I waited and waited for my friends to come. I looked out the window so much, my instructor took pity on me. 'They're not coming, Your Highness,' he said. 'The other parents decided they wanted their children in a separate class.' I begged and pleaded with him. 'Please bring them back. I'll be good. I promise.' But the teacher was adamant. 'You need to learn how to be a king, Your Majesty. You can't behave as normal children do.'"

Ire blazed in Acadia's chest. Even when Arnion was a child, Eiren had put so much pressure on him.

"That's terrible!" Ellio exclaimed, shaking his head. "I can't believe they did that."

Kaya scoffed and crossed her arms. "It doesn't surprise me. Eirenians are rule-followers to the bitter end."

Dragul leaned back and rubbed his chin, an uncomfortable look on his face.

Arnion drew a circle on the table with his fingertip. "I remember sitting alone at lunch, watching the butterflies in the garden. A servant brought my lunch on a golden tray. But I didn't have any appetite. Then I heard it—laughter. I peeked through the bushes and saw the other children, laughing and playing just as we used to. But when I stepped out to join them, they froze. And I could see it on their faces; they were afraid of me." His voice was rough. "I realized they thought I was going to get them in trouble. So, I turned and went back to my lessons." He blinked rapidly. "Alone." Arnion sighed and leaned back in his chair. "A few days later, Rhys turned up in my classes. My designated playmate." He laughed and ran a hand through his hair. "Thank goodness for Rhys. Without him, I would have gone mad."

He swallowed. "I've always wondered, since that moment, if being a prince meant I wasn't allowed to have friends. That Eiren always had to come first, even over my heart." Arnion's shoulders tensed. "What if, deep down, all people care about is my title and not the person underneath? I worried about it for so long, until I met you, Acadia." He brought her hand to his lips and kissed it.

Acadia's face burned and she looked down. She didn't know. Never in her wildest dreams had she imagined the prince of Eiren could be so alone.

"I'm serious," Arnion insisted. "In Gehenna, when I met you, you stole my heart completely. You had no idea who I was. And I knew you wouldn't have cared if you did. You would have treated me the same."

Acadia slunk down in her seat. "I treated you shamefully," she muttered.

"Frankly, it was a relief." Arnion laughed. "Too many people try flattery and insincerity. Your open hostility was a breath of fresh air. Besides,"—he leveled her with a grin that stole the air from her lungs—"I won you over soon enough."

Ellio leaned forward. "I wanna hear that story."

Kaya smacked him.

"Ow!" Ellio rubbed his arm. "What was that for?"

Kaya rolled her eyes. "Can't you see they're having a moment?"

Dragul chuckled. "Ah, the energy of youth." He shifted toward Kaya. "Forgiving each other, reconciling, healing. That's what families are for."

"What are you insinuating, you old fossil?" Kaya raised an eyebrow.

Dragul sipped his tea placidly. "Nothing."

Arnion and Ellio burst out laughing. Kaya spluttered.

"My, my," Zeliaris's voice cut in from behind. "You all look very cozy. I must say, Arnie, you exercise a shocking lack of formality with your staff."

"Eirenian cultural differences." Kaya waved her hand dismissively. Ellio elbowed her in the ribs.

Zeliaris cleared her throat, puzzlement written across her face. "Father's arranged for a tour of the city. I'm to be your guide." Arnion opened his mouth, and the princess held up her hand. "There's no point in asking to meet Father today. He's off playing clubs for the rest of the day."

Arnion frowned. "These delays are unacceptable. I must speak with King Atta. It's been a week since we arrived, and we haven't shared more than five words."

"Don't be cross, Arnie." Zeliaris molded her lips into a pout. "Come on the tour with me today, and I'll talk to him. Everyone knows I have Father's ear. One word from me, and you'll be meeting with him tomorrow morning."

Arnion gestured to his teammates. "Are we *all* invited?"

"Of course." Zeliaris tossed her golden tresses over her shoulder. "I know you wouldn't have it any other way."

Chapter 32

THE FIRST STOP ON Zeliaris's tour was the University of Melica, a series of grand marble buildings with an enormous courtyard in the center. Scholars garbed in red-and-gold robes walked among the buildings wearing tufted feather caps. Zeliaris caught Acadia staring and explained the color of the feather indicated their field of study. Red for medical, blue for technology, green for business, and purple for fine arts. She boasted that scholars traveled from all over the planet Elorah to study in Melica.

Next, Zeliaris led them to an immense building of pink-and-white stone. Acadia estimated it took up at least eight city blocks. The princess proudly declared this was Melica's premier city hospital, where they'd recently made major medical breakthroughs in organ repair and cellular regrowth. "We have over three thousand specialized med bots. And our researchers have made leaps and bounds in our blood-regeneration technology as well," Zeliaris bragged. "Our medical capabilities are on par with Eiren now."

Kaya rolled her eyes.

They walked past an imposing skyscraper. Zeliaris noted it was the city council building where the king and various ministers met to govern the country. "But that's boring stuff." The princess fluttered her lashes. "Let me show you somewhere more interesting."

Zeliaris took them up to the battlements of the city, declaring it was the best place to view the sprawling metropolis. She patted the rough-hewn stone of the parapet wall. "Melica will never have to worry about being attacked." She swept a hand across the view, chin lifted high. "Everything you see here is protected by our city's impenetrable defense grid, the Melican autonomous defense system, or M.A.D.S." She fluffed her hair and preened. "We can target anything moving within a stadion of the city. And the weapons system is energy based, so we don't have to worry about running out of ammunition. Melica is an impenetrable fortress. Those Kifans have no idea who they're dealing with." Her boastful tone and gestures reminded Acadia of the old rooster on her family farm. The poor thing had strutted about with its head held high, all the way to the chopping block, where it was made into meat pies.

Apprehension niggled Acadia's gut. M.A.D.S. had been on the plaque next to the server room Espina had asked her to hack into.

Kaya crossed her arms over her chest. "The Kifans are just trying to survive and feed their people. It looks like Avathys has more than enough resources without encroaching on their neighbors."

"The Vosna River delta has always been Avathysian territory," Zeliaris protested. "Those Kifans are squatters on land that belonged to our ancestors for hundreds of generations."

"It would help if you had any proof," Acadia muttered.

"What was that, Agidiot?" Zeliaris asked. "Did you say something?"

"It's *A-ca-di-a*." Kaya ground out the syllables. "Just how long are you planning to drag out that dumb joke? It's getting old." Zeliaris looked taken aback. Kaya had never objected to her teasing before, even though Arnion and Ellio repeatedly tried to correct her.

Acadia grinned. It was nice to be on Kaya's good side for a change. She squared off against Zeliaris. "I said, you and your ancestors make a lot of big claims, but you don't have any proof to back them up."

"The word of an Avathysian is enough." Zeliaris huffed. "Anyone with good breeding would know that. It's outrageous to even have to speak it out loud."

Kaya snorted. Ellio fidgeted with the sleeve of his robe.

"It might be bad breeding, but it's common sense to be able to support your claims," Acadia insisted. "On the world stage, you need evidence."

Zeliaris drew herself up, cheeks darkening. "I don't know why you insist on insulting my honor and the honor of my home while at the same time partaking of our generous hospitality." She sneered. "It seems Melican food is good enough for your tastes, even as you threaten our sovereignty."

Frustration simmered under Acadia's skin. She flexed her fingers to avoid scratching her knuckles. "That's not what I—"

"Acadia meant no disrespect to Avathys." Arnion stepped beside Acadia and laid a hand on her arm. "But Eiren is deeply concerned for the Kifans. The naval blockade is jeopardizing their food supply and families are suffering. On top of that, entire towns are disappearing, ransacked by an invisible hand."

Acadia glared at Zeliaris. "And there's reason to believe Avathys is involved."

"My father would never!" Zeliaris raised a hand to slap Acadia, but Arnion caught it. The princess ripped her arm free, her lips white with rage. "How dare you make such an insinuation. It's unforgivable." Her words ended in an angry hiss.

"It's not a wild accusation." Arnion reached in his pocket and drew out the energy cartridge. "Acadia and I found this at the Reditona site." He held it out to the princess.

Zeliaris grabbed the metal box and turned it over between her fingers. "What is it?"

Kaya stepped up beside Arnion. "It's an energy cartridge from a photon pistol."

Zeliaris's eyes widened. "That's . . ." Her fingers traced the etching on the side of the cartridge. "I recognize this design. It's from one of our manufacturing companies, but I didn't know they made weapons." She clenched the cartridge in her fist. "Why would this be in Reditona? My father has forbidden Avathysians from engaging with Kifu. The blockade was just to force them to the negotiating table."

Arnion nodded. "We're investigating the connection between this energy cartridge and the disappearances."

Zeliaris's hands trembled. "But anyone could have used this! Avathys trades throughout Elorah. Someone else could have bought it and used it in Reditona. It doesn't mean my country was involved."

"But it means whoever was in Reditona purchased this from Melica at some point," Ellio held out his hands in a peace-making gesture. "If Melican companies are engaged in black-market weapons trading, that's a serious problem."

"Between that and the grumbles of discontent from your nobles, you could be looking at a coup," Kaya said.

"Ridiculous!" Zeliaris laughed sharply, crossing her arms across her chest. "No one is discontent in Melica. We have the city council for people to voice their complaints."

"Not that it does them any good," Acadia muttered. Zeliaris narrowed her eyes and Acadia shrugged. "People will only let you oppress them for so long. Sooner or later, they fight back."

Zeliaris pursed her lips. "No one in Avathys is being oppressed. We don't force people to behave by punishing them."

"Then why are you trying to starve Kifu into submission?" Kaya shot her a condescending look.

Zeliaris's shoulders wilted, and she bit her lip. "The ministers told Father it would just be for a couple days. Long enough for Kifu to realize they were outmatched." Her chin quivered. "Are they . . ." She licked her lips. "Are they really starving?"

Acadia told her about the travel lodge she and Arnion had stopped at on the way to meet Dragul. When she described the toddler Finn and the anxiety etched in the faces of his parents, tears formed in Zeliaris's eyes.

The princess sniffled. "I didn't realize it was that bad. No one told me."

Arnion took her hands. "Maybe your father doesn't realize it either. That's why I must speak with him. There's also a risk that you are in danger."

Zeliaris nodded, blinking back tears. "I'll see what I can do."

Chapter 33

ZELIARIS WAS TRUE TO her word. Shortly after Arnion and his team returned to their suite, a messenger arrived bearing an invitation for the prince to meet with King Atta the next morning after breakfast.

Hope fluttered in Acadia's chest. At last, they were getting some results. Zeliaris wasn't as shallow and heartless as she'd imagined. Acadia pictured the tears in the princess's eyes as she heard the truth about Kifu's situation. Maybe there was hope for Avathys after all.

Acadia didn't expect the pulse that vibrated along her forearm that night. Espina hadn't contacted her for the last eight days, not since she had inserted the bacillus port in the server room. Acadia had assumed that intel had been sufficient for the Eirenians. She'd been relieved that she wouldn't be called on for any more acts of espionage. Her last gamble with the server room had been almost fatal.

What could Espina want? She should have all the data she needed by accessing the Melican palace's mainframe.

Acadia activated the data crystal and took a sharp breath. Espina wanted her to infiltrate the tech station in Tramak Hadril's home. He was the trade minister they had linked to the weapons cartridge from Reditona. Military intelligence was concerned about the possibility of black-market weapons trading and wanted her to investigate further. It was likely that Tramak had more incriminating data on his personal server. If anything was hidden there, the bacillus would be able to uncover it.

Acadia swallowed. She'd been lucky so far. The Kifan military base camp trusted her, and Ruah had helped her escape the Melican security system. Even Hadril's house was bound to have some security systems in place. What if she couldn't manage it on her own? If it wasn't for Ruah, she wouldn't be alive today. The mysterious spirit voice hadn't spoken to her again since then, and Acadia wasn't sure how much she could rely on him for help. If she was caught breaking into the trade minister's house, there'd be no excuse, no lie that she could use to cover herself. It would be clear to everyone she was a criminal, or even worse, a spy.

Was it worth the risk?

Acadia remembered how Arnion had smiled while they all sat in the palace kitchen earlier. He'd been so relaxed and at ease. Acadia wanted to protect that. She wanted to protect Arnion. If she could pull this off, he might not even need to worry about the war anymore. If Eiren discovered where the weapons were going, maybe they could find Lucien and deal with him too. Once Lucien had been stopped, she and her prince could have the happily ever after they dreamed of. Maybe she'd finally feel worthy of Arnion once she'd helped save the world.

Acadia steeled her shoulders and clipped her lock-picking hair clips on her bangs. She crept to her bedroom door and opened it a crack. No one was stirring. Acadia snuck into the suite and headed for the exit. When she opened the door, she collided with Ellio who was coming back in.

He let out a surprised yelp, and she smacked a hand over his mouth. One heartbeat went by. Then two. Ellio mumbled something against her hand, and she pressed her fingers down harder.

"Quiet," she whispered. Internally she seethed. *Of all the rotten luck! Now what am I going to do?* Ellio wouldn't forget her creeping around at night. What could she tell him? Acadia's mind raced. First, she needed to get him out of the suite before he woke anyone else. She jerked her head to the left. "Follow me," she demanded in a harsh whisper.

Ellio stumbled after her.

Acadia led him out to the gardens and sat on the rim of the fountain. She rolled her shoulders, trying to relieve the tension. "It's hard to sleep in there." She stretched an elbow behind her head. "I never like sleeping in a strange bed."

Ellio flicked a pebble into the fountain. "You were sneaking out, right?"

Acadia suppressed a flinch, but ice ran through her veins. She let out a choked laugh. "Why would you say that?"

"It's obvious," Ellio replied. "I know about the last time too."

Acadia froze. She looked at the water rippling in the fountain. It sounded so peaceful, but it did nothing to soothe the terror shredding her heart. "How?" Her voice warbled.

Ellio ran his finger over the seam in the fountain's pediment. He didn't meet her eyes. "Because I *do* have trouble sleeping. You sleep like a rock."

Acadia didn't know whether to laugh or cry. Ellio could destroy her life with a well-placed word. "Please don't tell the others," she pleaded.

Ellio met her gaze. She didn't like the mistrust she saw there.

"Give me a reason I shouldn't," he said.

There was nothing for it. She had to tell him the truth. It was clear Ellio wouldn't be satisfied with anything less. Acadia held out her forearm. "Press here."

Ellio's brows furrowed and he pulled away.

"Come on, Ellio. I'm trying to show you. Give me your hand." She grabbed his hand and drew it along her forearm. "Do you feel that?"

"There's a little bump. It feels like . . . a data chip." He turned puzzled eyes on her.

"It's a data crystal. Eirenian military intelligence injected it under my skin before we left. I'm working for them . . . as a . . ." Acadia cleared her throat. "As a spy."

Ellio's dazed expression would have been amusing if she wasn't trying to argue for her life. If he exposed her at the wrong time, it could cost her everything.

"Look." Acadia activated the data crystal and tweaked its settings so that it would be visible to anyone. Numbers and patterns flashed along her arm, as the data crystal scanned their surroundings and sent information back to Espina. "Now do you believe me?"

"If that's true, why doesn't Arnion know about it?" Ellio asked.

"What makes you think he doesn't?" Acadia forced herself to speak calmly, but sweat slicked her palms.

Ellio fixed her with a pointed stare. "I may be young, but I'm not an idiot. You're prowling around at night when you think everyone's asleep. And with the guilty way you look at him, it's clear you're hiding something."

"I'm not guilty," Acadia snapped. "Who do you think I'm doing this for? A prince can't get his hands dirty like this, but I can. I'm helping him stop a war, in case you hadn't noticed."

Ellio shrugged. "It doesn't look like you're doing much good."

Acadia scoffed. "That's just because Eiren has been gathering data. Once Avathys tries to make a move, they'll find themselves cornered and forced to the negotiating table."

"Is that how Eiren deals with its allies?" Ellio asked. "It sounds more like how you would treat an enemy."

Acadia threw out her hands. "Eiren is neutral. We're just trying to negotiate a peace settlement."

"Then why all the secrecy?" Ellio crossed his arms and frowned. "Zeliaris doesn't seem so bad once you get to know her. She kept her word and helped Arnion get an audience with the king. How do you know King Atta won't be reasonable like her?"

"You saw how he behaved at the dinner. He doesn't care about Kifu." Frustration needled Acadia and her face grew hot. Why didn't Ellio get it? "We can't count on his good will. We need leverage. What we're doing is right. The ends justify the means."

"If that's the case, why are you too ashamed to tell Arnion?"

"I'm not ashamed," Acadia said, but the desperation in her voice left even her unconvinced. "Look, I don't know how much you know about my past, but it's bad. Real bad. I used to work for Lucien." Ellio flinched, but Acadia forced herself to continue. "Not just work; I lived for him, helping entrap people in Gehenna. You've heard of his Jewels, right? Well, I was the queen of them all. Lady Sapphyre herself."

"You?" Ellio stuttered, his eyes wild. He tried to scoot away from her, but Acadia clutched his hands.

"Arnion already knows that part. You can ask him, I swear. But there's more. At my peak as Sapphyre, I threw myself a birthday party. The biggest, most decadent party Beulah had ever seen. Everyone who was anyone was there. Politicians, celebrities, even a foreign prince. Everything was perfect—or at least it should have been. I had the best food, the best music, the most lavish decorations." Acadia ticked them off on her fingers. "But something was off. The mood was . . ." She shook her head. "I couldn't figure it out. Everyone was smiling, but their smiles were fake. Like they were painted on. People were tense, ready to bolt at a moment's notice. It felt more like a hostage situation than a party.

"I had been looking forward to celebrating with everyone. What was wrong with them? Didn't they know how lucky they were to be around me?

"When one of my servers spilled a drink on me, I lost it. I screamed and beat her in front of everyone. While the other servants were dragging him away, I threatened to call in his debt because he was so useless." Acadia swallowed and scratched her knuckles. "It got so quiet. Everyone stared at me. And that's when I saw it. The fear in their eyes. I wasn't loved at all. I was hated. I tried to smile and pretend everything was fine, but I couldn't unsee it. Everywhere I looked, fear and hatred smoldered underneath the surface. It was terrible." Acadia buried her face in her hands.

"I ran from my own party, went into my bedroom, and sobbed my heart out. I've never felt so lonely and betrayed in my whole life. I'd given everything to Lucien. I'd sold out my family, my honor, my conscience; I'd done everything to be beautiful, but I could see in their eyes that no one thought I was beautiful. I was an object of horror to them."

Acadia looked up and met Ellio's eyes. "Soon after that, all my worst fears came true. Lucien threw me into Gehenna, and no one shed a tear. I was alone and hated. And, worst of all, I knew I deserved it." She took a deep breath. "Then Arnion came, and everything changed. He gave me a reason to live." Tears slipped down her cheeks, but Acadia didn't care. "When he died for me, I thought I would never smile again. It felt like all the color had left the world, and I was doomed to live in black and gray. But then he came back." She smiled, laughing through her tears. "My prince came back to life. And I vowed to never let him shoulder a burden like that on his own again. Not if I could help it."

When Acadia looked at Ellio, she was surprised to see tears shining in his eyes. "I . . ." His voice was hoarse with emotion, and he cleared his throat. "I felt something similar when I met Kaya. She gave me courage I didn't know I had."

Acadia let out a breath. "Then you believe me."

Ellio nodded.

"Good. And you won't say anything."

"I won't," Ellio promised. "I give you my word."

Acadia almost collapsed in relief. She felt drained, her energy puddling at her feet like old candle wax. She'd never told anyone about that birthday party. But she had needed to convince Ellio. And now she needed to rally her strength for Espina's mission. It could change everything. "Then you understand why I need to do this."

"I understand," Ellio said. "And I'm going with you."

Acadia shook her head. "Absolutely not. It's too dangerous."

"All the more reason for us to work together. I can help. I have some experience breaking into data systems." Acadia tried to protest, but Ellio spoke over her. "I also care about stopping the war and helping Arnion. The prince is my friend. I don't want him to feel like he has to solve everything by himself either."

Acadia opened and closed her mouth. She could already tell by the stubborn set of Ellio's jaw that there would be no convincing him otherwise. She sighed and rubbed her temples with her fingertips. "Fine, but don't blame me if we're caught and executed as spies."

"Then let's not get caught." Ellio tilted his head back and grinned.

Acadia had to admit, having Ellio with her was a huge help. Hadril's house had security systems beyond what her data crystal could handle. While Acadia used it to jam the video surveillance feed, Ellio took a small toolkit from his pocket and spliced into the electrical circuit on the side of the house. Within seconds, he had deactivated the security system. The back door slid open.

Acadia's lips parted, and she stared at him in wonder. "Why does it feel like you've done this before?"

Ellio scratched the back of his neck. "I'm just good with machines." But a suspicious blush painted his cheeks.

Together they crept into the entryway. Luckily, the house was quiet. Ellio and Acadia snuck down the hall and located the trade minister's office. Ellio stared around the room at the opulent surroundings.

"This is really something," he whispered, slowly turning as he took it all in. His shoulder bumped against an ornate vase. The antique wobbled, tipping off the pedestal. Ellio's eyes widened in dismay as he stretched out his hands, but he was too slow.

Acadia dove forward and caught the vase with both hands. She glared up at him from the floor. "This isn't playtime, Ellio! Stop messing around."

"Sorry," Ellio whispered. He took the vase from her hands, set it gently on the pedestal, and helped her up.

They walked over to the tech station, and Acadia plugged the bacillus port into the access point.

"What kind of port is that?" Ellio whispered.

"Bacillus," Acadia answered.

"Never heard of it." Ellio shook his head. "Some kind of backdoor-entry virus?"

Acadia shrugged. "Honestly, I'm not sure. I just know it gives Espina access to the information she needs."

Ellio looked concerned. "It's risky. If they have a sophisticated security system, it'll be detected."

Acadia's memory flashed back to the defense bot in the server room, and she suppressed a shudder. "Nothing I couldn't handle so far," she said, forcing confidence into her voice.

Ellio looked at the bacillus port as it blinked green. "It doesn't look like any Eirenian tech I've ever seen. In fact, I've never seen anything like it."

"How much Eirenian military tech have you come across?"

"Not much," Ellio admitted. "But I've never seen a port like this anywhere."

Acadia yanked the bacillus port out of the system uplink. "Let's go!"

They were about to exit the room when they heard male voices outside. Ellio's eyes widened in alarm. Acadia signaled for him to be quiet. Desperately, she scanned the room for hiding places, but there were none.

The voices were coming closer. Footsteps trod along the carpet in the hall.

Acadia jerked her neck toward the corner. Ellio's look told her that he thought they were done for. He wrung his hands, eyes wild. Acadia grabbed her panicking friend and marched him into the corner. She pulled him behind her, pressing into the wall.

The door began to open.

<Conceal,> Acadia whispered, and droplets of blue flame drizzled down on them until they blended completely into the background.

The office door opened. Tramak Hadril and another man stepped into the room. ". . . completely destroyed the server room," the trade minister was saying. "Thankfully, everything was stored in a backup location. But heads are going to roll. The military thinks it might have been an attack from Kifu."

Acadia felt Ellio squirm behind her. <It's all right,> her spirit whispered to him. Kaya had told her that Ellio was learning basic spirit communication but that it was difficult for him. Acadia wasn't sure how much he would understand.

<How . . . are they not seeing us?> His spirit voice was wobbly, fading in and out.

<I'm using my spirit to conceal us.>

<You can make people invisible?> Ellio's voice reverberated with awe.

Acadia laughed through her spirit. <It's an advanced spirit technique I'm learning. But I haven't mastered it yet, so don't distract me.>

The trade minister was still talking to the other man. "We're moving our ships into position. The trade blockade doesn't seem to be applying enough leverage on Kifu."

Dread froze Acadia's veins. Even after risking her life, Avathys was going to initiate a war. How was that possible? Espina had promised they would be able to prevent it.

Suddenly Hadril stopped talking. He was staring at the vase Ellio had almost knocked over.

"What's wrong?" his companion asked.

"That vase . . . Did someone move it?" The trade minister walked over to it and brushed his finger along the rim. "The sun should be facing toward the east." He turned the vase, pointing the sun image in what Acadia presumed was an easterly direction.

Then his eyes met hers. Hadril blinked and rubbed his face. "Does something feel off to you?"

"Hmm?" His companion tapped the vase and glanced up. "What do you mean?"

Sweat dripped down Acadia's back. Doubt swirled in her gut. If she and Ellio were caught now, it was over. And she would be responsible for bringing Ellio down with her.

Acadia's spirit wavered and the concealment flickered.

Hadril took a step toward them. "What—"

The office door burst open, and another man rushed in. "There's been an incident. King Atta is calling for us to report to the palace immediately."

The trade minister blinked and shook his head. "I must be crazy." He ran a hand down his face and turned to face the man at the door. "What sort of emergency?"

"Another Kifan village has been attacked. The Kifans could declare war at any time."

Hadril strode forward, and all three men exited the room.

Acadia slumped backwards, hands trembling. "That was too close," she whispered.

Ellio gave her a shaky nod.

They made their way back to Arnion's suite of rooms. Acadia collapsed onto her mattress, exhausted. Tears burned her eyes, and she threw an arm up over her face. Everything was falling apart. Nothing she'd done had made any difference. Their mission had failed. Avathys was determined to go to war.

Chapter 34

KAYA SETTLED INTO HER stance and prepared for Dragul's attack. It was still dark. The sky shimmered in the blue-gray of pre-dawn light. Last night, her grandfather had requested that she meet him early in the morning on the sparring field. Since he'd been on mission, they hadn't practiced shielding in over a week. Dragul wanted to check her progress.

Kaya knew it wouldn't be good. Her anger and strength made offensive techniques like spirit flames come easily. But the defensive technique of the spirit shield didn't make sense to her. She copied everything Dragul did, but her shield was always so weak, it shattered under Dragul's first punch.

She breathed out through her nose and settled into her stance. Dragul nodded and signaled for her to begin. Kaya closed her eyes and reached into her spirit.

<Shield,> she commanded.

A shimmering golden bubble coalesced around her, but Kaya could sense its fragility. The shield shivered in the air, like it was about to burst.

"Harden it." Dragul's voice cut through her thoughts. "Channel your strength into it, or it won't last."

Kaya gritted her teeth. She was already channeling her strength into the shield as much as possible, but the more she tried to force it, the more the shield wavered. Did the old fossil think she *liked* failing?

"Focus, Kaya!"

"I'm *trying*." She squeezed the words out between clenched teeth. "What does it look like?" The shield quivered, golden energy crackled along its surface. The hair on the back of Kaya's neck stood up.

The shield burst, showering Kaya with golden sparks. She yelled in frustration and kicked up a wave of sand from the training floor. "This is so *stupid*."

Dragul sighed and walked toward her. He held out a hand. "What are you thinking about when you're forming the shield?"

Kaya gave him a sidelong glance. "I'm thinking about making the shield strong enough to withstand your attack."

Dragul rubbed his whiskery chin. "What is the purpose of a shield, Kaya?"

Kaya groaned and turned away from him. "Not this again. Defensive techniques are as important as offensive techniques. I need to master all of them to be a successful warrior of Eiren. Blah blah." She waved her hand dismissively. "You've said it a hundred times."

Dragul took a deep breath. Kaya knew her attitude grated on his nerves, but he was always droning on about defense and self-control.

"I want the simplest answer. It's not a trick question, Kaya. What is the purpose of a shield?"

She turned back to him, arching a brow in just the way she knew aggravated him to no end. "To protect me from attacks, obviously."

"Maybe that's your problem. You're thinking here"—Dragul tapped her forehead with a finger—"when you should be thinking here." He pointed to her heart.

Kaya scoffed. "I didn't know you could be so sentimental, old man." She waited for him to lose his temper, to snap at her like he always did when she was being belligerent, but Dragul surprised her. He stared into her eyes, searching for something.

Kaya rubbed the back of her neck and looked away. "What?" she mumbled.

Dragul watched her intently. "I realize I've been a fool. I've been going about your training all wrong. I should know by now what motivates you." He pointed to her heart again. "Think with your heart. Who would you protect with your life?"

"Ellio," Kaya said without hesitation. She drummed her fingers on her forearm. "And the prince and Acadia, I suppose."

Dragul nodded. "Good. Now this time, when you prepare to generate your shield, think of Ellio, Acadia, and Arnion. Think about how you want to protect them with your life. Forge the shield with the strength of your desire to protect them."

Kaya grumbled and combed her fingers through her long bangs. "If you think it'll help." She tilted her head to the side, cracking her neck.

Dragul rubbed his hands together and stepped back. "Try it once more, with that in mind."

Kaya closed her eyes and breathed deeply. She pictured Ellio's face, then Acadia's and Arnion's. If anyone tried to hurt her precious friends, she'd protect them with her life. Kaya's pulse roared in her ears, and her spirit blazed.

"Well done, Kaya."

Kaya opened her eyes and activated her spirit sight. She gaped at the glittering golden sphere that surrounded her. Dragul walked forward and pressed his hand against the outside. The shield buzzed and blasted him backward.

"That's my granddaughter." Dragul smiled at her.

Kaya laughed, incredulous.

Dragul took up a fighting stance. "Now we can really train."

Kaya flung herself onto the grass. Sweat soaked through her biomesh top and covered her in a sticky sheen. Dragul handed her a cup of water and sat beside her.

"Thanks," Kaya said and took a big gulp. She leaned forward, resting her forearms on her knees. "You know, that was the first time one of our training sessions has been pleasant. I don't think I'll ever forget you calling yourself a fool."

Dragul's eyes twinkled. "It was a long time coming." He took a large swig of his water.

Kaya laughed. "I've been saying it for years."

"Yes." He nodded at her. "I suppose you have." His voice grew quiet, and he stared into the distance.

Kaya propped her cheek on her fist. "What are you thinking about?"

Dragul turned to her, startled. "I was thinking about your parents. You're definitely your mother's daughter. The two of you have the same taste. Picking up men in unusual places."

Kaya's skin tingled. Dragul never talked about her parents, but she'd always wondered. "Would you . . ." Her heart slammed against her rib cage and she dug her fingers into the grass. "Would you tell me about them?"

Dragul leaned back and propped himself on his elbows. "Your father was . . . rough around the edges. Not the Prince Charming I wanted for my daughter. Your rebellious attitude and cutting tongue are gifts from him, as is your propensity for black clothing. But Stryx had a sincerity, an unexpected depth of character and, in the end, he found his reason for living. He was devoted to your mother."

"My mother . . ." The words escaped Kaya's lips in a puff of breath. She flinched and clasped her hands over her mouth.

Dragul smiled. "Nia was my little angel. She could do no wrong in my eyes. But when she chose Stryx . . ." He sighed and covered his eyes with the back of his hand. "I was against their marriage. They were such different people, from different places. I couldn't imagine a future where Nia would be happy with him. Where she wouldn't regret . . ." Pain laced his words.

Kaya picked at the dirt under her fingernails and flicked it away.

Dragul took a shuddering breath. "I thought Stryx would bring Nia down. I thought he was ruining her life, but the truth is, he set her free. In a way, Nia had been a prisoner of me and my expectations. I thought if I could protect and guide her, she'd eventually find happiness. If she'd never met Stryx, maybe she'd be alive today."

Kaya tensed, and Dragul shook his head.

"But I don't think she would have been happy." A smile cracked through the tears running down his face. "It took someone as hard-headed as Stryx to break through all the barriers I'd set around her. He took that bone head of his and bashed through every safeguard I had set in place. At the time, I was furious, but now that I look back, it was actually quite impressive. He was never scared of me, though I tried my best to intimidate and humiliate him. Your father used to make Nia laugh like a schoolgirl."

A smile meandered onto Kaya's face.

Dragul continued. "I'd never known your mother to laugh. She was always a bit stoic and reserved. But your father would drag these huge belly laughs out of her. I'd never heard my daughter laugh like that. In a way, I was jealous that this stranger had opened up a side of her heart I'd never seen before." Dragul looked at Kaya with tears in his eyes. "I was wrong about Stryx. I failed them. At first, it was my prejudice, and then it was my pride that kept me from reconciling. And when I finally softened enough over the years to make the trip . . . it was too late."

Kaya reached forward and squeezed Dragul's hand. "Thank you for telling me. I always wanted to know . . ." Her voice choked with emotion, and she swiped at the tears forming in her eyes.

"I wish I could tell you more about Stryx." Dragul sighed. "I watched Nia grow up, but I think I forced her to mature and become an adult before her time. I have so many regrets, Kaya. But finding you and helping to raise you—I've never regretted it, not for one heartbeat." Dragul pulled her into his embrace.

A dam broke inside her. She sobbed, her tears soaking Dragul's shirt.

He rubbed her back until she quieted, then he whispered, "I'm so proud of you, my granddaughter."

Chapter 35

ARNION PACED THE ANTECHAMBER to King Atta's throne room. At last he would be able to speak with the king, and not a moment too soon. Narhast had contacted him via teleport early this morning. Another Kifan village had been raided. All the villagers had vanished without leaving any clue behind. Kifan medics were astounded by the strange properties of the berserker corpse, but their politicians weren't impressed. Lucien was an obscure threat to them, but Avathys with their naval blockade was a clear enemy.

Arnion rubbed his temples. The situation was rapidly falling apart. If he couldn't make King Atta see reason, their mission would end in failure—exactly what Lucien must want.

He thought about the members of his team. Kaya had incredible strength, but she was arrogant and immature. He couldn't count on her to be level-headed. Ellio was her anchor. If anything happened to that kid . . . Arnion shook his head. He wouldn't let harm befall his friends. Thinking of the blue-haired Kifan made him smile. Ellio had a heart of gold but struggled with self-doubt. He and Kaya made a good pair. If only Dragul could see that.

Then there was Acadia.

A lump formed in Arnion's throat. Every day it felt like she had slipped farther away from him. Dark circles ringed her eyes, exhaustion carved in the tightness around her jaw and shoulders. His chimad was carrying secrets wrapped so tightly about her, it had formed an impenetrable armor between them. Any time he tried asking her, she deflected. Arnion's heart wrenched painfully.

Hadn't she learned anything in Gehenna?

Didn't she trust him?

Her silence was like a knife slicing between his ribs, but if she refused to talk to him, he couldn't force her. She had to come to him on her own, otherwise how was he any different from Lucien?

At the thought of the Heartless King's name, Arnion's fist clenched.

He was certain that Lucien was at the center of everything, like a spider skulking in the shadows, waiting for its prey to get hopelessly tangled in the threads of its web before revealing itself.

What did Lucien stand to gain with this dispute between Kifu and Avathys?

The door to the throne room opened, and a servant beckoned him forward. "King Atta will see you now."

Arnion straightened his shoulders, determination flooding through him. He had to find a way to get through to King Atta.

"Welcome, young prince." King Atta stood before a large bulky object wrapped in a tarp and set on a marble pillar. He waved Arnion over. "I've got something to show you." He gestured at the object. "I commissioned something to commemorate your time in the capital. The sculptor brought it to me this morning." With a flourish, the king pulled the tarp away.

Arnion restrained a gasp. Standing on the pillar was a carved statue, with bulging muscles, a large cleft chin, and windblown shoulder-length hair.

Something about the face looked vaguely familiar.

Arnion squinted. "Is that . . ."

"It's you, my boy." King Atta clapped him on the back. "A little something to remember you by." He tugged his golden beard. "In truth, I wanted to arrange a grand unveiling, but Zellie insisted we skip it."

Arnion tilted his head, studying the sculpture. "It does bear a passing resemblance . . ." he tried politely.

King Atta laughed. "Of course, the sculptor took some artistic license. That's what we pay him for. No one wants to see reality. They want the idea of you. A reminder of the strength of Eiren and the indomitable power of our alliance."

"The power of our alliance?" Arnion stared at the sculpture. It was hideous. He didn't want people to associate him with some maniacal empire set on world domination. That wasn't what Eiren was about. He swallowed his frustration and tried to pin Atta down. "King Atta, I must insist that we talk about your naval blockade of Kifu. It is causing great harm."

King Atta flapped his hand dismissively. "Kifans are prone to being dramatic. I know for a fact they have food stores. Trust me, the moment they start to feel the pinch, they'll be knocking at our doors, begging to negotiate.

"You are gravely mistaken," Arnion said firmly. "Wealthy Kifans may have the resources to maintain a food supply in crisis, but the common folk do not. As Acadia and I traveled through Kifu, we witnessed people suffering because of your blockade. You are responsible for children going without food." King Atta's trademark smile fell, and relief coursed through Arnion. *Good. King Atta wasn't completely hardened. Maybe like Zeliaris, he was unaware of the truth.*

Arnion took a deep breath. "There's more. The disappearances in Kifu—"

"Avathys has nothing to do with that nonsense!" King Atta roared. His face darkened. "Are you accusing me of kidnapping innocent people in their beds? You insult me, Prince Arnion."

Arnion held up a hand. "No, King Atta. I don't believe you are responsible. But with tensions already high in Kifu, these attacks are a critical tipping point. Kifu is preparing to go to war."

"Preposterous!" King Atta huffed. "They can't possibly blame us for that. They have no proof."

"You launched a hostile naval blockade just one day prior. It's not a leap to assume you would initiate other hostilities if your demands weren't met."

Twin red splotches appeared on King Atta's cheeks. "It's one thing to engage in maritime posturing, but completely another to go about kidnapping people. It's without honor."

"Do you really think threatening a nation with your superior naval resources is an honorable tactic?"

King Atta loosened the collar of his robe. "It was only supposed to be for a couple of days, but those hard-headed Kifans! They'd sooner ram their heads against a wall than walk around it."

Annoyance zinged through Arnion, but he forced himself to temper his response. "When is the last time you actually spoke to a Kifan, rather than making decisions based on what your advisors suggest?" he asked.

King Atta harrumphed and turned away, focusing his gaze on the far corner of the room.

Arnion laid a hand on his arm. "Meet with the Kifan king. Talk with him. He's a man who loves his country and wants what's best for it, just like you. Stop letting other people form your opinions for you."

King Atta huffed and raised an eyebrow. "So, you think I don't know my own mind. Is that it, young prince?"

Arnion shook his head. "I only think you do not know your neighbors. You have much to gain from a peaceful alliance."

King Atta tugged on his beard. "Things would go much easier if Kifu was willing to negotiate. But how do you know they'll even meet with me? They're already sharpening their spears from the way you've described it."

Relief surged through Arnion like a physical force. The crushing weight along his shoulders lessened. He was getting through to King Atta. "I can arrange a meeting. I'm sure the Kifan king would prefer it to open war."

King Atta paced the throne room. "But where can we hold it? If we have it here in Melica, it suggests we're still holding the reins, but if we have it in Kifu, Avathys loses face." He stopped in front of a large tapestry along the wall. It was a faded map of Elorah with grinning dolphins stitched into the sea. King Atta traced his finger along the Vosna River that separated Avathys and Kifu. "There's an abandoned fortress here, about an hour's flight outside Birano."

Arnion frowned and turned his gaze toward the map. "What are you proposing?"

"A secret meeting. A peace pact. Let us meet with the Kifans and come to an agreement before word gets out to the people. The abandoned fortress is close to the border; you won't find more neutral ground than that."

Arnion rubbed his chin. "It could work. I will reach out to the Kifan king. We'll need to act quickly."

"As you say, Prince Arnion. I will notify my chief of security to begin making the necessary preparations. We shall be ready to leave at a moment's notice." He extended a forearm and Arnion clasped it.

"Thank you, King Atta." Gratitude rang in Arnion's voice. A feeling of lightness flooded through him, tingling from his head to the tips of his toes. There would be peace between Kifu and Avathys. Arnion was convinced that once the two kings met, they would find common ground. Soon, this mission would be over, and he would have the time to talk with Acadia. Just like the two kings, he knew once they sat down and really talked, a solution would present itself to whatever had been troubling her.

That night, Kaya turned to Acadia as they were brushing their teeth. "Did anyone ever tell you that you talk in your sleep?"

Acadia stiffened. "No. What do I say?" What if she accidentally revealed something about Espina's missions?

"Mostly nonsense." Kaya yawned. "But sometimes it sounds like you're being lovey-dovey with Arnion."

Heat exploded across Acadia's face. She must be blushing like crazy. She placed her palms on her cheeks and slapped herself.

Snap out of it!

Could she possibly be more embarrassing?

"I think it's cute." Kaya smiled at her. "You guys make a good couple. Why aren't you engaged?"

"It's complicated." Acadia sighed. "He's the crown prince of Eiren, and I'm . . ." she waved a hand, gesturing to herself. "I'm nothing."

"It doesn't seem complicated to me." Kaya shrugged. "You love him. He loves you. The rest is just details."

"Yeah, right." Acadia finished brushing her teeth and spat in the sink. She walked to the door, then turned back and waved at Kaya. "Good night."

"Night."

But that night, Acadia lay awake, thinking. All the things she'd kept hidden strained against the dam of lies she had built. How many more could she contain before the whole thing burst?

Chapter 36

THE SECRET MEETING WAS set. Arnion had personally contacted King Yarma of Kifu and convinced him to abstain from war until he at least met with King Atta. Both parties agreed to the location of the abandoned fortress, and a meeting time was set at dusk the next day. Absolute secrecy was required. Both kings would bring a small but elite security detachment and a scribe to record the meeting. Little else was necessary, unless the talks progressed further. Arnion wanted to minimize the chances of Lucien and his spies learning about the peace talks until they were finished. Acadia knew he was thankful to even get both kings willing to sit at the negotiating table. It had been centuries since the rulers of Avathys and Kifu had peaceably sat together in the same room.

On the day of their appointed travel, Acadia flew with Arnion and his team in the halcyon, following King Atta's security squadron. To avoid notice, King Atta refrained from flying in his luxurious red-and-gold royal aircraft, choosing instead to fly discreetly in a sleek gray plane. The king guided them to a clearing in the woods just below the fort where they could land their airships.

King Yarma arrived shortly after them in a boxy aircraft that spat black clouds of exhaust. The king of Kifu was tall and broad-shouldered, with a neatly trimmed military haircut and frown lines etched at the corners of his mouth.

King Atta led them into the old mess hall. It still had a serviceable table and chairs, recently dusted by one of the Avathysian security detail. King Atta waved them forward and both kings took a seat.

The meeting proceeded as expected. There was a bit of posturing on both sides that Arnion worked hard to mitigate, but eventually both kings settled into the business of negotiating.

Then, King Atta's scribe pressed a hand to her ear, listening to something on her telelink. Her face turned ashen. She scribbled a hasty note and slipped it to the king.

"You filthy two-faced dog!" King Atta bawled, leaping to his feet in a rage. You have the nerve to sit across from me, talking of peace, while your vermin attack my trade ships?"

King Yarma looked bewildered at first, but then a purple flush spread across his face and neck. He rose from his chair so quickly, it clattered to the floor. "I knew an Avathysian couldn't be trusted. I came here in good faith, only to be subjected to your baseless accusations."

"They're not baseless!" Atta roared, jamming a fat finger at Yarma. "Did you think we wouldn't find out? Did you think you could sit here smiling to my face while your cowardly soldiers stabbed us in the back?"

Arnion stood and slammed his hands on the table. "What is going on? King Atta, do you have proof of this?"

Atta's hands shook. "My people have just sent me an urgent message through my scribe. Our whole merchant fleet has been sacked. These were innocent men and women, not soldiers." The veins in his neck bulged. "And these despicable Kifan dogs weren't even smart enough to cover their tracks. Kifan weapon shells and spent energy cartridges everywhere. It's irrefutable—"

"What are you talking about, you blathering fool?" King Yarma interrupted. "I've ordered no such attack."

Acadia watched in shock as the conflict escalated. Avathysian trade ships attacked by Kifans? It didn't make sense. Why would Kifu attack Avathys after King Yarma agreed to meet? Why now, when the blockade could be lifted without violence?

A wave of dizziness struck her, and she held a hand over her mouth, suddenly nauseous.

Trade ships? Tramak Hadril was the minister of trade. But Espina had been searching for more information about his illegal weapons trade. Not shipping routes. Hadn't she?

Acadia's heart sputtered, anxiety suffocating her. She turned toward Ellio and grabbed his arm in a vice grip. "I've made a terrible mistake!"

The lights flared overhead. Then the electricity cut off, plunging everyone into darkness.

Chapter 37

HORROR TORE THROUGH ACADIA, and for a moment all she could hear was her own terrified breathing. They had tracked her! Espina had used the data crystal to follow her movements and find the location for the peace talks. She dug trembling fingers into the skin around the data crystal. If only she could tear it out.

Inhuman barks and snarls pierced the air. Acadia recognized those sounds. It was trividium-corrupted, hordes of them by the sound of it. The room erupted into chaos. Screams of terror tore through the air. People were stumbling all around her, crashing into furniture. Green flashes of light zinged across the room as someone fired a photon pistol.

Acadia blinked. Her eyes began adjusting to the darkness, and she made out a Kifan security guard beside her. He drew a flux sword, the blade humming with electric charge, before another sword cleaved through his chest. His mouth formed a wordless "O" and he crumpled to the floor.

Panic congealed in Acadia's stomach. Bodyguards around the table were slaughtered. King Atta slumped over the table, blood dripping down his golden beard into a puddle on the floor. King Yarma was crawling toward her when something jerked him backward. He let out a terrified cry that was cut short. His body fell to the floor, eyes glassy and unseeing, mouth twisted in agony.

Then she got a look at his attacker. Black sludge dripped from lips pierced by unnaturally long canine teeth. Corded muscles bulged through the tears in his clothing, and his inky-black veins throbbed under his skin.

A berserker!

He was bleeding from multiple wounds but seemed completely unaffected as he fixed a hollow stare on Acadia. He let out a blood-curdling howl and charged at her.

Acadia froze as the man's blade swung closer and closer.

She was yanked backward. Arnion thrust her behind him and parried with a glowing red flux sword. He must have grabbed it from one of the fallen Avathysian guards. The berserker lunged at him, and Arnion deflected the attack, slicing the man across his back. The berserker slumped to the floor, and Arnion turned back to Acadia.

His fingers shook as he touched her jaw lightly. "Are you okay?"

Numbly, Acadia nodded. "The others?" She barely dared to ask.

Arnion shook his head. "I don't know."

<Rally to me,> Dragul's spirit shouted through the room. <There is a concealed exit.>

Acadia grabbed an abandoned flux sword, and she and Arnion fought their way to Dragul. Acadia sagged in relief on seeing Ellio and Kaya with him.

"Quickly," Dragul urged and ushered them through the secret passageway. It was a dark hallway of cold stone. Acadia shivered as a cobweb brushed against her neck. But that was the least of her worries. The trividium warriors had completely overwhelmed the secret meeting. Both kings were slain. There was no recovery from this tragedy.

Their mission was a disaster, and scores of berserkers would be bearing down on them in seconds. It was hard to imagine anything else could possibly go wrong. And she was responsible. How would she ever be able to tell Arnion? If they even lived through it.

Acadia shook her head. They would get out. They had to. She just needed to focus on surviving the next few minutes with her friends. Later, she could find a way to fix this. Somehow.

Kaya and Ellio sprinted in behind them. Dragul thrust the door closed and shoved the wooden door bar across it. "That won't hold them for long."

Arnion gripped Acadia's hand and tugged her into the passageway. "How many do you estimate were in there?" he asked Dragul as they fled down the tunnel.

Dragul wiped a hand across his brow. "At least eighty. Maybe more. I didn't sense Lucien, but someone must be commanding them."

Arnion looked heavenward for a moment and closed his eyes. Then Acadia knew their situation was hopeless. There were too many berserkers for them to make it out alive. They had come to the peace talks unarmed as a show of good faith. Now, the only weapons they had were those they had scavenged off the murdered guards during the chaos. Kaya and Ellio were unarmed. She and Arnion had flux swords and Dragul had a pair of photon pistols. He handed one to Kaya as they ran.

Something large slammed into the door behind them. Thuds echoed down the tunnel, punctuated by screeches and barks.

They only had seconds before the berserkers would break down the door.

The tunnel opened into an antechamber that forked in three directions. Dragul nodded toward the middle tunnel. "That way will lead you to the exit." Arnion tugged Acadia toward it, but Dragul didn't follow. "Your Majesty, it has been an honor." He bowed low.

"What are you talking about?" Kaya's voice shook. "There's still time. We can all make it out."

Dragul's eyes glittered with unshed tears. "I'll be your rear guard," he said in a gravelly voice.

"No!" Kaya lurched forward, grabbing her grandfather's shoulders.

Dragul smiled and chucked her chin. "Little Kaya, you still have much to learn about when to fight and when to flee."

"I'll never run from a fight."

Dragul patted her head. "You must. Someone needs to warn the kingdoms about these trividium soldiers before the nations are overrun. You must tell Zeliaris about her father and shore up the defenses in Avathys, otherwise thousands more will share the same fate."

"No!" Kaya shook her head. Tears dripped down her face. "I won't leave you."

Dragul took hold of her shoulders and shook her gently. "I failed your mother and father when they needed me most. I won't fail you." He nodded at Arnion. The prince and Ellio each looped an arm around her and pulled her away.

"No!" Kaya screamed. "Ellio, let me go!" She tried to jerk out of their grip, but the two men held her fast. "Let me go," she pleaded, her voice breaking.

Energy blasts began to echo down the tunnel. Kaya's throat was scratchy from shouting, her sight blurry with tears. Dragul was buying them time, with his life. A heaviness weighed down her limbs. Her stomach twisted in knots.

All those times fighting with Dragul. Arguing with him. Blaming him for her parents' deaths, when it was no more in his control than it had been in hers. But she'd been so angry. She couldn't see.

She'd been so blind . . .

The photon pistol went silent.

Kaya tore her fingers through her hair and wailed.

Dragul's spirit was gone.

Arnion and Ellio continued to grip Kaya's arms as they made their way through the middle tunnel. A headache throbbed behind Acadia's right eye, her mind a disjointed jumble of thoughts. How could Dragul be gone? Just the other day they were laughing around the table eating spicy dumplings. She gripped her head. It couldn't be real.

Around her, each member of the team seemed to be processing their grief differently. Ellio cried silently, Arnion's face twisted in anguish, and Kaya strode forward with rigid, mechanical steps. Dragul's estranged granddaughter. She had been hit the worst of all by his death.

Acadia's mouth opened and closed, but she had no words.

Then an eerie laugh echoed from the darkness ahead.

"Scurry, scurry, little vermin, though it's all pointless in the end."

Acadia's mouth fell open, and she jerked to a stop. Sweat trickled down her spine, and the hairs on the back of her neck stood up. A figure was walking toward them through the darkness, blocking their escape route.

That voice.

It couldn't be.

"Espina." Acadia's voice trembled.

The creature that stepped from the shadows was something out of her darkest nightmares. Black veins crawled along Espina's skin. Hollow pits of darkness consumed her eyes. She smiled through dripping black lips.

"You *know* her?" Kaya bared her teeth.

Espina scraped long, talon-like nails along the cavern wall as she sauntered toward them. "Acadia is an old acquaintance of mine. One might say everything I've accomplished, I owe to her." She smirked and tossed her rotting purple hair over her shoulder.

Acadia felt Ellio and Kaya's gaze turn on her, shock and betrayal raging in their eyes. She couldn't bear to look at Arnion's face. "You used me," she whispered around the thickness building in her throat.

Espina stuck a hand on her hip. "Just like you stepped on thousands of people to get where you are today. Tell me, Acadia, how many lives did you destroy while working in Beulah? I bet it's so high that you've lost count."

"You work for *Lucien*?" Kaya hissed under her breath.

Panic gripped Acadia's lungs. "No!" She turned desperate eyes on Kaya. "Of course not. I would never—"

"Tut-tut." Espina snapped her fingers. "No one likes a liar, Acadia. Today all your deceit has come to an end."

"Acadia, what is she talking about?" Arnion asked. She could hear the desperation in his voice, begging her to deny it.

Icy cold hysteria dripped down Acadia's spine. "She's lying," Acadia stammered. "Please believe me."

"Really?" Espina smiled. Black ooze dribbled from her lips. "Then how do you explain the perfect flow of information I've been getting from her throughout this little trip?"

"What?" Kaya and Arnion said at the same time. Ellio's agonized gaze tore into her, his mouth open in shock.

"She's an Eirenian analyst. She works for Military Intelligence." Acadia wrung her hands and turned to Arnion, pleading. "She told me I could help you stop the war."

"By selling us out?" Kaya's voice was incredulous.

"No," Acadia said in small, broken tones.

"You traitor!" Kaya spat at Acadia. Her chest heaved with ragged breaths. "Dragul . . . my grandfather is dead because of you. I can't *believe* I trusted you." She shoved Acadia with both hands.

Acadia staggered back, her heart racing. It wasn't supposed to be this way. She was supposed to be the hero. But all she could see was betrayal and disgust written across her friends' faces.

Horror piled up in Acadia's gut, immobilizing her in panic and self-loathing.

"Aren't you going to say anything?" Kaya advanced toward her, murder in her eyes. Ellio stepped in front of her.

"Kaya, stop. There are things you don't understand."

"Ellio, I swear, if you don't move, I'm going to break your arm," Kaya growled.

Espina howled with laughter. "You people are a riot. Tell me, Arnion, were these children pathetic before you met them, or is this a side effect of hanging around *you*?" She slapped her hand on her palm. "That reminds me, Acadia, Lucien sends his regards." She blew Acadia a kiss. "You're on his naughty list, but he says if you come crawling back on your hands and knees, he'll consider forgiving you. Bonus points if you bring him Arnion's heart." She clicked her tongue. "I told him it was pointless, but you know men. They all think they're irresistible." Her eyes burned with a yellowish glow, and she looked down at her nails carelessly. "I suppose it doesn't really matter, seeing as you'll all be dead in a couple of minutes."

The howls of the trividium warriors were closing in behind them, and Espina was blocking off the tunnel they needed to escape.

Arnion stepped forward.

Chapter 38

ARNION FIRED HIS PHOTON pistol at Espina, but she moved out of the way with superhuman speed.

Espina laughed. "You didn't think it'd be that easy, did you?"

Arnion glared at her. "How are you not overcome by the trividium?"

Espina tossed her hair and laughed. "Not all of us turn into brute beasts. Some of us have enough strength to truly transcend." She curled her hand into a fist, dark flames dancing down her arms. "Spirit energy is laughable compared to this power."

Kaya broke free from Ellio's grip and lunged forward, not at Espina, but at Acadia. "You disgusting little traitor. I knew there was something off about you. I knew it all along." She curled her hand into a fist and swung.

Acadia ducked, bringing her hands up into a defensive posture. "If you'd just listen—"

"How many people are dead because of you? Soon there'll be millions more when Lucien unleashes his hoards on Kifu. Doesn't that mean anything to you?" Kaya leaped at her. Acadia dodged, panting.

Espina clapped her hands. Snarls filled the air along with the shuffling of feet. The berserker horde had caught up to them.

"Shield, Kaya!" Arnion ordered. When she hesitated, Arnion shouted, "Do it now, or we're dead!" He was still firing blasts of his photon pistol at Espina.

Kaya's spirit shield wrapped around Ellio and Acadia. The trividium soldiers slammed into it, gnashing their teeth. They were pressing in on three sides. Ellio and Acadia watched, wide-eyed, as the berserker soldiers hurled themselves at Kaya's shield.

Something broke inside Kaya, a swirling dam of emotions – sorrow, guilt, regret, rage. She focused on the rage. Rage, she knew. Rage, she could deal with.

Lucien's soldiers continued to ram into her spirit shield, and she snarled back at them. But she could feel it weakening. They were firing photon pistols now, energy blasts pinging off her shield and ricocheting into the stone walls of the tunnel. Kaya watched one soldier take aim, right where Acadia was standing.

Acadia.

Kaya seethed. This was all her fault. Why couldn't she have died instead of Dragul? Kaya's shield flickered, little holes opening as she lost focus.

The soldier fired, aiming at Acadia and somewhere, deep inside, Kaya was glad. A hole opened in her shield, directly in front of the traitor. A shock of blue hair blurred in front of Kaya's vision. Blood splashed across the floor.

Kaya blinked. *What?*

Ellio stood in front of Acadia. He swayed on his feet. Then Kaya saw it, the blood blossoming across his chest from the energy blast. Ellio fell to his knees, hands clutching his chest. Kaya could hear the blood gurgling in his lungs as he took a breath.

"Ellio!" Kaya screamed. She leaped toward him and caught him as he slumped to the floor. In a second Arnion was by her side, pressing his hands onto Ellio's chest. Acadia stood behind them. Tears poured down her face.

"Shields, Kaya!" Arnion shouted. "I can't save him if you don't shield us."

Kaya rocked back and forth, shaking her head. Arnion was pouring his spiritual energy into keeping Ellio's heart beating.

"Focus, Kaya!" Arnion's shout sounded like it was underwater.

Kaya stared at him dumbly. *Did he want her to do something?* She looked at Ellio. His eyes were closed, and his face was deathly pale. She watched his chest rise and fall until it stopped.

Darkness swallowed Kaya. Rage and fear and loss howled in her mind.

Arnion looked at her with wide eyes. He reached toward her just as she lost control.

Chapter 39

ACADIA TREMBLED AS DARK flames licked up Kaya's arms and exploded outward in a ball of fire. If not for Arnion's shielding, she and Ellio would have been consumed as well. The force of Kaya's blast smashed soldiers into the wall, where they fell in smoldering heaps of charred ash.

Even Espina had been consumed.

Kaya fell to her knees beside Arnion and Ellio, rocking back and forth.

Ellio cracked his eyes open. Blood trickled from his mouth. "Kaya?" he rasped.

Kaya gasped. She snatched his hand and pressed it to her cheek. "I thought you were . . ."

Arnion exhaled. "I was able to stop some of the internal bleeding, but he needs immediate attention. That strike will kill him if left untreated. We need to get him to the Melican hospital now."

Relief swept over Acadia. Ellio was alive. Then a wave of shame crashed over her, and she nearly stumbled to her knees.

King Atta.

King Yarma.

Dragul.

All dead because of her.

She looked at Ellio's pale face. Purple bruising rimmed his eyes, and his head lolled weakly. He knew she wasn't a traitor. He'd believed her.

That's why he'd jumped in front of her, saving her life. How many more people were going to die because of her stupidity? She had been so desperate to be accepted in Eiren, that she couldn't see Espina for what she was.

I hurt everyone around me.

Nausea roiled in Acadia's stomach. Darkness flickered at the edges of her vision.

Breathe!

She needed to breathe!

If Acadia didn't get outside now, she would suffocate.

She took one step back and then another.

"Acadia." Arnion flicked his gaze up to hers. Shame sheared through her at the anguish she saw there, as if she were ripping his heart from his chest. His eyes pleaded with her to stay.

"I'm sorry." Acadia turned and ran.

Chapter 40

AGONY TORE THROUGH ARNION as Acadia fled. He reached out to her, and Ellio spasmed beneath his hand, spitting blood. Ripping his focus off his chimad and forcing his concentration on the dying young man beneath him took every ounce of strength he had. Even then, his actions were mechanical as he pressed both hands back on Ellio's chest, directing his spirit to heal.

Had Acadia really betrayed them all? He would never get the chance to ask her. The expression on her face had told him she wasn't coming back.

Arnion's heart ached, and his eyes burned. He took a shuddering breath. Ellio let out a rattling cough beneath him. Arnion forced his grief to the back of his mind. He could process it later. Right now, Ellio needed all his attention. Using his spirit sight, Arnion assessed the wound. The photon blast had thankfully missed Ellio's heart, but it had ruptured a lung and caused serious internal bleeding. Without the constant flow of Arnion's spirit, Ellio would be dead in minutes.

Arnion poured his spirit into Ellio's body, white sparks infusing life and healing as they flowed into him. His spirit focused on the tear in Ellio's chest, knitting together the punctured lung. Ellio was still losing blood. The young man's face took on a bluish cast as Arnion searched with his spirit, sealing the torn blood vessels within his chest. It took all his concentration to stabilize him.

After a tense moment of touch and go, Ellio's body took to the healing. The internal bleeding stopped, and the bluish tinge left his skin. Arnion sat back, exhausted.

It hit him how completely their mission had failed. Both kings were dead. Acadia had left him. Lucien had played them at every turn and now had an army of berserkers and something even more twisted—people who were able to absorb trividium and gain supernatural power from it.

Arnion shivered, confidence withering inside him. There would be no peace. Elorah was about to be consumed by war. A wave of despair crashed over him, stealing his breath. He allowed himself to feel the pain of each wound, each betrayal for a moment, but then he cut it off. There was still good he could do. There was still hope. Ellio was alive and needed his help.

Kaya crouched beside him, motionless. Sweat dripped from her face. Her eyes were fixed on Ellio's chest with a feverish intensity, but she didn't say a word.

"Kaya." Arnion spoke softly, but she still flinched. "I've stabilized his condition, but we need to get him to Melica. Now."

Kaya stared at Arnion blankly. She knew the prince was talking to her, but her mind couldn't process the words.

Arnion grabbed her shoulder and shook it. "Do you understand?"

Kaya rocked back on her heels. The movement caused Ellio to stir. He opened his eyes and smiled up at her.

"Kaya."

She bent over him, tears dripping down her cheeks. "Idiot!" she whispered hoarsely. "Why would you do that? Why would you risk your life for her?"

"I didn't . . . do it . . . for her." Ellio's words came in little gasps and wheezes. "I did it . . . for you."

"What?" Kaya's voice trembled.

"I knew . . . you'd never . . . be able to . . . forgive yourself . . . if you let her die."

Kaya moaned and pressed her forehead against his. Ellio knew her better than she knew herself. His selfless act of love had almost killed him. "Don't you dare die," she whispered.

Dragul had known her too. Better than she could have imagined. He knew her rage. Her uncontrollable anger at having lost her parents. He felt the same at losing his daughter. But he'd been trying to protect her from the darkness. Trying to teach her self-control before she lashed out and hurt someone.

Someone like Ellio.

Ellio let out a pained breath. "Wouldn't dream of it." His hand twitched. Arnion grasped it, and Kaya took hold of it as well and squeezed.

"Ellio." Kaya wanted to scream until her vocal cords crumbled to dust. She'd done the one thing she swore she'd never do. Not only had she failed to protect Ellio, she'd been blinded by rage and lost control. She'd tried to kill Acadia, almost killing Ellio in the process.

For the first time in her life, Kaya realized she wasn't worthy. Dragul had been right about everything. And Ellio had paid the price for her folly.

Ellio's eyes rolled, and his head slumped to the side.

Panic stabbed Kaya's heart. "Ellio!"

Arnion stopped her from shaking him. "He's just unconscious. He's lost a lot of blood. We need to get him to the Melican hospital for a transfusion. Slide his right arm over your shoulder. I'll take his left and we'll carry him."

Chapter 41

ACADIA DIDN'T KNOW HOW far she ran. Sweat dripped down her back. Her breath sawed through her chest in ragged gasps. She pushed off against the tunnel walls with a dirt-encrusted hand.

Was Ellio all right?

If he hadn't stepped in front of me, I'd be dead. A chill trickled down her spine. *Kaya probably wants to kill me.* Her face had been murderous.

Acadia didn't want to think about the fourth member of their group. The one whom she'd most deeply betrayed.

The one who had looked at her like she'd cracked open his ribcage and torn out his heart. Acadia remembered Arnion's silent scream when Lucien had impaled him with a spear. He'd given her the same look. Only this time it was her thrusting the blade. Destroying him.

Arnion.

No, she couldn't think his name. She couldn't think about the love she'd just lost.

Survive. That was all she needed to focus on now.

Acadia burst out of the tunnels and into a familiar clearing bordered by woods. It was where they had secured their vehicles. There were no guards. Espina's berserkers must have taken care of that. The airships sat deserted.

Acadia wandered between them, her feet guiding her to the halcyon without conscious thought. She pressed her hand against the metallic orange hull. She had watched Arnion fly it multiple times and knew how to activate the autopiloting system. But could she really steal the halcyon from him? Bile surged up her throat.

He already hates me. What difference would it make?

Acadia glanced around at the unfamiliar Avathysian aircraft. She had no idea how to operate any of them. The halcyon was the only vehicle she could hope to fly. Self-loathing roiled in her gut. How could she even consider it? With Ellio injured, Arnion and Kaya would need to get help as quickly as possible.

But Arnion could fly one of these Avathysian ships. And they were close to Melica. Ellio would get the help he needed. Acadia was sure of it.

Self-loathing scorched her lungs and she took a ragged breath. The urge to flee overwhelmed everything else. She pressed her hand against the halcyon's hatch and stumbled inside. At the sight of the familiar bucket seats in the cockpit, she fell to her knees, gagging. She never knew a person could hate themselves so much.

And yet, she wanted to survive. She needed to get away before Kaya and Arnion emerged from the tunnels and stopped her.

Acadia heaved herself into the pilot's seat. Mimicking Arnion's motions, she was able to activate the startup sequence. The halcyon's onboard AI greeted her cheerfully. Hollowness swallowed Acadia as she pressed the buttons with numb fingers.

The halcyon purred to life. When the AI asked her for a destination, Acadia jabbed her finger to a random point on the map. She didn't care where she went, as long as it was far from here. The light harness snapped around her, securing her in place with bands of yellow webbing. There was a rumble beneath her as the thrusters activated, and then she was airborne.

Land flickered below her, and Acadia saw smoke and fire spreading across Kifu. Her mouth went dry, hopelessness sinking into her limbs. Of course, Lucien wouldn't send all his trividium soldiers to attack the kings. Just a few berserkers would be enough to take out the small number at the abandoned fort.

By now, Lucien had thousands of berserker soldiers. And he was using them to attack Kifu. With King Yarma dead, Kifu would be in a leadership crisis. It was the perfect opportunity for Lucien to strike.

Despair cinched around her neck like a noose.

Lucien had used her. He knew exactly where they'd be and how many of them there were. All because of her and that stupid data crystal. Acadia dug her fingernails into her arm. The data crystal was deeply embedded. She'd need a knife to cut it out.

Acadia unstrapped the light harness and pulled out the ship's emergency kit. Rooting around in the box, she found gauze and a sterile scalpel. Lucien was undoubtedly still tracking her movements. Maybe there was a chance she'd led him away from Arnion and Kaya's location in her reckless flight. But the crystal needed to come out. She was through being Lucien's pawn.

Acadia steeled herself and drew the scalpel across her skin. Burning pain seared her nerves, but she gripped the blade tighter and used the edge to pry at the chip. Agony exploded behind her eyes, and she blinked back tears. Little by little, the chip came loose until it fell to the floor with a clatter. Acadia flopped back in the chair. Her shirt stuck to her back with perspiration. Weakly, she grabbed the roll of gauze and twined it around the bloody gash in her arm. Then she ground the data chip to pieces under her heel.

Her arm throbbed. A migraine pounded behind her eyes.

Acadia tried to lean back in the chair and sleep, but she couldn't stop replaying the scene in the tunnels. The look of betrayal on Ellio's face, the hatred on Kaya's, the sorrow and disappointment in Arnion's eyes.

How long before her prince's love turned to disgust? She had betrayed him. Caused the death of Dragul. Worked as a spy for Lucien. And was directly responsible for the death of two kings and the failure of Arnion's peacekeeping mission.

Arnion must despise her.

How could he not? She despised herself.

Guilt slipped between Acadia's ribs and twisted like a knife in her heart. She clutched her side, gasping in pain.

She had an absurd desire to sit in Petra's kitchen, share a pot of tea, and ask the older woman for advice.

How can I be missing Eiren? They hated me before, and now that I've betrayed Arnion, I will never be welcomed back.

All the time Acadia had lived in Eiren, she'd felt out of place. But now she'd screwed up so royally that she would never be allowed back, she missed it. Almost unbearably so.

Arnion.

She almost reached out to him with her spirit but quickly crushed the thought, smothering the pathetic spark of hope that lighted in her chest. They would never see each other again. She'd destroyed any chance she'd ever had with the Eirenian prince. Regret shredded her to pieces. Tears streamed down her cheeks, and she covered her face with her hands.

Arnion had saved her life; he'd paid her debt with his life blood. And how had she repaid him? By stabbing him in the back, betraying him and his kingdom, and then fleeing. Leaving him to a broken heart.

Don't be delusional. He's not brokenhearted; he's angry. If he ever sees you again, he'll curse you to your face.

Acadia slid out of the bucket seat onto her hands and knees on the cold metal floor. Nothing mattered any more. What was the point in running from Lucien and his horde? She had nothing left. She curled into a fetal position, sobs wracking her body.

Chapter 42

ON PURE ADRENALINE, ARNION and Kaya carried Ellio's unconscious body through the tunnels. Arnion realized it was a mercy the young man had passed out. If he'd been awake, he would have been in agony.

They stepped out of the tunnel into a clearing, and Arnion exhaled slowly. He scanned the area, hoping to see Acadia, hoping she had turned back. But she was gone. Arnion struggled to keep his disappointment from showing, forcing his attention on Kaya and Ellio. They needed him. When he realized where they were, a slight hope flared within him.

The airships were here. They could get Ellio to safety.

Kaya let out a bitter laugh. "She stole the halcyon. That filthy traitor." Her nostrils flared.

Arnion fought back the despair that choked his throat. "It doesn't matter," he said in a rough voice. He nodded toward King Atta's gray ship. "I can fly that. Help me get Ellio aboard."

They flew to Melica in silence. With King Atta's airship, Arnion could land directly on the hospital's roof. As soon as the ship touched down, a trio of med techs rushed out.

"We've got one man critically injured. He took a photon blast to the chest," Arnion said woodenly. Weariness from the day's horrors was starting to overwhelm him. The hospital staff wheeled Ellio in and took him straight to emergency surgery. Arnion and Kaya sat silently in two blue plastic chairs in the hallway, their clothes and skin still splattered in blood.

Kaya wanted to scream. She wanted to spew insults about Acadia until she had no breath left in her lungs. But one look at the prince's heart-broken expression and the words shriveled on her tongue. She swallowed back the bitterness.

She couldn't worry about that traitor right now. Ellio needed all her focus. Flecks of his blood, like rust, had dried in the creases of her knuckles and underneath her fingernails. He had lost so much blood. Without Arnion's advanced spirit techniques, Ellio would have died in the tunnels.

Kaya looked at the crown prince. His chest heaved with every breath. Clearly, he'd exhausted himself saving Ellio.

Their team was in shambles. Acadia had betrayed them. Dragul had given his life. Ellio had nearly died. Arnion was spiritually exhausted and heartbroken. Whatever emotions Kaya felt about Acadia, it must be much worse for the prince.

Kaya remembered Dragul's words: "Eirenians mate for life."

If Acadia rejected Arnion's proposal, did that mean he'd be alone? Forever? What about the royal line? It was too much to think about.

A half hour later, the surgeon came to tell them the operation had been a success. The damage to Ellio's lung was minimal but he had suffered severe blood loss and shock. He had required ten pints of blood and plasma via transfusion, but he was expected to make a full recovery. A med tech guided them to the room where Ellio was sleeping. When Kaya saw the peaceful expression on Ellio's face and the way his chest rose and fell, her knees gave out. She collapsed on the floor beside the bed, her body shaking.

The sound of Ellio's breathing filled her with relief. He was alive. He was going to recover. She'd never forgive herself for letting him get hurt. Ellio was completely innocent. She'd wanted to hurt Acadia, but she'd lost control of her shield, letting her anger consume her. Ellio had paid the price.

Kaya wished she could trade places with him. Why had she hurt the one person she'd sworn to always protect? How could she? She was a monster.

As if sensing her thoughts, Arnion knelt beside her and placed a hand on her shoulder. "Kaya, are you all right?"

She tensed as if he'd struck her. "You're joking, right? Of course, I'm not! I nearly killed the person who—" She choked back a sob, slapping a hand over her mouth. Tears blurred her vision, and she blinked, desperately trying not to lose it.

Too late.

The tears came and Arnion rubbed her back.

"Kaya, he's going to be okay. I'm not going to let anything happen to Ellio."

"How can I even look at him?" Kaya whispered. "Look at what I've done. Dragul was right, about everything. I can't control myself. I can't control my spirit, and I nearly killed him."

Arnion pulled her to him in a tight hug. "It's going to be okay."

"I don't think so." Kaya's voice was small and afraid. "I don't think anything's going to be okay ever again. Even if Ellio wakes up, even if he's fine, he's going to hate me. I'm a monster. I'm a murderer."

"What are you talking about?"

Kaya curled her fingers around the metal frame of the hospital bed. "For a moment, in the tunnels, when my shield was failing . . . I *wanted* Acadia to get hit. I think my spirit sensed that. A hole opened up right in front of her. And then Ellio . . . he must have known. He knows me so well." Kaya sniffed and wiped her nose on her sleeve. "He knew I wanted her to die, and he stepped in front of her. Ellio is so good. Once he recovers and realizes what I did, he's going to hate me."

"Don't be ridiculous," Arnion said. "Ellio loves you."

"Dragul was right." Kaya rocked back and forth. "I wasn't ready. I'm just a stupid kid." She pulled away, staring at the beige hospital blanket tucked around Ellio's legs. "This is all my fault."

Arnion patted her head. "I think he had already forgiven you the moment you did it."

Kaya bit her lip to keep herself from crying. Arnion's words rang of truth. It was unbelievable, but she thought he was right. Ellio hadn't seemed angry with her. He'd been protecting her, from herself. That's what he'd said, right?

Ellio, you idiot! How could you? Why do you throw yourself in harm's way for other people, over and over again!

When he recovered, she was going to have a serious conversation with him about valuing his life more.

When he recovered.

Kaya pressed a fist to her mouth. *When. Not if.*

Ellio would recover, and then she would kick his butt for putting himself in danger.

Zeliaris burst into the hospital room, and Kaya stared at her in shock. Someone must have informed her of their arrival in the hospital. Zeliaris looked at Arnion and then Kaya. Her bottom lip trembled. "Where is my father?"

Kaya closed her eyes.

They would have to tell her about the trap. About what happened to her father and the negotiating party. Zeliaris was an orphan now, just like her.

"Where's Acadia?" Zeliaris asked.

Arnion flinched. Sorrow pierced his chest like a blade thrust between his ribs.

Zeliaris looked between him and Kaya wringing her hands. "What happened out there? You said my father was going with you to a peace talk. Where is he?"

Arnion's throat constricted. Grief weighed on him, making his limbs heavy, but he forced himself to his feet. "Zeliaris, let's step outside."

The princess's lips trembled. Her shoulders wilted, her eyes wide and fearful. "It's not . . . it can't be . . ." Gone was the haughty princess act. Her demeanor crumbled and she clutched Arnion's arm like a fearful child. "How?"

Arnion's heart ached for her. "It was an ambush. Lucien's corrupted soldiers were waiting for us."

The princess let out an anguished cry, pressing her hands to her lips. "But how could they have known? The location was supposed to be a secret."

Arnion's jaw worked for a moment before he had the strength to speak the words. "We were betrayed," he said softly.

Zeliaris whimpered and slid to the floor, her dress crumpling around her.

Sorrow flooded Arnion, crushing him like a lead weight. Stiffly, he crouched beside the Avathysian princess and put a hand on her shoulder. "There will be a time for you to grieve, but your kingdom needs you now," he said.

She sniffled and looked at him with tear-stained cheeks. "What?"

"Lucien will use this situation to his advantage. With King Atta out of the way, he will surely make an attack by nightfall."

"Nightfall?" Zeliaris blinked rapidly. "But that's only two hours away."

"Gather your guards. Rally your advisors. Make ready for war." Arnion helped Zeliaris to her feet. "I must contact Eiren." He reached for the door handle.

Zeliaris laid a trembling hand across his. "Is my father truly dead?"

"I'm sorry." Arnion's voice was gentle. "He's gone."

Zeliaris swayed on her feet. "This can't be happening. It must be a dream." She slapped her face with her palms.

Arnion clasped her hands and drew them down. "You can't fall apart. If you don't act, all of Avathys could be lost."

His words seemed to break through the cloud of despair surrounding her. She straightened her shoulders. "You're right. I'll summon the council and tell them what we know. We'll find a way to rebuff Lucien's attack."

"Good." Arnion exhaled a sharp breath. "We'll get through this together."

Zeliaris pushed open the door and turned back. "Arnion." She twisted her fingers together. "I'm so sorry about Ellio. I hope . . . I hope he's all right."

Arnion ground the heel of his hand against his eye, as if he could rub away the exhaustion building inside him. "He will be." He tilted his head toward the door. "Go swiftly. Time is of the essence."

Zeliaris nodded and dashed off.

Chapter 43

A VOICE WAS SHOUTING inside her mind. <*Acadia! Wake up.*>

Acadia stirred, groggy. Hair stuck to the side of her face, dried mucus crusted her nostrils, and her skin was sticky with dried tears. She sat up and rubbed her neck. Her body ached from lying on the halcyon's metal floor. Then it all came tumbling back. The secret meeting. The murders. Espina's betrayal. She curled her arms around herself.

<*Acadia, you must move now,*> Ruah's voice trilled in warning.

<Ruah? Is that you?> Acadia pressed her hands over her ears as if she could block out his voice. <Go away. Leave me alone.>

<*Get up now.*> Ruah's voice wavered. <*Before it's too late.*>

Acadia scoffed. <It's already too late. I've betrayed everyone.>

Ruah's voice hummed in her mind. <*It's not too late to save your family.*>

Acadia flinched. When thinking of family, her first thought was of Arnion's face. She remembered sitting around the table eating dumplings with Arnion, Ellio, Kaya, and Dragul. <Trust me, Ruah. My family never want to see me again.>

<*Your family in Cobasso. You can warn them. Save them from Lucien's corrupted.*>

Guilt settled like a stone in her stomach. Ruah was talking about her *biological* family. Acadia hadn't even considered them. *Was there no end to the number of people she would fail today?*

<*Get up, Acadia. If you stay here, you'll be caught.*>

A deep instinctual desire to survive drove Acadia to her feet. She almost laughed at herself. *What do I have to live for?* But the thought of Ma, Talon, and Dren kept her standing. She had seen how the berserkers tore through people. No one deserved to die like that.

It would never make up for the damage she'd done, but maybe at least she could see her family spared from Lucien's horrors. She stepped over the control panel and keyed up Cobasso. Her random flight path had taken her in the right direction. The halcyon had landed at the foot of the Meyhorn Mountains. Cobasso wasn't far. The navigation system beeped, calculating the optimum route. Acadia switched on stealth-mode. With Lucien and his soldiers tearing through Kifu, she needed to travel undetected.

Ruah guided Acadia, helping her avoid the berserker patrols as she flew to Cobasso. Along the way, he spoke to her more and more.

<*Ellio lives. Arnion and Kaya have brought him safely to Melica.*>

<How can you possibly know that?> Acadia shot back.

<*I am Spirit. I know,*> Ruah answered.

Acadia frowned. <What do you mean you're a spirit? Like a ghost?>

<*No.*> She felt Ruah chuckle inside her mind. <*Humans have a spirit wrapped in mortal flesh. I am Spirit entirely. Not bound by location or time.*>

<This knowledge would have been convenient earlier,> Acadia grumbled.

<*Would you have listened?*>

Her jaw fell open. She snapped it shut with a click. He had her there. Ruah had been trying to talk to her for ages and only now was she starting to listen. He spoke to her of the time before humans inhabited Elorah and warned that a great evil was coming to the planet. Something that made Lucien look like a child.

Before she knew it, the halcyon's onboard AI was landing on the outskirts of Cobasso. Acadia leaped from the hatch, sprinted to her family's home, and pounded on the door.

During the flight, Acadia had formed a plan. She would lead her family to Ysra Mountain Pass. It was too narrow for large forces to pass through and should buy them a little time. From there, Acadia and her family could flee to Dardak. It was a small island nation, isolated from the rest of Elorah. Acadia hoped it would be too insignificant for Lucien to trifle with.

The only problem was that she would have to ditch the halcyon. The Dardaki were known for being militaristic and suspicious of outsiders. They were also not allied with Eiren. If Acadia tried to fly an Eirenian craft into their airspace, there was a good risk she'd be shot down. They'd have to find a boat to sail across the Shoals. Acadia was no longer welcome in Eiren, Avathys, or Kifu, but she could save her family's life today if she could convince them to evacuate.

Acadia's mother and brothers were shocked by her arrival, and even more so by the terrible news she bore. They had heard rumors but nothing verified, other than the oily black smoke that rose in the distance.

"We have to hurry!" Acadia urged them. "Take only what you absolutely need. There's no time. Lucien is coming. We need to evacuate to Dardak."

At first, her mother and brothers protested loudly, but Kep stopped them. He studied her expression intently for a moment before clearing his throat. "Do what she says." His voice was rough.

There were no more arguments.

Acadia helped her family pack emergency bags with enough food and clothing to last a few days and prodded them toward the halcyon. The flight to Ysra Pass was brief and riddled with tension. When the halcyon landed, Acadia's heart leaped in her throat.

The docks were jammed with a sea of humanity. It would take a miracle for them to make it onto a boat. Kep straightened his shoulders and patted Ma on the arm. "I'll be back soon," he whispered.

Acadia watched him saunter through the crowd, projecting confidence. After a few moments of animated conversation with the ferryman, he walked back. "I was able to book us passage on the next one, but we have to board immediately."

Acadia's shoulders sagged in relief. *Thank goodness for Kep!* She followed her family to the queue of passengers waiting to board, when Ruah's voice pressed upon her spirit again.

<Arnion is in danger.>

<What are you talking about? You told me he made it safely to Melica.>

<There will be an assassination.>

<Impossible! Arnion's too powerful. He came back from the dead. There's no way . . .>

<His spirit is troubled. He does not hear me. He does not see . . .>

Acadia swallowed. So far, everything Ruah had told her had been the truth. He'd helped her stop wallowing in self-pity enough to evacuate her family and guided her safely around the berserker patrols. What if he was right?

Arnion was probably distracted right now. Enemies were closing in, and he was broken by betrayal. This would be the perfect time for Lucien to strike.

"Acadia, let's go!" Talon called. "The line is moving. We have to board now."

She smiled at her younger brother. "I love you, Talon." She ruffled his hair before crushing him against her in a hug. "But I can't go with you." She turned and looked in the direction of Melica. Arnion would have gone to the Melican hospital. It was Ellio's only chance; she was sure of it. "I have to rescue my chimad."

Even if Arnion never wanted to see her again, even if he threw her out on the street, Acadia would scream from the gutter so loudly that he would have to hear her warning. She wouldn't let Lucien hurt him again, even if it cost her everything.

Chapter 44

ACADIA PREPPED THE HALCYON for one last flight. She didn't know what Arnion would do when he saw her again. It wouldn't surprise her if he had her clapped in irons and thrown in prison. As long as she could warn him first, it didn't matter. She had never flown so fast. The halcyon soared through the air, the ground streaking below in a blur. Her heart was in her throat when the aircraft touched down outside Melica's hospital. She ran into the lobby, desperately searching for the front desk.

Then, Acadia heard a sound that awakened her heart and made her blood sing along her veins. Arnion's voice. His back was to her as he walked away down the hall.

He's all right. I made it in time.

Acadia's legs wobbled. She stumbled and caught herself against the wall. Arnion turned the corner, and Acadia caught a glimpse of his troubled profile as he moved out of sight.

He hadn't seen her.

Acadia's pulse hammered in her throat. She called out his name.

Rough hands seized her from behind, clamping over her mouth and jerking her backwards. Her attacker dragged her out through the hospital doors and around the corner into the hospital vehicle bay.

Acadia clawed at the arms restraining her, chest heaving. The stench of rotting flesh flooded her senses. She gagged.

Harsh laughter erupted from behind her. "I hoped we'd meet again, Acadia," a raspy voice whispered in her ear. The arms gripping Acadia spun her around and shoved her backwards.

Acadia stumbled, eyes widening as she caught sight of her attacker. The woman who stood before her was eerily familiar. Matted red hair clung to her scalp in clumps. Black veins bulged from under skin so pale, it was almost translucent. Her laughing gray eyes were fixed on Acadia's face, red lips curved in a sneer.

It was a face that haunted Acadia's dreams.

"Delilah?" Acadia asked.

"The one and only." Delilah flipped her hair over her shoulder. She sauntered toward Acadia. Her bare feet left inky black footprints along the concrete floor. She put a hand on her hip and clicked her tongue. "What are you doing here, Acadia? Isn't it enough that you've destroyed everyone's lives? I'm impressed you have the nerve to show your face." She smirked and black sludge dripped from her lips.

Acadia recoiled.

Delilah looked at her nails. They were inhumanly long, red, and sharp. Like claws. "I know this appearance takes some getting used to. Lucien has made me new. You can't imagine the power he has, Acadia. Power that makes your pathetic little spirit abilities look like parlor tricks." She curled her hand into a fist. "Eiren will fall. Your prince is going to die and, this time, stay dead." With each word, she took a step toward Acadia, dragging her nails along the wall. "Lucien thought you'd come in some pathetic attempt at heroism. He sent me to make you an offer. Join the winning side."

Acadia's mouth fell open. "You must be joking!" She shuddered.

Delilah tapped her nails along her forearm. "It's no joke. Lucien is pleased with the work you've done. Opening up a way to assassinate the monarchs of Avathys and Kifu was no small feat."

A metallic taste pooled on Acadia's tongue. She shoved a knuckle into her mouth, trying to force down her nausea. "That was an accident."

Delilah waved her words away as if they meant nothing. "It's shown Lucien that you still have some value." She gave Acadia a dismissive look. "Not that I see it." Delilah shrugged. "But it's not my call. He sent me here to offer you one final invitation. Join us."

Acadia stepped back. Her hands balled into fists. "I refuse."

Delilah smiled. Large canines poked from beneath her upper lip. "I was hoping you'd say that." She rolled her neck with a sickening crack. "In that case, I'm to take you by force and, once you're subdued, I'll assassinate that pathetic Eirenian prince."

"Assassinate! Are you crazy? It doesn't matter what Lucien's told you; you're no match for Arnion!"

"Really? I think I might surprise you." Delilah slinked toward her, and her features began to melt and blur. Acadia blinked and rubbed her eyes. Delilah's appearance was transforming. Her skin smoothed as the dark veins faded away. Her red hair twisted and curled, shrinking on her head until it was short and dark. Freckles blossomed across her cheeks. She closed her eyes, and when she opened them again, they were a brilliant sapphire blue.

Acadia gaped at a reflection of herself. Delilah had copied her physical appearance right down to the tiny scar barely visible on her chin. A cold sweat broke out across her skin. "I-it's a trick," she choked out. "Arnion will see through it."

"It's no trick." Delilah stepped forward and grabbed her arm with inhuman strength. Acadia gasped. If Delilah squeezed any harder, it would shatter bone. "Look. See. Feel." She forced Acadia's hand to stroke her short dark hair down to her silken cheek. There was no trace of the rotting skin or matted hair of Delilah's true form. Even the putrid smell was gone, replaced by a light floral scent. "This is the power Lucien has given me. The power of trividium."

Acadia's strength faltered. Her limbs gave out. If Delilah hadn't been holding her arm so tightly, she would have collapsed. "H-how are you . . ."

Delilah raised her chin in triumph. A malicious grin split her mouth. Acadia was unnerved to see such a twisted expression on her own face. "I've always been good at hiding who I am. At showing other people what they wanted to see. Trividium just enhanced that. I've heard you used to be a Jewel yourself." Delilah sneered. She grabbed Acadia's chin and yanked it to the side, considering her. "Not that I can see why with *this* body."

Acadia wanted to gag. Adrenaline sparked through her veins and every fiber of her being screamed to flee. Even her spirit shivered within her. A reaction, she realized, to being in the proximity of a trividium-corrupted being.

Delilah shook her. "Now do you understand the power Lucien has?"

"I see nothing but a cheap copy." Acadia made her voice cold and disdainful. "And that's all Arnion will see. I'd be surprised if he doesn't kill you outright. I didn't exactly endear myself to him and his team before I left."

Delilah patted her cheek. "Oh, he'll take me back, all right. He and Kaya have been looking for you diligently in between checking up on their sweet little mechanic."

Ellio!

Did that mean he was all right?

The last time she'd seen him, there was so much blood that Acadia had feared the worst. Relief spread through her at Delilah's words. Maybe Ellio was okay after all.

Delilah scowled, still wearing Acadia's face. Black ooze dripped from her lips. "I'm losing my patience. This is your last chance. Join us."

"Never." Acadia wrenched her arm out of Delilah's grip. She readied her spirit. It leaped to her call, forming a protective shield around her. "I'll never join you."

Delilah laughed, and Acadia's form dropped from her body like a serpent shedding its skin. She tapped the golden spirit shield surrounding Acadia with a long fingernail. Energy sizzled through the air, as Acadia's shield rebuffed her. "All right. Let's see if your precious Eirenian prince has taught you anything worthwhile." Her yellow eyes flashed, taunting.

Acadia drew on her spirit, coaxing it forward into arrows of blue-white light. They crackled through the air and shot toward Delilah. Lucien's acolyte howled with laughter, batting them away with her bare hands.

"Is that the best you can do?" Delilah scoffed. A dark-purple aura bled down her shoulders and arms. She crouched and extended her hands. Whips of energy, like thorny purple vines, unfurled from her fingers and lashed across the floor.

Acadia leaped backward just as the vines snapped toward her. She held up her arms, bracing her spirit shield as the whips of energy beat against it.

Delilah laughed. "You're going to have to do better than that."

Acadia reached for her flux sword but found only empty space. *Dral!* Her sword was sitting in the halcyon's weapon locker. She hadn't brought it to the hospital because she wasn't planning to fight. If Arnion wanted to arrest her, she had planned to surrender peacefully.

Curse Lucien. He anticipated my every move. I'm playing right into his hands.

Doubt wavered through Acadia's spirit. Her shield shivered.

Delilah flung herself at Acadia. Light and dark spirit energy crashed together. Purple and blue sparks exploded outward, releasing a shrieking gust of wind. Energy skittered over Acadia's skin. The hair on the back of her neck stood up.

Acadia swallowed. Delilah was more powerful than she'd imagined. What if trividium could overwhelm Arnion? At the thought of her prince, love flared through her heart. She couldn't let Lucien's plan succeed. She would protect Arnion with her life.

Power surged in Acadia's spirit, bolstered by the intensity of her feelings. Blue-white spirit flames engulfed her. Acadia seized Delilah's forearm. Her spirit blazed outward, scorching corrupted skin.

Delilah screeched. She clawed at Acadia's arm, her red nails gouging into the sleeve of her jacket.

Acadia lashed out with her other arm, slamming Delilah's chin in an open-palm strike. The corrupted woman staggering backward.

Delilah wiped her mouth with the back of her hand. "So, you can fight after all." She raised her hands over her head. A series of cracks—like bones breaking—split the air. Four black, razor-like limbs extended from Delilah's back.

Acadia forced herself to remain calm. She couldn't be defeated here, or Delilah would use her twisted power to lure Arnion to his death. She rallied her spirit, fists blazing with blue flame.

Delilah launched forward, arachnid limbs snapping through the air like blades.

Enhanced by her spirit, Acadia dodged them with supernatural speed. She darted forward, under Delilah's guard. The redhead's eyes widened, and Acadia slammed a fist into her chest, knocking her backward into the cement wall.

Acadia panted. An exultant flush heated her face. She was winning! A warm trickle dripped down her cheek. She brushed it with her fingertips. Blood.

Delilah drew her fingernail across her mouth, smearing blood on her lips. "Too bad, Acadia."

Did she scratch me as I was leaning forward for the strike?

The world spun and Acadia staggered backward. Why was she dizzy?

"Honestly, Acadia. I don't know what Lucien sees in you." Delilah let out an exaggerated sigh.

Acadia tried to blink away her blurry vision. Her spirit fizzled, blue flames winking out. "Poison?" Her voice croaked. Acadia's legs gave out, and she crashed to the floor.

Delilah shrugged. "I never said I'd fight fair." She loomed over Acadia. There was a ripple of energy. Her extra appendages folded up into her back, and once more she adopted Acadia's appearance.

Acadia's blood ran cold. She'd failed, and Arnion's life was at stake. Self-loathing rose in the back of her throat.

Delilah mirrored Acadia's look of horror before smirking and primping her hair. "What do you think your prince will do when he sees me? Do you think he'll cry?" Her mocking words thudded like daggers in Acadia's heart. "Maybe he'll sweep me up in a passionate embrace." Delilah tapped her lips, smirking. "Maybe he'll try to kiss me."

Acadia struggled to rise, but her limbs wouldn't respond. She flopped onto her side, helpless.

Delilah laughed, a harsh cackling sound. "One thing's for sure. He certainly won't be expecting my knife in his back." She leaned down and patted Acadia's cheek. "Don't worry. This time, I'll make sure he stays dead. I'll carve his heart clean out of his chest if I have to."

"No!" Acadia latched onto Delilah's ankle in a desperate attempt to trip her.

Delilah lashed out with her foot, kicking Acadia in the ribs. "You fool. There's nothing you can do to stop me. I am beyond you now." She snapped her fingers, and two men appeared in the doorway. "Take her to the absorption chamber. Let's see how beautiful she looks once her veins are pumped full of trividium."

"Let go of me!" Acadia screamed. "Somebody help!"

Delilah grabbed a fistful of Acadia's hair and yanked her head back. "Scream all you want. No one is coming to save you. And you've only yourself to blame."

Acadia's heart faltered. Delilah was right. She had destroyed every friendship, everything good in her life through her own actions. Despair coiled around her throat, stealing her breath. Delilah released her hold and Acadia's head slumped forward. Tears blurred her vision as Lucien's men dragged her away.

Chapter 45

"YOU EXPECT US TO believe the word of Prince Arnion? He's an outsider."

"He probably slaughtered the king himself and now he's trying to cast blame on Lucien."

The members of the Avathysian council sat around the table, with Zeliaris on the throne instead of her father.

"Are you out of your minds?" Zeliaris raised her voice above the clamoring ministers. "Arnion would never do that. Eiren would never betray Avathys."

"Eiren has grown weak."

"They probably murdered our king and the king of Kifu to seize our lands!"

The council members were getting whipped into a frenzy. Froth formed on their lips as they shouted.

"This is insane!" Zeliaris clapped her hands, desperate to regain control of the meeting. "Arnion is our ally. Eiren has always been our ally. Lucien is the real threat. Him and his murderous army. They're headed for us right now, while we're vulnerable. We need to prepare our defenses."

"You're a fool, princess, if you believe that. Even your father knew better."

Zeliaris raised a hand to her lips, horrified. "What are you talking about?"

"King Atta worked with Lucien."

"Liar!" Zeliaris shouted. "My father would never . . ."

"How do you think we learned about the ancient land disputes with Kifu? Lucien provided the documents. Lucien taught us the trade routes. And now, you're asking us to turn back from all the gifts he's handed us. Those Kifan dogs don't deserve the land. They're capable of nothing more than hard labor. People like that need a firm hand to lead them. An Avathysian hand."

"I call a vote." Zeliaris rose from the throne, eyes blazing. "We must revoke any ties with Lucien and recognize him as a threat to our nation. I vote to shore our defenses against attack and stand united with Eiren. We need to prepare to rebuff Lucien's assault immediately."

The ministers shifted in their seats. No one would meet her gaze.

Helplessness tightened Zeliaris's chest. "None of you will stand with me?" she asked in a small voice.

"Your Majesty!" A guard burst into the throne room. "An army is approaching the city, and the autonomous defense system has failed. It's as if the entire program short-circuited at once. Without it, there's no way our defenses around the perimeter can hold. Our technicians can't understand it. The enemy soldiers are throwing themselves in front of our guns like it's nothing, even as they're being shredded apart. I've never seen anything like it. It's . . . It's . . . insanity."

"We must make a treaty with Lucien!" one of the ministers shouted. "He'll spare us."

Rage boiled under Zeliaris's skin. She clenched her fists. "Are you out of your mind? He killed my father—your king—in cold blood! And now his troops are about to pillage our city! There will be no treaty."

"Your Majesty." The advisor tugged her over to a window where she could look out and see her city burning. "If we don't make a treaty, we have no hope."

"Lucien isn't here for negotiating." Zeliaris was firm. "We have nothing he wants. Nothing except the people. You're just bodies to him. Bodies to inject with trividium so he can control you like slaves."

"But with the power of trividium, we might save Avathys."

Zeliaris shook her head. "Trividium doesn't save. You heard the guard; people under its influence are insane. Anyone who comes under its power will have no love of Avathys in them. No promise Lucien makes is worth the suffering it will bring."

The ministers muttered around the table. Tramak Hadril rose. "Then, we must disagree, Your Highness. Monarchs are a dying breed. Avathys needs competent leaders, not those who haphazardly acquire it through birth alone. You are welcome to abandon this city, but we will not."

"I never said anything about abandoning . . ."

"You may leave with your precious Eirenians, but we, who remain loyal to Avathys, will strike a deal with Lucien to preserve our city."

"No! You can't!" Zeliaris protested.

Hadril signaled to his personal security and had her ejected from the room.

Arnion paced the hospital lobby, waiting for Zeliaris to return. When she appeared in the doorway, he knew her attempts to sway the ministers had failed. "Zeliaris, you did everything you could and still they rejected you. Eirenian transport ships are on the way to help evacuate your citizens."

"But we can't evacuate the whole city!" she pleaded. "There isn't time. There must be something we can do."

"If your ministers are unwilling to act, it's only a matter of time before Melica will be overrun with berserkers. We need to prepare to leave immediately."

"The ministers have stripped my title. They're going to ally themselves with Lucien. They think it will save Avathys." Zeliaris's fingers gripped the sleeve of his shirt. "I'm sorry, Arnion. I tried, but they've chosen Lucien. The ministers have forsaken Eiren . . . and forsaken me."

Arnion shut his eyes. Avathys had fallen. Not by the sword, but by compromise and fake diplomacy. By trying to be friends with Lucien, they would end up being his slaves, as surely as the Kifan nation was being overrun. And with two nations worth of people, Lucien would have plenty of fodder to supply his trividium experiments and conquer the world.

Zeliaris sagged against him. "How can I abandon my city and my people?" she sobbed.

Arnion laid his hands on the princess's shoulders. "We will save as many as we can. Do you have a public address system from here? Can you direct your people to rally at the hospital?"

Zeliaris nodded, tears streaming down her cheeks.

"Good. Send the message. Then meet me upstairs at Ellio's room."

"All right." Zeliaris sniffled and fled down the hall.

Arnion let out a breath and pinched the bridge of his nose. The betrayal of Melica's ministers was a harsh blow, but he couldn't let Zeliaris see how it had shaken him. Zeliaris. Kaya. Ellio. They needed him to maintain his courage if they had any hope of living through this.

"Arnion," a feminine voice said behind him, and his heart stopped. He would know that voice anywhere.

Chapter 46

DELILAH'S FINGERS CURLED AROUND the knife behind her back as she walked up to the prince. He looked at her eagerly, face brightening in hope. She slunk toward him, like a cat toying with its prey.

Foolish prince. His downfall would solidify all of Lucien's plans.

Delilah minced forward, allowing a small broken smile to flicker over her lips.

Arnion's eyes tracked her mouth. He smiled at her, and Delilah crept closer. He was within striking distance. Her hand tightened on the handle of the knife. She took one step closer, muscles taut to deliver the killing blow.

Her hand lashed out, quick as lightning, but Arnion stepped to the side and caught her wrist in an iron grip. "Who are you?" he growled. "And what have you done with Acadia?"

Delilah laughed. She tried to pull her arm free, veins straining against her skin as she forced trividium through her muscles. But the power fizzled out and the prince's grip held firm. That battle with Acadia had drained her more than she thought. Delilah didn't have enough strength left to fight. "Still thinking about your precious little princess?" she taunted. "I'd say Lucien's finishing up his experiment on her right about now." Arnion's grip tightened spirit flames dancing along his hand, and Delilah bit back a hiss.

"Where is she?" he demanded.

"I'm right here, Arni-poo. Can't you recognize your woman?" She rubbed against him.

Arnion shouldered her off, and swapped his grip, restraining her wrists behind her back.

Delilah pouted. "How could you tell I wasn't her?"

Arnion gave her a flat look. "When you're truly in love, you'd never fall for an imitation."

Delilah huffed. "Too bad for you, your gem is shattered. Once Lucien's through with her, there'll be nothing left.

Arnion shook her. "Where is she? Tell me if you value your life."

"Little prince, don't you get it? The Acadia you know is already dead. One way or another."

Fear pierced Arnion's heart with icy talons at the woman's words. "Who are you?" he demanded.

"I'm Delilah." The woman batted her eyelashes.

Delilah was lying. Lucien wouldn't . . . He couldn't . . . But the words rang hollow in Arnion's mind. The Heartless King was capable of unimaginable atrocities. He needed to find Acadia. Fast.

Delilah's lips thinned into a vicious smile. Black oozed from her mouth, and dark veins crawled along her skin as she shed the guise of Arnion's beloved in favor of her true appearance.

Arnion fought back the urge to retch. The stench of tar and burning hair had been covered up by Acadia's skin. Now that Delilah stood before him in all her wicked, trividium-infused glory, the sight and smell made him nauseous.

She seemed to revel in his discomfort, writing against his grip. Arnion marched her over to the guards stationed at the hospital. As they dragged Delilah away, she turned her head and called over her shoulder, "You know no prison here will hold me for long. And even if it could, there's no stopping what's coming. Avathys will fall, just as Kifu has. You can thank Acadia for that."

Arnion couldn't worry about that now. His thoughts were consumed with fear for Acadia, at the mercy of Lucien. Being tortured, injected with trividium. Would she try to absorb its power as Delilah clearly had? Or would she reject it, dying in agony? Arnion didn't want to think about which was worse.

There was no treatment.

There was no cure.

Either the spirit rotted away, or the physical body tore itself apart.

He had to find her. There might be a chance he could reach her in time. And if not . . . Arnion didn't want to think about what would happen then. Living apart from Acadia was painful enough. Thinking about her spirit being torn from this world was unbearable.

But what about the hospital? If he didn't stay to defend it, more innocent people would die. Was the life of his beloved worth more than others?

Arnion's forehead throbbed, and a tight knot twisted in his chest. What was the right answer? He had contacted Eiren. They were sending transport ships and aerial support, but it would take time for them to rally and travel, even at Eirenian speeds. They wouldn't get here in time to save the city.

What should he do?

<*The good shepherd leaves the ninety-nine sheep that are safe to go after the one that's missing.*>

Arnion started. <Who's there?> He cast his spirit around him in a searching net but felt no other presence. <Who said that?>

<*I am Ruah. You do not know me. But I know you.*> The voice echoed in his mind, full of power.

<Ruah?> Arnion frowned. <Who are you?>

<*I am Spirit,*> Ruah answered.

Spirit?

<*You asked what you should do, and so I reminded you. The good shepherd leaves the ninety-nine sheep to go after the one that's missing.*>

Arnion smiled. *So that was it.* He had been so concerned with balancing the needs of his kingdom and his personal relationships, but Acadia was part of Eiren. She was lost, and he had to go after her. Even if she continued to reject him, even if they had no future. He wanted her to know he would wait for her. Always.

<Ruah, can you lead me to her?>

<*Yes,*> Ruah's voice echoed in his mind. <*But you must hurry. She is running out of time.*>

Chapter 47

KAYA LEANED OVER THE rail of the hospital bed and gripped Ellio's hand. He was still sleeping peacefully, but for how long? She tried to summon her spirit, but every time she thought about it, she could picture Ellio's pupils dilating and his mouth opening in surprise before a fountain of blood gushed out of it.

It was her fault. Her lack of self-control had nearly killed Ellio, the kindest, most wonderful man on the planet. The thought of using her spirit nauseated her, but there was no way she'd be able to defend him without it.

A rumble shook the building, and the lights flickered. Ellio stirred, brow furrowing. He let out a small sigh.

"Ellio?" Kaya asked. "Are you awake?"

"Kaya?" His gaze was unfocused for a moment before it fixed on her face. "What's that sound?"

She looked away. "Lucien's trividium warriors are attacking Melica. We're in a hospital. You were shot. You're recovering."

Ellio flipped his hand up, pressing his palm against hers and tightening his fingers around hers. "What do we do?" He looked at her, and Kaya was amazed to see his steady gaze. Full of trust.

She wanted to smash something. Instead, she pulled her hand away. "I need to tell you something."

He tried to sit up and winced. She gently propped pillows behind him for support. "Kaya." He breathed out her name like a caress and rested a calloused hand against her cheek. "I *love* you. There's nothing you can do to change that."

"I almost got you killed! I saw the soldier taking aim at Acadia and I . . . the shield . . . I let it go." Ellio watched her silently. Kaya pounded a fist on the bed. "Don't you get it? I let go on purpose. I wanted him to kill her. But it wasn't Acadia who got hurt. It was you. In my moment of stupidity, I almost got you killed, and I'll never forgive myself."

He pressed both palms against her cheeks. "That's not what I want. If I can forgive you, who are you to keep holding a grudge against yourself?"

She pulled away with a huff. "I won't ever use my spirit again."

Ellio rolled his eyes. "Kaya, I'd never ask you to do that. Your spirit makes you who you are. I'd never ask you to cut it out of your life. Just like, I'd never ask you to, er, cut off your arm."

Kaya narrowed her eyes. "That's not—"

"It *is* the same thing!" he insisted. "Or it might as well be. Your spirit is a part of you! It gives you strength. It's one of the things I love about you."

Kaya froze. She walked away from him to the window and pressed a palm against the glass. "Melica is falling. We need to evacuate. But in your condition . . ."

"Leave me here." Ellio told her, his expression serious.

She whirled around to face him. "How can you even suggest that? I would never leave you. Never! I'm insulted you'd even have the nerve to say it."

"Then help me." He held out his hand. "Protect us and get us out of here."

She turned back to the window. "Arnion's gone to find Acadia. Eirenian ships are on the way to help Melicans evacuate the city. We just need to hold on until they get here."

"What?" Ellio sat up straighter.

"One of Lucien's minions tried to assassinate him. She had some strange power brought on by her infusion with trividium. She was able to mimic Acadia's appearance. She got close, but somehow Arnion spotted the difference. He stopped her. I guess he really loves Acadia, even after all she's done."

Ellio smiled at her. "I still love Acadia too." At Kaya's scowl, he hastened to add, "Different from how I love you. Acadia's like a big sister."

Kaya scoffed. "How can you say that after what she's done? Because of her . . . because of her . . . Dragul is . . ."

"Acadia really believed she was working with Eiren. Espina used her weakness, played on Acadia's insecurities to manipulate her. It's not that different from us."

Kaya snorted. "And what makes you the expert on Acadia all of a sudden?"

"I knew about it," Ellio admitted. "I even helped her with one of Espina's tasks. We thought we were doing the right thing. So, if you're going to blame Acadia, I'm equally guilty."

Kaya bristled. "Why didn't you tell me?"

"I gave her my word."

She huffed.

Ellio's hand found hers across the blanket and gave it a squeeze. "Is Acadia all right?"

Kaya looked out the window. "We don't know. But it's Lucien, so . . ." She trailed off and then brought her eyes back to his. "He's capable of anything. And Arnion went alone."

"We have to help him!" Ellio struggled to get up, and Kaya pushed him back down.

"Are you crazy? You're not in a condition to help anyone."

"But we're a team. How could you let him go alone?"

Kaya thought about Arnion. The incredible spirit power she'd seen. And how he'd confessed during their talks that he was troubled and having difficulty accessing his full spirit abilities. Something was blocking them. At the time, Kaya hadn't understood, but after her trauma wounding Ellio, she had a better idea.

Our spirits are intricately tied to our hearts and our emotions. When our heart is in disarray, our spirit can be easily led off track. I wonder if that's what's happening to Arnion.

Kaya remembered the pain in Arnion's eyes. The young prince had carried the sorrow of Acadia's betrayal, Ellio's injury, and Kaya's hate. He'd been bearing all their burdens. Kaya slapped a palm against her forehead. She'd been so oblivious.

She squeezed Ellio's hand. "Let's put our heads together. There must be some way we can help Arnion, even from here." She gazed out the window at the burning skyline. Worry constricted her throat. "I hope he makes it in time."

"Then let's hurry." Ellio attempted to get out of bed, wheezing.

"You really are impossible, aren't you?" Kaya put a hand on her hip. She pressed a button to activate the hoverchair in the corner. "But you're going to ride in this thing. The doctor said no strenuous activity for a few weeks, or your wound could reopen."

Kaya helped Ellio into the hoverchair. He tapped a few buttons, and the chair hummed with new life.

"Now what are you up to?" Kaya asked.

Ellio flashed Kaya a mischievous look, and she was reminded of all the time they had spent together in his shop in Beulah while he tinkered with appliances. "Overriding the speed inhibitor."

Kaya grinned back at him. "Of course." She cracked her knuckles. "Now, let's find a way to help our golden couple."

A medical bot rolled by them in the corridor, and Ellio grabbed Kaya's arm. "I have an idea. Help me find a tech console."

Chapter 48

ARNION CLENCHED HIS FIST and tried to summon his spirit sword. Energy crackled up his wrist, but nothing happened. Arnion sighed. So, he still couldn't use it?

Ruah led him into the city sewers. After a series of twist and turns, Arnion found himself before a gate with armed guards. He curled his spirit around himself, forming a protective shield. The guards were already on alert. He wouldn't be able to sneak past them.

White flames crept down his arms, and he readied himself for combat.

They fired photon pistols at him, but his shield held, deflecting the blasts into the walls on either side of him.

The guards shouted in alarm. They couldn't see his spirit shield, but they'd seen its effects.

Wait.

They were wearing some kind of special goggles; maybe they could see spirit activity after all. Lucien must have developed his own iridium-spectrum lens to share with his personal guards.

Arnion sprinted forward, hands clenching into a fist. Arrows shot forward from his spirit, pinning the guards to the ground. He got up close to them and pressed a hand to each of their foreheads.

<Sleep,> he commanded with his spirit.

The guards slumped over, unconscious.

Arnion continued through the tunnels, leaving a trail of senseless guards behind him.

When would Lucien make his appearance? So far, the protection within the sewers was ridiculously light. Almost as if Lucien wanted to make it easy for him.

Arnion could feel the Heartless King's presence. He was close. Arnion heard laughter. A voice crackled over the intercom system.

"Hello, Arnion." Lucien's voice purred over the speakers. "Let me guess why you've come. You're here to steal my Jewel away from me, aren't you? Just like you stole the people of Gehenna."

Arnion clenched his fist. "Where is she?"

"Sapphyre was my creation. She belongs to me."

"Acadia doesn't belong to anyone." Arnion whirled around until he caught sight of the camera in the left-hand corner of the hallway. "What have you done with her?"

"Left you too, did she? Fickle little thing." Lucien's gleeful laugh screeched over the speakers. "I understand how it feels to lose something precious." He clicked his tongue. "How do you know she didn't return to me of her own free will?"

"Acadia wouldn't!"

"You have to admit, there's a lot about her you don't know."

Arnion shook his head. "It doesn't matter. I want to see her."

"Are you sure?" Lucien snickered, and Arnion's stomach twisted. "She may not be as you remember."

"Where is she?" Arnion's fist smashed into the wall.

"Little prince," Lucien said gleefully, "never let it be said that I didn't give you what you asked for."

Ahead of Arnion, a series of electronic locks activated and a door creaked open.

"My little Sapphyre is resting in that cell. Don't be surprised if she doesn't wish to see you. She's been a bit snappish lately." Amusement and pleasure coursed through Lucien's voice. Arnion clenched his fist.

Lucien's laughter echoed down the hall, and Arnion rushed forward. He pushed the creaking door open and peered inside. Everything was dark. Arnion took a deep breath and stepped over the threshold.

Chapter 49

DARKNESS SWALLOWED ARNION'S VISION. His heartbeat pulsed against his throat. "Acadia?" he called out.

There was a buzz and halogen lights flickered on. Arnion stood in a ramshackle laboratory. Workbenches were clustered with scientific instruments. Flasks, test tubes, and wiring sprawled across every available surface. Arnion wrinkled his nose at the acrid stench in the air. A piece of paper crumpled under his foot. Arnion grabbed it and glanced over the scrawling chemical formulas written in a spidery, unsteady hand. Then his eyes caught on the other half of the room and he dropped the paper. The laboratory was split in half by a series of heavy iron bars.

A cage.

There was a door with a security light blinking red.

Locked.

A figure was huddled in the corner with her back to him. "Acadia!" Arnion rushed at the bars and tugged. "Acadia! It's me!"

Acadia flinched, curling tighter around herself. Her short dark hair was matted, and she was wearing a dirty hospital gown.

"Arnion?" Her voice was a whisper like dry leaves scraping along the pavement. Her shoulders hunched. "You should go."

"What are you talking about?" He grabbed the cage door and shook it. "I'm not leaving without you."

Acadia let out a strangled sob. She shook her head. "You don't under-stand. I'm not leaving with you. I can't."

Doubt squirmed in Arnion's stomach. Then he remembered Ruah's words. "Acadia, you are my heart, my family. Even if you don't want to be with me anymore, at least let me help you escape. Then you never have to see me again." His voice broke on the last word.

Acadia shuddered. "It's not that . . ."

"I'll find a way to get you out of there. Don't worry."

The intercom crackled again. "Sapphyre, my sweet." Lucien's voice was oily smooth. Delight dripped from his words. "You can push the button and release yourself any time you want." The lock hummed, and Arnion saw Acadia could indeed unlock it from the inside.

"Acadia! Come on! Let's get out of here!" He stretched his hand toward her, but she didn't move; she didn't even turn her head.

"I can't," she whispered.

"Ellio is going to be okay. And what happened with the kings . . ." Arnion's throat tightened and he swallowed. "We know Lucien was manipulating you."

Acadia let out a moan and rocked back and forth. "If only it were that. You don't understand." Her voice had a strange thrumming texture to it that Arnion had never heard before. "I can't go with you. You need to leave me."

"No!" Arnion shouted. "I'm not leaving you with Lucien. I won't! Even if I have to die here."

Acadia flinched as if she'd been struck. "You don't understand! I want you to go," she wailed.

"Acadia . . ." Uncertainty filled his voice and stole the rest of his words.

"Go away!" she screamed.

Lucien's laughter echoed through the intercom. "You heard the lady, little prince. Aren't you chivalrous enough to respect her wishes?"

Knives of pain flensed Arnion's heart. "Acadia." His voice was quiet. "I don't want to leave you. Please, don't send me away. Whatever it is, share it with me. I can help."

She shivered. "Nothing can help me." Her hand came up to tuck a strand of hair behind her ear. Her fingernails were cracked and bruised. Obsidian veins traced up her wrists.

No.

She turned to face him, and Arnion's eyes traced the dark lines throbbing under her skin. Her breathing was ragged and pained.

No.

Lucien had injected Acadia with trividium, and her body was fighting it. Destroying itself. Her eyes were watery and bloodshot. When she met his gaze, black tears slid down her cheeks.

"Now do you understand?" Her voice was resigned. "I didn't want you to see me like this. I wanted you to remember me as I was."

"Acadia!" He reached for her, and she smiled bitterly.

"Now you know why you have to go. Leave me here. It won't be long. My body feels like it's burning up from the inside out."

"No!"

She smiled at him. "I won't give in to it. Don't worry. I'd rather die than become one of those creatures." Her body spasmed. After a moment, the fit passed. She clutched her chest, taking great heaving breaths. "Go on, Arnion. It's okay. This is what I deserve."

Arnion pressed his lips together. Frustration coiled around his chest. He clenched the bars in a white-knuckled grip. "Do you still think so little of me?" he whispered, voice tense. "Of my love? Do you think this changes anything?"

She stared at him with wide, surprised eyes.

"I love you, Acadia! I traveled back from the realm of the dead to be with you. Trividium doesn't change anything. I love you! I'll always love you."

She started crying. "Why?" she asked. "Why do you love me? I tried so hard to be worthy of you, but nothing I did was ever enough."

Arnion shook his head. "I never asked you to earn my love. I gave it freely. And I always will. You don't have to do anything."

Acadia pulled back. "I can't atone for my past. For all the lives I ruined, all the people I've destroyed." Her shoulders shook with a rattling cough and she spit a wad of black phlegm on the floor. She whimpered, wrapping her arms around her shoulders. "How can you love me? Look at me. I'm a monster! Even before I was injected with trividium, I was a monster."

"No." Arnion stretched out his hand, trying to reach her through the bars. It wasn't enough. He couldn't reach her. "You're not a monster. You're my chimad. And I'll love you forever. There's nothing you can do to earn my love, and there's nothing you can do to take it away. It's my choice to love you, regardless of what you do. I always have and I always will." He pressed his chest against the cage, reaching toward her. It still wasn't enough. "I've never taken a single step away from you," he said earnestly. "It's always you who's running away from me."

Acadia looked at Arnion's hand in wonder. Could it really be as easy as that? No, not after everything she'd struggled with. How could it be that simple? She didn't deserve it.

"Take my hand!" Arnion shouted. "Whatever comes, let's face it together."

She looked at the lock blinking on the wall. Then she turned to Arnion's outstretched hand. Acadia knew Lucien was watching.

Her body spasmed in pain. Molten fire crawled through her veins, and her head throbbed. She hit the floor, jaw clenched. Her vision turned hazy. Her body was rejecting the trividium and tearing itself apart.

"Acadia!" Arnion's anguished cry swam to her as if she were underwater. Her vision blurred, but she tried to fix her eyes on her prince. His handsome face was wrought with pain.

I've hurt him again. How do I always manage to hurt the people I love?

<Love?> Ruah's voice echoed in her mind.

Yes. I love Arnion with all my heart.

With each breath, her ribs cracked. Her heart stuttered. Even now, when she was at her most repulsive —dirty, infected, and dangerous; a betrayer, a liar, a thief—Arnion was still reaching through the bars. Straining as though his life depended on it.

It's always you who's running away from me. His words echoed in her mind. It's true, she'd spent her life running from things. From her family, from her responsibilities, from the truth.

Acadia blinked, and her vision cleared. She could see Arnion, tears streaming down his face. He was shouting something. Reaching for her through the bars.

Arnion.

He'd come for her, in spite of everything she'd done.

Arnion, whom she loved. And who loved her.

With the last of her strength, Acadia stretched out her hand and reached for him from her prone position on the floor. It wasn't enough.

Their fingers couldn't touch. She took a deep breath and crawled toward him. Her heart seized painfully. She coughed and spat blood on the floor.

Arnion!

Acadia wanted to reach him. She stretched out a trembling hand, waves of pain radiating from her chest, bright lights exploding behind her eyes. The world grew dim; sounds faded to nothing. Her heart beat slower and slower.

Acadia stretched forward and felt her fingertips brush against Arnion's, sliding up his palm to his wrist. She felt him grab her hand and tug her toward him.

<*Now, Arnion,*> Ruah's voice shouted—faintly, like he was standing at the far end of a tunnel.

Everything went black. Acadia was swallowed by darkness.

A blast of white light burst behind her eyes. The ground roiled beneath her as if she were at sea. Acadia opened her eyes and watched the prison bars explode outward, embedding themselves in the wall. The security camera shattered and intercom crackled in half. Lucien no longer had access to his little show.

Acadia breathed out. She felt warm and safe. Someone was holding her tight. He smelled like pine needles and sweat.

Acadia turned and gasped. She and Arnion were glowing white. Arnion held her in a tight embrace, eyes closed. She looked up at his handsome face, dark lashed fanned against his cheek. She brushed a hand against his glowing cheek. Acadia was connected to him in a way she'd never been before. She could feel his every breath as if it were her own.

"Arnion," she whispered.

He turned his cheek to nuzzle her hand and opened his eyes. They crackled with white spirit energy for a moment before dimming to their usual molten gold. "Acadia?" He took in her face for a moment then crushed her to him. "The trividium! It's gone!"

She hugged him tightly. "Somehow," she murmured against his chest. "But I feel strange. Sort of tingly, like I'm floating in a pool of water and all my limbs have fallen asleep."

He pulled back and looked at her. "Me too. Like my spirit is buzzing with energy. I've only ever felt this way once before, in the realm of the dead."

Acadia swallowed. "Are we dead?"

Arnion flexed his hand and looked around. "I don't think so. We're still in Lucien's lab. Last time, it was different. Come on." He tugged her up and they both stood, examining the shimmering aura surrounding them. "It almost feels like . . . wait a minute."

Arnion stepped back and closed his eyes. He breathed out.

Acadia gasped. A ball of white light gathered in the palm of his right hand. Energy whipped around them in a vortex of wind, and in a moment, Arnion was clutching a great sword almost as long as himself. The entire blade from tip to pommel glowed a brilliant white and flames of spirit energy crackled along its edge.

"Arnion, your spirit sword! You're able to form it again."

Her prince opened his eyes. "You're right." He grasped the sword with both hands and gave it a practice swing. "My spirit feels settled and at peace. Whatever happened, I think I'll be able to summon it again now."

Acadia smiled. Energy blazed underneath her skin. Her spirit pulsed, tied to Arnion's. "Do you feel . . ."

"Like we're connected? It's like our spirits have joined together and I'm a part of you now. And you're a part of me."

"I feel so much energy. Like I'm ready to burst."

<Focus the energy on your palms,> Ruah directed her.

Acadia took a deep breath and did as he said. Spirit power burst out of her. She blinked and looked at her hands. In each was a curved scimitar, blazing with white hot flames. The blades were shorter than Arnion's, just a little bit longer than her arms. Elegant crossguards curved from the hilt up into the grip. "Arnion! Look! I was able to make a spirit sword. Two of them." She smiled and tested their weight. It was like they were made for her. Each one fit perfectly into her palm, and she twirled them expertly. Curved scimitar spirit swords, made just for her and her ambidextrous hands.

"Acadia, that's fantastic!" Arnion tugged him to her and gave her a toe-curling kiss. "But we can't stay here. Lucien's warriors are about to overrun the city. With our spirits joined and these new spirit swords, maybe we can stop him from destroying Melica. My father and the Eirenians are on the way, if we can just hold out until they arrive. We may be able to save Avathys from Lucien's grasp."

Acadia clenched her swords and nodded. "Let's go!"

Arnion kicked open the damaged door and they charged up the stairs.

Chapter 50

WHEN ARNION AND ACADIA emerged from the sewers, Acadia gasped. Outside was a war zone. Smoke billowed up from enormous craters pockmarking the street. Hovercars and jetbikes smoldered in the ruins. Fires ravaged the beautiful buildings and swarms of berserkers poured into the streets.

A trividium-corrupted soldier grabbed an Avathysian woman by her hair and dragged her backward, lifting a blade to her throat.

"No!" Acadia leaped forward. Her curved scimitars shimmered in her hands, white flames leaping down her arms. She swiped at the guard. Where her blades touched him, his skin crackled and frayed. The berserker yowled, clawing at himself as his arm disintegrated. He staggered to his knees, and white spirit flames consumed his flesh until he was nothing but a pile of ash.

The Avathysian woman was screaming. Acadia released her spirit swords, and they faded away. She took hold of the woman's shoulders and hauled her to her feet. "Get to the hospital!" Acadia shouted. "We are evacuating from there. Whatever you do, get off the streets."

The woman whimpered and ran off.

Another berserker lunged at Acadia, black drool dribbling from his lips. She called on her spirit swords. When the blades touched him, he crumbled into ash.

"Acadia, look out!" Arnion slammed into her, and the two of them crashed onto the sidewalk. A blast detonated right where she'd been standing. Another smoking crater exploded near their feet. "There! Behind us!" Arnion shouted.

A squad of berserkers had formed at the end of the street, lobbing detonation bombs at anything that moved. Another explosive hurtled toward them. Arnion deflected it with his spirit sword, and it went rocketing into a nearby building, dislodging a giant hunk of concrete and rebar. Debris rained down.

Acadia threw up her spirit shield. She marveled at the incredible power flooding her spirit. It was like connecting with Arnion had supercharged her. Was this how he always felt? Things she had struggled with before were now effortless.

And these swords . . .

Acadia glanced at the twin scimitars in her hands. The grips were wrapped in a sparkling white cloth. The curved hilts were engraved with chiksa blossoms. The metal felt as strong as steel, but it was pure white.

Arnion and Acadia charged the nest of berserkers. With every swing of their swords, the corrupted crumbled into dust.

A putrid stench floated on the breeze. Goosebumps prickled along Acadia's arms. A darkness was approaching, and it felt familiar.

"Acadia," a raspy voice called out.

Delilah.

She stepped out of the shadows, darkness flowing around her like a malignant cloud. "You've really made a mess of things." She stretched out her razor-sharp nails, poison dripping from her fingers.

A child screamed. Four berserkers were advancing on a group of small children trapped in a jetbus. The driver had crashed into a building and was slumped over the steering console.

"Go!" Acadia nodded at Arnion. "I can handle this."

"You don't learn, do you? I would have thought the great Sapphyre would be more intelligent." Delilah advanced on her. Threads of darkness coiled around her like serpents.

Acadia held her chin high. "I'm not Sapphyre anymore. Arnion has forgiven me for my past. It no longer has any hold on me."

"What a shame." Delilah shrugged, her yellow eyes blazing. "It was the only part of you that was mildly interesting." She stared at Acadia for a moment, shaking her head. "I'm not sure how you got the trividium out of your system, but it was the only chance you had. Why would you give up so much power?"

"Whatever you get from trividium, it isn't worth the cost."

"All I hear are the pathetic bleatings of a sheep about to be slaughtered," Delilah sneered. "The least I can do for Lucien is rid the planet of your existence."

Acadia stepped forward. Her scimitars blazed with white light.

Delilah snarled. "If you think those little glowing sticks are going to help you, you're more delusional than I thought. I will show you the true power of trividium." She held out her hands and darkness poured from her palms, forming into twin blades—black mirrors of Acadia's own. Delilah leaped forward, swords singing through the air.

Acadia met her charge, and their swords collided in a shower of white and black sparks. As the two women each grappled for the upper hand, a spiny appendage shot out of Delilah's back, curving straight toward Acadia's heart. Acadia leaped back. The razor-like protrusion missed her by a hair's breadth.

Three more segmented black legs unfurled from Delilah's back, like those of a spider. Delilah shrieked with glee at Acadia's aghast expression. She twirled her swords, blade-like limbs clicking in the air. "How long can you keep this up before you run out of strength?" Her arachnid limbs shot out toward Acadia, nearly slicing her in two. A blade cleaved toward Acadia's head. She jerked to the side just in time, and Delilah's sword barely grazed her cheek. Blood dripped from the wound, but at least it wasn't poisoned.

Acadia tightened her grip on her swords. She had to be stronger, faster. She remembered the pull of Arnion's spirit, the power that flowed through her when their spirits connected. That same power was flowing through her veins right now. She just had to access it. She could feel Arnion with her, feel his heart, feel his spirit. White flames burst along her arms. Acadia shut her eyes.

Delilah was laughing. Acadia could sense her coming in for the final charge. Acadia fired a spirit arrow that impaled Delilah, pinning her to the ground. Delilah writhed. When she tried to touch the spirit arrow, she jerked her hands back, and shrieked with rage. Black sludge dripped from her eyes and mouth. "It burns!" she screamed. Her torso began turning the color of ash.

"Do you want to be rid of trividium?" Acadia released her spirit swords and took a step toward Delilah. "You don't have to remain like that; you can be free."

"C-curse you!" Delilah howled. She threw her head back, spasming in pain. Acadia's spirit flared, burning white light pouring through the arrow into Delilah. It looked like her spirit was vaporizing the trividium. But Delilah clung to the dark substance with every cell in her body. As the spirit incinerated the trividium, Delilah was also being consumed. Her body blazed with white fire, exuding a stench of tar and melted hair. The charred husk cracked and crumbled into dust.

Then Arnion was back at Acadia's side, ushering the group of school children in front of him. Hundreds of berserkers surged onto the street.

Arnion's eyes were desperate. "We need to fall back to the hospital! Kaya and Ellio are there. The Eirenian ships can land on the roof to evacuate us."

Acadia drew up a spirit shield to surround Arnion and the children as they raced down the street. "What about Melica?"

Arnion met her gaze for a second, brows furrowed. "The Avathysian council has decided to cut a deal with Lucien. They're probably negotiating right now for a ceasefire. But that won't include anything to do with us or Eiren. As far as Avathys is concerned, we're fair game to Lucien. They blame us for getting involved."

"That's ridiculous!" Acadia spluttered in outrage.

Sweat dripped from Arnion's chin. He sliced through a berserker angling toward the children and urged them forward . "If we can get to the hospital, we can escape, along with anyone from Avathys who doesn't agree with the council's decision. Zeliaris has been broadcasting the hospital as a safe point for anyone still loyal to her."

"How could anyone work with Lucien? He experimented on the Gehennians, and now he's kidnapping people from Kifu to continue building his army of berserkers. With the collapse of Kifu, he'll have even more troops. After conquering Avathys, he'll have a whole new population to draw on. How could Avathys capitulate to him?"

Arnion looked at her sadly. "I've heard it directly from Zeliaris. The council has shut her out. If she's captured, it's likely they'll hand her over to Lucien, along with anyone loyal to her."

Acadia shuddered. Her stomach roiled at the thought of Zeliaris or anyone else in Lucien's clutches. "Let's move."

They continued fighting their way toward the hospital, alternating between shields and swords to protect each other and the terrified group of children. But every step was harder. Each time Acadia drew on her spirit swords, she felt more drained. And the berserkers kept coming. No matter how many they cut down, more flowed onto the street, clawing at their shields, teeth snapping. Acadia glanced at Arnion. They were both sweating profusely. Her spirit swords flickered beneath her fingers. Acadia didn't know how much longer she could maintain them.

"How long were you able to keep your spirit sword last time?" Acadia shouted to Arnion.

"I only had it for a few minutes. It seems that sustaining it for any length of time is a massive spiritual drain." Arnion panted and swiped at the sweat dripping off his brow. "But we can't give up. We're almost there."

They turned the corner, and Acadia could see the hospital at the end of the street. Hope fluttered against her ribs. They were going to make it.

Then she stumbled, limbs locking beneath her. Her spirit shield shattered. A horde of berserkers surged toward them. A woman dripping black ooze from her nose and mouth loomed over Acadia, swinging a blade at her head.

There was a clash of metal and Acadia blinked. A hospital med bot had thrust itself between her and the berserker. The blade slid off the bot's alloy shell. The med bot beeped. It raised a spindly metal arm and shot a stun bolt into the woman's chest. Her body seized, electricity crackling over her.

Acadia's eyes widened. Beside her, two nurse bots were restraining another berserker while a third wrapped him in a restraining belts. A surgical robot was tightly winding another trividium-corrupted in surgical gauze, tripping him up.

What on Elorah?

"You are in danger." The med bot's metallic voice chirped at Acadia. "Remain calm. Evacuate to the hospital." It slid past her, stunner aimed at a berserker charging toward them.

Arnion and Acadia regrouped with the children and continued down the street. Arnion summoned a spirit shield to protect them as they ran. He raised his brows at Acadia as another trio of nurse bots shot tranquilizer darts at the corrupted barreling toward them. Hospital bots swarmed the area, pulling Avathysians out of the rubble, herding them toward the hospital. There were even janitor bots dousing berserkers with volatile cleaning fluid.

Acadia laughed. "It must be Ellio. This has his name written all over it."

They made it safely into the hospital lobby, along with a cluster of Avathysians rescued by the med bots. A group of nurses took charge of the school children, herding them to shelter. Acadia looked around. "It seems like Kaya and Ellio have been able to defend the hospital from attack."

Arnion nodded. "Kaya is shielding the entire hospital." His eyebrows drew together in concern. "She must be exhausted. Defensive spiritual abilities have always been a struggle for her. I can't imagine how much she's strained herself to maintain a shield of this magnitude."

The hallway ahead was barricaded with a cluster of hospital furniture.

"Kaya! Ellio! Are you there?" Acadia shouted.

"Acadia, is that you?" Ellio's voice rang out from behind the barrier. "Thank goodness. I didn't think we'd be able to hang on for much longer. Kaya's here, but she's focusing so hard on maintaining the shield, she's no longer able to talk. It's like she's in a trance."

Worry flooded Arnion's face. "Her body is shutting down due to spiritual drain. We need to wake her and have her turn off her spirit shield immediately. Otherwise, her spirit could start draining her life force."

Ellio grunted. "Can you move this desk?" Acadia heard him talking to other people behind the barricade. There was a screech of metal furniture being dragged across the tiled floor. A hole opened up in the jumble of furniture, large enough for Arnion, Acadia, and the other evacuees to pass through.

"Ellio!" Acadia ran to her friend, heart lurching as she noticed he was sat in a hoverchair. "Are you . . ."

He reached out and squeezed her hands. "I'm all right. But what about you? When we heard you'd been captured . . ." His voice faltered and he swallowed, his Adam's apple bobbing. "I'm so relieved you're both safe. "

Guilt seized Acadia's throat. She swallowed against the dryness in her mouth. "I'm so sorry, Ellio. It's my fault you were hurt."

Arnion gestured to the hospital staff around Ellio. "How many of you are there?"

"Some of the workers fled, but most are still here," Ellio replied. "Since I sent out the bots, more and more people have been coming. I've been directing them to gather close to the rotopad on the roof, to make evacuation easier."

Howls and barks filled the air. It sounded like a wave of berserkers was heading toward them.

"We need to move!" Arnion urged. "Where's Kaya?"

"She's here." Ellio led them to her.

Kaya didn't look good. She sat cross-legged on the floor in a janitorial closet, palms pressed together, eyes closed. Sweat beaded her forehead and soaked her shirt. Her jaw was clenched, her lips were pressed together tightly, and dark shadows lined her eyes.

"Kaya, it's okay. Arnion and Acadia are here. You don't have to hold the shield alone anymore." When Kaya remained motionless, Ellio shook her shoulder. Her head lolled to the side, but she didn't wake. Ellio looked at Arnion in alarm. "What's wrong with her?"

"She's exhausted herself to the point that she can't wake." Arnion knelt beside Kaya and cupped her face in his hands. His palms glowed white for a moment, and Acadia could feel the push of his spirit. "Kaya, wake up!"

Kaya stirred. Her eyes scrunched and she moaned. "Oww." She rubbed her forehead. "My head is killing me."

"You're lucky that's all that happened," Arnion told her seriously. "You've exhausted your spiritual energy. Without giving it time to recharge, you would have used up your life force and died. You were already in a comatose state when we found you."

Kaya blinked at him lazily. Then her eyes slid to Acadia, and her gaze sharpened. "So, you're here too?"

Acadia fought the urge to look away. "Is that all right?"

Kaya rubbed her neck. "Ellio told me how Espina betrayed you." She swept an assessing glance over Acadia. "Are you okay?" she asked gruffly.

Acadia licked her lips. "From the looks of it, I'm doing better than you are."

Kaya grunted. Arnion and Acadia helped her up. She wobbled on her feet and Acadia kept a steadying arm around her waist.

"I'm sorry," Acadia whispered.

Kaya closed her eyes and scrubbed a hand over her face. "Me too."

A data pad strapped to Ellio's wrist pinged. He tapped the screen and looked up in alarm. "I'm losing bots like crazy. The berserkers are overwhelming them."

Arnion pressed his hands together. "I'm putting up a new shield now. We need to get everyone to the roof and be ready when the Eirenian ships arrive. We just need to hold out a little longer."

"Where is Zeliaris?" Acadia asked.

Ellio nodded toward the ceiling. "The princess is upstairs in a tech console. She's been broadcasting continually about the council's betrayal and urging people to flee the city and for those who can't leave to rally to her." Ellio's fingers swiped across his data pad, tapping furiously. "I'm sending her a message to meet us on the roof."

From the rooftop, they could see the horde of berserkers surrounding the hospital. There were hundreds of them. Arnion caught Acadia's eye, and she nodded. As one, they drew forth their spirit swords. Ellio gawked, and even Kaya looked impressed.

"Neat trick," Kaya said to Acadia. "You'll have to show me that move next time we're in the sparring ring."

Acadia pressed her lips together. If there would be a next time. There was no way she and Arnion would be able to hold off that number of berserkers alone. But they would die trying. She squared her shoulders and raised her chin.

A series of energy bursts exploded in front of the hospital. Acadia jerked her head up in surprise. The Eirenian ships had arrived! Defensive airships spread out in a ring above the hospital. Photon blasts pounded the berserker troops below, creating a secure perimeter around the hospital. A spirit shield shimmered into place, creating a further barrier of protection. They must have additional spirit warriors on board each vessel, Acadia realized.

Transport ships hovered above the rooftop landing pad. Arnion and Zeliaris directed the evacuees to board each aircraft as it landed. Arnion's team, along with Zeliaris, slipped on board the last ship. Then Arnion signaled to the pilot to take off.

As the ships flew over Melica, Acadia covered her mouth with her hand. Devastation welled up in her chest, numbing her limbs and making it hard to breathe. Fires spread across the city. Ornate golden buildings crumbled. Transport vehicles were smashed along the sides of roads and oily smoke tinged the air.

Zeliaris sat on Acadia's left, tears coursing down her cheeks. "It's all gone," the princess sobbed. "Melica is lost."

Arnion was on the other side of Acadia, his face troubled. "We failed."

Acadia squeezed his hand. "This isn't the end. There is still more of Elorah to fight for. And we have a new weapon." She called up a spirit sword and twirled it between her fingers.

Zeliaris gasped, and Kaya's eyes widened. "Your spirit." Kaya was staring hard at Acadia. "It's white now, not blue."

Acadia looked at the burning flames curling around her and flexed her fingers around the grip of her blade. "Lucien infected me with trividium. I was dying. But Arnion refused to give up. His spirit, his love flowed into me. I could feel it taking root inside." Acadia pressed a hand over her heart. "It's still there. I can still feel him within me." She breathed out and released her hold on her spirit. The flames winked out and her sword dissolved into the air. "Arnion's spirit is connected with mine. And somehow, it's given me the boost I need to produce spirit swords. In fact, all things regarding the spirit seem to come easier now."

Arnion curled his fingers around hers, determination gleaming in his eyes. "Acadia's right. The spirit sword isn't exclusive to me. But there's much we still need to learn. How to sustain it for longer periods of time and how to teach others to generate them."

Ellio perked up. "Does that mean . . . even someone like me could have a spirit sword?"

"Ruah told me it's available for everyone." Acadia smiled at Ellio's look of wonder. "Eirenian and non-Eirenian alike," she said with confidence. "This could give us the edge we need to defeat Lucien."

"Wait a minute." Kaya wrinkled her nose. "Who's Ruah?"

Acadia chewed on the corner of her lip. "I'm not sure how to explain. Ruah is complicated."

There was a beat of silence, punctuated only by the gentle purr of the shuttle's phylar engine. Ellio shifted in his seat, brow furrowed. Zeliaris turned her tear-streaked face from the window. Her lips pressed together in disapproval.

Kaya leaned forward, resting her elbows on her knees. "Complicated how?"

"Well," Acadia hedged. "He's not exactly human."

"What?" Kaya and Ellio exclaimed in unison. Zeliaris's eyes widened and she reached up to fiddle with the necklace around her throat.

Acadia brushed her fingers lightly over her knuckles. "He's Spirit. He's been talking to me for a while and he knows things. Things no one on Elorah could possibly know. He's been helping me." She repressed a chuckle at the way Ellio's jaw dropped and Kaya's eyes widened in shock.

A pallor crept over Zeliaris's face and she glared at Acadia with cold eyes. "And what makes you think this *spirit* can be trusted?" she asked with disdain.

Acadia flushed. "It's true I've made mistakes—"

Zeliaris scoffed. "That's an understatement."

"I've heard him too," Arnion spoke up. "At my darkest moment, when I learned Acadia had been captured . . ." Anguish flashed across his expression and he brought a hand up to cover his face. "I didn't know what to do," he said in a small voice. "But then Ruah spoke to me." He lowered his hand and met Zeliaris's skeptical glare. "His voice was unlike anything I'd ever heard. His words were truth and life," Arnion said earnestly. "He guided me to where Acadia was being held and when all hope seemed lost, Ruah helped me save her." He held out his hands, palm up. "I suspect he also has something to do with the spirit swords."

Zeliaris leaned back and crossed her arms. "I suppose time will tell if you're right." Her eyes flashed in challenge.

Acadia winced and Arnion wrapped an arm around her shoulders. "It will."

Kaya thrust two fingers in Acadia's face. "When we get back, the first thing I'm going to do is shower." She curled one finger down. "And then, you have some serious explaining to do." She looked back and forth between Arnion and Acadia. "Because clearly you two have been holding out on us and I'm tired of being left in the dark."

Guilt niggled in Acadia's stomach. She dipped her chin in acquiescence. "All right. I'll tell you anything you want to know. No more secrets."

Ellio's eyes lit up and he nodded vigorously. "No more secrets. After all, we're family."

When the transport ships arrived in Capital City, Rhys and Naileah met them. It was a somber greeting party.

Acadia's throat constricted. She wasn't looking forward to what came next. The council would expect to hear all the details of their mission and its disastrous consequences. Though it would be much worse for Arnion. All of their expectations were set on him. Thinking about it, her heart ached.

Naileah bowed deeply to the prince. "Your Highness, I have information to report." Arnion inclined his head for her to proceed. The analyst cleared her throat. "Lucien has overrun Kifu and overtaken the city of Melica. It is only a matter of time before he makes use of the Avathysian armies and technologies. We need to fortify our city. There are also indicators that he is furthering his advances into Alsehir and Mintra."

Despair fell like a stone in Acadia's stomach.

Kaya groaned. "No rest for the wicked."

"There is much I need to report to you and the other analysts as well," Arnion said. "There have been some critical breakthroughs in our fight and some critical losses. But first we need to take care of Princess Zeliaris and the Avathysians who have evacuated to Eiren."

"Of course." Naileah bowed. "In anticipation of your arrival, I have assembled a team and begun allocating resources for that purpose. I believe you will be satisfied with the results."

"Thank you, Naileah." Arnion's fingers shaped the Eirenian gesture for gratitude. "As always, your analysis was spot on." He patted her shoulder. "Please summon the council for an emergency meeting. I need to brief them right away. I would like you to attend as well, and share the results of your report."

Naileah nodded. "Certainly, Your Majesty." She looked questioningly at Acadia and Kaya.

Arnion, as if sensing her question, waved his hand over them. "Acadia and Kaya will attend, as will Zeliaris, princess of Avathys. Ellio, how are you feeling?"

Ellio rolled his shoulder. "I'm all right, Your Highness, but if it's all the same to you, I'd rather sit this one out." Kaya's eyebrows drew together and she looked at him in concern. Ellio ruffled her hair. "I'm all right. I just need the rest. You can fill me in later."

Kaya huffed, blowing her bangs out of her eyes with a puff of air. Acadia bit back a smile. Council meetings were never enjoyable and today's meeting promised to be worse. The younger girl would certainly rather spend the time fussing over Ellio if given the choice.

Arnion smiled and clapped Ellio on the shoulder. "Very well, my friend. Naileah?"

"Sire?"

"Please put out a call for an Eirenian med tech to accompany Ellio. He's still recovering."

"Of course, Your Majesty." Naileah bowed and stepped aside to summon emergency services with a spir-com.

Arnion, Acadia, Zeliaris, and Kaya made their way to the Eirenian council meeting. It was a bleak affair. Kaya recounted the battle to defend the hospital from berserkers.

Zeliaris shared about being overruled by the council, the Avathysian government's plan to surrender, and how her country had been working with Lucien to instigate land disputes with Kifu. Her knuckles whitened as she gripped the stylus she had been nervously twirling between her fingers. She confessed Lucien had been secretly performing his experiments in Melica all this time.

Acadia wanted to reach over and squeeze her hand, but she didn't dare. She knew Zeliaris didn't trust her, but her heart went out to the exiled princess. It couldn't have been easy for Zeliaris to admit that Lucien had a stronghold in Avathysian politics for years, unbeknownst to her.

Then it was Acadia's turn. Her heart was heavy as she reported on the extent of Lucien's experiments and how he had been using Gehennians as his test subjects. When he had run out of people, the Heartless King had resorted to kidnapping Kifans living in remote areas to continue his research. Fear chilled her blood as she recounted her first experience with a berserker and his mindless, murderous rage. When she described Espina and her ability to control the berserker soldiers, there was a collective groan of dismay.

"You mean to tell us Lucien has found a way to control people corrupted by trividium?" Advisor Genoas asked. "How is that possible?"

"I'm not sure." Acadia shook her head. "But Espina was clearly able to manipulate the soldiers she brought. It seems like Lucien has found a way for people exposed to trividium to maintain more of their sanity or even develop special skills." She went on to describe Delilah's shape-changing ability and how she was able to manipulate the darkness around her to form poisonous blades.

Advisor Ayam pressed her shaking hands on the tabletop. "If this is the situation, how were you able to escape?"

Acadia smiled. That was the one bit of good news they had to share. She looked at Arnion; they both nodded and moved to the front of the room. Together they activated their spirit swords.

The council members gasped.

"These are swords of the spirit," Arnion explained. "Somehow in the process of interacting with Acadia, our spirits were joined. Even after being separated, the connection remains. I can feel her with me, and she can feel me with her, always. As you can see, Acadia's spirit power is now white, like mine. And she can generate spirit swords. Although hers are different."

Acadia twirled her twin scimitars, the blades sparkling in the light. "It's like these blades were made for me. They are the exact right size and weight for my fighting style."

"We still don't know all that they're capable of," Arnion said. "But it appears other people will be able to generate spirit swords. This may be the miracle we need to defeat Lucien and the trividium berserkers once and for all."

The council erupted into cheers.

"How can she do that?"

"Do you really believe others will be able to generate spirit swords?"

"What can they do?"

"Did she really survive exposure to trividium? Is it possible that others can be saved?"

Arnion looked at the council. "I'm not sure what the implications are for those whose bodies have completely integrated with trividium."

Acadia shook her head. "In my fight with Delilah, the powers of the spirit burned her. She refused to relinquish her hold on trividium and exposure to high levels of spirit power destroyed her."

"But what of you?" Advisor Genoas asked. "You were exposed to trividium, and yet you stand before us, wielding the spirit."

Acadia bit her lip. "I was fighting it. Fighting the dark whispers inside my mind. I think as long as you're fighting, there is a chance you can be healed. But once you give in, there's no going back."

A few days later, Arnion and Acadia slipped away from the unending meetings to take a walk outside. Her prince led her beside a water fountain in a secluded courtyard. Acadia sat on the rim tracing her fingers along the edge. Arnion slid next to her and took her hand.

"I love you, Acadia."

She squeezed his hand. "I love you too." The smile that lit his face at her words was so brilliant, for a moment she forgot how to breathe. Acadia swallowed and looked down at their hands. "I didn't think it would be possible to sit with you like this again after what I did." She tilted her head to meet his gaze—a smoldering golden-brown that warmed her like the summer sun. A flush spread over her face and she curled her toes inside her slippers. "I kept waiting for you to realize I didn't deserve you." She brought a hand up to cup his cheek. "But now, it's incredible. I can feel your love, on the inside. I know you're always with me. That our spirits are connected." She closed her eyes and pressed her forehead against his. "Now I know without a doubt that you love me, that I never have to fear losing your love," she whispered.

"Acadia, does this mean . . ." Arnion's breath hitched.

She nuzzled her nose against his. "Arnion Huios Melek Elyon, are you still willing to call someone like me your chimad?"

Arnion's arm wrapped around her waist and he tugged her closer. "Always and forever. Will you marry me, Acadia?"

"Yes!" She tipped her head back and kissed him, a feathery warmth tickling her belly. "Yes!" She took his face in her hands, laughing. "Yes! I'll marry you, my chimad."

A radiant smile burst across Arnion's face. He looked happier than she'd ever seen him. He reached into the pocket of his jacket and drew out the matching engagement armbands he had forged. A frown clouded his face as he drew a finger across the sapphire eyes embedded in the golden lions of his house insignia. "Perhaps I should alter these . . ." He lowered the armbands.

Acadia covered his hand with hers. "They're perfect. I've accepted that part of my past, just as you've accepted me. I'm not Sapphyre anymore, but I've forgiven myself for being her once. The armbands are beautiful and carved by my true love. I'd be honored to wear them."

Arnion slid her armband over her wrist and up her arm. "Beloved, I, Arnion Huios Melek Elyon, pledge myself to you. Let not life nor death separate us."

Acadia slipped the armband up Arnion's left arm. "And I, Acadia Dannon of Kifu, pledge myself to you. Let not height nor depth, nor any power or principality, separate us." Acadia leaned forward and brushed her lips against his. Electricity tingled along her nerves. A feeling of lightness enveloped her, like she could float away on the clouds. Any lingering doubt had been washed away. There was only this truth: Arnion loved her, and she loved him. No doubt, no fear, no schemes of the enemy would ever separate them again.

Acadia sighed as Arnion pulled her closer. She wrapped her arms around him and twined her fingers in the soft hair at his nape. Breathing in Arnion's scent, feeling the gentle rise and fall of his chest, made her heart race. She pressed in closer, wanting this moment to last forever.

There was a cough. Acadia flinched and Arnion loosened his hold, resting his hands lightly on her hips.

Kaya and Ellio were there. Kaya smirked. "Sorry for interrupting."

Ellio was mortified. He stared awkwardly at the ground, tugging on Kaya's sleeve. "We should leave them be."

Kaya rolled her eyes. "Did you already forget? We were sent to fetch them. They want to start spirit-sword training with Ruah." Kaya turned to Arnion and cleared her throat. "The students are eager to get started, Your Highness."

Arnion chuckled and squeezed Acadia's arm. "It sounds like Ruah's ready too. Let's go."

Ellio coughed into his hand and looked up, a blush spreading across his face. "Congratulations on your engagement."

Kaya hooted in amusement. "It's about time. When's the wedding?"

Arnion stood and helped Acadia up. His eyes searched hers, willing her to understand. "When there's peace in Elorah."

"Peace," Kaya whispered, looking at the contrails in the sky left by Eirenian military aircraft. "After losing Kifu and Avathys, do you think that's even possible?"

"Of course it is." Acadia said, determination rising within her. "We're going to have a wedding. And we're going to have peace." She grinned at Arnion, the strength of their spirit connection humming under her skin. "When we're together, nothing is impossible."

Kickstarter

I owe a tremendous debt of gratitude to the *Beauty from Embers* Kickstarter backers who helped make this book a reality. Thank you for supporting an indie author and bringing new creative projects into the world. The map at the front of the book, along with the following bonus content, is all because of their support.

Abigail, Alexandra Corrsin, Amanda Balter, Anthony I. Henley-Shaw, April L. Miller, Ash Harrier, Bianca Tatjana Višić Ritorto, Carl Spitzer, Catherine McP, Chimichanga, Christina, Cristine, CSK, Darlene N. Böcek, Derrick and Juliana Hall, Dione, Daughter of Heaven and Earth., Emily F., Eric Buck, Giselle, Jayden Bell, J F Rogers, Kandi J Wyatt, Katherine Malloy, Kathy Brasby, Kayla Ann, Kitty Bucholtz, Krysta, Liz Reis, Lynn P, Madeleine Mozley, Marie Campbell, Marlene Renteria, Melissa B., Michael H., Mindy Hite, Nava Starling, Nicole Triptow, Rachael Ritchey, Samantha Newberry, Stephanie Shackelford, Vickie Grider, Wyngarde, & Z. R. McCormick

The Sapphyre Diaries

Deleted from the original manuscript, these bonus scenes provide a glimpse into the life of Sapphyre, Lucien's most notorious Jewel. These scenes have been unlocked by the support of the amazing *Beauty from Embers* Kickstarter backers.

Sapphyre drummed her lacquered nails against the frame of her palanquin. The rings on her fingers clicked together. A large, heart-shaped ruby glimmered on her left hand, a recent gift from the Marquis of Bergoth. She chuckled, remembering how the young noble had fumbled with the box when presenting it. But he was gone now, back to snowy Mintra nestled among the mountains, taking his shy smiles and bumbling courting attempts with him. Convincing him to spend beyond his means and steep himself in debt had been a simple matter, and Sapphyre couldn't deny she enjoyed his gifts. If only he hadn't been called away by reports of his mother taking ill.

Dratted woman.

Sapphyre half suspected the old crone had feigned illness to pull the marquis beyond her grasp. Without his fawning attention, how was she supposed to entertain herself? Life in Beulah had become so tedious.

Sapphyre hooked a finger around one of the violet curtains that hid her from view and pulled it back. The teeming city's nightlife assailed her senses. Transports hummed, stuck in the ever-present snarl of traffic. Her footmen's wooden sandals clacked against the cobblestones. Grid screens buzzed, advertising the latest fashions. A cloud of sycophants fluttered around her palanquin like butterflies, young ladies vying for her favor and swains hopeful to catch her eye. Their inane chatter grated on her nerves. The scent of grilled meat wafted through the air from a nearby street cart, undercut by the tang of ergon fumes of idling vehicles. Sapphyre wrinkled her nose and let the curtain fall back into place.

Even Aurea, Beulah's most affluent district, was far from perfect. Sapphyre shuddered to think of life in the lower districts. That was one of the benefits of having servants. They could do all the unsavory tasks and errands for her. Sapphyre never traversed beyond Aurea if she could help it. Even here, the roads were chaotic. She had a luxury transport at her disposal, and plenty of willing escorts to accompany her. But today she preferred to be alone with her thoughts.

She also enjoyed the prestige of being one of the few in the city to still maintain a traditional black lacquered palanquin and bearers. In case anyone was tempted to forget the power and influence she wielded. Sapphyre liked to remind the denizens of Beulah that she was here to stay.

The movement of the palanquin stilled and there was a gentle knock on the door.

"Mistress, we've arrived at the gambling hall," one of her attendants spoke through the curtain.

Sapphyre checked her makeup in a small tortoiseshell mirror. Blue eyes glittered in her reflection like gemstones, rimmed in black kohl. Her complexion was flawless, with a porcelain glow that came from hours of rigorous beauty treatments and a liberal application of pashir-shell powder to hide the freckles that speckled her nose. She'd dabbed her lips with a new tincture today, a sparkling ruby red designed specifically for her. The cosmetician had named it Sweet Temptation. Sapphyre admired the glossy sheen, a satisfied smile curving her mouth.

It was perfect.

Today she wanted to be the picture of seduction. It was her one-year anniversary of dominating Beulah's social scene and she planned to keep it that way.

Sapphyre rapped her knuckles against the palanquin and her footman opened the door, extending a hand to help her down from the platform. Silken robes tumbled after her in a rush. She always loved a good train on her robes. It wasn't traditional for Beulah, but it was an extravagance she indulged in. As a child, she had always wanted to be a princess.

Sapphyre turned her attention to the gambling hall. The elegant marble structure extended two full city blocks with archways and columns climbing five stories high. From the center of the corniced roof, an immense statue of fortune welcomed patrons with open arms and a benevolent smile. But more important than the building were the guests climbing up and down the steps. Judging by the number of security staff mingling among the guests there were some high-profile players today.

Senator Crollux hurried toward her. Sapphyre smothered a grimace. The senator was a balding man of about sixty with a bulging gut that spilled over the edge of his tailored pants. A sheen of sweat dotted his forehead as he reached for her. "Sapphyre, darling, so glad you could make it tonight." He squeezed her elbow.

Sapphyre inclined her head. "Of course, Senator Crollux. I wouldn't miss the chance to best you again at the card tables." She didn't like to be touched, especially by his perpetually damp, liver-spotted hands.

When he rested a wrinkled claw along her forearm, she fought the urge to cringe. Her stomach roiled at the sight of his yellowed nails touching her silk robe. Still, the senator was an influential figure. She tolerated him. For now. She batted her eyelashes. The jewels dotted along her lash extensions made them feel heavy, but Sapphyre knew they provided an allure that was hard to resist.

The senator's doughy face reddened and he swallowed. "Of course, m'lady. It's always a pleasure to lose to your gracious personage."

Sapphyre slid her jeweled fan from a pocket in her sleeve and fluttered it coquettishly. "One can only hope you'll have better luck tonight, Senator." She swept into a low curtsy, discreetly tugging her sleeve from his grasp. Once she'd extricated herself, she swept past him into the hall.

The interior of the building was a sumptuous combination of dark ruewood and red velvet. Despite its enormous size, the subdued lighting and cozy nooks around each card table made the space feel intimate. An enormous crystal chandelier twinkled above the staircase and golden sconces lined the walls. The scent of warm leather and wood tickled Sapphyre's nose. She rolled her shoulders. The gambling hall was designed to lull guests into a relaxed state. Even knowing that, she wasn't completely immune to its charms. A white-gloved servant appeared at her side, offering her a glass of her favorite sparkling wine on a silver tray. Sapphyre barely acknowledged him as she took the glass. Her eyes skimmed the room, looking for anyone of interest. Senators, enforcers, bankers, and businessmen. She knew them all and the vices that drove them. Sapphyre sighed, rolling the stem of the wine glass between her fingers.

How tiresome.

In only a year, she'd weaseled her way into Beulah's most influential social spheres. It was thrilling at first, but now Sapphyre was decidedly unimpressed. These people had no imagination. They were all so predictable. She wanted a challenge. Something to thrill her, surprise her, or at least ease her boredom somewhat.

"Welcome, Miss Sapphyre." Sheila, one of the hostesses, curtsied before her. "Which game would you like to start with today?" She was petite with long black hair that cascaded down her shoulders. She wore a red silk dress with a large slit up the right thigh.

Sapphyre waved across the room, a slight moue pouting her lips. "I don't know Sheila, it all starts to feel the same after a while."

Sheila flashed a vacant smile. "How about the basset tables, Mistress?" she said with a cheerfulness that had to be fake.

"Basset it is." Sapphyre snapped her fan shut, sliding it back into the pocket of her sleeve. She crooked a finger at the group of grovelers fluttering behind her. "Who wants to join me?" There was a flurry of activity but Sapphyre strode forward without looking back. She couldn't help but notice how people's heads turned to follow her.

All eyes were on her. Sapphyre held her head high as she sauntered across the room. She could almost hear hearts breaking.

As Sheila helped her into a chair, three victors from her cloud of sycophants slid into the chairs beside her. There was Melshack, a business man with a sharp sense of humor; Lady Guan, the scandalously young wife of banker Guan; and a youth whose name she didn't know. He was slender to the point of being uncomfortable with a pencil-thin mustache quivering above his sweaty lip. Disgust curdled in her stomach and she resolved to ignore him entirely.

The basset games were all the same. Sapphyre tapped her cards on the table. She didn't even need to cheat to win. The repetitive banality left a sour taste in her mouth.

"Miss Sapphyre, look." Sheila spoke up beside her and nodded toward one of the other tables. "Newlyweds. You can tell from the robes. They must be playing for their wedding gift."

Sapphyre's eyes narrowed.

Newlyweds?

"Aren't they cute?" Sheila sighed dreamily. "He only has eyes for her. I hope someone will look at me like that someday."

Sapphyre resisted the urge to swat Sheila with her hand of cards, instead placing them demurely on the table. "Dear little Sheila, how ignorant you are to the ways of the world. Why, that man is no more loyal to his bride than a stray cat. He's just one pretty face away from an affair."

"Oh," Sheila murmured, looking down.

"Come now, Sapphyre," Melshack spoke up, laying his cards face down on the table. "I say that a man can be loyal to his wife for at least a month."

Sapphyre leaned back, a smile twitching at the corner of her mouth. "Do you doubt my understanding of men, Melshack?"

"I find it a bit cynical." Melshack rubbed his chin. "The man's clearly in love. Anyone can see it. Feelings that strong can't be vanquished in an instant." He picked up his wine glass, twirling the stem between his fingers. A bitter expression twisted his face. "It takes time and hardship to chip away at it."

"Love?" The word bit into Sapphyre's tongue as she said it. She gave a contemptuous laugh to hide her discomfort. She held up her hand and gestured as if tossing something into the wind. "A feeling as fleeting as the air we breathe."

Melshack leaned forward, elbows on the table. "Care to make a little wager, my dear Sapphyre?"

Sapphyre stole a glance at the couple across the room. The young man was a bit blockish, but comely in a rustic sort of way. The young wife gazed at him with adoration, an innocent blush staining her cheeks.

I could do it.

Sapphyre knew she could snatch that man away. He wasn't in love. She was just the first girl who'd said yes. The first girl he'd ever asked, most likely. His wife was cute, but Sapphyre was irresistible. She smiled. A rush of excitement poured through her veins. This was the first interesting thing to happen to her in ages.

"All right, Melshack." She held out her hand. "You have a bet."

Sapphyre slid from her chair, silken robes trailing behind her. The fabric was designed to slip down over her shoulders, giving a tantalizing view of her elegant neck, powdered a shimmering white. She straightened, mentally prepared herself, and sashayed over to the man.

"What are we playing?" She looped her arm through his and flashed what she knew to be an adorable impish grin.

"Mistress Sapphyre," the man stammered in surprise. "What a delight! My wife and I were just playing a bit of Hots. Taking a quick chance on the cards before our trip to Avathys and the sea. A little extra coin never hurts, you know? After such a nice wedding ceremony, I feel like today's our lucky day, right, Katarina?"

Katarina turned, the light dimming in her eyes as she beheld Sapphyre's hand wrapped around her husband's arm. The young bride looked down. "Kern insisted," she murmured to the floor. "It didn't seem like it could do any harm."

"Certainly not." Sapphyre sniffed disdainfully. The girl would be no trouble at all. Timidity was a vice, not a virtue. If Katarina wanted to keep what was hers, she would have to learn to fight for it. "May I offer my congratulations on your nuptials." She ran a hand along Kern's arm; long bejeweled nails glittered in the hushed lighting. "How lucky you are, Katarina, to find such a handsome man." She gazed adoringly at Kern for a moment before looking away. "I only hope that I myself will be so fortunate one day."

"Oh, Miss Sapphyre," Kern gushed. "I'm sure there are men lining the streets ready to propose to you." He patted her hand.

"I'm honored you think so." Sapphyre molded her face to appear tragic and long-suffering. "Though I'm afraid you're sadly mistaken." She made a move as if to withdraw her hand and Kern's grip tightened. Outwardly she maintained her forlorn expression but inwardly she crowed.

Success.

This was a game she knew how to play.

"Stay with us a while longer, Lady Sapphyre, please." Kern flashed a broad smile at her. Katarina frowned.

"Oh no, I couldn't possibly. I don't want to impose."

"It's no trouble," Kern insisted. "We'd be honored if you would celebrate with us. You could be our good luck charm."

"Well..." Sapphyre hesitated. She exuded vulnerability, flashing Katarina a pleading look. Humble. Long-suffering. Innocent. She coached herself on which emotions should pass across her face and for how long.

The young bride worried her lip and pressed her fingers together. Sapphyre could almost see the gears turning in her mind, good nature winning out over suspicion. "Yes, Mistress Sapphyre, we'd be honored."

Little fool.

Sapphyre's outward expression was docile, but inwardly she sharpened her knives. It wouldn't take much to cut out this man's heart and squeeze it in her palm. People were so easily manipulated.

Sapphyre almost purred with delight.

The game is on. Melshack better be ready to pay up.

And, as an added bonus, she'd be able to ensnare more people in debt.

Lucien will be pleased.

Three days passed and Sapphyre maintained a daily presence at the gambling hall. The building throbbed with activity. Guests buzzed between the card tables like a displaced swarm of bees and Sapphyre sat at the center. Their queen. Her servants had set up a small raised dais with a beautifully carved chaise lounge that she reclined upon. A young Beulan noble was on his knees fawning over her. He'd traveled all the way to Entova just to bring her sky fruits because she'd mentioned briefly that she'd never tasted one before. A trio of rugged Mintran hunters glowered at him from a few paces back. They had brought her rare furs from the Ilyon mountains and were waiting for her acknowledgment.

But Sapphyre ignored them all. Her focus was on Kern. He leaned over the gambling table in front of her, one hand gripping the edge, the other clenched around a glass of spritz. Still in his bridal clothes, though now wrinkled, and reeking of sweat He hadn't left the gambling hall since the night they'd met. She'd made sure of it.

The dealer cast the dice. Kern swore and slammed his glass on the table, shattering it. A woman beside him shrieked, but Kern ignored her. He slumped down to his knees, blubbering.

The dealer glared at him, but before the staff could escort him out, Sapphyre held up a hand. "Allow me." She slipped from her little throne and stepped beside Kern, running her fingers through his grimy hair. "Darling, you must behave yourself." Her voice was a silken purr.

Kern clung to her legs like a child. "It's rigged!" He rubbed his face against her robe, leaving a trail of snot and tears. "It must be rigged." His shoulders shook.

Sapphyre clicked her tongue. Disgust welled in her chest, but she forced it down. "We all have our ups and downs." She forced her voice to ring with compassion. "How about I buy you another drink? This next round's on me."

Kern's bloodshot gaze slid to her. His face lit up and he clutched her robes. "Thank you, Mistress Sapphyre. I just need one more chance. I'll win back everything I lost. You'll see."

Sapphyre recognized the hollowness in his eyes, the tightness in his bristly unshaven jaw. Desperation clung to him. Kern would sign a debt contract soon. With each round, his addiction grew. His enormous losses only convinced him further that his luck was about to change. Soon he would care for nothing beyond the gambling tables. Sapphyre had already contacted Mr. Kinu, Lucien's broker. He had the blood contract ready and waiting to be signed. All it would take was her gentle touch to send Kern spiraling over the edge into Lucien's debt.

Sapphyre nodded to her servants and they helped Kern to his feet. She curled against him, tracing a finger along his jaw. "Win this one for me, darling," she whispered and brushed her lips against his. He tasted like sweat and stale lemons. She forced back her revulsion, kissing him until his hands, hot and sticky, crept to her waist. Sapphyre pulled back slightly and nuzzled his nose. "Don't get too distracted. You have a game to win."

Kern shivered and loosened his arms. A waiter brought him another spritz and he downed it in three gulps. Then he leaned over the gambling table, attention rapt as the dealer prepared to take new bets.

Internally, Sapphyre smirked. Life was a game and she played to win. She extricated herself from Kern's grip and draped herself back over her seat. She was about to wave over the Mintran hunters when a disturbance near the entryway caught her eye.

Katarina burst through the crowd. Security guards trailed half a breath behind her. The spurned bride launched herself at Sapphyre, hands outstretched like claws. "Monster!" she screamed.

Sapphyre's bodyguards materialized from the shadows and restrained the young woman. Her bridal braid was a frizzy tangled clump clinging to her neck. Dark smudges lined her eyes and her lips were chapped. Her chest heaved as she struggled against the guards, shrieking.

"I trusted you." Katarina sobbed. Her furious expression morphed into hopelessness and she collapsed against the guards' arms. "Why would you do this?" Her voice was small and broken.

"All right, let's go." The guards tugged her to her feet.

Sapphyre held up a hand. "Wait." Silk whispered as she stood and looked down at Katarina. "It was nothing personal." Her voice was hard. "You lost, I won. There's no point getting hysterical."

Fire rekindled in Katarina's eyes and she lurched forward. "You have everything! You have more than anyone can dream of, and still you took him away. The one man in this town that wasn't eating out of your palm. You couldn't stand that someone wasn't looking at you." Katarina wiped her dripping nose with the back of her hand.

Sapphyre's lips tightened, but she caught herself before frowning. Instead, she threw her head back and laughed. "No one likes a sore loser, Katarina." She gestured dismissively to the spurned bride. "If this is the best you can do, I wonder how earnest your feelings truly were." Sapphyre flipped her hair over her shoulder. "Honestly, if it wasn't me, someone else was bound to come along eventually." She waved her hand and the guards pulled Katarina to her feet.

"You think you're so beautiful, with your makeup and fine clothes."
Katarina's voice rang out as they dragged her away. "But underneath
you're a monster. You're the ugliest woman I've ever seen." The look in
her eyes was cold as ice. If the little wretch hadn't been serious about
anything in her life, it was clear that she meant those words.

The mask threatened to slip from Sapphyre's face.

*Ugly? Ridiculous! I'm the most beautiful woman in Beulah. Men travel
stadia to catch a glimpse of me.*

Sapphyre flounced back to her chair and reclined on the cushions. She
tapped one of the beaded tassels with lacquered fingernails.

Katarina was just jealous.

"Kern," Sapphyre called.

The young man turned from the gambling tables and grinned at her
with empty eyes. "Yes, Mistress Sapphyre?"

"Your wife was just here."

"Who?"

Sapphyre drummed her nails along the armrest. "Your wife, Katarina."
She enunciated each syllable of the name.

The smile fell from Kern's face and he looked uncertain. A greenish
hue seeped across his complexion. He mopped his forehead with a handkerchief. "Oh yes, Katarina. Can you..." He licked his lips. "Can you send
her away, Mistress? I'm not up for it today. She's always nagging me, you
know."

"Of course." Sapphyre blew him a sultry kiss. "I'll make sure she never
troubles you again."

"Thank you, Mistress." Kern sighed in relief. He gave a pleading look
at the gambling table.

Sapphyre waggled her fingers at him. "Go ahead, Kern. You're free."

He turned back eagerly, stumbling in his haste. Sapphyre watched for a moment, idly spinning one of her bracelets. Then she snapped her fingers. "Sheila." The hostess appeared at her side. "Write a note to Melshack. Tell him it's time to pay up."

"Yes, Mistress." Sheila curtsied and hurried off.

Sapphyre smirked. Kern had been right about one thing. A little extra coin never hurts.

Sapphyre checked herself in her hand mirror before ringing the bell. The servants had done an exceptional job on her updo tonight. She turned her head to admire her long black tresses pulled into glossy loops and curls that defied gravity, accented with jade pins. Her complexion was flawless. The smoky kohl used to darken her lashes made the brilliant sapphire of her eyes glitter like gemstones. Her maid had enhanced the effect by sticking tiny sparkling gems along her eyelids. The emerald green robe she wore was accented with golden thread and tiny white cranes with diamonds for eyes.

She looked perfect, like a creature out of a fairy tale.

Sapphyre pressed a lacquered nail to the doorbell. A servant answered. He had dark circles under his eyes and anxious lines around his mouth.

"I have an appointment with Lucien." Sapphyre coiled a loose tendril of hair around her finger.

"Of course, Mistress Sapphyre." The servant bowed and backed out of the entryway. "We've been expecting you. He's in the mayor's office. Up the stairs and three doors down on the right." He gestured behind himself to a large golden staircase dominating the foyer.

Lucien always commandeered the nicest house when he visited Beulah. The mayor's home was a beautiful three-story structure. Black marble pillars supported the veranda that curved along the outside. The interior was stylishly decorated with colorful tapestries and oil paintings in gilded frames.

As Sapphyre passed by the servant, he flinched. Fear danced in his eyes and he winced as if expecting to be struck.

Odd.

Sapphyre smiled brightly to put him at ease. It was almost like he was scared of her. That couldn't be right. People loved her. Maybe Lucien's presence had set him on edge. The Heartless King could have that effect on people.

They don't know him like I do. Sapphyre tapped her fan against her lips as she walked up the stairs. *I know how to deal with Lucien. He respects our partnership.*

She sashayed down the hallway and knocked on the door. Another servant opened it and gestured for her to enter.

Lucien stood beside a blazing fireplace, glass of blood-red wine in hand. At her entrance, he turned toward the door. "Sapphyre, my little gem! How are you?" He strode toward her in long steps and clasped her hand. "Fantastic work with Kern, my pet. We've got him bonded for forty thousand drakka. You always do such excellent work."

"'Twas nothing, my lord." Sapphyre curtsied, keeping her eyes downcast.

Lucien placed a cold finger under her chin and forced her to meet his gaze. "So demure as always, but you can't fool me, Sapphyre. I see the predator underneath." His eyes raked down her face, catching for a moment on the gemstones delicately placed along the rims of her eyelids. He brushed a tendril of hair back from her face and tucked it behind her ear. "I've forgotten how exquisite you are to look at, my dear. A shining example for all of what they can achieve with my gifts."

Sapphyre leaned in to his touch, looking at him through hooded lashes. Lucien liked it when she played coy. He released her chin and she dipped her head in a bow. "It's all thanks to you, my lord."

Lucien laughed. He tossed the remains of his wine into the fire with a flash. "I'm sure you would have found your way regardless. You are a resourceful little creature."

He set his glass on the mantle and turned to face her, steepling his fingers. "Sapphyre, you've inspired me. With your success generating debt contracts in Beulah, I've decided to expand. I want a jewel like you in every city." He waved his hand at her with a flourish. "Ambitious women of beauty and influence."

Sapphyre pouted. "Are you trying to replace me?"

"Not at all, my pet. You are a swan among carrion. There's only ever going to be one of you. Nevertheless, I will find suitable imitations to carry on the spirit of your work in other spheres of influence in Elorah."

Lucien paced. His eyes shone with glee. "I want you to train them, this network of jewels. Train them in the art of manipulation, seduction, of leading others to always want more without ever truly receiving anything. Train them to ferret out secrets, to blackmail, to use a person's weaknesses against them. Train them to hunt hearts as you do."

Sapphyre laughed. "My dear Lucien, I'm not sure those skills can be taught. They require a certain instinctual talent."

"Endeavor, my gem, for my sake." Lucien crossed his hands over his heart. "And remember, the more powerful I grow, the more treasures I can bestow upon you." He gestured to a series of boxes beside him.

Sapphyre gasped and rushed forward. Her fingers stroked the silky ribbon that decorated the top box.

Lucien came to stand behind her. He placed his hands on her shoulders. "Consider this a taste," he whispered into her ear. "I reward those who please me, and I am very pleased with you." He squeezed her shoulders once more in an iron grip so hard it hurt.

Sapphyre stilled. The warning beneath Lucien's words trilled under her skin. The Heartless King rewarded those who pleased him. And punished those who didn't. She needed to remain on his good side. Always.

The packages contained an assortment of luxury jewels and clothing, fit for royalty. Silk scarves, a joffa fur-lined cape, diamond and ruby hair pins, rare perfumes in alabaster bottles, glittering stiletto heels, and a golden necklace with an obscenely large emerald.

Sapphyre cooed, running her fingers along the extravagant gifts. "You always have such excellent taste, my lord." She sunk into a sultry curtsy. "I will endeavor to deserve such generosity."

Lucien traced a hand along her jaw. "I know you will." He flashed a wicked, cruel smile. "Now, my jewel, I must be going."

Sapphyre rose and escorted him to the outer door with all the fawning and ceremony Lucien loved. After she shut the door, the mayor and his staff crept out from wherever they had been hiding. She turned to thank them but they cowered away from her along the far wall.

Sapphyre frowned. *Such odd behavior tonight. Lucien's no longer here. Who are they afraid of?* She shrugged it off. Servants were difficult to fathom sometimes and the mayor was basically Lucien's servant as well. She snapped her fingers and pointed to the nearest servant, a young woman with watery blue eyes. "You there, have these boxes delivered to my home. My footman can give you the address." She leaned forward to whisper in the girl's ear. "And I'll know if even one hairpin goes missing."

The girl recoiled. She twisted her fingers together, staring at the floor. "Yes, Mistress," she stammered.

Everyone's so skittish tonight. Sapphyre puzzled over the strange behavior for a moment, before her thoughts turned again to Lucien's gifts.
That emerald necklace would go perfectly with her black satin gown
with the sweetheart neckline.

The Orpheus Ballroom had transformed into a luscious midnight
paradise. Sapphyre took in the scene, nodding in satisfaction. Dark purple draperies robed each pillar. Swathes of lilies cascaded from the balconies, bathing the room in their heady fragrance. The gilded ceiling had
been covered in cobalt blue silk and thousands of light globes dangled
from the canopy in a magical imitation of the night sky.

Sapphyre had spared no expense for her birthday celebration. Bluebell
oysters, shipped overnight from Avathys, sat on glimmering beds of ice.
Porcelain tureens of saffron soup simmered along the banquet table and
lavender ice wine fizzed in silver goblets imported from Mintra. She
nodded to the servants and swept into the entryway to welcome her
guests.

Everyone of importance in Beulah's social scene had been invited.
Excitement tingled along Sapphyre's nerves as she took in the crowd
waiting outside. This was going to be the most decadent party Beulah
had ever seen. Dignitaries and aristocrats were lined up, dressed in their
finest. She spied actors from a popular grid screen drama and a foreign
prince with a large plumed turban.

The soft sounds of a string quartet wafted out of the ballroom and
Sapphyre smiled. Their timing was perfect. She had planned melodi-
ous, light-hearted music to start the evening off. Later, when the drinks
flowed liberally, she'd unveil *Wave Renders*, a heart-thumping new band
she'd smuggled in from Dardak. Their style was fresh and energetic. And

this would be the first time they performed on the continent. Sapphyre couldn't wait to see the awe on everyone's faces.

The evening proceeded smoothly; every part of Sapphyre's plan was meticulously carried out by her servants. But agitation rose within her, like an unbearable itch beneath her skin. Something was wrong. The food and music were perfect, the guests all smiling, but an undercurrent of gloom soured the mood.

Sapphyre didn't understand. This was the biggest, most extravagant party ever held in Beulah. People laughed louder than necessary, and smiled exaggerated grins. It was as if they were performing an exaggerated pantomime of having fun. The artificial behavior left a chalky taste in Sapphyre's mouth. She gritted her teeth.

What was wrong with everyone?

She turned to investigate further and collided with a servant carrying a tray of goblets. Lavender wine splattered her snow-white robes. Fury curdled in her stomach and she smacked the man across the face. "You absolute fool! Look what you've done. Do you have any idea how much this robe cost? More than you'll earn in a lifetime!" She punctuated each word with another blow. Sapphyre's breath sawed through her chest. She stopped to glare at the cowering servant. That's when she noticed.

The room had gone absolutely silent.

Thousands of eyes bored into Sapphyre. She whirled around and the woman beside her flinched, face white. All at once, the charade dropped and Sapphyre could see the naked fear painted across each face. She froze, pinned to the spot by an incredible wave of hatred and loathing.

"I-I..." Sapphyre's voice cracked. She cleared her throat. "I apologize for that vulgar display of temper." Her voice warbled, hands fluttering by her throat like injured birds. "If you'll please excuse me for a moment."

She fled toward the exit, the crowd parting around her like she was an infectious disease.

Everywhere she looked it was written on their faces.

Disgust.

Hatred.

Fear.

Sapphyre ran back to her apartment on foot, destroying her designer slippers. She barely noticed as she flung herself onto her bed. Great sobs wracked her body. She had given everything to Lucien in exchange for one thing. To be beautiful. Sapphyre wanted to be loved and admired more than anything. But no one in Beulah loved her.

They despised her.

They hate me!

Now that Sapphyre had seen it, she couldn't unsee it. Everywhere she walked, everywhere she looked, she was met with fear. *I thought people loved me, but they were really just afraid.* She clenched her fists until her nails bit red marks into her skin. This wasn't right. This wasn't what she wanted.

Sapphyre went through a few days in a fugue. Just because she served Lucien didn't mean anyone needed to fear *her*. What was wrong with them? It made her angry. She lashed out at her servants more and more often. And their fear grew.

"You cowering lout! How could you make the same mistake twice in one day? If you don't learn, I will have you thrown into Gehenna." The threat slipped out of her mouth in a fit of rage. If she thought people were afraid of her before, now they were terrified.

People avoided her in the street. Old friends deliberately turned and walked the other way when they saw her coming. Sapphyre's heart twisted painfully in her chest.

The stench of fear in her servants was becoming unbearable. So she began walking the street alone. One day a small rain shower burst overhead and she was caught without an umbrella. Sapphyre cursed. She took shelter under the awning of a restaurant and decided to wait out the rain.

A commotion exploded from inside and a scrawny young girl was thrown out into the rain. A balding man, with a paunch and a whiskery beard loomed over her. "You useless welp. That's the last glass you're ever going to break. Someone call the Reckoners. I'll no longer take on this girl's debt."

"Please." The girl sobbed, clutching his feet. "Please give me one more chance. I won't do it again, I swear."

Sapphyre took in the girl's appearance. She was slender to the point of being emaciated. Dirty, lice-ridden, barefoot, and dressed in a ragged slip of a dress with holes. She was the most pitiful creature Sapphyre had ever seen.

"Please," the girl sobbed. "Not the Reckoners. Anything but that."

"Get off me, girl." The man kicked out, dislodging her from his foot and flinging her down into the muddy carriage ruts of the street.

A memory flared in Sapphyre's mind. Da's hand raised to strike her for her clumsiness. Ma watching silently from the shadows.

Sapphyre stepped forward. "Stop," she commanded.

"Mind your own affairs, you..." The man turned, swallowing back his insult as he took in Sapphyre's appearance. "M-mistress Sapphyre. I apologize." He clutched his fingers together and attempted a clumsy bow. "I didn't see you there. I'm very sorry for disturbing you. The kitchen staff is on break but I'll have them called back immediately."

Sapphyre thrust out a hand. "Enough of your groveling. I'm thoroughly disturbed already." An idea was forming in her mind. It was an absurd whim, but the more she considered it, the more it appealed to her. Surprise bubbled up inside Sapphyre and she liked the feeling. She squared her shoulders and addressed the restaurant owner. "How much is that girl's debt?"

The proprietor wrung his hands. "I'm very sorry, my lady. It truly is nothing to trouble yourself with. I'll have this trash removed from your sight immediately." He yanked the girl up by her arm and she let out a yelp. He grabbed the back of her hair and forced her into a low obeisance. He whispered under his breath, "Apologize to the lady, you little fool, before she has both our heads."

The girl stammered out an apology and Sapphyre smiled. Sometimes it was good to be feared.

"It just so happens that I am in need of a new servant. I'll buy her debt and take her off your hands."

"B-but my lady." The proprietor made a chopping motion with his hand. "This welp's not worth your time. She's clumsy and always daydreaming."

"I wasn't asking." Sapphyre snapped her fan open and pinned the man with an imperious glare.

The man bowed deeply. "Yes, Mistress. Anything you want, of course. Allow me to give the girl to you—"

"No," Sapphyre said firmly. "No gifts. I will purchase her debt outright. Or do you think I would be so foolish as to owe you a favor?"

Sweat dripped down the man's neck. His lower lip trembled. "I wouldn't dream of it, my lady."

"Then stop wasting my time." Sapphyre deliberately used her most scathing tone. "Bring the girl's contract and a stylus. Immediately."

The man jumped and ran inside. He returned promptly with the debt contract and stylus. Sapphyre made him crouch down while she used his back to sign it. She eyed the amount due and plucked out one of her hair pins. It was from a senator's son, a betrothal gift. She'd rejected the offer, but kept the pin. White sagrins pranced along the pin against a pink lacquer background. Pearls and diamonds dangled from it, accented with tiny golden stars.

It was beautiful, but pink never really was her color. That young fool should have known she preferred red if he wanted her to even consider taking his proposal seriously. She tossed the pin to the proprietor who fumbled with it and almost dropped it in the mud. "That pin's worth at least a thousand drakka. More than enough for the girl's claim."

"Mistress, I couldn't—"

Sapphyre clicked her tongue. "You bore me. One can only hope you're a better cook than you are a conversationalist."

The man's jaw snapped shut and beads of sweat stuck out along his temples.

"Come along, girl." Sapphyre snapped her fingers at her newly purchased waif. "Let's hope you make a better maid than a dishwasher."

The girl followed her mutely all the way home.

Well, at least she knew how to be quiet. That was something.

Sapphyre introduced her to her household staff and ordered a hot bath, a warm meal, and a strict training regimen starting early in the morning. As she turned to go, the girl took hold of the trailing fabric of her sleeve. Sapphyre turned, ready to strike the girl for her impertinence, but something in the waif's expression stopped her. The girl's face was red, eyes filled with tears. She was crying, but didn't look afraid. The girl swiped at her eyes and looked up bashfully. "T-thank you, ma'am," she whispered.

"Think nothing of it. It was a whim." Sapphyre waved her off. But as she turned, her pulse raced. This girl hadn't been afraid of her. In fact, the waif looked at her with something like adoration. Sapphyre's heart pounded and she pressed a hand to her chest.

What is this feeling?

She turned back to watch the girl as the housemaids clucked over her, bringing her to the kitchens and patting her on the head. The girl managed a watery smile at all the attention.

Sapphyre felt a smile tugging at her own mouth and stifled it.

Ridiculous.

It was just a passing whim. That's all.

"Sire, we've received communication from Mr. Kinu. Sapphyre let another one walk. A pair of twins, actually. Just twelve years old. She bought their debts outright and sent them home to the family farm with their pockets full of jewels. That's three debtors this week."

"She did what?" Lucien slammed his fist into the messenger's jaw. "What do you mean three debtors *this week*? Why didn't Kinu inform me the moment she breached contract?"

The messenger picked himself up off the floor, legs quaking. Blood dripped from the corner of his mouth. "Mr. Kinu thought it was a phase, my lord. An affectation. She's been increasing her household staff lately. Hiring people out of debt to come work for her."

"What?" Lucien roared. His hands clenched the edge of his writing table. *How dare she betray me!* Fury seethed in his chest. "Who does that little wretch think she is? Without me, Sapphyre is nothing." Lucien flung the table on its side. Contracts fluttered through the air. Inkpots shattered. The obsidian liquid pooled on the floor, filling the room with a heavy scent of earth and metal.

Lucien paced back and forth, thinking. He needed to deal with this rebellion swiftly. No mistakes. If word got out that one of his own had gone behind his back, his crown jewel no less, it could cause other weaker minds to suddenly grow a conscience.

No, no. This wouldn't do. He needed to make it public. He needed to make a scene. So that everyone would remember what happened when someone didn't play according to his rules.

"Tell Kinu to call in all her debts. Every last one. And contact Bucephalus. Tell him I want her picked up by the Reckoners first thing in the morning. I want it public. Bring out the old hearse, the one pulled by sagrin. Everyone needs to know what happened to Sapphyre when she crossed me."

The messenger bowed and scurried from the room.

Lucien resumed his pacing.

Sapphyre, Sapphyre, what were you thinking? You had it all, and you gave it up to suddenly grow a conscience on me.

Lucien sighed. How disappointing. He'd poured resources into Acadia, transforming her from a simple rustic into the most sought-after courtesan in Beulah. He rubbed his chin. Though he had to admit, the returns she had given him were considerable. She'd allowed him to burrow into the fabric of Beulan society. Lucien's stranglehold over the city went deeper than he had dared to dream. Even the staunchest holdouts weren't immune to her charms. She was the inspiration for his network of Jewels—beautiful, intelligent women of influence placed strategically throughout Elorah.

But there was no salvaging this. Lucien tipped his head back and closed his eyes. He knew all too well how things would play out. One small spark of defiance could quickly grow into a conflagration.

There was only one solution. Make her downfall so abhorrent that when anyone spoke her name, they would shudder.

Lucien opened his eyes and smiled. He was going to enjoy shattering Sapphyre.

World and Character Glossary

Acadia Dannon. (uh-KAY-dee-uh DAN-un) Raised on a humble farm in Kifu, Acadia rose to become one of Lucien's key influencers in the city of Beulah before she summarily fell from favor and landed in Gehenna. While a prisoner, she met and fell in love with Arnion, not realizing he was a prince in disguise. When her blood oath was paid, she moved to Eiren and is currently living in the Eirenian palace in Capital City. She has brilliant dark-blue eyes, straight black hair, and freckles. At the start of *Beauty from Embers*, she is twenty-seven years old.

Adept Spirit Class. Eirenians who have developed spirit abilities to help in their chosen trade or profession. A caster uses their spirit to operate specialized machinery like a crane. A conjurer produces certain items directly from their spirit. Conjurers have generated hallmarks of Eirenian technology including irradiated spectrum lenses. There are also adept users who specialize in sensing various substances.

Alsehir. (AL-say-here) A country to the far west of Elorah known for its dry climate, wide-open plains, and herds of sagrin.

Analyst. An Eirenian who specializes in interpreting data and using it to make diplomatic predictions and provide tactical insight on enemy maneuvers. Easily identified by their white robes. A Lead Analyst oversees each of Capital City's seven visio ports.

Arnion Melek Iustus Huios Elyon, Prince. (AR-nee-on Meh-LEK YOO-stus WHO-ee-os EL-ee-on) The only son of King Elyon, Arnion is the crown prince of Eiren. He undertook a daring undercover mission into Gehenna, a prison colony and stronghold of his nation's mortal enemy, Lucien. While there, he fell in love with Acadia, one of the prisoners. When Arnion realized Lucien held a blood oath over the Gehennians, he willingly sacrificed his life in exchange for theirs. In the afterlife, he was able to generate a miraculous spirit sword, which allowed him to come back to life. He has golden eyes, a bronze complexion, and brown curly hair. At the start of *Beauty from Embers*, he is twenty-eight years old.

Atta, King. (AH-ta) Ruler of the nation of Avathys. A large man with a great curling golden beard. Father to Zeliaris.

Avathys. (AH-va-thiss) Powerful sea-faring nation to the east of Elorah. Known for its fertile soil, abundant agricultural resources, and exceptional naval strength. Avathys is experiencing a technological boom with rapid advancements in medical and military inventions. Notable Avathysians: Zeliaris.

Bacillus Port. (bu-SILL-us) A small electronic surveillance device that infiltrates tech stations. It introduces a backdoor virus that bypasses security systems and allows complete access and ongoing monitoring.

Bereavement Transport. Eirenian aircraft specifically designed for funerary services.

Berserker. A person who has been exposed to a high dosage of trividium within their body. Driven insane by trividium's dark power and the destruction of their spirit, Berserkers are impervious to pain and are driven by the desire to destroy everything in their path.

Beulah. (BYOO-luh) The capital of the nation of Kifu.

Blasphemer. A person who has been exposed to a high dosage of trividium but has maintained their sanity. These individuals can negate or weaken spirit abilities and control berserkers. Trividium enhances their natural aptitudes, gifting them with special skills such as mind control or shape-shifting.

Blood Contract. The written proof of each party's willing entry into a blood oath. Only takes effect when both parties sign using their own blood.

Blood Oath. The highest level of oath in Elorah. The contract must be signed using blood from each participant to be valid. The binding can only be removed upon death via the Death Insurmountable Clause.

Breaths. An Eloran unit measuring time. Equivalent to five Earth seconds.

Brokers. The financial and administrative workers of Lucien's empire. Brokers maintain Lucien's finances, distributing money and resources to his debtors. They also draw up his blood contracts.

Butterchuck. A wild, hoofed mammal prized for its delicious fatty meat.

By Shreeve. An Eloran curse. Loose historical references trace Shreeve to a Dardaki warrior who refused to yield, even after all four of his limbs were hacked off. Currently used as a coarse intensifier.

Chiksa. (CHICK-sa) A beautiful flowering tree native to Eiren. In the spring it produces an abundance of tiny white blossoms with a sweet fragrance.

Chimad. (khee-MAHD) Peeking ahead, are you? This will get revealed in the story, but for those who can't wait: Chimad is an Eirenian term for "beloved." Eirenians believe that every spirit has their perfect match somewhere in the world, a soulmate. An Eirenian will only ever have one chimad in their whole life. It implies unconditional, all-encompassing love. There are extremely rare occurrences where the chimad bond is not mutual. In this case, the Eirenian will often choose to live alone rather than marry someone else.

Cira. (SEE-ruh) Acadia's maidservant in Beulah. She was rescued by Acadia while she was living under the Sapphyre persona.

Da. Acadia uses this rustic Kifan term for her father, who passed away from an injury in her early twenties. His death set her family on a path of financial ruin and led Acadia to betray her loved ones in order to escape the clutches of poverty.

Dardak. (DAR-dak) A war-like, island nation to the southeast of Elorah.

Data Crystal. Eirenian espionage technology. A small microchip embedded in the skin of the forearm. Fingerprint activated. The device can be coded to the optic nerve of its host, thereby only visible to the person wearing it. It has many features including encrypted communication, remote tracking beacon, scanning features across multiple wavelengths, nanoscopic recording system, mineral and sustenance locator, poison sensor, enemy surveillance detector, and calendars.

Data Tablet. An Eirenian portable electronic device capable of storing vast amounts of information. They virtually sync to virtual data storage every five breaths and are operated using a stylus.

Death Insurmountable Clause. The only release from an Eloran blood oath. When one or more parties become deceased.

Defaulter. A person who has failed to adhere to the terms of Lucien's blood oath, most commonly in the form of missing payments.

Delilah. A young Beulan debutante who fell out of favor with Lucien. She and Acadia were both picked up by Lucien's Reckoners and entered Gehenna on the same day. Acadia tried to befriend Delilah, but was betrayed by her during in-processing. When Gehenna fell, Delilah chose to follow Lucien even after her blood oath was broken. When exposed to trividium, Delilah was able to embrace its dark power and received the ability to transform her appearance to mimic others. Before transforming with trividium she had green eyes and beautiful red hair. At the start of *Beauty from Embers*, she is eighteen years old.

Dragul. (DRA-ghoul) Kaya's grandfather. A gritty and jaded spirit warrior of Eiren. He raised Kaya after she was orphaned at age five. When she showed promise as a spirit user, he began training her in warrior-class spirit techniques. He and Kaya are both extremely gruff and bull-headed, leading to frequent explosive arguments. He is bald with brown eyes.

Drakka. A heavy gold coin equivalent to twenty-five til. One drakka can be considered a month's wages for an unskilled laborer.

Dral. An Eloran curse used to express frustration, anger, or annoyance.

Dren, Dannon. Acadia's younger brother. The middle child of the Dannon siblings. He is serious and skeptical. Of all the Dannon family, he struggled the most with Acadia's betrayal. Dren considers Kep a father figure and dreams of pursuing medical studies. He has black hair and dark-brown eyes. At the start of *Beauty from Embers*, he is sixteen years old.

Eiren. (EY-ren) A central nation of Elorah and a technological superpower. Eiren used to have flourishing relationships with the other nations of Elorah, but after a bloody civil war instigated by Lucien, international relations suffered greatly. Now, Eiren is considered by many Elorans to be a mysterious and isolationist nation. It is rumored to be a utopia where the streets are paved with gold and that its inhabitants possess supernatural abilities that extend their lives. However, shifting undercurrents within the nation hint that it may not be the idyllic paradise it seems. Notable Eirenians: Arnion, Elyon, Naileah, Espina, and Dragul. Lucien is an exiled Eirenian.

Ellio. (EL-ee-oh) A young Kifan who grew up in the Downs, the worst district of Beulah. Ellio is a gifted mechanic with a kind heart, often helping his neighbors even when they can't repay him. After his father passed away, Ellio was able to maintain his family's repair shop, although he couldn't break free from the mountain of debt his father had incurred. *City of a Thousand Tears* is the story of how Ellio meets Kaya and their adventures escaping the city of Beulah together. At the start of *Beauty from Embers*, he is eighteen years old.

Elorah. (eh-LOR-uh) A vast planet divided into eight nations. Each nation is in a different stage of technological and economic development. Eloran geography is varied from verdant forests and lush coastal valleys to toxic wastelands and frozen wilderness. Its abundant wildlife is exotic—and often deadly.

Elyon Melek Iustus, King. (EL-ee-on meh-LEK YOO-stus) King of Eiren and Arnion's father. An excellent leader known for his compassionate nature. His large stature and broad shoulders make him an imposing figure, but one look at the kindness in his eyes dispels any fright. He has a craggy face and large jaw. King Elyon repeatedly sent ambassadors to Gehenna to set Lucien's captives free. Before Lucien's fall from grace, Elyon treated him like a son, giving him responsibility and training far beyond his other advisors.

Emissary Spirit Class. Eirenians who have developed specialized skills focusing on social and emotional aspects of spirit use. Emissary level abilities include emotional sensing and sway (detects and influences the emotional state of those around them), truth tone (detects lie vibrations in another's voice), and mind meld (searches another's memories—often used for healing trauma or discerning the truth when there are multiple conflicting testimonies). Emissary class spirit users are teachers, counselors, diplomats, politicians, and sometimes enforcers. Notable Eirenians in this class: Rhys.

Enforcers. Law enforcement personal on the planet Elorah. Each country has their own variation of enforcers. Lucien also maintained his own enforcers as guards within Gehenna, often recruiting notorious criminals with a pending death sentence.

Entova. (en-TOE-va) A volcanic island nation to the southwest of Elorah.

Eril. (eh-RIL) Former Gehennian. Eril is a Kifan young man who met Prince Arnion during his mission to Gehenna. Eril was one of Arnion's first allies in the prison colony. Eril has straight black hair and green eyes. At the start of *Beauty from Embers*, he is twenty-six years old.

Espina, Kartul. (eh-spee-NA) An Eirenian analyst for military intelligence with an off-beat and quirky personality. She obsessively followed Arnion's mission into Gehenna and kept meticulous details on everyone he came into contact with. She has a particular fixation on Acadia. At the start of *Beauty from Embers*, she is twenty-seven years old.

Fibro Jacket. An Eirenian protective jacket for riding in open-air, high-speed vehicles. The fabric is molded together from a series of lightweight, high-density ballistic polymer in a honeycomb pattern. Intelligent impact absorption deflects damage away from critical areas in the result of a crash. Has built-in heating and cooling regulation.

Flux Sword. A combat sword with a current of electricity running along the edge of the blade. Versatile and elegant, the flux sword has been wielded by many famous Elorans throughout history. The combination of energy and steel allows the user to deflect energy blasts and inflict devastating damage in close combat.

Fuga. (FOO-guh) An Eirenian stingray-shaped personal aircraft. A high-velocity, open-air vehicle that requires constant spirit connection to maintain power. Frequently used for racing and aerobatic stunt maneuvers. Leaves a trail of blue electrostatic discharge in its wake.

Gehenna. (geh-HEN-na) The kingdom of the Heartless King, also known as Lucien. Originally a dumping ground for the city of Beulah, there are still piles of refuse that continue to burn to this day. Lucien was drawn to the area because of its proximity to the Cursed Barrens and its propensity for trividium deposits. He built up a prison colony and used the pretext of mining kelsum to have his debtors unknowingly search the area for trividium. Lucien discovered a large trividium deposit in Gehenna just before Arnion broke his blood oaths and freed the prison's inhabitants.

Grid Screen. Similar to laptop or television screens in our world, grid screens display images and sounds using Elorah's energy-based system. In Eiren, adept level engineers have created grid screens that can project and record spirit activity using irradiated spectrum lenses.

Grimlock. A large, mountain-dwelling creature that makes its home among massive rocks. Notorious for its large claws.

Halcyon. (hal-SEE-on) Eirenian aircraft valued for its speed. Can transport up to eight people comfortably. The aerodynamic curves of the vehicle are reminiscent of a shark with a muted gray paint scheme and orange pinstriping.

Hand. An Eloran unit of measurement, using the horizontal width of a hand from the pinky to the area near the thumb. Roughly equivalent to 4 inches or 10.16 centimeters.

Has. (HAHS) Former Gehennian. Has is an old man from Mintra with a rustic accent. Along with Eril, Has was one of Arnion's first allies in the prison colony. Has has wisps of white hair around his ears, deep brown eyes, and a wide smile—although he's missing quite a few teeth. At the start of *Beauty from Embers*, he is fifty-eight years old.

Heartless King. See Lucien.

Incursion Craft. Eirenian stealth attack aircraft.

Innate Spirit Class. In Eiren, anyone with basic spirit training has innate level spirit abilities. This includes sending spir-coms and syna, along with powering simple Eirenian devices like the trilorid. More complex Eirenian devices require testing into a higher level of mastery.

Irradiated Spectrum Lenses. Technology created by Eirenian engineers to allow grid screens to see and record spirit activity.

Jetbike. A three-wheeled motorcycle powered by an ergon engine. Jetbikes are a high-speed and popular way to travel outside of Eiren. Advanced models offer limited hovercraft abilities.

Jetbus. A large passenger vehicle powered by twin ergon engines. Jetbuses are most commonly used in school and urban public transportation. Depending on the model, a jetbus can hold between forty and ninety passengers.

Jewel. Intelligent women placed in strategic positions of power and influence, under the support of Lucien. Jewels are beautiful and sought-after courtesans who have sworn their loyalty to Lucien and work to ensnare people into his service or debt. There are seven known Jewels in existence: Sapphyre of Beulah, Jade of Melica, Onyx of Narsla, Diamond of Solis, Ruby of Plisk, Amethyst of Nokdune, and Pearl of Bergoth.

Joffa. (JAW-fah) A cute and fluffy marine mammal of Elorah. Their fur is prized for its exquisite quality and softness, but their limited population and questionable trapping practices have made joffa fur harvesting illegal.

Kaya. Orphaned at the age of five, Kaya was raised by her grandfather, Dragul. Her mother was Eirenian and her father Kifan, causing a rift between Dragul and his daughter. Dragul trained Kaya in combat and survival for many years, before her anger became uncontrollable. They parted ways in Beulah. Shortly afterward, Kaya's temper landed her in enforcer custody after a vicious bar fight. A scout from the city's fighting guild, Retiarius, discovered her and manipulated her into the guild's debt. *City of a Thousand Tears* details the story of how Kaya met Ellio while rising up the ranks of Retiarius as the prestigious fighter, Silent Nyte. At the start of *Beauty from Embers*, she is seventeen years old.

Kelsum. A dense gray stone quarried in harsh environments. Durable and resistant to weathering, kelsum is often used in construction and fortification. Construction workers frequently describe it as "not beautiful but will get the job done." Its extraction is labor-intensive, requiring significant physical effort. Despite this, kelsum is an inexpensive building material due to its propensity to be quarried by prisoners. Gehenna was built around a kelsum quarry.

Kep. Ma's second husband. When Acadia's father died and left the family in debt, Kep found them and began helping them stay afloat. Eventually he and Ma fell in love and were married. He is like a father figure to Acadia's two younger brothers, particularly Dren. He is a slender, wiry man with a neatly trimmed beard and salt-and-pepper hair.

Kifu. (KEY-foo) A southern nation of Elorah. Large heavy metal deposits in the soil make it difficult to grow crops, so Kifans have evolved a robust international trading network through the seaport town of Birano. They supply other nations with minerals and stone in exchange for produce. Notable Kifans: Acadia, Delilah, Ellio and Eril. Kaya's father was also Kifan.

Kraggy. (CRA-gee) A small, reptilian scavenger often found in deserts and wastelands. Kraggies are resourceful survivors and will eat nearly anything. They have bulbous heads, forked tongues, and mottled gray, brown, or reddish scales. Their large protruding eyes give them excellent daytime and night vision.

Kryet. (CRY-et) A medium-sized desert sand cat with long tufted ears and a whip-like tail. Native to Kifu.

Lead Analyst. Distinguished analysts of superior skill, often set in leadership positions and responsible for the training of junior analysts. Silver robes are the mark of their station. Each of Capital City's visio ports is overseen by a Lead Analyst.

Light Harness. An Eirenian safety restraint for high-speed vehicles, made of web-like bands of energy that glow a soft yellow when activated. It automatically adjusts to the passenger's body and is highly responsive to movement. Most of the time, wearing it is nearly imperceptible, but during sudden movements or a crash, the light harness will contract, providing unbreakable and yet comfortable support.

Light Shield. An Eirenian safety device designed to protect the eyes and/or face from impact and debris. Worn as a discreet fob on the temple, the light shield activates at the press of a button, deploying a barrier of energy to protect the wearer's face. The light shield is unbreakable, offering superior protection in high-speed collisions or hazardous environments. Comes in a variety of colors.

Lucien. (LOO-see-en) Also known as the Heartless King because of a rumor he eats human hearts to stay young. Lucien is an Eirenian who used to be King Elyon's second-in-command. Elyon loved him like a son and taught him some of the sovereign class spirit techniques traditionally limited to the royal family. However, Lucien became obsessed trividium's dark power and instigated a coup to overthrow Elyon. When it failed, he and all his followers were exiled from Eiren forever.

Ma. Acadia uses this rustic Kifan term for Mother. Ma desperately tried to keep their family together after her husband's death but was unable to maintain the farm. After Acadia betrayed her family they lost contact and haven't seen each other in five years.

Maglift. An Eirenian device similar to an Earth elevator, used to ascend or descend floors in a building and powered by electromagnets. Extremely fast and silent.

Melica. (MEL-ih-kuh) The capital of the nation of Avathys. Home to the royal family.

Messenger. An Eirenian specialist in spirit communications. They provide discrete and reliable communication services and are renowned for their confidentiality.

Mintra. (MIN-truh) A mountainous country in the north of Elorah, nearly inaccessible to outsiders throughout the year due to heavy snow. Notable Mintrans: Has and Agatha.

Naileah. (NY-lay-uh) Lead Analyst for visio port six. She is very rational and highly attentive to detail. She is considered a prodigy, even among analysts, for her exceptional skills. When nervous, she twirls her stylus.

Nanocrystal Radiance. Eirenian technology allowing for extremely clear video recording and enhancement abilities on gridscreens.

Narhast, Emissary. (NAR-hast) A retired Kifan general currently serving as an emissary to Eiren. Never one to back down from a fight, his abrasive nature has some questioning the wisdom in appointing him to diplomatic duties. He walks with a limp due to an old war injury.

Narsla. (NAR-sla) The capital of the nation of Dardak.

Observers. Lucien's staff that oversee the in-processing of new residents to Gehenna. They wear dark-blue smocks with large goggles and slicked-back hair, and take detailed notes on their clipboards. Observers are methodical and devoid of typical human emotions. They are fanatical devotees to the Heartless King.

Pashir Shell. (PAH-sheer) A rare crustacean whose shells are ground down to make a fine powder capable of concealing blemishes and giving skin a pearlescent glow.

Passenger Conveyors. Large Eirenian transport aircraft. Passenger conveyors can transport up to four hundred people safely. They are without weapons systems. When used to evacuate hostile areas, they are accompanied by an aerial security detail.

Photon Pistol. A small, handheld weapon for close or medium-range combat. Photon pistols are powered by energy cartridges. They fire bursts of concentrated energy which can penetrate light armor and unshielded vehicles and sear through flesh.

Reckoners. The brutal muscle men of Lucien's staff, Reckoners collect and transport defaulters to Gehenna.

Requisitioners. Powerful and influential men and women who work with Lucien to ensnare others in debt. Before creating his Jewels, Lucien relied heavily on standard requisitioners to spread his influence across the planet Elorah. They are experts at subtly manipulating the people and culture around them. Their presence has been carefully woven into every level of society.

Rhys. (REES) An Eirenian ambassadorial advisor and close friend to Prince Arnion. Rhys works to support ambassadors, preparing them for missions and debriefing them afterward. He has an extremely caring and intuitive nature which leads him to take Acadia under his wing after she immigrates to Eiren. At the start of *Beauty from Embers*, he is twenty-eight years old.

Sagrin. (SAY-grin) A six-legged equine mammal, with leathery skin, floppy ears, and a prehensile snout. Originally bred in Alsehir, sagrin are now traded throughout Elorah. Wild sagrin are herd animals. Domesticated sagrin are frequently used as beasts of burden for farming or low-tech transportation. The tough and gamey quality of their meat makes them an unpopular food source but sagrin leather is a burgeoning trade on the planet.

Sapphyre, Mistress, Jewel. Acadia was the original Sapphyre of Beulah. Her success inspired Lucien to create a core group of powerful women influencers to aid his cause. When Acadia fell from favor, she was replaced by Chandra as the new Sapphyre of Beulah.

Shoalskin. Eirenian synthetic leather fabric. Extremely comfortable, breathable, and versatile, shoalskin is a fashionable alternative for animal-loving Elorans everywhere. Shoalskin slippers can also be adapted to allow the wearer to move silently on their feet.

Silvie. A petite maid-in-training at the Eirenian palace. Silvie is currently shadowing Tifa, Acadia's handmaiden. Silvie has auburn hair and black-rimmed glasses.

Skaklops. (SKAK-lops) A small river-dwelling amphibian. They secrete a dark-brown mucus that acts as camouflage and makes them extremely slippery. For those with nimble hands, their tender flesh is delicious roasted over an open fire.

Sovereign Spirit Class. Highest level of spirit mastery, only obtained by the Eirenian royal family. Requires innate spiritual gifting and an extremely high level of control. Sovereign spirit class users have a much larger spiritual well to draw on and are highly gifted in sensing abilities. Other sovereign class abilities include voice of the spirit (ability to amplify voice in volume and elicit emotions such as peace, courage, strength, fear, or panic in listeners), spirit of suggestion (ability to lull listeners into a state of peace or susceptibility to suggestion), and spirit bombardment (an offensive attack launching arrows of spiritual energy), as well as advanced healing abilities. Notable Eirenians in this class: Arnion, Elyon, and Lucien.

Spir-com. Short for spirit communication, spir-coms enable Eirenians to speak directly to another person's spirit without the use of spoken words. This can be an intimate conversation between two people or broadcast to an entire group. Spir-coms are an innate level spirit ability for Eirenians, typically mastered in childhood. However, it requires training to be able to send spir-coms over long distances. Skilled users are also able to broadcast images and memories. Inexperienced users may also inadvertently send a syna along with or in lieu of a spir-com.

Spirit Sight. A mid-level Eirenian spirit ability where users are able to temporarily see spirit activity around them.

Stadia. (STAY-de-uh) The plural of stadion.

Stadion. (STAY-de-on) An Eloran unit of measurement, specifically used for distance. It is roughly equivalent to 607 feet or 185 meters.

Stunner. A handheld Eloran weapon that makes use of electrical current to nonlethally subdue other humans and creatures.

Survival Transmutation. An advanced innate spirit ability. All Eirenians are taught how to generate bread and water from spirit energy. It requires a simple knowledge of Eloran chemistry and basic sensory training. Survival transmutation is an Eirenian high school graduation requirement.

Syna. (SIGH-nuh) A simple technique where the user conveys emotions through vivid images sent using the spirit. Can be sent accidentally when a user experiences strong emotions and lacks sufficient spirit mastery.

Tallo. A Requisitioner of Beulah who discovered Acadia and introduced her to Lucien. Under his training, Acadia rose to become a powerful influencer and the first of Lucien's Jewels.

Talon, Dannon. Acadia's youngest sibling. A good-natured prankster, Talon shares the same piercing blue eyes that made Acadia notorious in Beulah. At the start of *Beauty from Embers*, he is fourteen years old.

Tech Station. A data-processing hub featuring one or more gridscreens. Tech stations allow users to access, store, and manage vast amounts of information, support real-time analysis, and facilitate communication.

Tifa. Assigned to Acadia as a handmaid in the Eirenian palace. In addition to her regular duties, Tifa is also tasked with helping Acadia integrate successfully with all Eirenian customs. She has gray eyes and thick indigo hair, often worn in an impeccable chignon. She has a tendency to be excitable and overly emotional.

Til. A brass copper coin equivalent to a day's wages for an unskilled laborer.

Tog. (TAUG) A hoofed, four-legged Eloran mammal, bred for its milk and shaggy fur. Similar to a cross between the Earth species of sheep and yak.

Trilorid. (TRY-lo-rid) A three-wheeled Eirenian training vehicle for young spirit users who are still working toward mastering their abilities.

Trividium. (tri-VID-ee-um) A dark mineral substance of mysterious origin. Found in deep subterranean deposits on Elorah. Lucien discovered that incorporating trividium within the human body generates superhuman strength and pain resistance in his test subjects—at the cost of their sanity.

Tsochi Cloth. (SO-chi) A pale gray silken cloth of extremely fine weave. Used exclusively for Eirenian funeral services because of its unique soundless property.

Ulekrew. (YOOL-leh-crew) A plateau nation in the northeast of Elorah. Known for its tall, muscular inhabitants and their fierce warrior culture.

Ungalor. (UN-guh-lor) A large carnivorous mammal, in the hyena family. They have a shaggy pelt with a ruff of fur around their neck, hairless legs, and extremely powerful jaws. Ungalors are aggressive predators. Once their jaw locks onto something, often only death will cause them to release their grip.

Vello Bike. The Eirenian answer to standard Eloran jetbikes. A turbo-charged hovering motorcycle. Can be built for one or two riders.

Visio Port. (VIZ-ee-oh) Seven observational towers circling Capital City. These are staffed by minor analysts, messengers, grid screen technicians, logistics staff, and managed by a Lead Analyst. Visio ports provide vital reconnaissance data to Eirenian analysts.

Warrior Spirit Class. Elite Eirenian spirit users. They go through a rigorous selection and training process before being paired with a mentor and taken out on field missions. Warrior class spirit abilities focus on combat techniques, both offensive and defensive, although wielders are expected to always attempt diplomacy first. Warrior techniques require the highest level of mastery outside of special skills reserved only for the royal family. Notable Eirenian in this category: Dragul. Kaya, and Acadia are in training.

Zeliaris, Princess. (zell-ee-ARE-iss) Daughter of King Atta and crown princess of Avathys. Zeliaris is beautiful and intelligent but naïve.

She is the apple of her father's eye which has allowed her to become a bit spoiled. She's lived a sheltered life in the Melican Palace and in her boredom often causes mischief to those around her. At the start of *Beauty from Embers*, she is twenty-three years old.

Author's Note

Thank you for adventuring with Arnion and Acadia once again!

Beauty from Embers continues Acadia's story after she was rescued from Gehenna and begins a relationship with Prince Arnion. Freed from her debt, she enters the beautiful and prosperous country of Eiren. In this new place, Acadia feels an immense pressure to be perfect. Arnion's sacrifice set her free and yet she struggles with doubt, self-worth, and old habits.

This story is a loose allegory for what our lives might look like after we begin a personal relationship with Jesus as our Savior. Sometimes we can feel pressure to be perfect, to never have any more bad habits or selfish behavior, to always be smiling and happy. But even though we have a relationship with Jesus, we're human. We still struggle with many things. Just like Acadia. She worried that she had to earn Arnion's love and maintain her good behavior to keep it. Sometimes we can fall into that same lie.

It takes most of the story for Acadia to realize Arnion will never leave her or forsake her. Just like Jesus will never abandon us. He knows every detail of our past, every dark corner of our hearts, and still chose to die in our place. The journey Acadia goes on is meant to be a picture of the same journey we experience. Every day is a battle to live according to our new identity in Christ rather than our old ways. There's a fancy church word for this—sanctification. It's the process of becoming a little more like Jesus every day.

Sometimes it's easy and we fly through life on a high. But sometimes it's hard. Really hard. Bad things happen. Disappointments. Failures. Loss.

When things go wrong, it can be tempting to think there's something wrong with us. (Why am I still struggling with eating/drugs/alcohol/pornography/self-worth/etc.?) Or that there's something wrong with God. (If God really loves me, how could he let this happen? Why doesn't he do something?)

I wish I had all the answers to share with you, but there are some things we will never understand on this side of eternity. What I do know is that you are never alone. Jesus is always with you and he always loves you. He understands that we are not perfect and loves us anyway. We never have to put on a show or pretend with him. Because Jesus experienced life as a human, he understands our struggles and all the temptations we deal with. Even better, he's promised to help us through them all.

My deepest wish is that you would know this love that surpasses understanding.

If you would like to invite Jesus into your life, it's easy. Just ask him! It can be as simple as saying something like this:

Dear Jesus, I want you in my life today and every day. Please forgive me for the wrong things I've done. I want to turn away from them and toward you. Forgive me. Save me. Lead me. Help me to love you and to know how wide and long and high and deep is the love of Christ—to know this love that surpasses understanding and be filled with all that God has for me. Amen.

The prayer above contains an excerpt from one of my favorite verses, Ephesians 3:16-19. If you've never read the Bible before, I encourage you to check it out. You will be amazed at the promises God has for you! He says he will never leave you or forsake you. That he has good plans for you. That he sings over you and has your name written on the palms of his hands.

There are some tough parts too. The Bible isn't a bed of roses and poetry. But it *is* the Living Word of God, and it has the power to transform your life. There's no other book like it.

If you were impacted by this and want to reach out, you can contact me through pamelahartwrites.com. I would love to meet you!

Share Your Voice

Thank you for reading *Beauty from Embers*! If you enjoyed the story, please consider leaving a review. Reviews help readers discover new books and are especially crucial for independent authors. It also helps me learn more about creating stories you'll love.

Get Connected

Sign up for Pamela's newsletter to get a free short story at
pamelahartwrites.com

You can also find her @pamelahartwrites on Instagram, Pinterest, &
Facebook!

Acknowledgements

Kudos to you for reaching the acknowledgements section, particularly if you're not directly related to me or the book production in some way. It takes dedication to make it this far and I salute you, intrepid reader. It's people like you who make it a joy to write. I weave secrets between my words and tuck Easter eggs in the crevices for you to find. Thank you for journeying with me through Elorah.

There are many people who loved and supported me while I wrote *Beauty from Embers*. Without them, this adventure would never have come to pass.

Thank you again to my wonderful Kickstarter backers who took a chance on this book before it was even published.

Thank you to my husband, Joe, for your scrumptious Saturday morning breakfast croissants and for supporting my dreams.

Thank you to baby Jake, for bringing so much joy into my life and reminding me of the hundreds of little miracles to celebrate every day.

Thank you to my friends at Pizzeria da Carmine for all your support and for fueling me with delicious pizza. The *Al Volto* with pumpkin and black truffle is the best!

Thank you to my fabulous beta readers Birgit Lehmann and Lisa Hatfield for making this story better.

Thank you to my editors Debbie and Makenna for your patience when I'm late on my submission deadlines and for doing amazing work catching all my misplaced, commas. (That one was on purpose to make sure you're still, with, me.) Any remaining mistakes are my own. (If you find any typos, dear reader, please email me and I'll fix them!)

Thank you, Jenny, for taking such good care of Jake. You gave me the gift of time. Time to breathe. Time to refresh. And time to write. Your friendship is a blessing.

Thank you to my writing buddy Krysta Maravilla for being a cheerleader, an encourager, and an advocate. Thank you for always reminding me to be kind to myself and for pushing me to make life more difficult for my characters. Acadia probably isn't too happy about it, but she's stronger because of it.

Thank you to my fantastic critique partners from Word Weavers Page Six: Kim Miller, Susan Simpson, Eva Marie Everson, Cindy Sproles, Audrey Frank, and Penny Hunt. You ladies are an inspiration to me. Your faith, wisdom, and incredible writing talents never cease to amaze me. I am so thankful and humbled to be a part of your group. I learn so much from your example. Thank you for putting up with all my strange fantasy words that are difficult to pronounce and thank you for helping me hone *Beauty from Embers* till it shined bright.

I would also like to thank Anthea Sharp and the Facebook groups Kickstarter for Authors and (Experienced) Kickstarter for Authors Cross-Promotion for teaching me the Kickstarter ropes. Running the Kickstarter for *Beauty from Embers* was a blast. Thank you for all your encouragement and for introducing me to an exciting new way to engage with readers. Cheers!

About the Author

Pamela grew up on a steady diet of fantasy, science fiction, and anime. She spent the majority of her childhood failing to acquire a Boston accent. Since then, she has slurped ramen in Ikebukuro, stampeded through flamenco lessons in Granada, and splashed her way across a fishpond for the Milkman Triathlon in Dexter. During her travels, she tends to overpack horrendously, but never regrets cramming her backpack full of books to devour along the way. She wanders the planet with Joe, the love of her life, Jacob, her sunshine baby, and her adorably maniacal Boston terriers, Willy and Marvin.

Pamela is the author of *Beauty from Ashes*, *Beauty from Embers*, and *City of a Thousand Tears*.

For more information, find her at: pamelahartwrites.com